A Brok

Across the Ice

Dana Fraedrich

Other titles by Dana Fraedrich:

SKATEBOARDS, MAGIC, AND SHAMROCKS
Skateboards, Magic, and Shamrocks ~ Summer 2012
Heroes, Legends, and Villains ~ Autumn 2015

BROKEN GEARS
Out of the Shadows (Lenore's storyline 1) ~ Autumn 2016
Into the Fire (Lenore's storyline 2) ~ Autumn 2017
Raven's Cry (standalone prequel) ~ Spring 2018
Across the Ice (Lenore's storyline 3) ~ Autumn 2019

Dana Fraedrich

This book is a work of fiction. Any references to historical events, real people, or real locales are used fictitiously. Other names, characters, places, and incidents are the product of the author's imagination, and any resemblance to actual events or locales or persons, living or dead, is entirely coincidental.

Maps by Hannah Pickering and Heather Boyajian

Cover digital scrapbook pieces courtesy Doudou's Design

Content Warning: This book contains sexual harassment, domestic violence, torture, and references to suicide and sexual assault.

ISBN-13: 978-0-692-98176-4

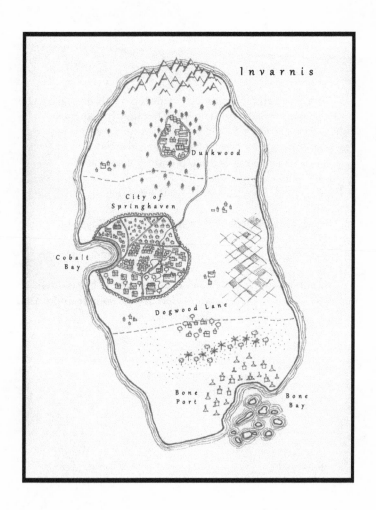

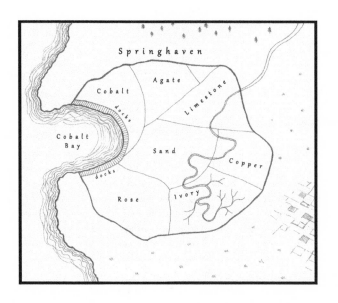

Contents

Dana Fraedrich

7

1

~Morning Meetings~

The cheerful brightness of morning light filtering through the windows belied the crisp air beyond. It painted the walls in shades of butter and sunflower. Lenore gravitated toward it as she ran her fingertips along the book spines in Eamon's and her library. She raised her face to the sunshine, bathing in the little warmth it offered. If only she could soak it up and store it away for more difficult times.

Hearing footsteps on the stairs, she spun and headed for the doorway.

"Good morning." Lenore did her best to sound cheerful. She even managed a half-smile.

Eamon looked at her for a moment. "Morning." He didn't return the smile.

"Would you like to walk to work together?" She took a step forward. "I thought I might get an early start."

"No, thank you." He adjusted his cravat. "I hope you have a good day."

He continued out of the house without looking back. Once he was gone, Lenore's face crumpled; it'd been this way for the last several weeks. She sank into a stiff leather armchair and allowed herself to weep.

"You must accept your feelings," Mina had counseled her. "Allow yourself to process them."

Lenore hadn't told Mina, Neal, or the rest of her adoptive family what had transpired between Eamon and herself the night of the Halls of Justice attack. She could tell they had an inkling, however. Eamon's anger at discovering Kieran's existence followed by Lenore's increased presence in their home must have told them enough.

"What did he say?" Neal had asked not long after that dark night.

"He's upset with all of us," was all Lenore would betray.

She hadn't wanted to risk angering Eamon further by "airing their dirty laundry," as Eamon's mother often phrased it. Later, however, she'd told him about Neal's question. Eamon had barely hidden his contempt.

With Bitsy curled up in her lap and Majesty at her feet, Lenore allowed her mind to wander. A distant lone zeppelin glided by the window, possibly on its way to Bone Port. She wondered if the passengers could see the sweep of white-clothed protesters spilling across the Parliament building lawns below. Their ranks had swelled after the Enforcers had been given temporary extra funding in response to the attack. The thought weighed Lenore down even more. She tried to follow Mina's instructions, though Lenore's old thief-self warred against it.

Stuff it down, the voice inside her said. *Don't let yourself break like this.*

She let loose another sob and pushed the instinct away. Lenore remembered her mother, the hope just before that small office wall had exploded. It hurt, but she let the pain pool inside her heart. Her loss was worthy of her tears, so she honored it.

The sharp emptiness of the house cut into her heart. Thank the stars for Bitsy and Majesty—they were the only support she had left here. After Lenore had cried her tears into their coats, she opened her pocket watch. Neal and Mina's precious gift, with its exposed gears and smoked glass face, gave her bittersweet news. Given that she'd risen early to catch Eamon, she'd be right on time.

)(

Camilla shifted her doctor's bag to one hand and knocked on the grey-blue door. She chanted the prayer that had become a ritual with these visits: *Please let him wake up today.*

Every day that Falcon remained unconscious eroded hope for his recovery. Camilla cursed the explosive that had blown him off that window at the Halls of Justice. The event had killed hers and Lenore's mothers, Adelle and Twila, and left Falcon comatose, though only Camilla and a few others knew the full truth of it.

She focused on the door to re-center her thoughts. Its knob was black, the trim white. Falcon's mother had painted it to resemble a blue jay's plumage. The door opened, revealing Falcon's father, Scholar Jacob Smoke.

Without preamble, he informed her, "No change since the other day."

Camilla's heart sank, but she molded her expression to one of comforting encouragement. Following a gesture from Scholar Smoke to enter, she headed straight down a corridor into Falcon's makeshift sickroom.

When they had transported him home, Mina had recommended he be moved as little as possible. Since his usual room was up a grand flight of stairs, the Smoke family had fashioned a space for him in a small conservatory at the back of the house.

"He's always loved the view from this room," Rhea, Falcon's mother, had said. "Perhaps the sunlight will be good for him."

At the moment, Camilla was concerned about the chill seeping in through the windows. Embossed birds on striped wallpaper swooped along panels of sunshine, and the family had placed cheerful flower arrangements around the room. Camilla laid another blanket over Falcon's unconscious form. She checked his vitals and performed other necessary hygiene tasks. As Jacob Smoke had said, no change—unconscious but stable.

After her ministrations were complete, Camilla pulled up a chair next to Falcon. "It's been difficult without you," she whispered. The Smokes often popped in during her visits, so she kept her words between Falcon and herself. "Emily Lee's parents have sent her away to a boarding school in the north. I understand it's an excellent institution, and it gets her out of the city. I suppose Mrs. Lee is protecting Emily in a way, even if Emily hates everything about it. Mina tried speaking to Mrs. Lee about Emily's position again, but Mrs. Lee still refuses to hear any argument for it. I think she's fairly well written Mina off, but I wrote to Emily this morning. She made me promise to keep her updated on things here. Eamon wasn't much help. He's still upset with Lenore about the Halls."

As well as Kieran, Camilla mentally added.

She stroked Falcon's hand. He'd worked so hard to keep them safe that night. He could have turned them in or at least abandoned them, but he had put himself in harm's way instead. He'd even gone so far as to try to help Adelle and Twila escape—prisoners he was meant to keep incarcerated. And this was his reward. He had hurtled back, fallen, as everything flew apart in that fiery blaze.

"I want to thank the stars you haven't had to answer for anything that night, but it's not worth... this. The Enforcers have questioned Mina and me as to your state. They're questioning everyone about the attack. I thought attending Fourth Hawkins' funeral would bring me some closure. Then I thought perhaps it was just slow in coming." Camilla's voice cracked. She took a deep breath to collect herself. "You know how I hated him, and yet... Blast it all." A few tears rolled down her cheeks. "I thought at first this was about my mother and you, but... Why, Falcon? Why am I mourning him? He was the worst kind of monster."

She dabbed her face with a lace-edged, clumsily embroidered handkerchief. In echinacea pink floss, the letters HCA blared against the white silk—the C for Camilla being larger than the other two letters. Mina had counseled Camilla and Lenore together on processing their feelings, but it wouldn't do to fall apart when the Smoke family was in their own pain, not to mention the possibility of appearing unfit to treat Falcon.

"I miss you," she whispered. "Please, get better. There's nothing more I can do on this end."

Camilla's throat tightened, and she paused to collect herself. Taking deep breaths, she reclaimed distance from her patient, hating the need to do so with every inhalation.

)(

As soon as Lenore entered the Arc-Tech department, she headed for Neal's desk. She often left work late nowadays, so everything looked exactly as it had when she left the evening before. Tidy stacks of papers and correspondence stored in their respective envelopes hunkered behind rulers and pen cups—barriers Lenore had erected in the battle to keep the center of Neal's workspace usable. She knew what her mentor had on his agenda, having looked over his diary last night, but she gave it another check anyway.

"G'morning, Nori," came a gruff yet soft voice beside her.

A familiar, exquisite scent tickled Lenore's nostrils and dragged her attention to the stout figure standing a few paces off. Copper held out a paper cup and wrapped parcel. She said nothing and kept her eyes glued to the cup.

Their relationship had become rather complicated these last few weeks, ever since Lenore had learned Copper had enabled the Reaper's Collective to blow up pieces of the Halls of Justice. He'd cut ties before the attack, when the Collective tried to kill him. They'd used what he had taught them, however, to take out innocents, including members of the museum staff and Lenore and Camilla's mothers. Having learned Copper's reasoning, Lenore couldn't entirely blame him, but he still had blood on his hands. Then again, he'd been a dear friend and supportive mentor, so she didn't always know how to interact with him.

"Neal told me where to find that place that does up coffee," Copper continued. "Thought you might like some."

Lenore finally raised her eyes to Copper's face. "Thank you," she said, and took the proffered gifts.

Copper shifted from foot to foot. "Neal told me how you liked it. I hope I did it right."

"Thank you." She tried to hold Copper's gaze, to think of something more to say. With each passing moment, more heat flooded her cheeks. "I'm sure it's lovely," she mumbled before turning away again.

"You going to Neal's do tonight?" he asked.

Neal and Katerina Holmes were co-hosting a soirée to drum up support for their Enforcer reform initiative. They'd recruited as many of their family and friends as possible to help give the attendees a positive experience and inform them of the reform's goals.

Lenore nodded, not wanting to discuss the event with Copper. It was too close to the disaster he had helped engineer. She grasped for a different topic and swept her eyes over Neal's desk again. Her eyes landed on his open diary. "We've got new graduate student interviews today."

"Aye. Let's hope this lot is better than Dempsey."

Lenore gave a strangled laugh and glanced back at Copper. His mouth ticked up into something that almost resembled a smile.

"Would you believe he was the best of the last lot?" he said.

"No," Lenore replied, perhaps a bit too emphatically. "I really don't."

Copper didn't know Dempsey, their former colleague, had hired a shadowy coterie of assassins to kill Lenore. The contract had finally been dissolved, but Dempsey had escaped and disappeared without a trace.

"It was his grades," Copper explained. "Top marks from university. We knew he was a prat from the get-go, but on paper he was the best candidate. And his daddy was a generous donor."

Lenore made a disgruntled noise of acknowledgement and lifted a folder from Neal's desk. She'd scrawled *Grad Student CVs* across the tab.

Offering the folder to Copper, "Want to see what we're working with this time?"

Copper's brushy beard perked up as he took it from her, and he motioned to the research corner on the far side of the room. She grabbed her coffee and unwrapped the accompanying parcel— pound cake. Companionable ease joined them at last as they sat, occasionally commenting on the applicants' qualifications.

Lately, Lenore found her job trying. On top of the awkwardness with Copper, assisting Neal with the Archeology department's sunken temple project had its own problems. The congenial facade Eamon donned at work cut her like splinters of ice, which melted beneath the heat of their colleagues' knowing glances.

While she and Copper worked, Lenore had to push back tears. Only once, though, thankfully. Anything could set her off nowadays. In this case, it was gratitude that she and Copper had managed to connect.

)(

Winter was good to Kieran, with its longer nights and fewer people outside. The cold air felt like a mild breeze on his skin. It was odd to think summer used to be his favorite, back when he'd been mortal. He crouched against a tree trunk, balancing effortlessly on a sturdy bough. Below sat a tiny but tidy back garden. Kieran gathered shadows around himself for camouflage. He dearly wished he could go inside, but ever since her purging, Annabelle made every room as bright as daylight. She only turned the lights down before bed, and humans were deadly boring to watch sleep, no matter what some of those over-romanticized novels said.

He chuckled. As children, she turned up the petrolsene lights in his room at night when he'd annoyed her, knowing he didn't sleep well except in total dark. At least that hadn't changed.

Annabelle was making dinner for herself and her daughter, who was elsewhere in the house, probably painting or updating business expenses for Annabelle. When they were in the same room, Kieran sometimes hid beneath the closest window and listened. He sighed. It was pathetic, yet it was the only way he knew to retain a connection with his older sister, tenuous though it was. Neal and Mina had suggested on many occasions that, perhaps, he should reveal himself, but if a time for such things had ever existed, it had long passed.

Annabelle had turned herself in for purging for her daughter's sake. That hideous practice—"cleansing" a criminal through torture and confession—had cost Annabelle's hand. Kieran hadn't been there for her then. Now that she'd pulled herself up by her bootstraps, it wasn't his place to upend her life. She'd thought him dead for over a decade, seemed to have made her peace with it, so he remained a silent observer. He saw her happy, and that was enough.

)(

Three black-clad figures walked into Rook's office as silent as shadows. Rook was already standing, Dmitri just behind him. Garrick stood behind the desk, ready to pull switches rigged to hidden crossbows around the room. Rook hoped it wouldn't come to that.

He'd been forewarned of the dark trio's arrival, and he mentally ticked each of the goons stationed at various posts outside his office. One, a behemoth called Grunt, covered the door. That was standard. But the rest, the plants pretending to peruse the market's wares or even selling items, were not.

Rook smiled and spread his hands in welcome. "Good to see you, Reaper. I trust the outside world wasn't too terrible to traverse."

He extended his hand, but the Reaper made no move to take it. They didn't even tilt their bird-masked face to look at it.

No one knew the strange figure's real identity. They didn't even claim a gender. With their robes pooling beneath them like squid ink, Rook wondered if the creature had some kind of horrible, slimy, cephalopod face. That certainly would explain the ridiculous getup.

Rook retracted his unshaken hand, shrugged, and turned, one eye always on his guests.

He made sure to use Dmitri's code name. "Ermine, drinks, if you please. Absinthe, yes?" Rook winked at the visitors. "If the rumors are anything to go by anyway."

The Collective members gave no indication of having heard him, much less of being impressed. Their round, soulless, glass eyes, which bulged from brass and leather masks, stared forward. Metal grates served for their mouths. Dmitri, almost as stone-faced, headed over to the drinks table. He remained behind the invisible line Rook drew with his body.

"May I invite you and your associates to sit?" Rook asked, and glanced at the two Crypt-Keepers behind the Reaper.

"No," one replied.

"You prefer to stand and drink?"

The other Crypt-Keeper pointed at Dmitri. "We came only for him."

"Really? I'm disappointed." Rook did not at all look disappointed. "Your note made it sound like you wanted to establish new business dealings. 'You have something of mine,' I believe it said?"

"No one leaves the Collective," the first Crypt-Keeper replied.

"I understand the pain of losing one of your flock. Believe me, I've been through it. But you know what they say. If you love something, let it go."

Dmitri returned with two small glasses and handed one to Rook. Rook clinked his against the one Dmitri still held. He then leveled his eyes at his guests as he took a sip. Dmitri continued to hold the other glass in silent challenge.

"This worm belongs to us," the first Crypt-Keeper said.

Rook's eyes narrowed. "I'm done talking to you grunts." A sound from the goon at the door. "Oh, not you, mate. You stay out there. Thank you." Rook looked back at the Reaper, who rose almost as tall as him. "I want to hear from the big dog."

A long pause passed. Dmitri took a sip of his absinthe.

A deathly wheeze rattled from the Reaper. "Do not test me."

"I assure you, there is no test in play." Rook's tone was deadly calm. "This is business. Ermine works for me now."

"His interference has taken one of my children from me. His life is mine."

"Your ill-conceived attack on the Halls of Justice cost this city much more. The Enforcer ranks have swelled. How many of us will lose people thanks to you? You're not the most popular person at the moment."

"Will you kill me then? Call your planted soldiers in here and strike me down?"

A smile curled up Rook's face. "No, but I can't speak for anyone else. I want a truce between us instead."

Another pause.

"Indeed."

Rook waited, but the Reaper didn't elaborate. "That's not an agreement."

"It is not a refusal either."

The Reaper turned and left without another word, black robes whispering over the floor as the Crypt-Keepers followed. Rook waited until the door was closed again and the sound of feet on the stairs outside had subsided.

He placed his glass on the desk. "*Glech*! How does anyone drink that swill? Garrick, post additional lookouts. I want to know the moment one of those morbid morons enters the Char district."

Garrick grumbled and shot Dmitri a venomous look as he left.

"Thank you. I still love you, even if I do have a second second-in-command now," Rook called to Garrick's retreating back. He sounded uncannily like a parent of small children. "Let's try to remember to play nice with one another. I need you all at your best." He pointed at Dmitri. "You watch yourself. I think that freak would sooner flay themself than give you up. Although, who knows? It might enjoy that."

"Yes, sir," Dmitri replied flatly.

Rook stole one final glance at the broad window that looked down over the market. Should he have just killed the Reaper and been done with it? No. Even if he'd succeeded—far from a sure thing—it would have started a war. One he wasn't sure he could win.

2

~Gathering Support~

L enore pulled her coat more tightly around her. A fierce winter wind tugged at her hair and shook a bevy of russet leaves from their branch. They swirled over Lenore's head and onto the museum's roof. Lenore watched them go, gazing up at the imposing building.

"Are you ready to go?" came a voice like sunshine cutting through rain.

Lenore turned and gave a small smile as Camilla and Mina approached.

"Yes." She motioned to her skirt, waistcoat, and blouse hidden beneath her coat. "I hope this is sufficient for Neal and Katerina's gala."

"It's not." Mina squeezed Lenore around the shoulders. "But not to worry, darling. We brought something for you that will do."

Camilla held up a trio of garment bags. "We'll have lots of time to change beforehand."

Lenore took one from her and nearly dropped it, expecting it to be lighter. "I should try sparring against you. You look as if these weigh next to nothing."

Camilla's eyes brightened with pride. "It takes a good bit of elbow grease to saw through solid bone."

Lenore made a noise in her throat as her stomach turned.

Given the size of their party and parcels, the three traveled by growler instead of the cheaper hansom cab. Within its privacy, Mina schooled them on everything they needed to remember that evening, though Lenore wondered if it was mostly for her benefit.

"Remember, she is *Lady* Katerina tonight. Or Lady Holmes. Use your discretion. We must appear both proper and approachable."

Lenore wished for a guidebook, or at least a checklist, for determining which to choose in each situation.

"Who will be there?" Camilla asked.

"Goodness, I wish I could remember them all," Mina said.

Lenore's confidence returned. This she could do. "Neal had me quizzing him with flashcards today. Cambridge, who's coming tonight, is good friends with Jones, who isn't. They're on opposite sides of the argument. Laurel has already pledged his support, and Evergreen is firmly ambivalent, but he's coming for the free food."

"I'd like you to stay close to me tonight, please," Mina said. "Goodness knows I won't know who's who in there."

Lenore inwardly sighed with relief. She could follow Mina's lead regarding titles. "Is this normal? Garnering support by throwing a party?"

"Apparently," Mina said. "I went to one of Katerina's soirées years back, when she pushed for looser travel restrictions."

"Did it work?" Lenore asked.

Mina held her hands up like scales. "Part of her proposal eventually passed, but she had to surrender the other part and offer support for someone else's scheme to make it happen. To be honest, I didn't try terribly hard to keep up with all the associated intrigues."

"Zeppelin restrictions loosened, but trains remained the same," Camilla said. "And she voted in favor of higher tariffs on goods shipped from Duskwood." Silence met her explanation. "It was very exciting the way Beatrice told it."

Dread curled like smoke into the back of Lenore's mind. Tonight had all the portents of being frightfully dull, but Katerina and Neal's goals were more important than her own comfort.

The growler pulled up to the Holmes manor, a stately building of whitewashed stone with an elaborate water garden in the back. A white-gloved, black-tuxedoed footman greeted them with a perfectly lukewarm tone and led them to a guest room to change. Several vanity tables lined one wall, and Lenore wondered if they were usually here. As many events as Katerina and her husband, John, hosted, it was possible they always kept this room

19

ready for such situations. The Allens normally attended only their New Year celebrations.

Not one minute after the ladies had been deposited, Beatrice, Katerina's daughter, entered and whirled around the room like a congenial cyclone.

"Doctor Allen," Beatrice cooed, kissing the woman on each cheek. "I can't tell you how delighted we are that you came."

"It's lovely to see you again, dear," Mina said.

"And Camilla." Beatrice pronounced each syllable of her name like she was savoring it. "I never tire of seeing your sweet face."

Camilla laughed like silver bells. "Nor I yours."

"Lenore, I've missed our lunches of late. Where's Eamon? I heard he's not coming tonight."

Lenore caught the sympathetic glances Mina and Camilla threw her and forced a smile. "He has a prior engagement at the Badger Club."

Beatrice gave a measured yet playful roll of her eyes. "How disappointing. Of course, this is why I'm still single. I haven't the patience for anyone who doesn't support my endeavors a hundred percent. If he were mine, he would be on the verge of losing me, but you, my dear Lenore, are far more patient, which is what makes you such a jewel."

Lenore blinked as no less than three conflicting emotions assailed her. "You are in top form tonight, Beatrice."

"Thank you. Now, how can I make you ladies shine? Not that you need much help, but we need to dazzle the other magistrates tonight." She flickered her fingertips through the air. "Dazzle their top hats right off!"

Beatrice laced and styled and perfected, somehow not displacing a single strand of hair while doing so.

"Lenore," Beatrice said as she placed glittering gems artfully throughout Camilla's hair, "you're acquainted with that Varick chap, yes? Friends even?"

It took Lenore a second to realize Beatrice meant Rook—the name sounded alien coming from her friend's mouth. She covered the pause by pretending to focus on her makeup. "I am."

Beatrice set the rest of the hair gems onto Camilla's vanity table. "Here, darling. Could you finish with these, please? Your taste is ever so good." Without waiting for an answer, she trotted over to Lenore and slid what looked like a fascinator from a reticule hanging from her wrist. The hair accessory made Lenore do a double take. "I commissioned this especially for you."

"It has gears on it." Lenore batted one of the fascinator's swaying feathers with a finger. They were black, sturdy, and tipped with gold. A few glass gems glittered here and there, but the bronze, silver, and gold gears sprinkled around the piece instead of the usual flowers held Lenore's gaze.

"Yes, to signify your position," Beatrice explained. "It matches the pocket watch Neal gave you, doesn't it?"

"It does, rather well actually, but the gears don't serve a purpose."

"Of course they do. I just told you."

"Yes, I know, but I mean functionally. They don't do anything. That's the whole point of a machine part, to work."

Beatrice chuckled. "Oh, Lenore, pragmatic as ever. It's *art*." Lenore didn't know how to respond to that. "I'll just clip this here… Perfect. As I was saying, Varick Pendragon is a friend of yours, but do you know who his father is?"

"We don't really discuss his family," Lenore said. The truth of the words made them effortless to say.

"And I'm not surprised. That whole purging business left quite the stain on their reputation."

Lenore traded a surprised look with Camilla. Purges weren't usually spoken of in polite society, at least not so openly. In hushed whispers behind fans and hands, yes, but never so matter-of-factly, and especially not by fine young ladies. Even amongst the middle class, it was treated as a bit of a dirty word.

"I don't mind telling you, though," Beatrice continued, "that his father is none other than the Speaker of the magistrate council."

Even Mina spun in her seat, half-painted lips hanging open.

Lenore recovered first, eyebrows still bobbing. "*The* Speaker? Of the entire council?"

"Does Neal know?" Mina asked.

"Indeed." Beatrice's eyes danced. "I'm surprised you didn't."

Mina gaped. "He never told me. Though, to be fair, I never asked. That is…"

"Shocking," Camilla finished.

"I know. It positively rocked us when we found out. Of course, the Pendragon family tried to keep matters quiet when Varick disappeared, and doubly so when he came forward." Beatrice placed a delicate hand to her lips, feigning embarrassment. "Anyhow, I was wondering if you, my dear Lenore, might have a chat with your friend about mending some fences, as they say. Get back into his father's good graces and convince him to throw us a little support."

"The Speaker is meant to be an unbiased party," Camilla said.

Mina returned to her vanity mirror. "But he's been known to support Enforcer causes before."

"And Lenore here can remind him of that, maybe nudge him toward nudging his daddy into a more bipartisan position, hm?"

Lenore laughed. "I'll talk to him about it, but I wouldn't count on it." Camilla made a noise, though Lenore couldn't quite decipher it. "Saying that, will Speaker Pendragon be in attendance tonight?"

"Oh no," Beatrice scoffed. "He wouldn't deign to attend a pitiful gathering like this. Besides, he's supposed to be a neutral party, remember?"

)(

The ballroom sparkled like sunlight on rippling water, while low chatter mimicked the sound of a babbling brook. Wine flowed in every shade. From light topaz to citrine to dark amber. Pink sapphire and rose quartz. Warm ruby, cool garnet, and nearly amethyst. It loosened lips and billfolds—something Lenore had grown accustomed to seeing but could never quite accept. Lowly plebeians like she had once been only ever had enough money to come in coin form. She couldn't understand how flimsy paper was somehow worth more than solid metal, yet she didn't hear a jingle all night.

As promised, she shadowed Mina like a faithful cat. Not dog. Dogs didn't slink and watch like Lenore did. She provided what information she could as they circled the room, chatting and glad-handing and discussing the "Enforcer changes," as Katerina and Neal had taken to calling them. Changes they desired, changes they disliked, always letting their party guests fill in their own interpretations whenever someone flung the phrase into conversation like a baited hook. Neal and Katerina's main goals tonight were to garner favor, take temperatures, announce their next event—a masquerade for which they hoped to acquire numerous commitments—and perhaps even drum up a few donations to the cause. If they failed to pass their motion at the next regular magisterial council meeting less than three months away, they wouldn't get another chance.

Beatrice claimed Camilla as her partner for the evening, and the two ladies left Lenore to charm everyone they met together.

Lenore quickly decided she didn't like this type of party. She kept stealing glances at the long table at the back, laden with food, and willed her stomach not to grumble. She hadn't had time to grab dinner, so she barely sipped her wine, wanting to stay sharp.

"Bring me a salmon toast and I'll love you forever," Lenore whispered to Camilla as their paths crossed again.

"You already do," Camilla whispered back.

"A cheese straw. *Anything!*"

A new voice called Lenore's attention away. "Mrs. Lee." This was Magistrate Warren, if memory served her. "Where is your husband tonight?"

Lenore glanced at the ring shining painfully bright on her finger. She'd recently begun going by the surname Blackbird-Lee, though Neal didn't seem keen on using it, nor did she expect this gent to care much for a correction.

Thinking of Eamon, bitterness spiked within her, but she kept her countenance cool and pleasant. "Working late. He's also an apprentice, but in the Anthropology department."

"Ah, well, once he completes his apprenticeship, I'm sure you'll be able to spend more time at home," Magistrate Warren replied.

Lenore's smile widened, though it felt more like she was baring her teeth. "I couldn't. My job is far too fun."

He chortled and slapped Neal on the back. "I suppose this old chap mustn't be too dreadful a boss then. Eh, Magistrate Allen?"

He laughed again, and Lenore snuck a glance at Neal. She knew how much he hated his political title. Like her, he smiled, but she caught the same tightness in his features she felt in hers.

Magistrate Warren and Neal continued to chat, and Lenore's eyes drifted back to the refreshments table.

)(

Lenore did a circuit around the house when she returned home that night and found Eamon sitting at a table in the library with no less than four books open before him. Shelves towered around them, while a fire crackled in the fireplace. The licking flames had eaten nearly all of their wooden fuel, but the resulting warmth still hung around. Majesty lay curled beneath the table, golden eyes shining. Bitsy, who hung around Lenore's neck, growled at the canine. In response, Majesty lolled out her tongue and wagged her tail. Lenore petted Bitsy's head to quiet him. Her shoes tapped on the wood floor, but Eamon didn't look up from his work.

"Did you feed Maj?" she asked.

The regal wolf replied with a look that said, *No. No one ever feeds me.*

"I did," Eamon said. His focus remained on making notes in a small journal. Majesty huffed and laid her head back onto her paws.

Lenore couldn't help but smile at the leggy canine. Her smile faded, however, when she turned her attention back to Eamon. "Long day?"

"Yes. Still at it too."

"Beatrice asked after you." When he didn't reply, she added, "People might get suspicious if we keep not appearing in public together."

"You're the one who said you can't pretend everything is fine, which is curious given how easily you lie about everything else."

Lenore opened her mouth to protest, but no sound came out. The effort to keep herself from crying again demanded too much.

Eamon spared her a glance. "In any case, it's not as suspicious as you think. You obviously haven't known many upper class married couples."

Lenore remembered her conversation with Beatrice earlier that evening. How patient was she really? She wasn't sure how long this toxic environment could last before she forced a change.

"Did you really go to the Badger Club this evening?" she asked.

This time, Eamon looked at her properly. The cold, thin line of his lips and the contempt in his eyes made Lenore's anger rise, but she clamped her mouth shut.

"Of course I did. I said I was going, didn't I? What were you expecting?"

Lenore took a deep breath and barely managed not to huff as she released it. "I was just trying to be communicative. Your plans might have changed for all I know." The haughtiness in Eamon's expression remained. She decided to try one last time. "I can tell you've got a lot of work to do, but would you like to share a cup of tea? Just for a few minutes before I go to bed?"

"No, thank you."

The words clanged against Lenore's ears. She barely managed to utter a civil goodnight before quitting the library.

)(

The sun struggled to spread its shine over the waking city as it crested the distant buildings. The Copper quarter's white plaster and red brick appeared sullen in the dim light, but coaches and cabs bustled over the cobbled road, spry as spring rabbits.

As Camilla and Mina walked to Mina's clinic, Camilla spied Ginger Oran walking arm in arm with her twin sister, Mint. They came from the other direction across the road, toward their mother's apothecary shop. Ginger waved her arm like a flag in a gale. Camilla smiled; Ginger had always been the best at mornings. Camilla and Mina returned more demure though no less friendly, finger waggling responses.

"Be right back," Camilla said. She broke away from her aunt and crossed the road to her friends.

Ginger waited for Camilla, while Mint went to unlock the door. Just as Camilla reached their side, Mint called her sister's name. She sounded concerned. Camilla turned her attention to the older twin, who stood at the apothecary's entrance.

Leaflets covered the shop's stoop. Dozens of them. The sisters picked up one each and compared them. Identical, the leaflets were printed on black paper and bore the image of a flexed arm in white ink with the word "*FIGHT!*" written underneath. Smaller print below read,

The Enforcers are death. Show them we won't take their abuse any longer.

The twins exchanged a concerned look.

"Could this be from the protesters?" Ginger asked.

Mint shook her head. "They're supposed to be peaceful."

Camilla wished the flyers were from the protesters, who still occupied the Parliament building's lawn day in and day out. Instead, she suspected these came from the strange organization Dmitri had joined—the Reaper's Collective. She turned to see Mina at the clinic's door with another black leaflet. A moment later, Stephen, Mina's other assistant, appeared over the rise at the top of the road. Even from this distance, Camilla could make out the black sheet of paper he carried.

The sight of Mina on the other side of the gulf bred a plague of terror in Camilla. A similar tableau had played out just before her mother had been killed. Camilla dashed into the road, heedless of traffic. A chestnut gelding hauling a cab reared up on its hind legs as she ran right into its path. The horse pawed the air. Camilla froze as its hooves descended toward her. She felt herself yanked back and found the twins hanging onto her. They were on the walkway again. The cab driver shook his fist and shouted at Camilla, but she couldn't hear him over the screaming realization that she had almost just died.

"Milly!" Ginger gasped. "Are you alright?"

Camilla could only nod dumbly.

Mina appeared beside them and checked Camilla for injuries. "Darling, what were you thinking, darting into traffic like that?" Anger and relief vied for top spot in her tone.

"I'm sorry. I… I got scared." Visions of her mother across a different gap, just before Camilla had lost her forever, burst before her eyes. She looked to Mina. "Are *you* alright?"

"Yes, dearest, I'm fine. Well, not quite fine." She held up the leaflet, still gripped in her hand.

"They're all over," Stephen puffed, pulling up to the group. "Bloody things are on every doorstep."

Camilla couldn't tell if he hadn't seen the almost-accident or if, since all was well, he'd redirected his focus to the next emergency. He might not have had the best bedside manner, but he was certainly good with triage.

She turned to Mina. "Can Neal do anything? Or Lady Katerina?"

"I don't know. Maybe…" Mina stopped to think. "Stephen, go to the museum and find my husband, Engineer Neal Allen, in the Archeotechnologics department. See what he makes of this."

"Doctor Allen, I'd be faster," Camilla said. "I know where to go."

"I want you here with me," Mina said, "not out there by yourself."

"Mina," Camilla pressed. The rest of the group looked taken aback at this breach in their usual propriety. "This is too important."

Mina pressed her lips together and shook her head. "Stephen will go."

"But—"

"But nothing, young lady." Mina fixed Camilla with a hard look that referenced events they couldn't speak of here.

She willed her simmering emotions to steady while Stephen hailed a cab. Camilla was surprised at how cross she was with her beloved aunt, though the fear thrumming underneath superseded.

Mina asked the twins, "Is your mother coming soon?"

"She'll be along," Mint said. "She asked us to open the shop so she could deliver some orders."

Mina pressed her fingertips to her forehead. "Are you two sure you'll be alright by yourselves?"

Mint and Ginger exchanged a look before Ginger said, "Doctor Allen, we've opened the shop plenty of times. We'll be fine."

"I know that. What I mean is… That is to say…" Mina took a deep breath. "Of course. If you need anything, though, please don't hesitate to come over. Even if you feel silly about it."

Mint laid a hand on Mina's arm. "Don't worry, Doctor Allen. We'll look after each other."

Mina watched as the twins unlocked and entered the apothecary shop. She then herded Camilla back across the road and into the clinic. Once inside, she leaned against the wall.

"This can't be happening again," she muttered.

Seeing Mina so weary doused Camilla's anger. Camilla hugged her, squeezing a little longer than usual. "We'll get through it, whatever happens. Shall we prepare the clinic?"

Mina took one more moment to breathe before straightening up and giving herself a little shake. With a stronger voice than before, "Yes, of course, darling."

Despite their hopeful words, unease jangled Camilla's nerves. True, Neal and Katerina were doing something about the Enforcers, but no one was doing anything about the Collective.

)(

The Arc-Tech department was quiet this early in the morning. Only Lenore occupied the huge workshop, which also served as office and reference library. Sitting in the comparatively tiny research corner, she gripped a cup of tea between her hands, trying to ward off the chill slithering over her. The familiar presence of her favorite squashy chair and nearby bookshelves comforted her a little. The sheet of black paper lying on a low table before her, however, radiated raw malice.

The sound of the door opening and shutting on the other side of the workshop made her lift her head. She recognized Copper's heavy footfalls. Unexpected anger sparked, pulling her features into a scowl. Leaflet in her free hand, she marched to Copper's desk, where he always started his day. He watched her approach with an inscrutable expression.

She slapped the black paper onto the desk and jabbed a finger at it. "Do you know anything about this?"

Copper barely looked at it. "Why would I know anything about it?"

"Because you worked with them. What do they want? Why are they trying to incite violence?"

Copper picked up the flyer and examined it. "We don't know who made these. It might be—"

"You know as well as I do the Reaper's Collective is behind this!"

Copper's eyes snapped to hers. His mouth thinned into a stern line. "How do *you* know who they are?"

Lenore leaned back against the desk and crossed her arms. Neither had ever said to the other who *they* were. She sipped her tea and decided not to say anything more.

Copper's face transformed like a heating teakettle. His finger popped up under the pressure, and he shook it at Lenore. "Now you listen here, young lady—" Lenore's eyebrows shot up into her hairline. "You heard what I said. Whatever you're mixed up in, I want you out of it. Those people won't hesitate to kill you for even knowing who they are."

"I'm not mixed up in anything," Lenore shot back. She knew her chances of being believed were slim at best, given she'd told Copper she'd been inside the Halls of Justice the night of the attack. "And don't speak to me like a child. You're not my father."

"Well, *someone's* obviously gotta talk some sense into you."

The sound of the door opening again stopped them. Lenore took another sip of tea, listening to the shuffling footsteps she was fairly certain came from Ezra. Sure enough, her fellow apprentice shambled into view a few moments later and gave them both a sleepy wave.

"Morning."

Lenore assumed as pleasant a tone as she could muster. "Good morning, Ezra. Neal's out. He's gone to speak with Lady Katerina and the protesters." She shot Copper a look that said, *So be a bloody professional and let's get on with it.*

Copper's answering glare was angry but resolute. He wadded up the leaflet and chucked it into the bin beside his desk.

3

~The Hollow Tower~

The small sitting room was warm, almost uncomfortably so, with a fire crackling away in the hearth. Lenore, however, was pleased for the excess heat. The sky, a flat sheet of steel eking watery light through the windows, was conspiring with the wind, which had bitten especially hard on her journey over. She still felt the cold beneath her skin. Their chairs, circled around a small table, were as cheerful as the fire, embroidered with colorful flowers and twining green vines.

Lenore giggled as Lowell nudged her with yet another biscuit. She was quite pleased with herself, considering she hadn't cried once all day, and Lowell had more than made up for her rotten journey over. His sunshiny personality practically beamed light into her. She was having tea with him and Felicia and trying to forget all the nasty words that had been exchanged lately.

"I know you too well, my tinker belle," Lowell teased. "Biscuits always make you happy. Have another. Have two more!"

A second joined the first in their silly pestering, and Lenore laughed again. Perhaps she wasn't as good at hiding her feelings as she'd imagined. Then again, Lowell usually seemed able to tell when she needed cheering up. She didn't really have the energy to protest—not that she would have protested extra biscuits anyway—and accepted the baked goods.

"Thank you." Turning to Felicia, she added, "Thank you both, for always being so willing to open your house to me. It's such a nice escape from the rest of the world."

"We certainly think so," Felicia replied. She smiled as she sipped her tea, but no warmth reached her eyes. Felicia didn't wear her heart on her sleeve like her brother. "I have to go out later. Do you have plans to stay here?"

Lenore shifted her gaze. "If that's alright." She left off the words "with you", knowing Felicia held some modicum of control over Lowell's life. Lenore being alone in the house with him wasn't quite what upper class society considered proper.

"You know you're always welcome here." Lowell patted Lenore's hand. "Day or night, you come whenever you need a respite." She watched Felicia's face from the corner of her eye, but the woman betrayed nothing. Meanwhile, Lowell turned to his sister. "We've got some smashing new designs drawn up. I finally received those materials I sent for ages ago. The box was so heavy it nearly pulled my arms from their sockets!"

Felicia didn't answer Lenore's query. Both ladies sipped their tea while Lowell waxed poetic about the contents of his long-awaited shipment.

When she'd finished, Felicia said a few perfunctory farewells and swept out of the room. As she left, she called back over her shoulder, "Don't break anything important."

Lenore couldn't tell if she was being serious.

)(

Rook entered Fetch—or Felicia, as few knew her—and Lowell's house through the conservatory, around the back of the house. He could have used the front door, but that required knocking and he just couldn't be bothered. He wanted sleep, and the Thorne manor had the advantage of being closest to his last meeting. That, and Lenore had started coming round more often since the Halls of Justice attack.

He had just hung his coat on the rack in the receiving hall when a voice broke through his drowsy thoughts.

"Your friend Lenore," Fetch said.

Rook turned and bowed to the woman, who stared down her nose at him. She stood with hands on her hips partway up the staircase—a queen surveying a lowly servant of her queendom.

"How may I assist?" he drawled.

"Are you aware of her situation?" Fetch asked. "The issues in her marriage?"

Rook forced his smile to remain in place, but his eyes turned cold. "I am."

"I am appalled! Is he having an affair?"

"Not to my knowledge, and believe me, I've looked into it. Why do you mention it?"

"Because the poor thing is completely cut up about it. It's upsetting Lowell. I'm going to have to start *buying* biscuits at this rate."

Rook crooked an eyebrow at her. "And store-bought biscuits are the worst."

"Pure dreck. The whole thing's casting a pall over my house. When are you planning to do something about it?"

Rook threw back his head and laughed. "Why on earth do you think I'm going to do something about it?"

Fetch descended the staircase and began donning her coat and gloves. "Because of what she means to you. To be honest, I'm surprised the man still has all his pieces attached."

A sly smile sliced across Rook's face. "If I could manage it without upsetting the balance, I would happily deprive Eamon of an appendage or two. There are Lenore's feelings to consider, however."

"How tiresome." Fetch rolled her eyes and turned to walk out. "Just do something to brighten up my house."

"I'll see what I can manage."

"That was not a request."

She shut the door with a decisive snap. Rook sighed; his nap would have to wait. He headed for the place he would most likely find Lenore.

She, Rook discovered when he walked into Lowell's workshop, was elbow-deep in a wooden box of iron ball bearings. Always tidy, Lowell's tools hung along the walls like regiments of soldiers ready to serve. A pleasant mélange of scents drifted through the air: wood, oil, and gingerbread—a leftover treat from tea, Rook guessed. Quietude sat in attendance like a soothing companion. Rook knew its presence had fled Lenore at her house, the museum, and the Allens' manor, turning Lowell and Fetch's home into a refuge.

Rook sidled up to her. "And what sort of mischief are we up to today?"

Before Lenore could answer, Lowell exclaimed, "Oh, good! So glad you're here. We really needed a third, and you know Felicia has less than no interest in assisting."

Rook smirked, but his eyes remained half-lidded with tiredness. "And you assume I'm keen? This looks precisely like the sort of thing I've proven to be rubbish at."

"He's right." Lenore grunted as she shoved a hollow metal cylinder down through the ball bearings to sit flush against the bottom of the box. "He was useless in Bone Port."

Rook watched as she began removing handfuls of the ball bearings from inside the cylinder to outside it. "Why didn't you just empty the box and refill it around your... whatever that metal tube thing is?"

"Because it's too heavy for me, and we don't have that kind of time." As if in response, the sky rumbled like a coal engine with indigestion. She looked at the ceiling. "We need to hurry. Rook, could you finish this, please? Lowell, is your assembly ready?"

Lowell brandished several metal spikes, the very picture of a general celebrating victory. "These are, but I need to bang a few more into shape."

Lenore trotted over and donned a pair of protective goggles. "It'll have to be messy."

His brow furrowed, making his good eye squint behind the smoked glass of his customized protective eyewear—customized because it had to fit over the usual mask he wore.

Lenore brushed his arm as she passed. "I know, my mechanical marvel, but it won't look nice once we're done anyway."

"I never agreed to this," Rook called after them. Despite his words, he worked with deft fingers, eager to see how quickly he could complete his task.

)(

It was a lucky thing indeed Rook had come along when he had, and not just because he'd gotten to show off. With nary a grimace, he'd lifted the box that had reportedly nearly pulled

Lowell's arms from their sockets. He could also keep an eye on Lenore and Lowell, who must have each taken out their good sense to play with and lost it.

On the rolling lawn of Fetch and Lowell's back garden, surrounded by stone musicians, the three hurriedly erected a ramshackle framework—a hollow tower of metal piping. Clouds as heavy as the hammered iron they resembled rolled above. The sky grumbled at them for daring to test its power. Rook's lower back tingled not for the first time.

"I'd like to reiterate," he called over the wind, which blew his hair into his face and stung his eyes, "that this seems like a phenomenally bad idea."

He also wanted to point out Lenore had another tool for this—her curio—but he suspected doing the project with Lowell had benefitted her more. If this failed, she could always fall back on the strange lightning-shooting weapon anyway. As Rook understood this insane undertaking—and he barely did—if it worked, the ball bearings would somehow become hundreds of charged ferrousites and stick together like magnetite or lodestone. The how and why behind it all eluded him, however.

Lenore maneuvered another rod into the cylinder inside the box. "Almost there." The top of the rod, like those around it, sat against the tower's inner framework, resembling dry noodles against the edge of a pot.

"You've said that three times now." The sky flashed white fangs above. Rook twitched as the oath living inside him snarled in reply. "That's enough now. We have to go inside."

Lenore began to protest, but Rook stopped her with a faint touch on her elbow. His eyes fixed on her as hard as the statues' around them.

Her gaze traveled to where his hand pressed against the pain in his back. "Okay. Lowell, we're ready. Let's go in."

Lowell looked back as Lenore tugged him along. "Do you think we need to adjust any of the central conductors?"

"The forces of nature aren't that fussy, so we don't need to be either."

They tucked themselves into the conservatory with a perfect view of their setup in the distance. Lowell volunteered to get something to sip while they waited. Rook wondered if an agenda existed behind the man's insistent refusals for assistance.

"Stronger than tea, if you please," Rook said to Lowell's disappearing back. He turned to Lenore and lifted her hands to his lips. He kissed her knuckles. The gesture rasped against the edges of propriety given their situations. "Thank you."

Lenore smiled but gently pulled her hands away. "I never want to cause you pain." Rook's smile cracked like a rusted beam, and Lenore heaved a sigh. "Never more than I can possibly help."

She looked outside at their creation. The sky flashed, creating its own pyroprismatic show, and rain began to patter against the windows around them.

"About Eamon..." Rook rolled different word combinations around in his mouth and imagined the possible outcomes of each. "I've seen how he's acting. It's hardly convincing anymore."

Lenore's shoulders tightened, and he feared he'd chosen poorly. Her voice was soft when she answered. "It's still what's expected of me." Rook made a disgusted noise at that. Lenore turned her green eyes back to him, their color dimmed. "I know, but it's what's safest for everyone. And I made a commitment." Rook opened his mouth to object, but Lenore cut him off. "I lied, Rook. I've lied to him about so much, or at the very least kept secrets. I'm trying to make amends. I tell him where I'm going. Eamon knows each time I'm gone where I'll be and with whom, when I feed Kieran and... and what passes between you and me. It's the only way I can think to fix this."

I could kill him. I could just kill him, and no one would have to know, Rook thought. *Or just punish him a little.*

"Does he ever tell you no?" he asked.

Lenore's smile threatened to break Rook's careful control. "No. I think even he knows that's too far."

Too far for her or him?

Rook's fingers itched to grab one of his knives. Or to punch something, but no good targets volunteered themselves. Instead, he brushed his fingers against hers as the weather darkened further. The rain poured heavier, matching his mood.

"Just be sure you don't give up anything you can't stand to lose." Now it was Rook's turn to interrupt Lenore's protests. "I know, I know. Believe me, I have every faith in your ability. It's your willingness I question. You're too good."

His spirits lifted as Lenore turned back to him. A challenging glint lit her eyes. He didn't care if she was deflecting. He was all too happy to see fire in her, something that had been sorely but understandably missing of late.

"You're one to talk," Lenore said. "You don't even want to get rid of your oath."

Rook matched her gaze and leaned toward her. A lock of hair fell over his eyes. "The oath has its downsides, yes, but it also has some strong advantages."

Lenore smirked and brushed the rebellious lock back into place. "It robs you of choice. Besides, if you want to protect me—"

"I do."

"—then wouldn't it be better to get rid of it and do so without pain?"

"If you stumble upon a way to release me from the pledge I made to your father, we can find out."

Caw! Caw!

His grin disappeared into a confused pucker as they looked to the noise. Their heads cocked in sync at the sight of a raven roosting in an upper corner of the room. It fluttered to the back of a chair and croaked again.

"Has that been here the whole time?" Lenore asked.

"I didn't see it when we came in," Rook said, "but I was more concerned with making sure you didn't accidentally get yourself killed." A fragment of his smile returned while he watched her try to formulate a defense. His vow had spoken; that was difficult to argue with.

The familiar sound of Lowell clomping back claimed their attention.

As he reentered the conservatory, Lenore asked, "Lowell, are you aware you have a raven in here?"

The bird cocked its head at them, giving Rook the distinct feeling it was studying them as much as they were it. Lowell glanced at the chair-turned-perch and got back to refusing Lenore's help with the refreshments tray.

"Thank you, petal, but you just make yourself comfortable. Yes, she comes around now and again and makes for excellent company."

"She?" Lenore asked.

The raven flapped her wings and cawed.

"She," Lowell said.

Beyond the conservatory's glass walls, the clouds slashed the air with claws of searing white light, which streaked down to the hollow tower. A split second later, the box beneath the apparatus exploded in time with a great crack of thunder. Lenore screamed as smoking wood shrapnel flew in all directions, trailed closely by some of the ball bearings. Without thinking, Rook pulled her into his arms and held her tight as she began to shake.

He whispered into her ear, "Shhhh, it's alright, little bird. We're all fine."

"I say, looks like our lyrist might have lost his nose." A comical grimace stretched across Lowell's face. "Felicia will *not* be happy about that. I can't see any other damage, though. At least not from this distance. And our work hasn't been in vain. Best if we wait for the storm to pass before checking the results, I think. If what those chaps in your Environmental Kinetics department said is right, we should have far more ferrousites than we need, eh?" Lowell finally turned back to Lenore, who nodded, seemingly unaware that Rook still held her. "My dear tinker belle, I didn't know you were afraid of thunder. Here, sit down and have some spiced wine. It's simply the best for settling one's nerves."

Rook reluctantly released Lenore so Lowell could usher her to the sofa. Rook saw Lenore gathering her wits in her slow inhalation, re-establishing her walls in the firm set of her jaw. Strong though she was, strong and radiant like a steel lily, he wanted to draw her back into his arms and fight her fears for her. To give her rest the way Lowell had.

"It surprised me, that's all." Her voice still trembled. "You said this is spiced wine?"

"Nice and hot." Lowell placed an earthenware cup in her hands. Tendrils of steam rose out of it and caressed Lenore's face. "Oh my stars and garters, you're shuddering. How is my brave sweet pea, who's faced murderous brutes, so afraid of a little storm?"

"Felicia will be furious you broke into her stash," Rook cut in. He took a cup and a seat for himself. The spiced wine would likely do him in after the day he'd had, but he welcomed it. With a wink, he added, "Perhaps we shouldn't tell her."

The raven squawked and ruffled her feathers at them.

"Oh, are *you* going to tattle on me?" Rook laughed at his own joke.

4

~Shots Fired~

The dark wood walls of Scholar Bates' office reflected the light from the petrolsene sconces and lamps around the room like moonlight on snow. The radiator hummed and burbled in the corner. Sweat prickled the back of Lenore's neck, but it wasn't thanks to that modern heating system. Her heart pounded in her ears, and the tea Scholar Bates' assistant had served tasted like too-warm nothing.

Lenore had received a note earlier that day requesting her presence for an afternoon meeting in his office. She'd paced the Arc-Tech department, wanting to ask Copper if he knew anything about it. In the end, given the last conversation she'd begun with that question, she'd decided against it. Instead, she'd helped Ezra with improvements to the Subaquatic Sloop copy—SS for short.

After everything that had happened at the Halls of Justice, the project that had once been a passion was now a source of pain. The crate it had traveled to Springhaven in had clued her in to Copper's involvement with the attacks.

Watching him explain a complicated mechanical concept to Ezra as they lay on the floor beneath the SS copy, she'd wondered again if she should speak to him. Lenore could have asked if he'd heard any rumors—didn't matter what kind—or the biggest question plaguing her: was Scholar Bates firing her? Then again, what if her behavior toward Copper was the reason for this meeting? Fear and anger warred within her as she had watched Copper mentor Ezra.

Now she sat stewing in her regret and perspiration as Scholar Bates discussed some administrative matters with his assistant. Her eyes roved over every inch of the room, seeking any clue as to the reason for her being there. She only just stopped herself from jumping as someone rapped against the doorframe.

"Ah, Neal! Copper! Come in, come in." Scholar Bates beckoned them inside with great sweeps of his hand. To be fair, the mountainous man did everything large. "Close the door behind you, please."

The sweat on Lenore's neck froze. What had she done?! She tried to review her recent work performance, but events were moving too fast. While Scholar Bates' assistant served Neal and Copper tea, Neal set down a file folder he'd brought with him. Lenore homed in on it. She thought she spied her name printed along the top, but he set it face down before she could be certain. The folder's blank back glared at her from its place on the low table between her and the others.

"How's the sunken temple research going, Neal?" Copper sipped his tea, sparing hardly a glance at Lenore.

Neal was so busy nowadays the two men rarely had a chance to speak, and Lenore avoided the subject at all costs. Any time it came up, she couldn't think about anything except what the members of the Anthropology department must whisper about her and Eamon behind their backs.

"Slow as always, but exciting nonetheless," Neal replied.

While they buzzed on about that, Lenore scrutinized the folder's edges. Was that the tip of an envelope sticking out from the side?

"Scholar Smith is nothing if not meticulous," Neal said, carrying on about the Anthropology department head.

"Well, he's right to be concerned." Scholar Bates folded his hands across his ample belly as he leaned back in his chair. Lenore resisted a groan; he was settling in for a long explanation. "It's not really best practice to move artifacts too much, but there just aren't the same facilities in Bone Port as there are here." He looked to Lenore, who tensed. "You know, Neal and I, along with some others, have explored options for partnering to expand the Bone Port Historical Society, but…"

Scholar Bates trailed off as Neal cleared his throat. The two men exchanged a knowing glance that made Lenore's hammering heart trip over itself.

The Head Curator chuckled. "Forgive me, Lenore, my dear. As usual, I've let my thoughts run away with me."

"It's fine," she said.

It's not fine! her anxiety snapped.

"Let us get down to the purpose of this meeting then. Engineer Allen, Engineer Cooper, and I have been discussing your role here at the museum."

Neal pulled not one but two envelopes from the file folder. Lenore swallowed hard. Her gaze swung to Copper, who gave her an apologetic smile.

I'm getting sacked. Her heart turned into a millstone and crashed into her stomach.

)(

Camilla sat by Falcon's bedside again. Her voice held steady as she read aloud, but her attention remained divided. Darkness pressed against the windows as if eager to hear the story too. Camilla pulled her shawl tighter around her. It was colder here, a disadvantage of using this space as a sickroom. Perhaps that was why Falcon's vitals had measured better today.

It could just be a fluke, Camilla's doctor-brain advised. *The human body changes in response to all manner of stimuli.*

Still, she'd advised against another blanket when Rhea asked earlier that night. Seeing hesitation in the woman's eyes, Camilla had volunteered to stay for a few hours to monitor him. Falcon's sisters, Lark and Wren, ambled in at various points and sat doing their own projects—both drawing at the moment—as they listened to Camilla read.

"Do you think he hears us?" asked Wren. Her words jolted through Camilla's recitation.

Camilla lowered the book and found both girls' eyes on her. She gave her best comforting smile. "There have been accounts of patients waking to say they'd heard everything that transpired around them."

"But what do *you* think?" Lark pressed.

Wren's eyes flicked between Camilla and Lark, tense as a tourniquet. Camilla suspected Wren thought her younger sister was being impertinent, so Camilla gave an easy tip of her head.

"I can't be certain, but I choose to believe he at least knows we're trying."

"Is there anything more you could be doing for him?" Lark asked.

Years of practice kept Camilla's voice even. "What do you mean?"

"Mother and father have had another doctor coming in here."

"Lark!" Wren said. "They said not to tell."

Camilla resisted the urge to ask which doctor, though that didn't stop her mind from rolling through the possibilities. "It's very common to get a second opinion, especially in complicated cases. In fact, Doctor Allen often recommends it. If you don't mind my asking, though, have we done something to offend your parents?"

Wren's cheeks flared a gentle pink as she glared at her sister. The glare went entirely ignored.

Lark half-shrugged. "Not that I know of. I think they just want Falcon better."

Camilla offered her hands to both ladies, who accepted the gesture without hesitation. "I don't blame them one bit."

"I don't like him. Neither does Wren, though she's too polite to say so."

Wren gave her younger sister a disapproving look. In return, Lark pulled a face, which set Wren giggling and made Camilla smile.

Despite her amusement, unease gnawed at the back of Camilla's mind. She couldn't help but wonder if she and Mina being women had influenced the decision to seek out another physician. If she knew more, had more expertise, perhaps she could be a better doctor for Falcon.

Camilla returned her attention to the sisters. They were showing each other their drawings and describing them to Falcon. Their optimism swept away Camilla's dark thoughts like cobwebs. She was grateful for their company and made it a point to tell them so.

)(

Rook was going over some paperwork with Dmitri when the door to his office burst open. His head snapped up, a sharp reprimand coiled on his tongue. Garrick stood there, panting and holding his side. Blood soaked a dinner-plate-sized area along his ribs, and Rook's rebuke died unspoken.

His voice was hard and cold as steel as he asked, "Are you in danger of dying?"

Garrick wheezed. "Nah, just a flesh wound."

"Good. Explain."

"Those gloomy bastards attacked us. Whistler's dead."

"Reaper's people, you mean?"

"Aye." Garrick leaned against the doorframe.

Rook had never seen him show weakness like that. He swore and slid a thumb along his sleeve, where a small blade lay concealed. He stopped himself from offering the older man a seat on his couch; Garrick wouldn't appreciate that sort of gesture.

"Where?" Rook asked. "When?"

"At his post. I was headed to meet him for drinks after duty. They weren't expecting me. It's the only reason I got away."

"Any damage to them?"

Garrick started to shake his head but winced. "Nah. There were three. Whistler went down, and they saw me."

"So you couldn't recover his body?"

"No, sir."

Rook paced. When he spoke again, a serrated edge rasped in his voice. "Garrick, get yourself stitched up."

Dmitri began to tidy the paperwork, though his gaze remained on the other two men in the room.

"I'm fine." Garrick pushed himself off the doorframe. "It's but a scratch."

Rook gave him a hard look. "I'm not done. Tell our people to drink to Whistler's memory tonight. On me. Let them know this won't go unpunished. They'll get more orders later."

Garrick sounded half-mollified. "Aye, sir."

Something else tugged at Rook. Against his better judgment, he added, "And Garrick?" The man turned back to his employer. "Good job keeping yourself alive tonight."

Garrick grunted and left. It was a more positive reaction than Rook had expected.

Next, he locked eyes with Dmitri. Rook's lips pulled back into a snarl as he slipped the knife from his sleeve. Dmitri's focus went straight to the blade, and he took a step back. Rook, however, spun and hurled it at the wall. The tip embedded itself in the wood while the rest trembled.

Rook squared his gaze back on Dmitri, his eyes a shade darker than usual. "No more lone patrols. If we have to pay extra, so be it. And set Chrysalis on Lenore." Rook's petite master of disguise had laid low since being locked in a cell during the Halls of Justice attack. Knowing how badly the experience had shaken her, he'd given Chrysalis a bit of a holiday to recuperate. "Tell her this is her only assignment until further notice. I want full reports. If a new plant grows in their garden, I expect to hear about it."

"Yes, sir," Dmitri said, his voice even. "Anything else?"

Rook took slow breaths. "Contact Lowell. Get him working on some miniature crossbows for me. Small enough to carry concealed. Top priority."

"Should he use the one from that assassin—Mercy?—as a guide?" Dmitri asked. "I understand it didn't do much damage."

"I don't care. I want our people equipped with some kind of ranged defense as soon as possible. He's free to make improvements so long as it doesn't slow him down. Am I understood?"

Dmitri nodded. Rook didn't miss the slight bob in his throat.

"Let's get one thing straight, mate. I don't blame you," Rook said, though his voice had lost none of its edge. "Just so long as *you* don't turn on *me*. Treachery may be part of our world, but I won't tolerate it. Got it?"

"Of course." Dmitri still looked tense, but the twitch in his eyebrow told Rook it was more from injured pride than fear.

Dmitri returned to the paperwork while Rook retrieved his knife.

)(

Grey light filtered through the window as the rain outside dripped like molten silver. Cold seeped from the glass, but huddling by the fire on a tufted footstool kept the worst of it at bay. Bitsy lay like a stripey pile of frayed yarn on the mantle above. His dark eyes were narrowed to sleepy slits. He wasn't even bothered about Majesty, who sat next to Lenore and her footstool. The regal wolf kept bumping her head against her mistress' hand; however, two letters occupied Lenore. One was from her harrowing meeting yesterday. The other was from Oya—her friend and pen pal from Bone Port—and had been waiting beneath the mail slot when Lenore had gotten home not long ago. She kept rereading a certain passage, unable to keep from smiling.

I've been wanting to tell you since I heard. My father told me over dinner a few days ago. I'm saving this letter until he tells me I can finally send it. I really hope nothing changes between then and when you get it. Otherwise, I'll either ruin a surprise or create a very awkward situation. If the former, surprise! If the latter, um, well, I don't really have an answer for that.

Lenore extended a pinkie to scratch the insistent wolf behind her ear. She felt Oya's excitement in the dried ink. Feelings as bright as a rainbow frolicked inside Lenore. She lifted her head when Eamon walked in. A gloom that matched the one outside rolled across her rainbow. He stopped when he noticed her; one of the armchairs around the fireplace must have blocked her from view at first.

"Apologies." He walked to the library's table, where his research materials lay strewn about. "I just need to pack up my things for work tomorrow."

"You don't need to apologize for walking into the same room as me." Lenore's frustration tugged at its leash. She strained to keep her voice level. "That shouldn't be how we are." Eamon began to respond. His scornful tone told Lenore far more than the few syllables he managed to utter before she cut him off. "I've been trying, Eamon. Very bloody hard. I don't know what else I can do."

Eamon didn't look at her as he collected his papers and books from the table. "I don't have time for this, Lenore. I'm meeting my family for tea in an hour. Are you still planning on visiting yours today?"

"Yes, dinner and sparring with Rook, but we need to talk first." Lenore rose from her seat, immediately missing the warmth of the fire. Eamon didn't reply. She resisted the temptation to threaten with cornering him at work. Instead, she brandished the letter she'd been reading. "Oya's travel paperwork is finally processing."

Eamon turned to face her, condescension etched across his face. "And? We've known about Oya's plans to come work here since last autumn."

Lenore ignored the barb. "It's finally gotten approved. Neal pushed for it. Instead of a temporary researcher, she's coming under an apprentice visa."

Lenore saw the wheels in Eamon's head turning. If Neal was the one pushing for the visa, he'd be listed as the responsible party, but Kieran lived with Neal.

Eamon shook his head. "She can stay elsewhere. There are loads of other staff members who can host her."

"The approval has conditions. Only Neal and I are listed as acceptable hosts. With some of the magistrates pushing for tighter borders after the Arnavi landing, it was the only way to get it approved."

Confusion dug deeper lines across Eamon's face. "Why would you be listed as a host? You're an apprentice too."

Lenore looked down. Hope flailed its hands as expectation tried to drown it. Stars, she wanted this to go well. She looked back to Eamon and lifted the other letter. The words surged to burst out of her, but she measured their release. "I've been promoted."

Eamon stared back, his face blank.

After a long moment, she said, "Please, say something."

Eamon took a deep breath and gifted her a fraction of a smile. "Congratulations. It's well-deserved."

Lenore's chest tightened. Not as bad as she'd expected, but also not the reaction she wanted. Tears stung her eyes. To shoo them away, she thought back to the Allens' private celebration for her the night before. They'd had cake and wine and countless hugs and tales of excruciating secret-keeping.

Eamon's smile disappeared. "I suppose we have no choice then. It's not like she can stay in the same house as a Vampyre."

"Precisely." She missed that smile already. Anger smoldered underneath. "So what do we plan to do?"

Eamon went back to collecting his research supplies. "What do you suggest?"

You could stop holding this over my head. She took a moment to breathe before speaking.

"As I said, I don't know what else *I* can do." Unspoken words hung between them, pressing like twin ferrousite poles.

"You could have been killed, Lenore." Eamon's voice sounded as it had the night of the Halls of Justice attack. "You could have been turned—"

"I told you, neither of those are—"

"—so how am I supposed to trust you again? This isn't a lie about your identity or where I send a little money for our personal protection. You placed that creature above me."

Lenore balled her fists, crumpling the letters, and forced her words through gritted teeth. "He's my friend, Eamon. He has as much a right to protection as you or I. And his name is Kieran."

"And this is why I can't move on."

Lenore's anger bubbled, threatening to boil over. "Because you don't see Kieran as a person."

"No. I—"

Lenore didn't stick around to listen to the rest. She turned on her heel and stormed out of the room.

)(

Cold snapped its teeth at Rook's face while he balanced on a tree bough next to a shape of nothingness. They gazed through the windows, though they didn't see anyone inside the Allens' manor from this angle. Darkness shrouded him and the petite shape as they squatted there.

"Remain unseen." Rook kept his voice low. "They have… extra protection. You might not see it, but it's there. If you do see it, though…" He hesitated, wondering if he sounded like a lunatic. "Just mention my name. They know me here." Blazes, this coordination would be tricky if he was going to protect Kieran too.

Chrysalis resembled a cat, perched upon their shared tree branch and dressed in her sneak suit. Though he couldn't see her face, her irritation was evident when she whispered back, "I know what surveillance means."

Fair enough. After what had happened at the Halls, Rook probably didn't need to worry about her rushing inside should something seem amiss.

He smirked. "I know, but your target is prone to getting into scrapes. I'm just trying to look out for you."

Chrysalis looked away. Rook wondered if she was blushing or rolling her eyes.

"You need anything from me before I go in there?" he asked.

"A blanket?" She glanced in his direction. "It's only... Never mind. I'll be making a warmer version of my suit soon."

Rook muffled a laugh against his arm. "Look who's feeling spicy tonight." She turned back to him. "I'll get you something nice and hot later. This is an important assignment. I value your diligence."

"Spicy? Thanks, Gramps." Was that trepidation in her voice as she delivered the joke or just the cold?

He chuckled. "Gramps? How old do you think I am?"

She shrugged. Her voice shivered less this time. "My Gramps was nice, looked out for me. My dad, not so much."

Rook raised an eyebrow at her. This was getting awfully informal and hit a shade too close to home for him. "How about you just keep calling me Rook? Now, eyes up."

Chrysalis nodded. She stiffened, sharpened her focus. Rook skulked to Lenore's old bedroom window and snuck in the same way he had so many times before. From there, he did a short silent circuit of the upstairs. The thick carpet smothered his footfalls as he checked every corner for Collective members. Once done, he headed into the library. True, he could sneak down the stairs and through the back hallway to the kitchen, but Kieran would know if anything was amiss on the lower floors. And this was good practice.

Rook scanned book titles as he strolled. How long would it take someone to notice if he nicked a volume or two? The scent of old paper wafted from the shelves, but it didn't bring Rook comfort. Rather, it dredged up old memories he'd rather keep buried, but he could take his time placing them back into their boxes.

Camilla still didn't want Rook in the house. Because Lenore refused to let him visit her in secret at night and because she was currently having dinner with her adopted family downstairs, he'd have to steal whatever leftover moments with her he could later. After losing Whistler, he itched to see her, to feel she was whole and safe. Of course, the oath's silence told him that, but it wasn't the same. At least, even in her pain, Camilla couldn't ask Kieran to turn Rook away. Not when Rook's blood made it possible for the Vampyre to remain in the city.

"I won't punish my family for what he did," Camilla had said.

To Rook's knowledge, no one had pointed out that Adelle had insisted Twila go first, and even he questioned the wisdom of bringing it up.

A sound like the rustle of a curtain whispered behind him. Hand on his dagger belt, Rook turned to see Kieran standing there.

"Aren't you meant to be downstairs with everyone else?" Rook asked. "You're being very antisocial, skipping out on dinner like this."

"I told them my dinner's waiting for me. I just didn't tell them he isn't where he's supposed to be." Kieran gave Rook a warning look. "Why are you up here?"

Rook gave a shrug reminiscent of a child trying to wriggle out of trouble. "I got bored." He grinned and shook his arm at Kieran. "Hungry? We can get this over with now."

Kieran spent a long time examining Rook's face. "You look tense. Has something happened?"

Rook let himself sigh. "Oh, you could say that."

"Is my family in danger? Is there anything I can do?"

Rook considered it, but no ideas came to mind. "As to the first, I don't think so, but I'm being cautious. I'll let you know about the second."

Kieran nodded and motioned Rook to follow him. Rook still practiced his sneaking as he went. Kieran, of course, made no more noise than a moth would.

They took the back corridor to avoid the dining room and entered the kitchen through the butler's closet, which served as a causeway between the kitchen and conservatory. Esther eyed them as she placed a slice of steaming apple crumble onto Rook's food tray. She'd begun fixing one for him any night he was scheduled to come over, feeding Kieran or not.

"I hope you have a good reason for breaking Miss Camilla's rule, Master Pendragon," she said. "Otherwise, I might decide you don't deserve this." She lifted the dessert plate from his tray and held it hostage.

Rook molded his face into a perfect façade of sheepish contrition. "I—"

"Don't lie to me, Master Pendragon."

Rook opened his mouth, moved it like he was talking, but no sound came out. He couldn't tell her the truth, but blazes, that crumble smelled good.

Esther tapped her foot. "I'm waiting, Master Pendragon."

Rook softened. "I can't talk about it, but I was worried for Lenore, for all of you." That second part was stretching it a touch, but he was sure truth lived somewhere in there. "I was checking upstairs for anything amiss."

Esther lowered the plate back to the tray and clasped her hands before her plump midsection. "I understand, but we have Kieran here. Miss Camilla has made herself clear. If I catch you where you're not supposed to be again, I'll drag you out by your ears. Do we understand each other, Master Pendragon?"

"Yes, ma'am. Perfectly."

He looked at Kieran, whose jaw hung loose as he stared at the exchange. Rook reached over and pushed the Vampyre's mouth closed for him.

Meanwhile, Esther pulled over a couple of chairs. "Sit here now. It's dreadfully cold downstairs. Kieran, you too."

Rook couldn't help but smile as he took his seat. Kieran followed, and they sat in silence as Esther bustled around the kitchen. Lenore eventually appeared with Camilla, both of them carrying the dinner dishes.

"Oh," Camilla said, as if she'd just discovered a slug in her apple crumble. "I didn't realize tonight was one of your nights."

Rook tipped an invisible hat to them. "Evening, ladies."

"I asked Master Pendragon and Kieran to stay up here," Esther said. "No one wants to eat while freezing their noses off."

"I see," Camilla said.

Lenore set down her dishes and took Camilla's from her. "I've got these." Camilla gave her a quick thank you before leaving again. "Esther, would you like help washing up?"

"No, but thank you, darling." Esther smiled, rosy cheeks like apples. "Sit and entertain your guests."

Rook's eyes followed Lenore, happy to see her safe and with people who cared.

5

~The Crime Lords Meet~

The city's reigning crime lords rarely met—too much opportunity for bloodshed. The last time had been just after Rook entered that world, after First Iago had come into power. No surprise, the Enforcers were the subject of tonight's meeting as well.

Rook leaned against the edge of his desk and gazed around his office, ticking names as he took in faces.

Twigs, a ludicrously tall gent with hair like fire and enough freckles to map the night sky.

Prince, Duke's son and most likely to either thank Rook or try to kill him. Rook had never been able to get a read on how Prince felt about Rook offing the old man.

Carver, a man with bronze skin and arms big enough to hurl a steer across a field. Rook knew him best of the group. Carver was a bit like a personnel agent for criminals. He'd built his network solely to connect people. Rook had found a handful of his employees, including Grunt, thanks to Carver.

The visitors sat around the drinks table. Each had, of course, brought their own goons, who clustered in a semi-circle behind their handlers. No one removed their weapons. The idea that any of them would go unarmed was laughable, though no one looked ready to crack a smile. Tension hung in the air thick enough to spread over the toast points plated artfully on the table. Rook had recommended everyone bring a bottle of their favorite drink— they'd never trust anything from his cabinet—but he still provided food. He didn't expect anyone to partake, but he was nothing if not a generous host.

Dmitri and Garrick stood behind Rook, one on either side of the desk.

He pulled out his pocket watch and checked the time. "Apologies for the delay, gents. It seems our fifth is running a little late. In the meantime, please help yourselves."

Rook snapped his fingers at Dmitri, who walked over to load up a plate. His face remained indifferent, though Rook caught a spark of disdain in Dmitri's eyes as he returned.

Rook lifted a cocktail sausage speared on a toothpick to his newest second. "Cheers, mate." As a show of goodwill to the other crime lords, he shoved the sausage into his mouth and smiled.

Despite this demonstration, no one made a move for the food. A few more minutes passed in silence, each of them marinating in the tension. Prince produced a flask and took a swig. Carver pulled a collapsible cup from a bandolier pouch across his chest, followed by a small bottle of red liquid. Twigs, drinkless, only glowered.

Rook motioned to Carver's cup. "Sloe gin? Excellent stuff. One of my folks downstairs puts her own spin on it. I can introduce you if you like."

Carver's eyes flashed golden in the dim light. "Genevieve?"

"The very same," Rook said.

Twigs stood. He looked like a candle with his bright hair, pale skin, and skinny form. Everyone else at the table followed, knocking back chairs and pulling weapons. The thugs behind them stepped forward, doing the latter.

"Steady on, gents," Rook soothed, though steel edged his voice.

"I'm done waiting," Twigs snapped.

Just as he turned to make his way out, Grunt opened the door and motioned a newcomer inside.

"Ah, there you are, Nieva," Rook said. "Welcome. Won't you have a seat?"

Nieva looked around the room, dark eyes sparkling against her olive skin. She wore a smile made of sugar and roses, paired with an unassuming dress that looked like it had come from one of the nicer shops in the Copper district. Behind her loomed two gents in modest cravats and waistcoats, their shoulders broad as a bear's.

Prince growled. "What the blazes is this?"

"Good evening," Nieva chirped. "I'm so pleased to make your acquaintances."

Rook motioned at the new arrival. "Gentlemen, allow me to introduce Ms. Nieva Barker-Nares, owner and operator of Springhaven's largest courier company."

Twigs folded himself back into his seat. "I think you took a wrong turn at the jewelry stall, Ms. Nares."

Still smiling, Nieva brushed an invisible something off her sleeve and flicked her hand in Twigs' direction. "It's *Barker*-Nares, if you please." She strolled over to the table with the sort of languor usually reserved for touring the city gardens. One of her bodyguards pulled out an empty chair for her. "Thank you, Monk. Bruno, wine, please."

Bruno pulled a bottle of wine and a silver cup from a satchel at his side and served. The others kept their eyes trained on Nieva.

"So what do you really do?" Carver leaned forward into the pool of light provided by a merrily flickering oil lamp at the table's center.

Nieva sipped her wine. "I provide a service in exchange for money, nothing more."

Prince pointed at Rook with a finger so thick and tobacco-stained it resembled a cigar. "What are you playing at?"

"I'd wager more money passes through my hands than anyone else's in Springhaven," Nieva said. She plucked a cheese square from the platter in front of her and handed it back to Monk. He sniffed it, licked it, and then popped it into his mouth.

"Listen, sweetheart," Prince said. "This meeting's for big boys. I—"

"She cleans money, numb-nuts," said Carver. His pearly smile shone with its own brilliance. "Ms. Barker-Nares, how disappointing we haven't met before. I'd love to discuss business with you later."

Nieva flashed her own luminescent smile and whipped out a business card from her sleeve, making everyone else twitch for their weapons. "Of course. Please come by my office anytime." Nieva then took a cheese square for herself, presumably since Monk hadn't dropped dead.

Twigs and Prince glared at Carver.

"There will be plenty of time for other business later," Rook said. "For now, let us turn to the matter at hand." He sat at the table and snapped at Garrick, who served him a glass of caramel-colored whiskey. "How many of you have experienced difficulties since the Reaper put on that little pyroprismatics show at the Halls of Justice?"

Twigs, Prince, and Carver each raised a hand. Their attention turned to Nieva.

Palms up, she gestured sugar-coated innocence. "To be honest, business has been booming." She pressed contrite fingertips to her lips. "Apologies. Pun not intended."

Rook's eyes lingered on her, trying to figure out if she was being sincere. He thought he caught the barest shimmer of a smile behind her hand, and turned back to the rest.

"I've lost a handful of people since the attack," he said. "One to the Reaper and the others to the Enforcers. I'd like to offer you all a partnership."

All around, eyebrows cocked, brows furrowed, and fingers steepled. Rook explained his idea: a two-pronged strategy, one piece focused on locking the Reaper out of business deals and slowly starving the Collective of resources, the second behind the scenes to grow the movement pushing for Enforcer reform. It would take people, coordination, and money. A lot of it.

"What about his other enterprises?" Prince asked. Cautious curiosity peeked out from behind tough veneers. "His chop shop."

Carver poured his fourth drink of the night but looked as steady as ever. "You mean those purported medical services? 'Organ replacements,' I've heard them called."

"Organs?" Nieva asked. "As in livers and hearts and the like? Oh dear. How icky."

Twigs shot her a suspicious glance.

"I'm trying to get more details on that," Rook said. "Dmitri here worked in the Collective for a spell, so we have some information, but not nearly enough to stop it. If any of you hear anything, I would welcome the help."

"We haven't agreed to this idea of yours yet." Prince leaned in and gave Rook a one-sided glare supposedly meant to be intimidating. "How do we know you won't double-cross us and hang up our bits as trophies?"

Rook wrinkled his nose. "Ew, can you imagine the smell? Look, Prince, it was me or your old man. I think everyone here would have done the same in my position."

"Mailing him in pieces was a touch on the strong side," Twigs said.

Carver shrugged. "I'da done it."

Rook spread his hands before him. "My plan benefits all of us. Even you, Nieva. I understand the Enforcers have gotten a mite enthusiastic about stopping couriers to search them."

"That is true." She sighed. "It's starting to chip away at my turnaround times."

"First Iago has publicly stated he wants to give the Enforcer order even more power," Rook said. "My sources say he's got some magistrates drafting a proposal for him as we speak. If it passes at the next council session, it's all our necks on the line."

"I've got a better idea." Prince lit a cigar and blew the smoke into the air above him. He waggled the cigar at Rook, dropping ash onto the table. "We do this, Katerina Holmes' motion passes, and you step down."

Rook blinked at him. "I'm sorry, I must have misheard you. I thought you suggested I step down."

"This is how your dad got done," Carver put in.

Nieva and Twigs glanced between Rook and Prince, poised to spring back.

"I don't see the problem," Prince said. "You can't beat the Reaper yourself, nor can you garner the necessary political support without us. A service for a service. We'd all be better off without you in the game."

"I take it that's your price?" Rook asked.

Prince tipped his head. "It is."

Rook looked around the table. "Can I count on the rest of you?"

"I won't agree unless we're all in." Twigs' answer came so quickly Rook suspected him and Prince of conspiring together. Then again, Twigs had always been skittish.

Carver crossed his arms, and his voice thrummed like a clock tower chime. "I'm happy either way, but I reckon Twigs is on to something. You won't get far without all of us, so I'm gonna need us all in too."

Nieva's tone was an apologetic knife across Rook's throat. "I'm afraid I don't know much about this side of things, but they do sound sensible."

Rook's jaw tightened as his movements slowed. Careful, while his mind whirred through different scenarios.

He smiled like poison spreading in hot chocolate and leaned back in his chair. "I'll step down now, but if either initiative fails— Lady Katerina's or the one to take down the Reaper—I'm back. Fair?" He didn't love his new plan, but it would have to do for now.

"And who will take your place?" Carver asked, a keen glint in his eye.

Rook jerked a thumb behind him. "Ermine."

"What?" Dmitri and Garrick said together.

Rook felt their eyes boring into the back of his head. "I'll need to assist with the transition, of course." Prince sneered at him, and Rook waggled his eyebrows back. "I'm sure *you* understand how difficult a sudden change like this can be. Just for a little while."

The others around the table exchanged looks.

"Sounds okay to me, assuming he actually follows through," Twigs said.

"I don't believe he will," Prince said, "but it'll make it that much easier to kill him if he doesn't."

He stuck out his hand, which Rook shook enthusiastically. Both men bared their teeth in feral grins as they tried to squeeze the life out of each other's hands.

Carver also shook on it, though far more cordially. "Let me know if you need anything."

Twigs and Nieva followed suit.

"Now, you'd all best get your ducks in a row," Rook said. "Ermine here will be in touch. If you'd like to stay, though, I can order more goodies."

No one took him up on his offer, and his office emptied within minutes. Once they were good and gone, Rook turned back to his right- and left-hand men.

"Just what are you playin' at?" Garrick demanded. "I ain't working fer this little snot."

"I hate to tell you, old man, but that little snot is your new boss," Rook said. He turned to Dmitri. "No offense."

"Are you out of your mind?" Dmitri asked. "Rook, I can't run this place."

"That we agree on," Garrick grumbled.

Rook had to tamp down on his smile. Seeing the usually stolid Dmitri in such a flap was positively delicious, but vexing him further right after thrusting greatness upon him wasn't the right move, no matter how entertaining.

"Relax, gents. All will be well." Rook hoped he was right. "Have I ever steered you wrong?"

6

~Breaking Oaths~

Night painted every surface and corner with ink as it soaked into the fibers of the city. Kieran swam through it like water. The deeper the dark, the faster he swam. Where the odd rays of petrolsene or firelight permeated, the dark grew thin and slowed him. Kieran gathered stray shadows and became one himself in these areas.

He hadn't known what to expect when he received Cali's version of a calling card—calling him over to her flat, in their case. She never failed to surprise him, but tonight had been especially shocking.

When Kieran returned to the Allen manor, he paused in the kitchen's back entrance. Someone, almost as much a shadow as himself, slipped toward a tray of food waiting on the counter.

Rook.

Kieran's mouth pulled up into a grin. Esther often left the lights low to conserve petrolsene, and he moved like breath through the murk toward the creeping crime lord. Kieran scraped the sole of his shoe along the floor, drawing Rook's gaze, and flitted to the other side. Kieran caught the faintest whiff of a familiar scent.

"Boo." He shed the shadows like a jacket and materialized next to Rook.

Kieran saw Rook's attack coming as if in slow motion and dodged easily. Rook's dagger sliced through empty air. He leapt back, eyes scanning for danger. When he spotted Kieran, Rook loosed a growl between gritted teeth.

"What the blazes do you think you're doing?"

Kieran cocked his head. "I believe it's called 'playing a prank' in some circles. Haven't you heard of it? Or do you always stab first and ask questions later?"

"It's worked for me so far." Rook sheathed his dagger, grumbling under his breath.

"You seem... tetchy tonight. Is everything alright?"

Rook leveled dark, impatient eyes on the Vampyre. "What is this? A cross-examination?"

"This is a friend concerned for a friend."

Rook's lips twitched as he glanced sideways at Kieran. "I've had a bugger of a day."

He turned back to the tray, but Kieran swept in front of him. "Not so fast."

This time, Rook didn't mask his feelings. His brows dipped and nostrils flared like a bull ready to charge. "I'm. *Hungry*."

"You smell like someone else."

"Like who?"

"I don't know, but I caught their scent on my way in." Kieran spun his finger toward the garden. Rook's features betrayed nothing. "Is it one of your people?" Still nothing. "Is it related to why you're in such a foul humor?"

Rook finally blinked. "Maybe."

"I need to know if my family is in danger." Something dark tinged Kieran's voice.

"This one's no danger, just a pair of eyes for me when I'm not around, so maybe take some extra care not to be seen." Rook paused. "Maybe you can help me, though. There are some people I need taken care of." Kieran narrowed his eyes. "They're very bad people, I assure you." Rook gave him a smooth smile, as if that would seal the deal.

"It's been enough of a struggle to hold on to my humanity." Kieran moved away to distance himself from the offer both physically and metaphorically. "I won't be your attack dog."

Rook leaned against the counter and crossed his arms. "You don't think the reason makes a difference?"

"I attacked Lenore in a moment of panic for my own safety. Do you think that excuses me?"

"Touché." Rook's careless wave made Kieran think he was deflecting.

He watched as Rook tucked into the meal Esther had left. Rook's glibness, left hanging in the air, poked at a tender place.

"Careful, Rook, or I might forget to be gentle."

"Oh, I like it when you talk dirty, night stalker."

The sound of someone approaching through the conservatory drew their attention.

Lenore smiled at them as she entered. It was warm, but weariness touched her eyes. "I thought I heard you two in here."

"Hello, little bird," Rook said. His muscles tightened as he kept his hands at his side. "Tell me something good. I need it today."

Lenore took his fingers in hers. "Is everything alright?"

He gave her a crooked smile. "No, but it's better with you here."

"Do you want to talk about it?"

"I do not, but I sense *you* have an extra bit of sunshine to share today."

Lenore exchanged a knowing look with Kieran. She pursed her lips in a weak attempt to control her smile. Rook's answering smirk took her hidden grin by the hand and led it out again.

"I couldn't tell you before. All very hush-hush until the official announcement was made."

Rook leaned closer. "You're teasing me. What is it?"

"I got a promotion at work." She bashfully bit her lip.

Rook's face lit up like a star. He threw his arms around Lenore and nearly lifted her off her feet. Kieran caught Rook stealing a kiss on her head as Lenore squeezed back. Her laughter filled the room like bells.

Neal would want Kieran to call for an end to their embrace, to play his part as pseudo-guardian and remind the two of propriety and their positions, but the words died on his tongue. He couldn't bear to steal this moment of unfettered happiness. It was contagious and lifted his heart too, especially after the sorrow of these last few weeks.

The two finally broke apart, and Rook raised his mulled cider to Lenore. "Expect flowers at work soon. Big ones."

"You see? This is why I couldn't tell you."

At last, Kieran cleared his throat. "She's not the only one with good news."

"Oh?" Lenore asked.

"You could have mentioned that earlier," Rook said, before shoving a buttery dinner roll into his mouth.

"It's better I keep you on your toes." Kieran flashed a fanged grin. "Besides, it concerns both of you."

Rook's brows perked up as he chewed. Lenore stood waiting for more.

Kieran took a deep breath. "I know how to get rid of Rook's oath."

Lenore's eyes bugged out of her head while Rook froze. Mouth still full, indecision flashed in his eyes. Indecision over whether to believe the words or how to react, Kieran didn't know.

"We... we can really release him from it?" Lenore asked.

Kieran nodded. "We can try, anyway. In the end, it's up to the universe whether or not to grant our request."

Lenore deflated, but Rook chuckled. "Oh, that's mighty convenient. If it doesn't work, we can just assume the universe wasn't in a generous mood."

Lenore's lips made an uncertain little pucker. "Well, this rather puts my thing in the shade, doesn't it?"

"Not in the least," Rook said. "I've said my vow's a benefit, have I not?"

"Yes, but you shouldn't be bound to me in that way."

"Are you saying you wish I were bound to you in some other way?"

Kieran's eyebrow ticked up, though he couldn't tell if Rook or Lenore noticed. Celebrating was one thing. Such outright flirting was quite another.

"Aren't you already, by our friendship?" A challenge twinkled in her eyes. "Or is that all the oath's doing?"

Rook relented. "Perish the thought."

"Never actually existed in the first place." Lenore gave his arm a little rub as if smoothing down real feathers.

Rook jerked his chin at Kieran. "This is a very sudden development. How'd you come by this alleged solution?"

"It's rather... complicated."

"As all ancient mysteries must be," Rook quipped.

"Let's just say a little birdie told me."

Rook nodded in understanding. Lenore, however, looked like she wanted to press for more information. She grimaced and picked at her fingernails instead, but stopped when Kieran continued.

"An oath's strength is determined by what is described as the 'heart of the oath-taker'—that would be your father, Lenore—and something referred to as the 'price demanded.' Are you following me so far?"

Lenore's head bobbed.

Rook gave a sarcastic wave and said, "Oh yes. This is all making perfect sense so far."

"Good. Now, it is apparently neither the oath-maker nor the oath-taker who holds a pledge after it's made. Rather... Hmm, this part is a little more difficult to understand."

"The universe?" Lenore suggested.

"In a way. It's the energy that forms magic itself. It's a force, like gravity, but almost sentient in that it acts."

"You're beginning to lose me," Rook said.

"Is it the thing that makes you a Vampyre?" Lenore asked.

Kieran smiled wryly. "I have tried for a long time to understand exactly how that works. Mina believes vampyrism might be a sort of, shall we say, condition. And from my short career as a medical student, I think there's potential in that argument. That's beside the point, however. This energy, for lack of a better word, is something else."

"Something your source refused to explain to you?"

Kieran bared a fang at Rook. "Remember what I said earlier." Rook only smiled back. "All that said, to break an oath, we must appeal to the force that holds it."

Rook's brow transformed into a series of quizzical lines. "You mean to say we simply have to... to pray to magic itself and ask it to release me? Never mind that it sounds ludicrous, I feel like we've sort of done that before."

"There's a bit more to it than that. We must present a case. The more people involved, the stronger the case that can be made."

Rook chuckled, which turned into full-on laughter. "Shall we make it a party then?" Turning to Lenore, "I imagine your family would love that. Us all getting together and talking about how awful it is that I'm bound to you."

"Rook." Lenore frowned. "It's not like that."

Rook reined in his laughter, but his words still cut with a sharp edge. "Isn't it, though? Mina and Neal and Camilla would all be thrilled not to have me tangled up in your life. Eamon, well, he'd be the first in line for this little experiment."

Lenore's voice sank to a pained whisper. "Rook, they don't hate you. Camilla is angry, yes. She needs a direction for her grief, but none of them can forget the risk you've taken for me. They know I would be dead without you."

"I can attest to that." Kieran crossed his arms. "You would do well to remember we all consider Lenore a member of this family and want to keep her safe, I daresay as much as you. And what you do comes with danger."

A knowing glare passed between him and Rook. The latter took Lenore's hands in his. His voice had lost its sharpness but rang just as sure. "All the more reason the oath needs to stay. Without it, I wouldn't have been able to save you."

Lenore sighed. "It's your choice, but I don't think it's right. It hurts you."

Rook shook his head. "Small price to pay."

"And what about the price to my own conscience? I hate seeing you suffer. No amount of rationalization will stop that."

"I don't have an answer for that." It was his turn to sigh, and he gave Lenore's fingers a squeeze. "But I know how important this is to you."

Kieran was surprised Rook's heartbeat maintained its usual tempo as he considered the decision. If Rook was at all concerned, he hid it well.

Lenore squeezed back. "*You* are important to me."

Ah, that *made his heart skip,* Kieran noted. *And hers too.*

Rook gifted her a gentle smile. "I'm not worried about anything between us. You know that, but I worry about you."

"I know, but as you've said, your vow isn't a fortune teller. You can't protect me from everything, and you shouldn't have to suffer for it. I'd rather work with you than be at odds. The oath will never let us do that. Partners, not shields, remember?"

His smile grew. "Partners then."

Lenore smiled back. "Yes. Partners."

)(

They decided they'd make the case the following week in the Allens' dining room, being large enough to accommodate everyone. Camilla and the Allens were willing, though not nearly with the fervor Rook had predicted.

And Eamon, according to Lenore's account, was on a whole other level about it.

"Truly?" he'd asked, his face agog before splitting into a huge smile. "We can cut him from our lives? Well, I say if there's a chance, we should take it."

"Eamon," Lenore had snapped, "you do realize Rook is one of my closest friends?"

"I don't know, Lenore." She hadn't been able to tell whether he was ignoring her or tone-deafened by joy. "He never really got on well with others as a child, and we don't know how the oath might have affected him, especially in regard to you."

Lenore was sorely tempted to disinvite Eamon, but her concern for Rook outweighed her anger.

Rook, meanwhile, had thought he'd have to order Dmitri to attend and was surprised when Dmitri only asked who, where, and when.

"Yes, Camilla will be there. And at their house," Rook said. "Now, I don't want to fight with you about this, but—"

"I'll be there."

Rook stared at him. "You'll what now?"

"I'll be there." Dmitri's words were cold and clipped. "Once you're free of the infernal thing, you can focus on what's actually important."

Rook smiled like the slow drawing of a dagger. "You think once it's gone, assuming this isn't the asinine hogwash it sounds like, I'll just cut ties?"

"Yes."

Rook laughed and told Dmitri to be there on time. "And dress nicely." He wiped a tear from his eye, still chuckling. "You're still on duty for me."

)(

Silence weighed down every particle of air in the dining room and clung like humidity. Lenore observed everyone while trying to look like she wasn't observing anyone. Dmitri stood at one end of the room and stared at an invisible spot on the table. Camilla, who hadn't seen him since that horrible night at the Halls of Justice, threw sharp glares at him and Rook from the other side. Lenore, Eamon, Mina, and Neal stood in the center, while Kieran joined Camilla.

Lenore clasped her hands under the table. If she weren't so hopeful for the chance to free Rook from his oath, she might have called the whole thing off. If this went well, perhaps they could do the same for Eamon, assuming his had actually taken—they'd never seen any sign that it had. She dared a glance in his direction and remembered how he behaved when she'd approached him about this venture. Anger like smelted ore bubbled inside her. She stamped it down, though, and looked at Rook.

Focus, she told herself.

Neal looked around the group. "Shall we sit? Esther has made us some lovely treats."

Though the family had said it wasn't necessary, Esther had insisted on fixing "a few plates of nibbles" for the event, not to mention brewing up some strong tea.

"You can't battle ancient magic on an empty stomach," she'd proclaimed against every objection.

Lenore had tried to explain they wouldn't so much be battling it as entreating it.

"And I shall treat you all," Esther had cackled.

In response to Neal's suggestion, Rook asked, "Can I have Kieran's portion?"

Camilla's mouth snapped open, likely to fling some insult him, but Mina stepped in before Camilla could utter a syllable. "You can't honestly be worried there won't be enough to go around."

"A few plates of nibbles" apparently meant small mountains of food.

"My apologies, Doctor Allen." Rook inclined his head. "I was only trying to lighten the mood."

They sat and helped ensure Esther's hard work didn't go to waste. Kieran told Dmitri he was pleased to see him and asked how he was keeping.

"Well enough." Dmitri didn't expound.

Lenore exchanged a look with Rook.

"To address the elephant in the room," Rook said, "no. Dmitri isn't working for those insane death worshippers any longer."

A breeze of relief washed into the room.

"I work for Rook now," Dmitri said.

And back out it went.

"I think that went without saying," returned Rook. "They can tell by uniform. You've never looked so dapper in all your life!"

Rook slapped Dmitri on the back. Lenore suspected Dmitri wanted to return the gesture across Rook's face. He didn't, but that might have been due to Neal's interference.

"Lenore, would you like to take us through the process?"

She nodded and took a steadying sip of her tea. "Kieran, please jump in and correct me if necessary. Essentially, we will join hands and, um, reach out to the magical energies of the world."

One of Camilla's eyebrows crept upward, while Rook unsuccessfully tried to squelch his growing smirk. Eamon placed a hand on Lenore's arm. She resisted the urge to shake it off but pulled away to fold her hands beneath her chin.

"As it will be easier to do this with something to focus on, we should all focus on Rook."

A shameless grin flashed across his face. Throwing his head back, he held both arms wide like he was basking in the sun.

Camilla's teacup shook in her hand. Kieran placed his atop it.

"Rook's strutting aside," Lenore continued, "it's the oath we need to… address, for lack of a better word. We'll each take turns making our statements, starting with me, working our way around to Rook, and then finally me again. The order has something to do with, ah…" She looked to Kieran for help. "Investment?"

"Or consequence," he said.

"Thank you. That."

A windy silence swirled around the table. Camilla looked at Neal and Mina, then Kieran, and finally Lenore. "And then what?"

Lenore hunched her shoulders in uncertainty. "And then we say thank you?"

"Manners are important, as I understand it," Kieran concurred.

"But how do we know if it worked?" Camilla asked.

"Precisely what I was thinking," Dmitri said.

Lenore opened her mouth only to close it. She tried again. "I don't know. I mean, short of someone trying to hurt me…"

"Well, that certainly won't happen," Mina said. "Either it works or it doesn't. And even if it does, what happens after the fact is entirely up to Rook."

Even so, everyone looked to Kieran. He shrugged. "Oath-bonds were rare and poorly understood even in the Old World, thus the uncertain nature of the ceremony. You all now know as much as I do on the subject."

More looks exchanged between those gathered. Sighs whistled, digits fidgeted, and every eye roamed to Rook. He was sitting coolly in his seat as if debating another cup of tea.

"Are we ready then?" Neal asked.

Acquiescent mumbles went round, and the petitioners joined hands.

Lenore looked at Rook and concentrated on the invisible shackles linking them. She saw them like heavy chains around his shoulders and wrists, razor-edged and capricious. "Forces of magic, of the elements seen and unseen… um, may we please have your attention? We have come to make a case against the vow Varick Pendragon swore to Edgar Crowley. Thank you for hearing us."

Lenore ignored the shudder of suppressed laughter in Rook's shoulders and looked to Dmitri.

He took a deep breath and spoke with shocking confidence. "The weight of this promise is detrimental to Varick. He cannot live his own life. Edgar never meant for Varick to undertake the trials he has. Edgar never imagined the sort of danger Lenore would be in. Varick was only meant to protect her from Enforcers. Given the circumstances she's found herself in, it demands too much. This undertaking should be his choice and his alone."

Lenore tried to force her concentration not to waver. She mostly succeeded but bristled at Dmitri's presumption to know her father's will.

Kieran went next. "Lenore is my dear friend. Though I never want ill to befall her, I know what it is like to be trapped in a life one has not chosen for themselves. Choice is a beautiful thing. Lack of it is oppression. Rook shouldn't be forced to choose between suffering and protecting Lenore despite promises made or how any of us feel for her."

After that came Camilla followed by Mina, Neal, then Eamon. No one mentioned Rook's character or lifestyle, but they did say Lenore should be able to live her life, whatever choices that entailed, without the guilt his pledge caused, and that it wasn't fair to punish Rook for her decisions.

When it came to Lenore, she grasped for the right words. She stopped and started and stopped again before they all came tumbling out. "Rook is a permanent piece of my heart, welded into place by our experiences. As much as the idea of losing him hurts—because *believing* and *knowing* our friendship is built on more than just this vow are two different things—it hurts even more to consider the prison that is this oath. I want no part of his captivity. Even if everything between us evaporates, even if we forget everything we've shared, I still want his freedom." Her voice had begun to crack. She gripped Rook's hand so tightly she worried she might hurt him. "I am Lenore Crowley, daughter and heir of Edgar and Twila Crowley. If this promise is my inheritance, I call for its abolishment."

A crease appeared above Rook's nose. His mouth set in a grim line. When he spoke, his voice was low and clear. "Go ahead. You've heard the arguments. Do whatever you think is right. For my part, continuation or dissolution, I will never forget or abandon Lenore. I will continue to guard her because she is precious to me, and you cannot change that."

Lenore held her breath. A few moments of stillness passed. "Thank you again, forces of magic, for hearing us." Another pause. "And, um, have a good evening."

A snigger broke out down the table. Neal tried to contain himself, but laughter bounded out of him. "Have a good evening?"

"I was being polite!" she replied, though she was already laughing as well.

Kieran chuckled with them, though his eyes were on Rook. Camilla and Mina smiled and shook their heads, as did Dmitri, though without the smile.

Smirking, Rook stood. "Well, that was very entertaining." He placed a hand over his heart. "Thank you, everyone, for your heartfelt words. I am…" He pretended to sniff and made his voice falsetto. "…truly touched."

Concern drove Lenore's laughter away. "Nothing happened?"

He shrugged. "Not that I can tell. Now, if you will excuse me, I've had a good bit of tea."

)(

As Rook left the dining room, he felt every eye follow him. He headed for the nearest water closet, which was tucked away from the main entertainment areas of the house. Locking the door, he sank to his knees and unleashed control over his features. His breath quickened as the entity living in the small of his back moved. It had begun at the table as a niggling while they'd laughed. At first, Rook had wondered if the oath was simply annoyed they tried to evict it. Then it had changed. As he knelt on the floor, it began to roil, grating against his bones, dragging barbs beneath his skin.

No, please. Don't leave me. He wasn't certain that's what was happening, but he'd never felt anything like this. *I wasn't serious. I need you to… Please, I ca—*

Rook bit back a cry of pain as invisible talons penetrated his lower back. They rent through his flesh but left no marks.

Don't. Please. Don't take her from me.

Tears escaped his eyes, indiscernible from the sweat dripping off his forehead. The force squeezed, stealing Rook's breath. No air left to scream. The claws plunged, speared through Rook's spine, and wrenched the oath free. His back arched as spirit-tendrils of weight and responsibility pulled taut before soundlessly snapping. Nerves made of watchfulness splintered, exposing raw ends.

The force left him. Rook felt lighter but also broken. A gaping unseen hole pulsed in his back.

Lenore. Lenore. Lenore, he repeated to himself. *I love you. I know you. Bone Port. Halls of Justice.*

Rook recounted times they'd spent together, in danger and in joy. He fixed his mind on the memory of her laugh, the feel of her skin, the sound of her voice, as his breathing returned to normal. He looked where Lenore had gripped his hand. The indentation of one of her rings had yet to disappear. He brushed a finger over it before tidying himself as much as possible. When he opened the water closet's door, he found Dmitri standing outside.

His eyes roved over Rook's appearance. "I thought you'd gotten lost."

"Do me a favor," Rook said. "Punch me."

"Beg your pardon?"

"Stop pretending and pu—"

Rook stumbled back under the force of Dmitri's fist. He pressed a hand over his throbbing eye socket. It replaced the residual ache in his back, which was dissipating like fog on the ground. And it served an alternate purpose.

"We'll discuss this later, you worthless cur!" He made sure to shout loud enough for it to carry.

Dmitri failed to suppress the satisfied smile stretching across his face. Sneering, Rook left him and re-entered the dining room.

"Everything alright?" Neal asked. He zeroed in on Rook's eye. "Would you like some ice?"

"Yes, please. In a glass. Covered with alcohol."

7

~ *"He lives!"* ~

Lenore stayed late at the Allens' manor. She wanted to speak with Rook, but he'd left with barely a goodbye shortly after getting into a scuffle with Dmitri and downing a drink from Neal. His hasty departure would have bothered her more if she hadn't been so distracted by other thoughts. Kieran also hadn't tarried, most likely for Eamon's benefit. He, Mina, and Neal had headed upstairs to the library with glasses and a bottle of wine. Eamon sat in the front parlor making polite small talk with Dmitri. Resentment thrummed through Lenore as she listened from the dining room. Why should *they* chat like old friends? Dmitri had been the one to guide their excursion through the Halls of Justice.

She shoved another miniature sausage roll into her mouth and chewed angrily. Footfalls shushed over floorboards behind Lenore. She could tell it was Camilla who sidled up to her by the soft tread.

"Join me upstairs?" Camilla whispered.

Lenore nodded and grabbed a few more leftover treats. They went through the back hallway. Eamon and Dmitri stood next door in the receiving hall when the ladies appeared.

Before either gent could speak, Camilla said, "While Lenore is here, I'd like her assistance with my masquerade outfit. I'm sure you understand."

"Don't feel obligated to wait for me," Lenore added. "I'll get a cab home." She hadn't meant to sound so callous, but she wasn't that sorry either.

When Camilla shut the door to her room, Lenore released a sigh. It had been coiling in her chest, ready to become something far more rancorous. She flopped onto a settee near Camilla's crackling fireplace.

Camilla crossed to her wardrobe. "Are things any better with Eamon now that we've tried this little experiment?"

"I don't know. I told you what a disgustingly happy boor he was about it. I haven't been able to speak to him since." Camilla made a noise in her throat that told Lenore they weren't in total agreement on the subject. "I understand why he hates Rook, but he could be more polite about it."

Camilla pulled a white gown from her wardrobe, layers of pearly faille fluttering as she did. "Perhaps he just needs more time."

Lenore groaned and rubbed her face. "He doesn't want resolution, Camilla. And I'm so tired of living with his constant scorn. I… I've considered…"

Camilla placed the dress across her bed. She walked over, knelt down, and took her adoptive sister's hands in hers. "What is it, Lenore? Whatever it is, you know you can tell me. We're family."

Tears burned in Lenore's eyes. The words surged up in her throat, warring against blockades of shame. She squeezed Camilla's hands and looked into those bright, earnest, blue eyes.

And she told Camilla what had secretly taken root in her heart.

)(

Chrysalis watched through the window as Camilla and Lenore descended the steps. Lenore's eyes were red and puffy, and Camilla held Lenore's hand as if lending strength. Concealed by her sneak suit and the thick darkness, Chrysalis remained hidden while Camilla escorted Lenore outside and into a cab.

The little spy had only just arrived. Rook had sent a message earlier that she was needed back at her post. She knew she should head to the townhouse Lenore shared with Eamon, but her feet remained rooted to the spot. Dmitri had asked Camilla if he might speak to her privately. Chrysalis could just make out their words within the parlor as she pressed against the wall and peered through the window's bottom corner. Dmitri stood when Camilla re-entered the house. She stared him down with eyes like shards of a clear winter sky.

"You wanted a word?" Camilla asked.

"Yes. I wanted to ask how you're doing." Dmitri's bearing was stiffer than usual. "We haven't spoken since… that night."

"Thank you for your concern. I'm fine." Camilla clipped her words like popping stitches.

Chrysalis felt the tension ripple. It urged her to mind her own business, so she pressed closer, her nose nearly touching the glass. The branches attached to her head for camouflage swayed gently.

Dmitri clenched his fists as silence swooped through the room like a mute banshee. "I know it's been difficult for you, losing your mother. I just want you to know I'm sorry, and if—"

"You *know*, do you?" Camilla's voice cracked through Dmitri's words like ice over a frozen pond, threatening the skater atop it. "Have you had Rook keeping tabs on me? I'm not a child, Dmitri, and I certainly don't need *you* coddling me like one."

Dmitri's voice strained to remain level. "I haven't done any such thing. Lenore talks to Rook, who talks to me, much as I'd like him to keep his mouth shut most of the time."

"So tell him not to."

"He's my employer."

"And it's my *life*! If I wanted you privy to it, I'd invite you back in, but you blew that to smithereens, didn't you?"

"Take it up with Lenore instead of blaming me."

"Lenore? It's hardly Lenore's fault our relationship ended. Perhaps it wouldn't have if you hadn't been such a child."

Chrysalis wished she had popcorn for the show. She saw by how Camilla shook that she was barely holding the threads of her frayed patience together.

Dmitri snarled, "I wasn't the one who ended it."

"Yes, you jolly well were! You said not to contact you again."

"Because I would contact you! *You* broke it off with *me* in a bloody letter."

"That was after the fact. And you don't get to decide when we communicate and when we don't."

Dmitri pressed his lips together and looked away. He took slow, deep breaths, shoulders tight. When he spoke again, it was with a heavy measure of control. "So you never intended to break things off with me?"

"Not at the time," Camilla said, cold as frostbite. "Though now I see it was for the best."

Chrysalis gawped, her eyes wide.

Dmitri pressed his fists against his thighs. "Blazes. I wish I had known. I never would have—"

"It was for the best," Camilla repeated. "There's no point in looking backward. If it means that much to you, ask yourself what we can salvage."

"This isn't… Dammit, Camilla! We can go back. We can try again."

Camilla was already shaking her head. "No, we can't. We're in different places now, Dmitri. We've both changed."

"But I want—"

"I don't."

Dmitri's face went stony, the way Chrysalis was used to seeing him. His eyes, though, couldn't shake their regret. "For what it's worth, I'm sorry."

"I'm sorry too," Camilla said softly.

A long pause passed between them.

Dmitri broke it, quiet and stern. "I meant to offer you support tonight, and I still do. What do you think can be salvaged?"

"I don't know. If you'd like to come around for tea, once we've both let our heads cool, we can see."

Dmitri gave a sad smile. "I'd like that very much."

Camilla nodded. "Don't you dare bring Rook."

Dmitri rolled his eyes. "Ugh, I wouldn't dream of it."

As his gaze spun, it landed on the window. Chrysalis ducked back beneath the sill. She listened as Camilla and Dmitri said their goodnights, and the front door opened a few moments later. Chrysalis retreated farther into the darkness. Dmitri's footsteps approached. She barely made out his silhouette against the light of the front porch. His voice scraped against her ears, but given the distance between them, she suspected he couldn't see her.

"You have *one* job, Chrysalis. How about I don't tell Rook you're slacking off, and you don't share any of what you've just witnessed?"

Chrysalis didn't hesitate before whispering back, "Deal."

)(

Gauzy light glimmered through the heavy bed curtains. A single petrolsene lamp burned in the room beyond. Mina was barely aware of being awake. The goose down coverlet beckoned her back to sleep, but a faint memory told her she couldn't just yet. From the corner of her eye, she saw Neal slowly rise to consciousness. A thumping noise from downstairs refused to stop. Ah, that was the memory. Mina had willed it away, but its persistence had woken her properly. She had a short list of maladies for which she made house calls, but her home address wasn't public.

She abandoned the warmth of her bed for duty. Neal watched blearily as she donned her dressing gown.

"No, no, I'll go," he mumbled. "You stay here."

Neal half-tumbled off the mattress. A clock on the wall said it was just past three in the morning. Despite his offer, Mina didn't return to bed—it would be such a disappointment to have to get right back up again.

The knocking continued as they made their way downstairs. When they opened the front door, Mina was shocked to see a young girl, no older than thirteen, standing there in slippered feet.

"Lark?" Mina exclaimed. "Are you alright, darling? Has something happened with Falcon?"

"He's awake!" Lark bounced on her toes, her face a mixture of concern and relief.

"Good heavens! Neal, my bag, please."

Neal was already halfway into the front parlor. Mina turned toward the staircase and called for Camilla. They all moved upstairs for easy communication. Mina and Camilla hurried to change into something presentable while Neal offered to look after Lark.

"I don't need looking after," Lark said. "Shall I help Doctor Allen? It might get us there faster."

Neal made a few faltering objections about hospitality and propriety but couldn't sustain them in these circumstances.

"If you're offering, you can assist Miss Camilla." Mina shouted from her bedroom. "Neal, hail us a cab, please."

They arrived, sans Neal, at the Smoke residence within the hour. Lark was practically running. Mina and Camilla followed at a slightly more decorous pace.

The younger girl skidded into Falcon's sickroom. "I've brought Doctor Allen and Miss Camilla."

"Lark!" her father scolded.

He began to say more but trailed off as Mina swept through the door and took in the scene.

Falcon was smiling weakly and sitting up, supported by a mountain of pillows. His mother bent over him. She helped him drink a little water. Meanwhile, Wren sat nearby wringing her handkerchief in her hands.

Mina turned to Jacob. "How long has he been awake?"

"My deepest apologies, Doctor Allen. I specifically instructed Lark not to rouse you." Jacob turned a piercing glare onto his youngest daughter. "She will be punished for this terrible disturbance."

"All part of the job, Scholar Smoke." Mina gave him a comforting smile. Camilla did the same as she stood back, ready to assist. "Now, how long has Falcon been awake?"

"He started calling out a little after midnight, but—"

"He just woke up? All on his own?"

"Yes, ma'am, but you really needn't be here. We've called for Marcus Gillespie."

Confusion froze Mina. Wren had been watching this scene unfold with her shoulders hunched by her ears. She took this opportunity to slip out of the room like a freed coal mine canary. The sound of the door shutting behind her shook Mina out of her stupor. Camilla had mentioned something about this but hadn't gotten many details.

"Doctor Gillespie?" Mina asked. "Whatever for? I have been Falcon's attending physician all these weeks."

Jacob shot Lark another look. This time, she shot one back.

"He's recently become our new family physician," he said. "Now that Doctor Phillips has retired, you see."

Mina smiled again. Not with her usual warmth, but as an automatic gesture after so long in this field. "Well, I am here now. Shall we get on with it?" She didn't wait for an answer. She was definitely overstepping her bounds, but if she was going to be ejected anyway, she might as well do some good while she could. Mina approached the sickbed, her smile warming like a spring morning. "Hello, dear."

Falcon slowly rolled his head over the pillow. It took a moment for recognition to light in his eyes. "Hello, Doctor Allen." He was already searching behind her. When he found Camilla, he smiled wider. "Milly."

Mina saw Camilla restrain herself, keeping her smile and motions professional. Had it not been for the blow from Jacob a moment ago, she might have encouraged her apprentice not to stand on ceremony.

"Hello, Falcon," Camilla said. Her smile got away from her, but the respectful incline of her head tempered it. "How are you feeling?"

"From what my parents have told me, I'm better than I should be." His voice croaked a little as he spoke, and his mother urged him to drink more water.

Mina got to work checking his vitals and neural functions. The latter were a little slow but in working order. Camilla wrote down every word and hopped to every instruction.

Doctor Marcus Gillespie arrived with his son, Barry, in tow just as the ladies began testing Falcon's strength.

"Good evening, all," Marcus said. "I hear someone's still a bit under the weather." He gave Falcon an exaggerated wink.

"I'm afraid Mister Smoke is more than under the weather," Mina replied. "His cognitive abilities—"

"Yes, thank you, Miss Allen," Marcus said. "I shall be performing all the necessary examinations this evening. Or shall I say morning?" He chuckled at his joke.

Mina couldn't manage a smile this time, not even an automatic one. Not that she wished to. Instead, she held up her notes. "No need, Doctor Gillespie. I have results to share with you."

Marcus waved her words away and sidled up to the bed. Barry followed, slipping between his father and Camilla. He turned to find himself nose to nose with her.

"Would you mind moving, please?" Barry said.

"I'm perfectly fine, thank you. This spot has served me well all night." Her face was pleasant, but her eyes were sharp.

Falcon's gaze swayed around the growing group. "Why are the Gillespies here?"

Rhea stroked his hair. "They're our new doctors, dear."

Falcon's brows crossed. "He's not my doctor."

"Nor mine," Lark agreed.

Falcon looked to his youngest sister and then around again. "Camilla is my doctor. She was here."

Every eye turned to Camilla before dubiously returning to Falcon.

"You're confused, my boy," Marcus said. "Miss Camilla isn't a doctor."

"I know." Falcon's cheeks flushed with exertion. "She's not yet, but she's been here while I've... Since the insurrection."

"That's true," Mina put in.

"Actually," Marcus said, "she's only been here intermittently. You are mistaken, Mister Smoke, but that is understandable given your—"

"You know what he means," Lark cut in.

"That is enough, young lady!" Rhea snapped. "Go to your room."

"He shouldn't even be here," Lark insisted. "It's Doctor Allen and Camilla who've—"

"You heard your mother!" Jacob was nearly shouting.

Lark dipped her chin, but her mouth remained set. "But—"

"But nothing. Do as your mother says. We'll discuss your behavior later."

Lark huffed and stomped out of the room. After she was gone, Rhea turned back to Marcus.

"I'm so sorry, Doctor. She's... Ever since her brother... Well, she's had trouble adjusting." Rhea smiled again, though it wobbled. "Hopefully, things will be better now."

Marcus replied, "Think nothing of it, Miss Smoke. Young ladies are prone to—"

"No! Shut up!" With a grunt, Falcon pushed himself halfway upright. "I don't want you here, so get out."

"Falcon," said his father gently.

"He's full of..." Falcon slumped back against the pillows, took a deep breath, and started again. "I want Camilla. Or Doctor Allen with Camilla in assistance if Camilla isn't allowed."

"Allowed to practice medicine, you mean?" Marcus asked.

Falcon rubbed a hand over his face. "Yes. Of course that's what I mean."

"I'll show you out, Doctor," Jacob said.

As Barry turned to follow, Falcon squinted at him. Barry returned an inquisitive expression. After a moment, Falcon asked, "Is your nose crooked?"

Barry scowled at Camilla before hurrying after his father. As peace returned to the room, Camilla looked to Mina.

"Shall we continue?" Mina said.

They resumed their examination without further issues. When conversation had been flowing pleasantly for a while, Wren reappeared. She curled up against a corner of the couch and slipped into the exchange as if she'd never left.

With the morning light came yet another visitor. Falcon's grandfather, Harding Smoke, hobbled in as everyone was settling down with some tea.

"He lives!" wheezed Harding, punching the air with his fist.

Rhea rose to meet him. "I'm so glad you made it, Father."

Jacob joined her and extended his hand. "Good to see you, sir."

"Morning, Grisham." Veins bulged from Harding's hand as he took Jacob's.

Camilla leaned toward Wren and whispered, "Grisham?"

"That's my father's original surname," Wren said. "Grandad insisted he change it so his name could continue on through Mother, lest he forbid them from marrying."

"Interesting." Camilla moved closer to Mina as Wren stood to hug her grandfather.

"And good morning to you, princess. Wherever is your partner in crime?"

Wren's easy shrug belied the earlier tension. "I think she's sleeping upstairs. It's been such a night for all of us."

"So I gather. And these two lovely ladies? Who might you be?"

"Doctor Philomena Allen." Mina realized too late Harding had meant to kiss her hand, a practice Mina found both silly and unhygienic. She gripped his awkwardly positioned hand and shook it like a dead fish. "I'm Falcon's attending physician. This is my assistant, Camilla."

Camilla's eyes darted to her mentor. She'd likely noticed that Mina had left the Hawkins surname out of the introduction. Camilla made no effort to address the gaffe, however. At least Harding seemed to have caught on to the idea of shaking a woman's hand and did so with her. Or rather, he went through the motions, but they felt empty.

"Allen, eh?" Harding's voice grew gruff. "Any relation to that soft pup running a smear campaign against our brave Enforcers?"

"Magistrate Allen is my husband," Mina said.

"Indeed? You have my sympathies then."

"Not necessary."

Harding muttered something indiscernible. Turning back to Falcon, "Tell me how you're doing then, lad. How long till you're back in the fight?"

"Doctor Allen says, if all goes well, she'll have me try walking soon."

"It will take time for you to regain your strength," Mina said.

"Is that so?" Harding asked. "Let's hear it then. What's the plan?"

Mina looked at Falcon, Rhea, and Jacob, who all nodded. She outlined Falcon's new treatment strategy, and Harding's expression showed approbation and dislike by turns.

)(

Lenore turned slowly to take in the entirety of the Arc-Tech department. She saw every shelf, tool, and broken piece with new eyes. Her new position as journeyman—the title was a holdover from the Old World—wasn't that different from her time as an apprentice. Neal had long entrusted her with more than most mentors did. Even so, she felt the responsibility resting on her shoulders like a mantle she had yet to grow into.

Neal, for whom she was waiting, had gotten caught up in a meeting. Again, she envisioned the conversation she planned to have with him and devised arguments for various reactions. She'd offered what she thought were sound ideas before, only to have the results blow up in her face. Lenore hoped this wouldn't be one of those times. She and Neal walked on good ground again. She swallowed hard; this too might damage their relationship.

When Neal walked in, uttering his apologies and usual complaints about the managerial life, Lenore made herself smile and gave all the right responses. Given how early winter nights swept in, they took a hansom cab home. Lenore began to recite her practiced words as soon as the driver shut the door behind them.

"I hope I'm not making a huge mistake by starting down this road…"

"Always a good way to open a conversation." A gentle smile curled up Neal's cheeks. "I am well prepared now."

Lenore's expression fell. "It's about Eamon."

"Ah, I see." Neal straightened. "Any better since our conference with Rook?"

Lenore resisted the urge to slump. That was another issue—she hadn't seen Rook since that night. He'd sent a note yesterday to say, due to some business matters—whatever that meant—he couldn't come over to feed Kieran. Yet another reason she was heading home with Neal.

"Eamon was thrilled with the whole endeavor, but that's not the issue. He's still hung up about me not telling him about Kieran. He says he can't trust me while I continue to believe I was right."

"You were right." Neal leaned forward and offered his hand across the cab. "I know it doesn't help things, but I want you to know I stand by you."

Lenore accepted the gesture. "Thank you. It's… It's such a poisonous environment at home. Every time I'm there, I feel so… unwanted."

"Oh, poppet."

Lenore shook herself. Despair had sunk cold claws into her again, trying to suck away her energy. She made herself sit up straight, tightened her jaw, and lifted her eyes to Neal's. "There's something I need to ask you. You and Mina actually. It's important."

Neal squeezed her hand before pulling his away to fold them in his lap. "Of course."

"Please don't be angry." And Lenore haltingly unfurled the request, feeling her bridge back crumble behind her with every word.

8

~All the Wrong Choices~

Dmitri slipped past the door, which was disguised as a wall, and into Rook's little hideaway. A single cracked petrolsene lamp lit the bare room. He stopped dead as the door clicked shut behind him. *This* was where one of Springhaven's most feared crime lords laid his head? The walls of Rook's office back in the Char district showed age, true, but it was well kept and filled with furniture chosen to impress both guests and enemies. The fixtures were kept in good repair, and bloodstains were cleaned away after examples had been made. The word *dismal* came to Dmitri's mind as he took in his surroundings. Nothing more than a pallet on the floor served as a bed. The walls—chipped and naked stone—radiated cold.

Rook had only recently trusted Dmitri with this location. This first visit made him wonder if Rook wasn't a little ashamed of it. Although, security was more than enough reason to keep it a secret too.

The man in question slouched over a splintered table off to the side. A half-filled glass and bottle of cheap whiskey, nothing like the good stuff Rook usually drank, sat with him. He kept one hand tucked beneath the tabletop. Any manner of weapon likely hid there. Rook's eyes were already on his visitor, and a slow smile slid across his face.

"Well, hello. To what do I owe the pleasure?"

"I'm here to check on you," Dmitri said.

Rook chuckled mirthlessly. "How kind of you. Unnecessary, but kind."

Dmitri stared at Rook for a long time. Rook stared back, and neither said a word.

Rook eventually returned to his drink, motioning to the seat opposite him. "Would you care to join me?"

Dmitri remained where he stood. "You've skipped work the last two days. What's going on?"

"Can't a man take a break?" Rook leaned back in his chair and took a long sip. His other hand remained concealed beneath the table.

"This is you we're talking about. You don't take breaks, not from work, and especially not with rivals breathing down your neck. They've sent more messages. You have to progress with the plan soon."

Rook shook his head, smirking. "You think you know me so well? You've barely shaken the wetness from behind your ears. I have everyth—"

"Cut the act."

Rook snapped his eyes back to Dmitri. Ice drenched his every next word. "You giving me orders now?"

"Stand up. Let me see you properly."

"Go fu—"

"*Now.*"

Rook smiled again, his eyes glinting. He slowly set his drink down and stood. No longer concealed by the table, Dmitri saw what he never could have imagined. Rook's shirttails hung out, sweat stained the armpits, and his waistcoat was wrinkled. The scent of a fish barrel, two days old, wafted over to Dmitri. On the hand Rook had hidden under the table, his knuckles were bloody.

"Happy?" Rook asked. His smile disappeared and his eyes darkened.

Rook trudged over to the pallet; he wasn't even wearing shoes or socks. He folded himself onto the pathetic excuse for a bed, bowed his head, and let his hair fall over his face.

"I don't feel anything anymore." Rook's voice rasped empty and broken. "Everything the oath gave me, it's all gone."

"All?" Dmitri asked.

"Not that," Rook snarled, scowling at him. "Lenore means the same to me as she always has, much as you might disapprove. I mean what the oath did for me. It was like a thread that connected us. Even when she was safe, there was a signal letting me know all was well. Now there's... nothing."

"Welcome to the world the rest of us live in."

"If you're going to insist on being an ass, get out."

Dmitri still didn't move from his spot.

Rook ran his hands through his hair and whispered, "This isn't what I wanted."

"Then why did you agree to it?"

"Because I didn't think it would bloody work! Nothing that absurd has any right to." He rubbed his back, fingers lingering on his spine. "I want it back."

"You know that's not possible."

Rook squeezed his eyes shut and grunted. "Not. Helpful."

"Then go see her."

"She can't see me like this. She can't know."

"Why not?"

Rook threw up his hands. The rest of him followed, only to pace. "How do I know she doesn't let me hang around because of it? If she knows it's gone..." He banged his bloodied fist against the wall a few times, then shuddered.

Dmitri had to restrain himself from outright gawping. Instead, he narrowed his eyes in thought. "You think so little of her affections?"

"She chose Eamon. She *married* the git. She stays with him despite... *him*."

"You said the marriage was a strategic move on her part."

Rook took up pacing again. "It was at first. I don't understand why she's still there. Maybe I underestimated her feelings for him. Maybe *she* did and it influenced me. No, Dmitri, I can't risk it. Not without knowing how it will play out."

With a sigh, Dmitri's shoulders slumped, and he unhooked his thumbs from his belt—his old Enforcer stance. His voice softened. "You didn't see her when you turned yourself in for purging. She very nearly tore my head off for letting you. She was sick for a week and pale for weeks more. That's not a passing affection. You are precious to her, married or not."

Rook leaned against the wall but offered no rebuttal.

"Go see her," Dmitri said.

"Why the blazes do you care? You wanted all this ended."

"Yes, I did. I thought your feelings for her would disappear." He paused. "I was wrong. It turns out you're better with her."

"I don't want… If I tell her the truth and she…"

"So you'll stay here? Hiding like a coward? Yes, that seems like an excellent plan."

In one smooth movement, Rook spun and flew at Dmitri. He grabbed Dmitri by the lapels and pushed him against the doorway.

A ferocious snarl twisted Rook's face. "I am no coward."

"Then prove it." Once again, Dmitri's tone was as flat and even as a pane of glass. "Don't be stupid. If she makes you better, then do what it takes to be better."

"I can be just as good without her."

"I don't doubt it, but it's on you to make that happen. Just get back to doing your job, whatever that requires."

Rook glowered at Dmitri, releasing him. "You're just scared if I'm gone too long the Reaper and their cronies will come get you. You're the coward."

"It'd be foolish of me not to keep that situation in mind. That's me being smart, not scared."

Rook growled from deep in his chest. "Get out."

)(

A gust of icy wind chased Lenore as she let herself into the Allens' manor. Camilla's note had sounded rather urgent:

Please come to the house today as soon as you're able. Love, C

Lenore's stomach twisted as her mind suggested the worst possibilities. After everything lately, the list of potential disasters had grown uncomfortably long.

With her heart in her throat, Lenore called from the receiving hall. Mina answered from farther back in the house. Lenore found her sitting in the conservatory. Surrounded by Esther's plants and hunched over the table, Mina resembled a drooping flower. She wore what Lenore recognized as her "lazy day dress"—an olive out-of-fashion piece from before Lenore had come into their lives.

Mina wore it when even she tired of keeping up with society's constantly changing whims.

Mina gave Lenore an anemic smile and rose. "Hello, dear." She pulled Lenore into a hug and kissed her head. "I'm glad to see you."

"Is everything alright?" Lenore said.

Mina's smile wavered like the air around a focused torch. "I'm afraid not." She sat back down at the table. Lenore followed but said nothing, sensing Mina needed a moment. "I need to do something to feel like I'm holding back the darkness."

"But you do that every day," Lenore said.

Mina's smile grew stronger. "Thank you, darling."

Esther came in from the kitchen with a tea service.

Lenore asked, "Can I help you with anything?"

"I've got it well in hand," Esther replied. "You just make yourself comfortable."

"I offered as well." Mina looked gratefully at the older woman. "You'll at least join us, won't you, Esther?"

"Of course, ma'am."

The doctor sank into herself again. Memories of the last year fueled Lenore's fretful imaginings: the grisly reports of last spring's riots, the black powder sabotage at the museum, the explosions at the Halls.

Her patience from a few minutes ago fled. "Mina…"

Camilla calling through the house interrupted them. Lenore waited as they exchanged greetings and Mina asked how Camilla's classes had gone that afternoon. Mina held onto her niece's hands for longer than usual, and her smile splintered at the edges as she listened. Camilla, with her perfect nurturing instincts, responded in kind with a touch more care than usual.

Esther returned with the rest of the teatime goodies and served everyone before taking a seat. Lenore looked around the table. Everyone had a melancholy tint in their eyes, but she couldn't identify the reason.

"Mina, has something else happened?" she asked.

Mina took a deep breath, deep enough to straighten her spine out of its exhausted curve. "Sometimes I worry I've made all the wrong choices. If I had done something differently, perhaps things would have turned out better. Or perhaps not. Not knowing is one of the hardest parts."

"Will you run another free clinic day?" Camilla asked. "Those are always so good."

"It's scheduled for next week. Stephen is organizing the entire thing, bless him." Mina gave a hollow laugh. "I need a new Emily. Stephen's abysmal with administration." She looked around. "If you all know anyone, *please* send them to me. My billing is already a week behind."

"I'll ask Copper to check with his wife," Lenore said. "She's how we got Ezra."

She'd decided against telling the rest of her family about Copper's part in the Halls of Justice attack. Much as they loved him, she couldn't be certain how they would react. Lenore didn't fancy seeing any more relationships broken. She also hadn't told Copper how much Neal and the rest of the Allen clan knew about her real identity, nor had he asked, which seemed to suit them both just fine.

Esther sipped her tea. "If paperwork's all that needs doing, I'm sure I can find someone."

"I'm afraid it's a bit more complicated than that, but thank you," Mina said.

Camilla added, "If you really can't find someone, I can come in between my classes and visiting Falcon to catch you up."

Mina shook her head. "No, dear, but thank you. I know what it's like to be young and have your life consumed by school and work. I don't want that for you."

"It's really fine," Camilla said.

"No, but thank you."

Mina's gaze was distant and pained. She'd been grieving her sister, Adelle, of late. They were all mourning someone, but this felt different. Whatever was wrong, Mina was being uncharacteristically reticent.

"Grief will make you feel as if you're all alone in the world," Mina had once said, when she'd taken up the mantle of being the strong one. "That's a lie. Don't let it isolate you. We must be here for one another."

What could make the strong, confident doctor Lenore knew hold something back?

"What do you think you could have done differently?" Lenore asked.

Camilla and Esther looked to Mina, who rested her head against her clasped hands for a moment before meeting Lenore's eyes again. "We had a young lady delivered to the clinic today. She made an attempt on her life. I did what I could, but…" Mina took another deep breath. "She didn't make it."

"Oh, Mina." Lenore placed a hand on her arm. "I'm so sorry. I'm sure you did your best."

Mina nodded and brushed away an escaped tear. "She reminded me of a young woman I knew, when I was about your age. I believe I once mentioned how I was one of the only women in my program at school. Most were studying to be nurses or physicians' assistants. One, Phoebe, also wanted to be a doctor. I didn't know her well. She wasn't in many of my classes, and we ran in different circles."

"Do you mean she didn't come from money?" Lenore tried to ask the question carefully but wasn't certain how successful she'd been.

Mina simply nodded. She stood and walked to a cabinet standing discreetly against the wall. The piece held an assortment of items: some of Esther's indoor gardening tools, old table linens, dishes they didn't like but kept for propriety reasons, and a myriad of objects without a home. Mina returned, carrying a framed image-still. It depicted a group of people Lenore's age in faded sepia tones. They were mostly men, but Lenore picked out a younger version of Mina. Her jaw nearly dropped when she spied Kieran, human, there too. He looked almost exactly as he did now, minus the vampyric features. She hoped to study the picture further, but now wasn't the time. Perhaps she'd quietly dig it out later.

"This was our class." Mina pointed at a young woman with unruly curly hair. Lenore suspected by the shade and her generous freckles that she might have been ginger, but it was impossible to tell. "Kieran knew her better than I did. He even met her younger sister, Zoe, and the rest of their family. And he defended her. Things got worse after he was turned."

Mina went quiet.

"They were cruel to her, weren't they?" Lenore asked. "The people in your program. The same way they're cruel to Camilla."

"Terribly." Mina dabbed at her eyes with a handkerchief. "She not only dared to want to be a doctor, but she was *poor* and wanted to be a doctor. I should have done something. I knew what was happening even before Kieran had to leave. I should have reached out, should have supported her."

Camilla put a hand on Mina's arm next to Lenore's.

Lenore's throat had gone dry, but she croaked out a burning question anyway. "What happened?"

Mina closed her eyes and placed a hand over her mouth. Her tendons flexed as she tried to hold back more tears, but they forced their way forward. "She was such a bright girl. Kind but sharp. The instructors should have done more. *I* should have done more. She… she killed herself a year before graduation."

Esther too extended a hand and joined Lenore and Camilla in their comforting circle.

"At the time," Mina went on, "I wanted to think I could absolve myself, that there was nothing I could do. I told myself I didn't have time between studying and looking for work, but the truth is, I was afraid. My life was already hard enough. It wasn't really, not in the grand scheme of things, but I thought, 'Why invite more hardship?'"

Camilla, Esther, and Lenore sat quietly while Mina cried. When she'd collected herself a bit, Camilla squeezed her hand.

"You've obviously learned from Phoebe's loss. That's good."

"Have I?" Mina asked. "I hope so, certainly, but some days feel as if I'll never do enough to make up for it."

Lenore raised a shy hand. "I don't know where I'd be without you. And your payment system helps underprivileged patients get the care they need."

Mina managed a smile and wrapped her arms around Lenore. She kissed the top of Lenore's head. "Oh, darling, I can't imagine not having you in my life."

Mina hugged Camilla and Esther too, and Camilla suggested they all discuss ways to put brightness back into the world.

)(

Dear Oya,

Neal is still working through the details for your visit. I wish it were going faster, but he's pretty occupied with things here. Magistrates Jones and Smoke came out publicly with intentions to offer a counterproposal to Lady Katerina and Neal's, one that would increase Enforcer oversight. Just watching Neal work is exhausting. If neither Camilla nor I wish to take up his title, I wonder to whom he'll pass it. Maybe Copper? Or one of Copper's children? Can you imagine, though? Lady Lenore/Magistrate Blackbird-Lee. Ugh!

Lenore looked up from her letter and wondered how much time she could fill with writing it. Neal was off attending to magistrate council business *again*. She sighed, thankful for her promotion but feeling like she'd been dropped into a blank canvas without inspiration. As a journeyman, she was expected to set her own projects, within reason—yet another way this new position wasn't that different from her apprenticeship. Ezra was off for a family event, so the SS copy sat in a corner for the moment. Lenore returned to her letter.

Do you think the museum would let me travel? Not right now, of course. Not while we're trying to get you here, but in a couple of years. All I really want to do is explore and discover. I suppose that doesn't contribute as much as they'd like, though. Let me know if you have any suggestions. In truth, I think the sunken temple project would yield some interesting ideas, but...

Lenore paused. During their time together in Bone Port, she and Oya had discussed all manner of subjects, including Eamon. More recently, Lenore had told Oya about her problems with Eamon in the vaguest possible terms. She hadn't shared the latest development, however—the idea she'd confessed to Camilla and Neal and Mina. Shame burned her cheeks again. Perhaps she should keep it to herself for now, just until everything came out. Then again, she was fairly certain how it would end. The thought made heat prickle in Lenore's eyes.

The door opening and closing sounded. Lenore folded her letter and put it in her pocket for later. Personal correspondence wasn't exactly part of her job description. Recognizing Copper's footsteps, she didn't look up and wondered what new awkwardness awaited them. She'd never cursed the smallness of her department more. Given her promotion, though, there was room for a new apprentice. Perhaps that would be a safe subject.

"Nori," Copper grumbled by way of greeting.

Lenore tried not to bristle at her nickname. Copper using it had never bothered her before, but his tone this morning gave it a bitter, hollow sound. She told herself he was likely just grumpy about the meeting from which he'd just returned. Neal being gone again meant Copper had to pick up the slack, and he hated administrative balderdash more than Neal did.

They worked in silence for a while. Lenore brainstormed project ideas at Neal's desk. Maybe building herself one instead of always using Neal's should go on the list. Although, that did mean people would want to put things on it.

While Copper organized paperwork at his workstation, he mumbled, "Bloody nuisance. Need a form to even blow your nose. Neal should be here doing this, not off lunching with her ladyship."

"He's trying to keep the Enforcers from becoming even worse than they already are," Lenore said, her voice strained.

"Seems to me he should have been doing that a long time ago." A similar thread of suppressed tension ran in Copper's voice.

Lenore turned toward him. "Care to share with the whole class, Engineer Cooper?"

He met her cold stare, both standing at their desks like islands. "Neal's done diddly-squat as a magistrate since his father passed. You'd think he might have already made a move against the Enforcers, considering how many lives he's seen them destroy."

Anger growled in Lenore, more so when she realized a little part of her agreed with Copper. "Perhaps you should mention this to him."

"Aye, I have, lass. We don't agree, but at least we can discuss it civilly. Something you could learn a thing or two about."

"Well, maybe you wouldn't have to shoulder his responsibilities if you hadn't helped those monsters blow up the Enforcers' precious prison." Silence slammed down between them. Not a second later, in a much calmer tone, Lenore said, "I should not have said that."

Copper's nostrils flared, lips pressed together so hard they'd gone pale. She wasn't sure which would be worse: if he turned back into the hollow shell he'd been after the museum's black powder incident, or if he started shouting her down.

"I'm sorry, Copper. I really shouldn't have said that."

He looked away, still as tense as an overwound pocket watch. Lenore waited.

Nothing.

Her blood turned to acid as she saw one more person slip away from her. She turned to retreat to the other end of the workshop.

"Don't you walk away from me, young lady." Copper's voice was tight but even.

Lenore faced him again as words and heat bubbled in her throat. No, that wasn't the way to handle this. She tried to form them into something less volatile and forced her voice to soften. "Please don't call me 'young lady.'"

Copper took a deep breath. He too sounded calmer. "Let's have it out, shall we?"

"No. Please, just forget I said anything."

"I care about you, Nori." This time, regret tinged the way he said her nickname. "And this won't get fixed if we don't talk about it."

A tidal wave of something like relief washed over Lenore—how good it felt to hear someone say those words. Tears came unbidden to her eyes. She wiped them away only for more to replace them, but she was able to keep her voice mostly steady. "Go on then."

"I'm not sorry for wanting the Enforcers gone, but I am sorry for getting mixed up with the Collective. I knew what they wanted to do, except for the part about killing me once I'd done my part. And I still think they've got a point." Lenore opened her mouth to object, but Copper held up a hand. "Let me finish, please. I hope to the heavens Neal and Lady Katerina's efforts work, but I'm not

confident the Enforcers will roll over just because we pester them."
He paused. "There now. I'm done."

Lenore weighed her words. Her voice shook, but she held it
together. "You knew there were innocents inside. You knew they'd
arrested my parents."

"Aye, and I'm sorry. I thought the price would be worth it,
that the Enforcers would have no choice but to change. I was
wrong, and now we're all paying for it. I'm trying to do better."

Lenore swallowed hard. Copper's words reminded her of
Mina's from the other day. Would Phoebe's family feel like
Lenore did now if they'd heard Mina speak?

"And I'm sorry if you feel like I'm trying to be your father,
lass," Copper said. "I would never presume to replace him. Like I
said, I care about you, and I know you've been going through a lot.
I reckon I slipped into parenting mode."

Lenore nodded. This was easier to answer. "Thank you. I
appreciate that. And I care about you too. I'm fortunate to have
such an excellent mentor."

Copper scratched his beard. "You still can't look at me the
same, though, can you?"

Lenore sighed so heavily it pushed her back into Neal's desk
chair. She hesitated. "I saw her die, Copper. One minute she was
there and then…" Lenore's voice caught as the memory of the
explosion played before her eyes.

Copper's throat bobbed. "I'm sorry, Nori. Truly. If I could
take it back, I would."

Lenore blew her nose. She used the time to pull her fraying
ends back together. Mina might have told her to allow herself to
process her emotions, but now wasn't the time. She wanted this
fixed too, and she wouldn't find out if that was possible if she sat
here sobbing.

A question burned in Copper's eyes, but he was too good to
ask it—what had happened to her father? Edgar and Copper had
met when Lenore was small, too young to remember. Of course
he'd want to know. How would Copper react if she told him an
Enforcer mole and a dear criminal friend had worked together to
poison Edgar? All because her father, should he ever get caught,
had made her friend swear to do so. The whole thing sounded so

ridiculous it almost made Lenore laugh in a hysterical sort of way, except it triggered another memory.

Her mother had been meant to die then too.

Rook once told Lenore that Edgar had wanted to leave Twila out of what he did. She'd refused. And Dmitri had said things hadn't gone to plan when he poisoned their food, that Edgar had died but not Twila. Lenore had forgiven them all. Well, Dmitri was still a lout, but she didn't blame him for anything her parents had endured. Hm, perhaps not directly. Alright, that was an issue for her to disentangle another time.

Lenore looked at Copper. She didn't want to lose any more people. If she could forgive Rook and Dmitri, how could she refuse to forgive Copper?

"I choose to stop blaming you," she said, knowing it probably sounded strange.

Nevertheless, Copper gave her a small smile. "Thank you."

Lenore wiped her face again. The smidgen of cosmetics she deigned to wear for work was well and truly done for. "I'd like us to get back to how we were. I know it won't be quick or easy, but I want that."

"I'd like that too." Copper cleared his throat, making himself sound almost as boisterous as he used to. "As I am one of your mentors, where've you needed guidance lately?"

Lenore shrugged. "Figuring out my next project."

"Ah, that'll be a cinch. As you're actually Neal's apprentice, though, could I bother you to help me with this paperwork?"

Lenore gave him a crooked but genuine smile. "If they're the budgeting request forms I think they are, I'm not authorized to complete them." Copper's head fell back and he groaned. "I'll deliver them for you once you're done, though."

He made a disgruntled noise in his throat. "It'll have to do. Right, let's put them off for now and focus on you."

Lenore chuckled and turned back to her list of ideas so she and Copper could discuss them. Awkwardness still draped over them, but she was determined to ignore it and look forward.

)(

Camilla's level two Diagnosis class let out with a collective moan of relief. The current subject—the epidemiology of endemic diseases—was complex and boring. Even Camilla, who had always enjoyed school and made excellent marks, was struggling. Memorizing symptoms, the different ways they presented, their corresponding maladies, and their myriad sources was enough to make the most dedicated student question every life choice that had led to this.

She walked outside and sat on a bench, thrilled to be out of that stuffy classroom. The campus was simple—paved footpaths through green lawns, plain brick buildings, and furniture that was entirely function over form. It was modern too, which meant radiators. They weren't a problem in her other classes. Her Diagnosis teacher was a thin grouchy man, who was either always cold or liked to see his students sweat both literally and metaphorically as he shot questions like crossbow bolts. At least he didn't care who his students were. Male, female, rich, poor—the only thing that mattered to him was knowledge. Camilla appreciated that, even if he did refer to everyone around him as idiots.

No breeze blew today. It was still frigid, but bright sunshine cut through the cold. Camilla basked in the light, intent on taking a few peaceful minutes for herself before her next class. She didn't move even when someone she didn't recognize sat next to her. As it wasn't Barry Gillespie or any of his cronies, Camilla didn't much mind. She and the odious Barry didn't share any classes this term, and he hadn't done anything to torment her since she'd punched him in the nose, but she wouldn't let her guard down.

With a voice as pleasant as the sunshine, the woman said, "Alright if I sit here?" Camilla nodded. "I'm Aisling. Nice to meet you."

Aisling looked slightly older than Camilla. The woman's hazel eyes and honey-colored hair sparkled. She wore an unfussy frock of evergreen with black accents and a hat with matching feathers.

Camilla smiled at her. "Camilla. Lovely to meet you as well."

They shook hands.

Afterward, Aisling pulled a stiff ivory envelope from her bag and offered it to Camilla with a warm smile. "I have a message for you."

Camilla's years of learned propriety warred against recent experience. She looked around to see if Barry lurked nearby, but she saw neither him nor any of those she knew he counted as friends.

Turning back, she gave an apologetic smile. "Forgive me if I seem skeptical, but might I ask what this is for?"

Aisling's smile turned mischievous. "You have to open it to find out."

Camilla looked around again. Was one of her other horrid classmates trying something on? She wasn't so naïve as to think those with a desire to be cruel would suddenly give up being so.

"It's perfectly safe, I assure you," Aisling said. She barely moved, just sat there patiently.

Camilla finally decided to get it over with and took the envelope. It bore her name in heavy, swooping black ink. She slid her thumb beneath the wax seal and pushed the creamy paper back. Red glared from the interior—the note within had been written in ink as bright as blood.

Camilla Hawkins,

Your superior achievements have not gone unnoticed. Consider this your official and only invitation to join our exclusive society. Should you decide to join, please follow the enclosed instructions. More information will be provided.

"Well?"

Every alarm bell inside Camilla's head rang. "What is this exactly?"

Aisling leaned even closer. "So glad you asked. We're a bit like a secret society. You know the type, right?"

Camilla had heard of them, yes. Most involved rich men's sons sitting around, drinking and discussing how they'd run things once their fathers died off. Tales circulated of groups that took part in more sordid activities as well. As a young lady of gentle birth and without friends at the university, whispers were all Camilla heard. Not that she was curious anyway. She was certain, however, neither sort would be interested in her, thus proving this was some kind of hoax.

She narrowed her eyes at Aisling. "I shall have to decline, thank you."

She tried to hand the letter back, but Aisling kept her hands folded in her lap. Failing that, Camilla laid it on the bench between them. She stood to leave but paused when Aisling spoke again.

"I'm not with those vermin who tease you."

Camilla lifted her chin with pride. "Are you a student here?"

"No, but you're a woman working to become a doctor. I don't need to attend to know some will abuse you for such a notion. Whether or not you choose to join us—though I hope you will—don't let them get you down. Keep fighting."

The words settled over Camilla like a warm shawl. Silly as it seemed, she didn't believe anyone here would stoop to encouraging her just to pull off a prank. She tucked the invitation into her bag.

"I shall have to consider it. In any case, I will let you know what I decide."

Aisling smiled. "That's very polite of you."

"Thank you," Camilla said with a return smile. "Unfortunately, I have another class, so I must go. I hope you have a lovely day, Aisling."

"You as well."

With that, Camilla walked off, curiosity budding within her.

9

~Dangerous Truths and Lies~

The townhome felt vast and empty as Lenore sat hunched over her sketchbook. She tried chatting with Eamon when she'd returned home that afternoon. He seemed interested as she'd shared the new project ideas she was playing with. As soon as the subject of Kieran had arisen, however, Eamon shut down again. Lenore had explained she still hadn't heard from Rook and wasn't sure how that might change the feeding schedule, and Eamon had actually turned his back.

Now she sat tucked up in the little room that had been reserved for her. She and Lowell had big plans for the ferrousites they had created. Lenore immersed herself in her sketches and tried to ignore the miasma of enmity pressing in on her from every wall. If it weren't so late, she would have gone over to Lowell's house to work. Not that he would have minded, more than likely, but Lenore didn't want to take advantage of his generosity or get on Felicia's bad side.

Lenore heard the doorchime ring, heard Eamon answer it, and kept on drawing. A soft knock sounded on the doorframe a few minutes later. Eamon, a scowl carved across his face, stood there with Rook behind him.

"You have a visitor," he said. "Despite the late hour."

Lenore's expression remained impassive. They'd agreed long ago that Rook was as welcome as any other guest. In the interest of making peace, she thought about asking Eamon to stay, even opened her mouth to invite him, but his next words stopped her.

"I'll be downstairs."

Was he just communicating or was there a warning in his words? She thanked him and listened as he walked downstairs. When her eyes returned to Rook, she summoned a tired smile.

"How are things?" she said. "I haven't heard from you since we tried to break the oath."

Rook smirked. "Peachy."

"Really?" Curiosity and disappointment blended into her tone. "Has there been no change? We didn't take time to discuss things afterward. We should have been more organized about it."

A soft chuckle bubbled in his throat. He looked away, ran a hand down the plum wallpaper, but said nothing.

A deep crease etched itself above Lenore's nose as she watched him. She reached out, hesitated, and drew back. "Rook?" It was as if he hadn't heard her. "Is everything alright?"

Rook sighed. When he finally turned back, the smile fell from his face. "No, it isn't."

"What's wrong?" Lenore asked, almost whispering. "What's happened? Is it the Enforcers? Or the Collective?"

He shook his head. "No, no. That's… something else. This is about… I…" He took another deep breath and lowered his eyes for a moment before lifting them back to hers.

Lenore stiffened when she saw fear in them. What could scare Rook, of all people?

He sat in the chair beside hers. She swallowed hard, steeling herself for whatever blow he had to deliver.

"The oath is gone."

She gaped, unable to find words at first. "It's gone? Completely?"

He nodded as if his head was too heavy. Lenore's wide eyes scanned the room as if the oath was simply hiding nearby.

She started and stopped speaking several times before settling on one path. "We should test it to be certain." She looked up at the room's single petrolsene sconce. Reaching for it, she kept her eyes on Rook.

"No, don't." He took her hand in his.

They stopped, looked at one another. He scooted so close their knees touched and clutched her hand to his chest. Lenore had fought hard to quash certain feelings Rook excited in her. She had been mostly successful, especially when she and Eamon had been on good terms. With things as they were now, however, and in this small room, those feelings stirred again, familiar and warm. She pushed them back with reminders of commitments made, but she didn't pull away.

And she most certainly did *not* pay attention to the feeling of Rook's heart beating against her hand.

"I know it's gone," Rook said. "I feel it missing, like a void. There's nothing but silence where it used to be."

Joy pulled at the corners of Lenore's mouth, but the look on Rook's face stayed her. She reached out with her other hand and clasped his.

"So why do you look like that?" she asked.

He struggled to keep his eyes on her, but he did, and his voice was softer than ever when he answered. "It was my connection to you, a bond that couldn't be broken. That I *thought* couldn't be broken. I can't bear to lose you, but without it, what tethers us together?"

Lenore blinked at him. Hurt and hope clashed in her heart. "Rook." It was almost a plea. "We have us. Everything we've been through, our... fondness for each other, our shared interests. An Old World oath is not the only true bond there is."

He smiled, sad and weak, as if saying goodbye for the last time. "We have very different perspectives of the world, little bird. I'm afraid I've not had much luck with those other sorts of ties."

He released her and stood. Lenore followed right behind. His smile had charged something in her, and it flared like a focused torch flame. She grabbed Rook's hand. When he turned back to face her, she stared hard into his eyes.

"Don't you give up on me, Rook. You said yourself the vow didn't rule you before, so don't let it being gone rule you either."

Rook's lips ticked upward, and his eyes flashed sharp like a blade in the night. His words, solid as iron now, tried to push Lenore away even as he stepped closer to her, hands still clasped. "And if you don't like something I do? If I tell you something about me you disapprove of? Will you suffer to keep me around now there's no bond like before? We both know you don't know everything about me, for good reason."

"Please." Lenore rolled her eyes. "I've long known about big, bad Rook, infamous killer criminal. I could have cut ties with you at any time. This changes nothing between us."

Rook's face twisted into a hard, scornful mask. Lenore closed the short distance between them, matching his intensity even as she had to tilt her head up to look at him.

"Stand down, Rook. If you don't know how to have a normal friendship, then learn. Let me teach you, and stop making excuses."

Rook's eyes ran over the tight set of her jaw and jagged emerald eyes. Lenore felt him shift, ready to spring away, possibly out of her life forever. She tightened her grip on his hand. His smile reappeared, soft and warm, as his shoulders relaxed.

He leaned toward her again. "Very well. I surrender. I'll try to be an easy pupil, for your sake, but I can't make any guarantees."

"I think you overestimate your difficultness."

"Do I?"

Rook reached out his free hand and brushed his knuckles against Lenore's. They'd gotten so close during their little tiff. He smelled faintly of leather and peat. Lenore wanted to draw closer to that scent, to press against him...

No. She couldn't indulge those thoughts. Not with the promises she'd made. She released her grip on his other hand and retreated. Sinking back into her chair, Lenore tried to ignore the way his dark eyes followed her. Heat rose in her neck. She gave what she hoped was a nonchalant wave.

"Or you underestimate yourself," she said, "depending on how you look at it."

He slipped his hands into his pockets. "I never underestimate myself."

Lenore adjusted her expression into something more serious again. "Do you want anyone else to know about this new development?"

Rook rocked from foot to foot before taking up a position against the closest wall. The very picture of casual ambivalence.

"Good question. It's always been the sort of thing that's better kept secret, but I'm sure your family is wondering."

Lenore made a face. "The subject has come up."

Rook rubbed his chin. "I suppose tell them the truth when it comes up again." He didn't sound happy. "They'll be relieved for a while, maybe even give me some sympathy until they realize how attached to me you are." Rook flashed a devilish grin, and she mimed swatting the comment away. He picked a piece of lint from his waistcoat. "Speaking of your family, shall we join Eamon? He looked like a shunned puppy when he left."

Lenore straightened. "If he'll have us, I'm willing to try. Maybe this news will do some good—with your permission, of course."

"For you, yes."

Lenore gifted him a grateful smile and stood. "By the way, Oya said hello in her last letter. And she says she wants a rematch."

"Oh, fun! I do hope we'll get in a few jabs at each other soon." He followed Lenore downstairs to the townhouse's main living area.

"It'll have to be here if you do, whenever she arrives, but you can't break anything. Most of this stuff isn't mine." And she certainly didn't want to provide Eamon yet another reason to dislike her or Rook.

)(

Water dripped from bare branches like outstretched fingers. Despite the soggy cold, the sun had exploded through the clouds not long ago and was shining brightly. Camilla smiled at it from within Falcon's conservatory before turning back to her patient.

"Wiggle your toes for me," she said.

Falcon sat with his legs hanging over the side of the bed. He was dressed in fresh pajamas and looked far better than he had days ago. Being able to attend to the most basic hygiene tasks himself helped enormously.

He flexed his toes and looked at Camilla for approval.

"Excellent. Now I'm going to push against your feet. Try to resist me."

Camilla stooped down and pressed her hand against the bottom of Falcon's bare foot. He jerked, almost kneeing Camilla in the face. She yelped and yanked her head away.

Falcon bunched up his shoulders like the puffy sleeves that were so in fashion. "Sorry! It tickled. Sorry, sorry, sorry! Are you okay? Did I hit you?"

Camilla laughed. "I'm fine. That's not the worst thing that's almost happened to me in this job."

Falcon lowered his shoulders and chuckled the tension away. "I suppose you have faced your fair share of accidents."

Camilla reached for his foot with more care this time. "Oh, it's not always been accidental."

Falcon's eyes widened. "Wait, have patients *tried* to harm you? As you were treating them?"

"Push," Camilla said. He obeyed while she returned equal pressure. "Some have, yes. It's incredible what people will do when they're desperate or frightened."

"Aren't you scared to go back to work after that?"

"Good, we'll try standing next." Camilla straightened and held out her arms for support. "Slowly. Hang on to me first. Yes, it's unsettling, but what else would I do? Give up my profession?"

Falcon grasped Camilla's arms and slid off his bed. His legs wobbled but didn't give. "If I ever doubted your passion, I stand sorely corrected."

"You stand marvelously." Camilla smiled up at him. "Do you feel strong enough to take a step?"

Falcon nodded, and Camilla took half a step back. He concentrated on his feet. They took a few more together before Camilla steered him back to the bed. She instructed him to try a few on his own.

"I don't love my job like you do." Falcon's voice was lower than before. He grabbed Camilla's arm once or twice for balance and kept his other hand hovering over the bed, but he managed a few shaky steps on his own. She had him sit back down before she responded to his statement.

"I know. You remember all the conversations we've had about that, yes?" She searched his face for signs of neurological symptoms. None of the physical markers, like a lack of pupillary reactivity, showed, but memory loss was a possible indicator too.

Falcon gave her a crooked smile—he was probably happy with her concern but perhaps not the question. "I do remember. What I meant was… Well, I've been doing a lot of thinking. Had I

105

not been there that night, what might have happened to you? Perhaps some good has come of me being an Enforcer."

Camilla walked to a small table where she'd set her things. Falcon's file sat amongst them. She made some notes in it, not answering him.

"Milly." She heard fabric shift behind her.

Camilla spun to see Falcon trying to stand and walk to her on his own.

"Don't!" She hurried to support him.

Falcon looked down at Camilla. His eyes gleamed with pain. "Milly, I'm so sorry for what happened. I... I assume they didn't make it."

"You remember that then?" she whispered.

They hadn't spoken of the chaotic night he'd caught her and the others running through the burning Halls of Justice, searching for Camilla and Lenore's mothers. They hadn't had the opportunity.

"Yes. And your father, he died in the attack too, didn't he?"

Camilla nodded. She wasn't certain if Falcon had seen the body or just heard about it after. "He sacrificed his life for... us."

"For you," Falcon said gently.

Why? Her father had never wanted a child, had never been a good person from all she'd seen. It made no sense.

"I wish I could ask someone about him," she said. "Someone who knew him well, but I don't even know if he had friends." She looked at Falcon. "Do you?"

He shook his head. "I'm sorry, I don't know. He didn't share with those of us under him, and I understand he started managing his own diary after Dmitri, erm, left the order. One of his peers might know more, but friendship isn't exactly encouraged in our ranks."

Tears burned in Camilla's eyes. She flung up the usual fortifications when emotion tried to interfere with her job. Despite her efforts, Falcon must have seen through her—he had gotten rather good at that before the accident—and held out one arm, hanging on to the bed with the other to stay steady. Camilla sighed and tightened her hold on her feelings. She accepted the embrace, awkwardly hugging Falcon around the side.

"This is terribly unprofessional," she mumbled. He squeezed her with more strength than she'd expected, and she logged this away as a good sign.

Falcon broke away and whispered, "My grandfather and some Enforcers are coming around to interview me today. I have a... version of events prepared for them. I don't expect too many issues given the circumstances, but do you mind if I run it by you?"

"Please do."

Camilla doubled her efforts on Falcon's rehabilitation while he spoke. It was a simple enough explanation—he'd chased after some particularly nasty criminals before getting caught in a blast. To catch potential inconsistencies, Camilla reviewed with him what she and the rest of her family had said in their own testimonies. Falcon didn't ask for more details about her actions that night, and their conversation wandered back to his part.

Falcon looked out of the window. "I remember the noise."

Camilla thought the sunshine a rather inappropriate backdrop for such a story.

"I remember seeing the fire and flying back. Then nothing. No, not nothing, just... bits. Mostly sound. I remember your voice, Milly. I remember that most clearly."

Camilla was relieved when the doorchime rang just then. She heard Wren answer it, followed by Lark leaping down the stairwell and greeting her grandfather.

"They're in the conservatory," Lark's voice chirped from down the hall.

Wren's voice wafted behind. They were walking toward the room. "Miss Camilla is helping Falcon regain his strength."

"Excellent!" Harding boomed.

The trio walked through the doorway. Wren and Lark each held one of Harding's arms as he leaned on a cane, which was topped with an eagle-shaped brass handle.

Two Enforcers trailed behind.

)(

Falcon didn't recognize the two Enforcers with his grandfather, which struck him as odd. He'd always made it a point to know the names and faces of as many of the order as possible. It helped that he'd attended multiple Enforcer functions. Falcon wondered if Camilla's earlier look of concern about his memory had some basis.

"Falcon, my boy." Harding extended his hand, while Lark and Wren took seats on a nearby sofa.

Falcon stood up straighter, leaning against the bed for support. Thankfully, Harding had come close for the greeting. Falcon shook his grandfather's hand, gripping it firmly.

"Need to work on your handshake," Harding said. He turned away to hack a thick, gluey cough toward a potted plant. Afterward, he fixed his gaze on Camilla, who stood a few paces away. "You make sure your regimen or what have you includes that."

Camilla gave him a professional smile. "We aim to get him back to peak condition, sir. Don't you worry."

"We, eh? That means you and Mrs. Allen. I hope she isn't as soft as her husband."

"You met Doctor Allen, sir. I'll leave that estimation to your judgment." Camilla's voice and expression reminded Falcon of spun sugar with steel threads woven into it.

Amusement lifted a corner of Harding's mouth the merest bit. He turned back to his grandson. "Falcon, my lad, these here are Reserve Sixths Fenton and Clark."

"Reserves?" Falcon looked between his grandfather and the two Enforcers. Neither of them moved. "As in, some of the temporaries hired after the attack?" He considered voicing concerns about assigning people to this case who'd not been Enforcers at the time of the attack. Given he'd been unconscious these last few weeks and likely didn't have all the facts, he decided against it.

"The very same, though First Iago and I hope they'll be made permanent after the next council session. This is a good opportunity, you know, for the people to see how important we are. Not that they should need reminding, but you know how people are." Harding had another coughing fit. Then he unscrewed the top of his cane, drew a small cup out of the staff, and poured a golden liquid from the eagle. He took a sip and smacked his lips. "Ah, that's the stuff." To Camilla, he said, "I'm not worried about you carrying that little tidbit back to Lord Allen. We've been very vocal about what this city needs."

Camilla bobbed her head but said nothing.

Harding then explained Falcon needed to provide a statement to the Sixths about the night of the attack.

"We're just about done here for the day anyway," Camilla said. "Falcon, you're making excellent progress. Just be sure to keep up with your exercises."

"We'll make sure he does." Lark beamed at her brother.

"Actually, Miss Hawkins," said Sixth Clark, "we need you to stay. We have some questions for you as well."

"Even now?" Wren asked. She looked to her grandfather. "After all this time?"

"All part of the process, princess," Harding said.

Camilla sat next to the sisters and made an innocent gesture with her hands. "Very well."

The Enforcers turned back to Falcon, who fell into his own professional manner as he recounted his tale and answered questions. After he'd finished, they returned their attention to Camilla.

"We have record of you visiting your father that evening, Miss Hawkins," Sixth Fenton said. "Our records indicate you were there for marriage advice."

Every eye turned to Camilla, and the peaches in her peaches-and-cream complexion turned into strawberries. "Yes, that's correct."

Heat rushed up Falcon's neck as everyone's eyes swung to him now.

Lark gasped. "Were you and Falcon—"

"Not the time, pet," Harding broke in.

"Sorry, grandfather," Lark said, though her eyes still flicked between Camilla and Falcon.

Relief cooled Falcon's flush as they deviated from the subject of marriage. The new thread, however, was hardly better.

"The first blast occurred not long after," Sixth Clark said. "We also have some reports of a young lady matching your description in the Halls during that time."

Camilla's angelic face puckered into confusion. "I don't understand what that has to do with me."

"Did you follow Fourth Hawkins into the Halls, ma'am?"

"Into the Halls?" Camilla repeated. "As in, *toward* the explosions?"

"What a mad question," Falcon said. Harding shot him a nasty look, and Falcon pretended to slump with exhaustion, which wasn't far from the truth. If necessary, he could always claim he'd forgotten himself in his weariness.

"That's completely insane," Lark said.

"Lark," Harding began, but she barreled on.

"You've probably got all kinds of barmy reports. It was pure chaos in there. Everyone knows it."

Wren put a hand on her sister's arm. "Larky."

"You still don't even know who did it. If there was someone who looked like Camilla, which is dubious, it was probably one of them."

"Lark," growled Harding.

"Before she got shuttled off, Emily Lee told Joy Pendragon who told my friend Claire that Doctor Allen's clinic was so packed with people coming in and out that anyone might have come through."

"But you weren't there for most of the evening, were you, Miss Hawkins?" Sixth Fenton asked. "At least, Fifth Jones reports that you weren't."

Falcon resisted looking at Camilla. He tried to keep his face impassive but had no idea how successful he was. He'd never liked lying, probably because he was rubbish at it.

"No. I was attending to a personal matter with a friend," Camilla said.

Falcon looked at his grandfather to gauge his reaction. Harding sipped from his cup, seemingly no longer interested in stopping his granddaughter from speaking.

"What matter?" Sixth Clark asked.

"And with whom?" added Sixth Fenton.

Falcon recognized the strategy as the Sixths began lobbing questions at Camilla in tandem. Quick and alternating, it was meant to trip up a suspect. Camilla, however, fielded the volley with aplomb.

"We covered all of this in my initial statement," she said. "You all have important things to do, and I don't see how rehashing this is a good use of your time."

"We'll decide that, ma'am. Answer the question."

Camilla nodded. "Very well. I was with Lenore Blackbird-Lee."

"And those personal matters were more important than assisting Doctor Allen?"

"I'm afraid it was quite bad," Camilla said. "Quite bad indeed."

"What were they, exactly?"

She paused before her features settled into resigned duty. "You gentlemen won't have experienced this, but when a woman's cycle begins—"

"Thank you, that will do," Sixth Fenton interrupted.

"Will it?" Harding eyed Camilla. "It must have been life-threatening to ignore your mentor's summons."

"Imagine an empty room, Lord Smoke." Camilla gestured with her hands to illustrate. "The room, in this case, is a woman's uterus."

Falcon no longer hid his reaction, as it matched the Sixths'. His eyes went wide as he realized Camilla's discourse led into delicate territory. Harding remained unfazed.

"Truly, that is sufficient," Clark said, almost barking.

Camilla settled her hands back into her lap, while Lark failed to suppress a laugh and Wren colored up to her ears. Fenton's, Clark's, and Falcon's cheeks were red as beetroots.

"Do you have any other questions, gentlemen?" Camilla asked.

They did, though not for Camilla. They shot a few more queries at Falcon as if taking out their embarrassment on him, repeated some of their earlier questions, and finally declared the interview over.

"I still think there's something off about Miss Hawkins' testimony," said Harding. "Perhaps it's something First Iago, Lord Allen, and Lady Holmes should discuss."

"I can provide a comprehensive medical explanation if that will help," Camilla said.

Harding grumbled. "Not necessary." He heaved himself out of his seat, ignoring Wren and Lark's offers to assist, and followed the two Enforcers out of the room.

Falcon watched them go, but his mind was on Camilla and what his grandfather had said about her story.

)(

The air in Rook's office stagnated with unrest. The crime lords were sitting around his table once again, a duplicate of the scene from over a fortnight ago. All had the same trappings as before, whether it be drink or cigar or fronts or tics.

Again, Rook smiled and leaned against his desk. "Thank you all for coming back," he said. "And on such short notice. I know how tedious reorganizing one's schedule can be."

"Just get to the point," Prince said. "You said you're stepping down, so what is this?"

Rook took a slow, deep breath and bowed. "I'm afraid my time in the spotlight has ended. My understudy, Dmitri here, takes center stage."

Dmitri walked forward and gave the assembly a curt nod.

"Not a man of many words, as you can see," Rook said. "The transition has been underway since the moment you last left, as some of you may have heard. Apologies for the delay, but these things do take time."

"You still talk like you're in charge," Twigs grumbled. "Let's hear from the organ grinder, if that's really what he is now."

"Of course. Exeunt, stage right." Rook bowed again and stepped behind Dmitri.

"Gentlemen, lady." Dmitri folded his hands before him. "Given that the terms of this agreement have been met—"

"Permanence dependent on the passing of Lady Katerina and Lord Allen's motion," Rook put in. "*And* successful dismantling of the Reaper's Collective."

Dmitri's expression flattened. "Given that the *initial* terms have been met, I presume everything is in order to begin the next phase?"

"Rook had better style," Carver muttered.

"Now that you're in charge, you don't have to follow through, you know." Nieva quirked her rose-painted lips at Dmitri.

"Ma'am, I made a commitment to this organization, and I intend to fulfill it."

"And what does Rook get out of it?" She leaned her cheek against a gloved hand. "I almost can't believe he's really gone through with it."

"Yes, what is the little bootlicker getting out of this?" Prince asked.

"Besides getting to see the Reaper fall? Protection." Dmitri locked eyes with each person. "That means the protection of the entire company. Am I understood?"

Twigs looked like an unhappy scarecrow as he crossed his thin arms. "I don't like it. Who's to say Rook isn't still calling the shots from behind the scenes?"

That was precisely the plan. Not that any of them needed to know that.

Rook winked at Twigs. "I like the way you've continued my theatre metaphor."

"Rook," Dmitri snapped. "Get out."

He resisted the urge to glare at Dmitri. This was *not* part of the plan, though Rook couldn't blame him. It was a viable option for the current situation. Not the one Rook would have chosen, though, which rankled.

"Yes, sir," he said, keeping up his cheerful persona.

"Don't go far," Dmitri said. "I'll call for you when we've sorted everything."

Rook strained to keep his eyes forward as he left his own office. Standing on the other side of the door, not being able to hear what was happening within, felt surreal, like this was some kind of bad dream. He looked over the market. A prickle of embarrassment crawled up his spine. He wanted to escape, to avoid every vendor and employee, but there was nowhere to go. Standing on the metal landing with Grunt and looking down at them as they moved about like the cogs of a great machine seemed the least horrible option.

At least he could take comfort in knowing he had a well soundproofed office.

Rook tried not to check his pocket watch, tried not to strain to hear even one word inside, but failed miserably. Grunt asked him the occasional question—"You planning any nice holidays now that you're no longer in charge?" and "Who do you reckon would win in a fight? Fifty normal sized squirrels or one squirrel the size of fifty?"—and Rook was glad for the diversion. At least the squirrel one gave him an idea for a side hustle should all this go pear-shaped.

At last, Garrick opened the door. His thin, grey brows bobbed when he saw Rook there.

"Dmitri said not to go far," Rook said, "so I didn't."

"I still don't like it," Twigs said from within.

Carver growled, "But you agreed a deal's a deal. I'm tired of talking about this."

Rook looked in. The party was preparing to leave.

"The decision was simple," Dmitri said. "They'll progress if you're out. Completely. From this point on. I've agreed, and they're off to get started."

"Completely?" Rook barely managed to keep the growl out of his voice.

"You'll still have our protection, but you won't even be a runner for me. You'll provide me information as necessary, but only when I contact you. Re-employment is not an option."

"And the final caveats?"

Nieva answered this time, her voice as sweet as arsenic-laced honey. "We're not planning on that being an issue."

All Rook could do to contain his anger was ball his fists and glare at Dmitri. A thousand ideas of how he might have gotten to this point spun in his head. Was this a ploy for Rook's benefit, or had Dmitri double-crossed him? Made a side agreement with one of the other crime lords?

Rook's finger scraped the tip of a blade hidden in his sleeve.

Prince clapped Rook on the shoulder as he made his way to the door. "Tough luck, chap."

Rook redirected his glare and reminded himself why he couldn't afford to snap off the offending hand. Prince smiled with straight, gleaming teeth—a snake's smile. He walked out. Nieva left Rook with hopes they'd work together again in some capacity.

Rook didn't hear what Twigs or Carver said over the blood roaring in his ears.

"Rook, you're dismissed," Dmitri said. "I'll send a note if I require anything."

Rook backed out of the office, keeping his eyes on the weasel who'd just usurped his throne. On the stairs down, he forced himself not to run, though he expected a knife between his shoulder blades at any moment.

10

~A Hedgehog, a Starfish, and a Lion Go to a Party~

The masquerade party, like its predecessor, glittered as if sprinkled with diamond dust. This one, however, had attracted more people, all of whom wore masks and matching outfits. The guests weren't just rich contributors and fellow politicians but merchants, artisans, and writers. The Holmeses and Allens had invited anyone and everyone who could contribute something to the cause. Given the broader income spectrum, Lenore was pleased to see a more colorful—literally and metaphorically—array of materials, accessories, and manners on display. She might have been nervous about it, given the greater chance for her to be recognized by someone from her old life— Springhaven was a massive city, but one never knew who they might serendipitously run into—but she felt only a tinge of apprehension. From behind the safety of a hedgehog mask, complete with bronze sparkle-tipped spines, she gazed over the collected supporters.

"Why a hedgehog?" Lenore had asked when Beatrice presented her costume.

"Oh, hedgehogs are brilliant," Beatrice had replied. As she'd spoken, she tested the mask's fit. "They're immune to poison, they have these little spines for protection, and everyone thinks they're cute."

Lenore had given her friend a sideways look. "Have you researched all the animals you've done masks of?"

"No. I'm seeing a chap who studies them. Before you ask, no, he doesn't work for the museum, and no, he's not coming tonight. So, no, you can't stick to him and chat about science or what have you all evening."

Now, dressed in her pointy-nosed mask and matching bronze gown, plus spiny fascinator, Lenore was meant to be charming the guests. She didn't know what that meant, nor had anyone given her a straight answer about it. Across the way, Camilla orbited the room like a moon. Dressed in a gauzy pearl-colored gown with a swan mask and feathered accessories, she made the task look effortless. Copper was around too. Lenore had briefly caught sight of him sporting a grey suit and a donkey mask. She'd known him by his uproarious laughter.

Lenore sighed. She didn't think her current strategy was cutting it. That strategy being to loiter near a corner of the room and pretend to admire the hanging decorations: artificial tree boughs meant to give the impression of being in a forest. She'd initially been attracted by the wind machine meant to simulate, well, wind. From what she could see, it looked more like an oversized chimney bellows.

"I'm the same way at parties," grated a voice next to her.

Lenore turned, hoping she made it look like an elegant spin. Lenore recognized the woman next to her by her mechanical hand. She smiled as the irony of the costume—a starfish—hit her.

"Gadget! Good evening," Lenore said. "How did you know it was me?"

"An easy guess. Not many young ladies would risk being caught more interested in a machine than anything else at a party. I understand, although my weakness is for furniture. All these chairs, barely more than sticks slapped together."

Lenore chided herself for getting caught up in her curiosity. She was supposed to be helping host, after all, and grappled for a new topic. "Neal said he'd invited you but wasn't certain you'd make it."

Gadget's sandpaper voice rasped as she said, "Your friend Varick was good enough to watch the shop for me tonight."

"I'm pleased to hear it. Did your daughter come too?"

"She did, though she isn't keen. Doesn't like coming out much. Takes away from her studies."

Lenore scanned the crowd but stopped when she realized, with all the masks, she wouldn't see anyone who resembled Gadget. She turned back to the craftswoman. "Would you introduce me, please? I'd love to meet her."

"I was hoping you'd say that." Lenore followed Gadget across the ballroom. "So Neal and his friend hope getting all of us together will change things, do they?"

Lenore recognized her chance and tried to channel Beatrice's charisma. "Lady Katerina, and yes. They'll say a few words later and mention how we can help."

"It's quite a large ship to turn, isn't it?" Gadget adjusted her mechanical hand, curling and then uncurling the fingers in the same pensive way someone might scratch their chin.

"It is, but I believe they can do it. Will you help us?"

"I'll do what I can, though I don't expect people to give me much credence. It's pretty clear if anyone has an axe to grind, it's me."

"But you have one of the most compelling stories to tell."

Gadget stopped in her tracks. "I have one of the most *compelling* stories to tell?"

Cold horror drenched Lenore. Her eyes flicked to the crowd around them. Thankfully, everyone nearby looked engrossed in their own conversations. "I don't mean that in an insensitive way."

"Then how do you mean it?" Gadget too seemed aware of their surroundings and lowered her voice. "Because it sounds like you want to spin my experience for your own agenda."

The spangles on Gadget's cerise gown sparkled like pyroprismatics exploding in the air. Lenore gulped. The woman suddenly appeared fearsome, even with her starfish mask.

"I promise that's not my intention. I only meant you personally know how cruel Enforcer methods are. You can convince people to support our movement by sharing your firsthand experience." Heat rushed to Lenore's face, melting the previous cold and beading her forehead with sweat. "I didn't mean... Um, I... Firsthand was a terrible word choice. I'm not very good at this. I-I-I—"

Lenore snapped her jaw shut when Gadget chuckled. "You certainly aren't."

The inside of Lenore's mask felt like a boiler. "I'm sorry I offended you. I really didn't mean to be callous."

Gadget had stopped chuckling, but Lenore imagined her smirking behind her mask. "Let's leave it at that," Gadget said. "Neal's already made noise about wanting me to be a poster child, but unlike you, he hasn't come right out with it."

"Oh, I didn't realize." Lenore made a mental note to tell Neal after the party how she might have ruined one of his schemes.

"I'll tell you now, I'm not keen on challenging them head-on. It wouldn't take much for our *mighty defenders*—" Gadget practically spat the words. "—to decide I'm breaking a law and lock me up again. And I have too much to lose."

Gadget's actual crimes—forging identity paperwork like what had given Lenore her second chance—were, of course, a far bigger risk. Not that Lenore was so foolish as to mention that. The craftswoman's fear wasn't unjustified, though. If the Enforcers decided to silence Gadget with false claims, it would be a life sentence, unlike with her purging.

Lenore felt she'd done enough damage for one night and nodded.

"There you are."

Gadget looked toward the new voice and said, "Ah, here comes my unhappy little offspring."

A young woman, almost the same height as Gadget, stalked through the crowd. She wore a bat mask, complete with enormous ears, over the top half of her face and a simple black gown. Her chestnut hair fell in a silky straight curtain past her shoulders. The sour line of her mouth spoke volumes.

"Mum, this place is awful. Can we go yet?" She sounded perhaps a few years younger than Lenore, though that could have been the petulance.

"Rowan, I'd like you to meet Lenore. She's Mr. Allen's cousin. Lenore, my daughter, Rowan Wilson."

Lenore extended her hand. "A pleasure to meet you, Rowan."

Rowan looked Lenore up and down. Her keen, dark eyes gave Lenore the distinct feeling of being measured. She barely returned Lenore's handshake and turned back to her mother. "Can we go? *Please?*"

Gadget stroked her daughter's hair. "Don't be rude, Ro."

Rowan crossed her arms and huffed.

"Your mother tells me you enjoy studying," Lenore said. "What do you study?"

"Art."

Lenore cocked her head. "How does one study art? Oh, do you mean the paints used and their application techniques?"

Rowan fixed her with a sideways look, clearly knocking points off Lenore's rating in her head.

Gadget chuckled. "Let's go get some refreshments. Perhaps you'll be less grouchy with a bit of food. Excuse us, Lenore."

Lenore flashed what she hoped was a charming smile before she remembered her mask hid it. "It was lovely meeting you."

"You too," Rowan mumbled, and Gadget herded her away.

Lenore's smile inverted to a grimace. *Well, that was a bloody disaster.*

"I don't think that went so badly." Lenore was surprised to see Felicia beside her. She wore a colorful butterfly half-mask and a dress that looked made of rainbows. Felicia sipped from her cup of mulled wine, then tapped its side. "What I stock is better, but you already knew that."

Lenore blanched beneath her mask and sent a silent thank you to Beatrice for it. "Would it be best to just beg forgiveness?"

Felicia smirked and sipped again. "Don't worry, pet. I can just have our mutual friend get me more, with interest."

Lenore relaxed a little and tried to remember how to be charming. "I'm surprised to see you here, though I am pleased for it. Do you know Katerina?"

"Oh yes, we're good friends," Felicia said. "Friends? Well, we certainly have an excellent relationship."

Lenore decided it was better not to know what that meant and veered away from the subject. "Any chance Lowell is here too?"

"So you two can go off together and build something while the rest of us do all the work? Heavens no." Felicia gifted her a warm smile.

Encouraged, Lenore said, "We have plans later on this week, actually."

"So I'm told. You know, he's always been ambitious, but never with other people."

Lenore wondered if, perhaps, Felicia's tight rein had hindered Lowell's opportunities with others. It was for his protection, surely—people could be cruel—but Lenore knew personally how limiting safety could be. She worried Felicia was doing more harm than good.

She was trying to think up a safer response when Felicia narrowed her eyes at her. Lenore looked down at her dress for whatever was offending Felicia. "Sorry, did I spill something on me?"

Felicia looked back to the room. "Just don't burn the house down, if you please."

Did I do something? Lenore wondered. Felicia was already swanning away, waving at someone else.

Lenore decided to take a break from helping Neal and Katerina's effort and went to find Beatrice. She'd regroup, perhaps get some advice, and head back out. That last one made Lenore's insides twist as her mind suggested new ways she could foul up.

She spied her friend off to one side of the room, laughing with a group of young men, and hesitated. Beatrice had forgone a mask in favor of having her face painted like a fawn's and, inexplicably, also wore a set of demure antlers. She looked busy working her magic but spotted Lenore and waved her over. Lenore went, trying not to slink as apprehension clenched her shoulders.

"Gents, allow me to introduce the incredibly talented Lenore Blackbird-Lee." Beatrice pulled Lenore the last few steps to her side. "Darling, you need a drink in your hand." She called over a roving server and handed Lenore a cup of steaming mulled wine from the silver tray. "There now." She then introduced Lenore to her group: a painter, a son of a magistrate, and an heir to his family's shipping company.

Lenore had briefly explored the possibility of a romantic relationship with the third one, Sebastian Kincaid. She hadn't seen him since their last outing and hoped her rejection hadn't hurt him too much; Lenore had tried to be kind in her letter. Thankfully, Sebastian was quick to bring up his fiancée, a girl called Mabel from a good family of grain farmers.

"She lives just outside of the city," he said. "I knew I'd found my soul mate when we first commiserated over our respective regulations. The Enforcers keep such an awfully close eye on both people and items traveling in and out of the city."

"I'm so pleased for you," Lenore said. "She sounds lovely."

Sebastian might have been flaunting how much better off he was without her, but Lenore didn't care a whit. Better he be happy and smug than bitter and vindictive.

The group made polite conversation as masked dancers whirled and spun nearby. Lenore found it ironic how much she enjoyed wearing her disguise, given how much her invisible one exhausted her.

Another gent sidled up to them. "A... shrew?" he asked in a nasally voice.

He wore a lion mask replete with a golden mane that matched his tawny suit and brown waistcoat.

"A hedgehog," Lenore said. She thought she recognized and definitely didn't like the voice chortling behind the lion mask. "They're very tough little animals."

Beatrice eyed the newcomer.

"Indeed," the nasally voice said. Then, quite abruptly, "Shall we dance?"

Given she was in the middle of a conversation that was going well, Lenore did her best to sound coy and not annoyed. "Tell me your name and I'll give you a dance."

"Give me a dance and I'll tell you my name."

The thought of helping Neal and Katerina achieve their goal pushed Lenore to agree. Stars, she hoped Neal didn't plan on passing his magisterial responsibilities on to her.

Her lion-headed partner led her to the dance floor. They went through a few steps in silence before Lenore spoke again, doing her best impression of Beatrice. "I believe you promised me a name, sir."

"Dempsey."

Those hissed syllables shot through Lenore and pinned her feet to the floor. Quick as a viper, Dempsey pulled her closer and dragged her through the movements.

He growled, "Keep dancing. You wouldn't want to make a scene, would you?"

Lenore forced herself to lift her feet, to hang on to Dempsey's hands instead of pummeling her fists through his mask and into his face. She almost laughed—Rook had once tricked her in a similar way. If all shady gents planned on cornering her like this, she'd have to swear off dancing forever.

"Awfully bold of you to show up here," Lenore whispered. "Come to beg for your old job? Because Neal gave it to me."

Dempsey squeezed her hands so hard they hurt. "You think you can goad me, little witch?"

"Blazes, are you still on about that?" Lenore dug her fingernails into Dempsey's hands.

"I've found far better employment anyway." Lenore heard the manic grin behind his mask. "The Reaper recognizes true talent when he sees it."

"The Reaper?"

"He's quite the character. Well, he goes by 'they.' One of his quirks, you know? It adds to the mystique. A bit much, I admit, but he gets results. You see, he's a crime lord, like your friend Rook."

Lenore wanted to snap that she knew perfectly well what the Reaper was but decided to play Dempsey for information instead. "Rook?"

"Also known as Varick. One and the same."

"I don't understand."

"No surprise there," Dempsey said. Lenore pressed her lips together, once again grateful for her mask. "In any case, your little friend Varick is of interest to us."

"Why?"

Lenore heard his eager intake of breath. "Oh dear. I regret to inform you he's still a criminal." Dempsey's eyes flashed behind his mask.

She measured a pause. "What? No, that can't be true."

"I'm afraid it is." He sniggered. "You think he turned over a new leaf? He's one of the *worst*."

"What do you mean?"

"I've only heard stories, of course, but I trust their source. He chopped up a competitor to get back on top. He actually cut a fellow human into pieces and *mailed* them to his rivals."

Lenore dropped her gaze to feign shock. She'd heard the story before.

Dempsey pulled her close again before turning the motion into a twirl. "This is where you come in." She looked back up. "My colleagues have informed me you were at the Halls of Justice attack with him. Why?"

"Why what?"

Dempsey tensed. Lenore wondered if he'd just resisted shaking her, or worse. "Why were you there with him?"

Given public knowledge and her previous performance, there wasn't much for it. "Because he asked me to go. He's my friend."

"You ran into a burning prison to help your friend?"

The memories of that night thickened Lenore's voice. "Isn't that what friends do? They help one another. Dempsey, you didn't see him. Whatever his reason for going—he never told me—it was killing him." She swallowed hard; the story sounded thin.

"Stars, you are stupid." She heard the sneer smeared across Dempsey's face. "That makes this part easier, though. You're going to get closer to him. You'll learn every secret of his you can and report back to us."

"How?"

"Don't worry. I've devised a system even you can't foul up. Just follow the instructions."

"No, I mean, how am I meant to get him to tell me anything? We're obviously not the friends I thought we were."

Dempsey narrowed his eyes. "Now you're just playing stupid. Use your powers."

"My powers?"

"Yes, you little pythoness. Take whatever tricks you used to get everyone at the museum to eat out of your hand and use them on Rook." Lenore began to object, but Dempsey stamped on her toes, silencing her. "Just do the job."

"Or what?"

"Or the Reaper will make life very painful for you."

Dempsey pulled a folded sheet of paper from his pocket. After pressing it into her hand, he spun her off balance. Lenore caught herself, but it took her a moment to reorient. She swept her gaze back and forth. There was no sign of the tawny suit or lion mask. She stuffed the paper into her dress and headed back to Beatrice.

"Who was that, my dear?" asked her friend.

"No one who can help us," Lenore said.

"Shame. Oh, speaking of people who can help us, have you talked to your friend Varick about speaking with his father?" Beatrice beamed all sunshine and roses.

Lenore tried to return the smile, but her mouth refused. "I'll contact him tomorrow. He and I need to have a chat anyway."

11

~Facing Death~

Gravestones surrounded Camilla. Winter had dulled all color here. The grass, dead and brown, poked at frost-bleached grey and black memorials. Thin, unhappy clouds washed the sky. Mist crawled along the ground and wreathed itself around her ankles. It seeped between the seams of her shoes and chilled deeper than her bones.

Seeing the broken monuments, most so old their inscriptions had worn away, Camilla thought of her mother. She envied those who could come here and commune with those they'd lost. The Enforcer order had offered Camilla Fourth Hawkins' ashes after they'd recovered and burned his body. She'd accepted, because what else could she have done?

But there was nothing left of her mother. The thought filled Camilla with something like the lingering heat of a burn, warm but painful.

She'd never been to this part of the Cobalt district. It certainly seemed an appropriate setting for a secret society. Only because many of these groups had connections had she finally followed the instructions included with her invitation. Harding Smoke's threat had frightened her enough to risk being pranked.

Her surroundings did nothing to quiet the uncertainty in her heart, however. The War of Light had produced more bodies than the city's crematoriums could manage, so other disposal measures had been taken. Magic had quickly dug a complex warren of catacombs. Those with the means bought their deceased private grave plots or even personal tombs. The rest were simply chucked in.

Camilla kept looking at the vast crypt's heavy stone doors. Something more chilling than cold radiated from it, and she decided to keep the entrance in her periphery just in case. She looked at her pocket watch again, feeling more foolish by the minute. Within a day of sending her acceptance to the indicated address, she'd received a reply:

Come to the main catacombs entrance in Cobalt at sunset tomorrow.

And so Camilla had, hoping this wasn't another puerile trick.

She looked to the horizon, obscured by processing plants, shipbuilding yards, and cargo houses. Camilla guessed the sun was nearly down, but it was impossible to tell from this angle.

Footsteps behind her made her turn. Aisling stood there with a smile on her face. What on earth was she wearing, though? Black leather and cloth wrapped around the woman like death shrouds. A brass and leather mask hung from her belt.

Dmitri had worn a similar uniform the night the Halls of Justice had been attacked. It belonged to the Reaper's Collective.

Camilla opened her mouth to scream. A gloved hand wrapped around her face, followed by one around her waist and arms.

"Welcome," Aisling said. "Thank you for being on time. Right this way."

Aisling headed straight for the catacomb's doors. Heart pounding, Camilla fought her assailant, but her shouts muffled into the glove and her elbows barely moved under the iron grip around her. As she was pushed forward, she indiscriminately stabbed her heels. She connected with something solid once; it barely slowed her captor. After passing through the door's stone maw, Aisling closed it again with a bone-jarring *bang*. Darkness surrounded them. The noise of Camilla's prison shutting reverberated off unseen walls as loud as her pulse.

The hands released Camilla. She spun and headed back to the doors, praying she hadn't lost her direction. She found a person instead. Camilla yelped and jumped back.

Light flared a moment later. A single lantern lit a narrow stone corridor. It was plain save for littered detritus along the floor. The holder of the lantern wore a mask with round, soulless glass eyes and a metal grate for a mouth. When they spoke, it was with Aisling's voice. "Let's be sensible now, shall we?"

Fear filled Camilla's legs with lead. "Are you going to kill me?"

"Of course not," Aisling said. "We invited you here. The *Reaper* invited you here."

Camilla failed to keep herself from shaking. "What does he want with me then?"

"They. And that is something only the Reaper themself can tell you."

Tears bashed against Camilla's eyes. She thought of Mina's bravery and made herself stand as straight as possible. "Let me go, please. Had I known who sent that invitation, I never would have come."

Aisling cocked her head. "Yes, we know. That was rather the whole point behind the deception."

Camilla took a deep breath and lifted her chin, but she couldn't keep her next words from trembling. "I won't work for you people. If that means you'll kill me, then please do so already."

Aisling shook her head and motioned Camilla to follow. Camilla turned back to the doors, but a stout figure in the same getup as Aisling blocked the path.

A male voice echoed from within the mask. "Go on." He crossed his arms over his barrel chest.

Camilla hurtled herself at the door. The man merely grabbed her wrist and pulled her along. She beat against his arm with her free hand, but he grabbed that too and joined them. His meaty palms swallowed her slender wrists, so she kicked. His knee buckled beneath her boot. He caught himself and spun. On his wrist sat a large metal beetle with glinting green eyes. He clenched his fist and, quick as a flash, the beetle's legs extended. Less than a foot from her face, Camilla realized they were razor-sharp blades.

"Behave," he warned.

Camilla swallowed hard. A tear slipped from her eyes. The weapon swept her earlier bravado away, and she allowed herself to be pulled down the tunnel. Aisling opened another heavy stone door.

The other side was an entirely different sort of place.

Damp licked at Camilla's face. Dripping water reverberated ahead. Strange blue-green lichen washed the walls in a ghostly light, while blazing braziers periodically added their own orange glow. Human skulls lined alcoves in the wall. Who had these people been? How had they died? Where had the rest of their skeletons gone? The noise of her boots scraped against the ground and bounced back at her.

"By the way," Aisling called over her shoulder, "that's Beetle. You can call me Nightmare. We're Crypt-Keepers."

Any hope Camilla might have had fled when she saw more people. Every one wore Collective uniforms, and not one of them looked at her with human eyes. Nothing but flat, dead circles of malevolence and suspicion stared at her as they made their way through the tunnels and burial chambers. Camilla stuck closer to Beetle.

At last, the Crypt-Keepers reached a heavy wooden door. Mercifully, it led to an area that looked like familiar territory—a laboratory. Its tidy organization did more for Camilla's nerves than anything else had. Although, that wasn't a big victory, given she was certain her skull would soon join the others she'd seen.

This laboratory and Mina's had several marked differences. Mina's was bright with white walls and ample lighting. This room, like the rest of the catacombs, was dim and cold. Multiple lamps scattered along every surface, ready to be lit when needed. Camilla looked past the beakers and flasks and shelves but saw no one else in the room.

"Over here." Nightmare beckoned with a hand.

With the door shut and Beetle guarding it, he released Camilla. She looked at him. He shook his head and she slunk over to Nightmare, who stood at a large window. Drawing closer, Camilla realized it looked into an operating theatre. A table stood in the center. A rather obese woman lay on it, covered with a cloth and staring at the ceiling with half-lidded eyes. Camilla could tell she'd been drugged but couldn't say with what. A tray of gleaming medical instruments laid in a neat row on a wheeled tray beside the table. A door on the other side of the room opened, and in walked a figure who could only be the Reaper.

They wore a mask with round glass eyes like their Collective members. This one, however, had a long beak. Legend had it, in the Old World, certain magi possessed the ability to commune with the dead, sometimes even called back a departed soul if the timing was right. Those magi wore masks like the Reaper's to denote their rank and power. What was the Reaper really about? They wore surgical gloves over their death shrouds. A promising sign, at least.

When the Reaper came to face the window, Nightmare bowed. An urge to scream at the creature before her struck Camilla, to break the glass, destroy the laboratory, but the woman lying in the operating theatre stopped her. Instead, Camilla dipped her head in acknowledgement. The Reaper gave no indication of approval or disapproval and turned back to the operating table. Several Collective members, also wearing surgical gloves, entered and gathered with their leader. Camilla watched the woman's covered chest rise and fall. Good. She looked stable. One of the Collective members lifted a flap in the cloth, revealing a section of marked skin where the woman's liver resided, and handed the Reaper a scalpel from the tray.

With sure hands, the Reaper sliced open the flesh and inserted a speculum into the wound. Camilla observed with bated breath as the Reaper and their assistants sliced, clipped, mopped, and flushed the woman's insides.

Eventually, one of those assisting called, "Ready for replacement."

Another came through the doorway carrying a basin full of ice. Something pink and fleshy sat amongst the frozen pieces. Camilla craned her head to get a better view.

Her attention was pulled back to the patient, however, as the Reaper lifted the woman's liver out of her body. They showed it to Nightmare and Camilla.

She frantically grabbed Nightmare's arm. "What are they doing? She'll die without her liver!"

Camilla looked around and spied a door, a dark blot against the barely lit stone walls. She turned to it, but Nightmare stopped her with a grip as strong as steel.

"Don't," she said.

Camilla pulled, but it made no difference. "How can you work for someone like that? That woman will die! Don't you care about anything?"

"Wait," was all Nightmare said.

The Reaper set the woman's liver into a smaller bowl, also filled with ice. The organ looked diseased. It slumped, enflamed and discolored, in its frozen bed like an oversized dead slug. The Reaper reached into the larger basin and removed what Camilla realized was another liver, this one pink and healthy. They placed it where the other had resided and began, unbelievably, to reattach the connections.

Camilla pressed herself against the glass to get a better look. The work was fiddly and delicate. A Collective member placed a curious pair of spectacles with multiple lenses over the Reaper's mask. Every so often, Camilla heard a soft hiss, and one of the assistants performed an action. She couldn't make out words but assumed the Reaper was giving their aides instructions. Time passed. Hunger and thirst demanded attention, but Camilla's awe shooed them away. Her toes had gone numb, and she shifted just enough to get blood flowing again.

"That should do it," said one of those assisting. Holding a scalpel in reserve between his pinkie and ring finger, he removed one of the many tiny clamps.

The scalpel slipped.

It hit one of the thin arteries tracing back and forth within the opening. Blood welled up and began to pour from the incision. The man loosed a colorful swear, and the others rushed to stem the flow. Only the Reaper seemed to know what they were doing. The rest might as well have been chickens with how they were flapping around.

Camilla shot for the door, lost her coat along the way, and found the closest sink. She yanked up her sleeves and called for gloves as she scoured her hands with soap and water. Someone fitted her with a pair of surgical gloves. Then she rushed to the patient and got to work. She was unaware of anything but shouting orders and trying to save the drugged woman. Finding the source was the biggest problem—the cut, probably no more than millimeters long, hid somewhere beneath the pooling blood. Precious moments ticked by before she located it. Camilla had told one assistant to get her a cauterization rod, which she used to stop the bleeding. Black-gloved hands joined her. Once the immediate danger had passed, the Reaper took over the transplant process again. They rasped instructions as she worked. Seeing the use in each directive, she did everything she was told to a T.

A Collective member took her place when only stitching up the incision and cleaning everything remained. All fairly basic tasks. Camilla wiped sweat from her brow with her arm and looked around.

The Reaper stood no more than a few feet away. They stared at her with those dead eyes. Now that the patient was safe, the ramifications of what she'd done sank in.

"You did well," the Reaper said, their voice like a death rattle.

The Reaper remained still as Collective members removed their leader's gloves and smock. Camilla watched the aides, who took her gloves as well. She hadn't been wearing a smock, so her dress was streaked and spattered with blood.

"You have passed," the Reaper added.

Camilla's eyes widened. Nightmare had come into the operating theatre and looked at her. Of course, it was impossible to read the expression on Nightmare's face with that blasted mask in the way. Other Collective members still milled about, finishing up with the operation and beginning to clear out. Camilla heard her heartbeat in her ears. The urge to lash out at the Reaper struck her again, but she cooled these emotions for the time being. She folded her hands before her, making a mental note to change and wash as soon as possible. She ignored the thought that it might not be an option.

"This was a test?" Her voice rang flat and even.

"It was," hissed the Reaper.

Camilla forced herself to be so calm she might have been delivering a lecture as she motioned to the woman on the table. "This patient's liver was genuinely sick, though."

"Yes. Risk was the price for her cure."

Camilla closed her eyes and pursed her lips. She urged herself to cage her emotions the way Mina did. "You endangered an innocent woman's life for your *test*?"

"That was the price."

The admission, delivered so coldly, turned up the petrolsene flame burning beneath Camilla's heart. She wouldn't be able to hold her temper if she continued down this line of questioning.

She opened her eyes again and fixed the Reaper with a hard stare. "Will she be alright?"

"The operation was a success, but recovery is always hard for the body."

"So people come to you, in need, and you... you..." Camilla couldn't bring herself to say *help*.

The Reaper beckoned slowly with a hand. They wore a second set of gloves beneath their surgical ones. In fact, not an inch of skin showed. Camilla followed the Reaper back into the laboratory and through the door Beetle guarded. She wanted to keep an eye on the patient, but there was nothing for it. She had no bargaining power here, nor skills to fight them off.

They traveled down a short hallway and into a little sitting room. Plush rugs in muted colors, like the vibrancy had been sucked out of them, covered the stone floor. It was almost enough to make her forget they were in a mass grave. Decorative hangings covered the walls. Armchairs ringed a small circular table, upon which sat an incense burner. Its smoke hung thick and heavy in the air, illuminated like fog as candles cast a golden glow over everything. How many candles a week did they go through down here? The incense smelled of carnations and lilies. Funeral flowers.

Camilla hung back near the door, and Nightmare stayed close to her. The Reaper removed something from their back. It looked like a gnarled walking stick, as dark as the gloom around it. They placed it on a shelf at the back before settling into an armchair. Their robes spread around them like liquid murk.

They beckoned again. "Please, sit. Nightmare, Beetle, you too. You have done well."

Camilla cast a bitter glance at the Crypt-Keepers as they passed. She took a step toward the door.

"Do not try to escape," the Reaper said. "You will fail."

Camilla took a deep breath and immediately regretted it as the stale scent of damp and decay invaded her nostrils. She held her chin high and stepped forward. Closer to the chairs, she realized their wooden frames had been carved to resemble bones—

at least, she hoped they were wood. She tried to school her expression of distaste but didn't feel confident of success.

"I'd prefer to stand, if it's all the same to you," she said.

"It is not. Sit." The Reaper motioned to the chair again.

Camilla swallowed hard and sat. The incense was stronger here. She was happy to breathe it in, given the other option.

"You have borne witness to a great feat of medical science," the Reaper said. "You have never seen an organ transplant, have you?"

Camilla shook her head. "I've never even heard of such a thing being achieved."

"The liver, rescued from a cadaver, served the living even in death. That woman, assuming she recovers, will not die within a year now."

Camilla took another deep breath, trying to collect herself. She was pleased with how much calmer she suddenly felt. "That is incredible, yes, but you put a patient's life at risk. Do you call yourself a doctor?"

A long silence as dark and deep as a grave passed.

"No. I am more. I am the Reaper. I hold the keys to life and death."

The words hit Camilla like a mallet to the chest. What was this creature? Her head spun. She closed her eyes, tried to breathe slowly to steady herself.

Think, Camilla, she told herself. *Be rational.*

Was it irrational to believe the Reaper might be something like the Old World death-speakers? Oaths were very much alive, as were Vampyres. Why not this too?

The Reaper's voice pulled her out of her thoughts. "Regarding tonight, we needed to see what you could do. I am impressed."

"Thank you." The words were automatic. She hadn't opened her eyes yet, still hoping to make sense of all this.

"You've seen us replace a sick organ with a healthy one. Would you like to see what else we can do?"

Camilla opened her eyes. The soulless, black mask stared right through her, piercing her heart and soul. She found herself nodding.

The Reaper motioned with a hand. "Follow."

Camilla followed the Reaper back into the catacombs. The smell of the incense drifted off their robes like petals on the wind. In the laboratory, they showed her a potion they called Verisap. It would "draw pure truth from even the most unwilling lips." They showed her diagrams drawn on a rollaway blackboard. The drawings explained how the organ transplant worked. More outlined a process for transferring blood from one person to another. Camilla gaped at the information before her.

"Not all blood is the same," the Reaper said. "I know how to read the markings within."

"This is incredible," Camilla said. "Do you know what this could mean for the medical community? Think of all the lives—"

"They are not worthy," the Reaper snarled.

"But people…"

The Reaper shook their head at her. "*I* hold the keys. If I give them away, I give my power to the undeserving."

Camilla didn't agree, but she also couldn't bring herself to argue with the Reaper. They were more awe-inspiring the more she learned.

"I would be willing to share it with you, however."

Camilla stared, certain she had misheard. "I… I beg your pardon?"

"You have risen above adversity. You have shunned this world which would hold you back from your true potential, force you into a mold it has chosen for you."

"I haven't done it alone," Camilla said.

"The members of this Collective are chosen. I have chosen you."

The Reaper drew close. The smell of their incense was stronger than ever. When Camilla breathed, she couldn't help practically drinking the heady scent. They cupped their hands around her face without touching her.

"Join us, Camilla. Join us, and I will share my keys with you."

Camilla flapped her lips like a fish, searching for words. It was difficult. The Reaper's presence took up not just physical space but an unseen intangible space too. She felt it might suffocate her if she remained in it too long.

After a few moments, she said in a wobbling voice, "I want to learn."

"Good. I am glad to hear it."

The Reaper drew away, and the pressure receded. Camilla took a deep breath and regretted it a little. The Reaper had moved on, and the air tasted stale and mildewy again.

"We will begin soon," the Reaper said. "You are dismissed for today."

Camilla realized what she had agreed to, what she was going to learn, and she wasn't afraid. Instead, peace filled her.

12

~"*News you won't like*"~

R ook trotted up to Lenore's door. Apprehension somersaulted in his stomach—he hadn't seen her since confessing about the oath. It had been just over a week, but lingering insecurities made it feel longer. They'd sent a few short communications back and forth. Nothing serious, just checking in with each other. Even with that, though, a voice in the back of Rook's head taunted him.

She's done with you.

With everything that had happened lately, he'd practically leapt when she'd sent her card to Gadget's shop. It had become his primary haunt of late. Rook had made the courier wait while he scribbled a promise he'd be over that very afternoon. No reply had come back, but he assumed it was fine. Manners and his current patience level didn't go hand in hand. Dmitri had yet to contact him after their last meeting, and each passing hour shaved another slice off Rook's nerves. He barely felt the cold as he rang the bell, and again a few seconds later.

When Lenore opened the door, he couldn't help but smile. "Little bird, you are a sight for sore eyes."

Lenore gestured him through. "My, you are eager today."

"I'm always eager to see you."

Lenore sighed and led him into the parlor. "You should sit. I'm afraid I have news you won't like."

Rook floated into the nearest chair and crossed a leg over his knee. "Oh, good. I was hoping for an excuse to stab someone." He chuckled. "Of course, I'm kidding." He stopped when Lenore gave him a look that almost, just almost, gave him permission. "What's going on?"

"I ran into Dempsey last night."

Rook sprung out of the chair and crossed to Lenore to check she was unharmed. He retreated when another thought shunted that one away. She wasn't hurt; he could see that. He ran his hands through his hair. His nerves frizzed like a fuse. Despite the evidence, he asked in a low voice, "Did he hurt you?"

Lenore shook her head. "No. He was just very much himself."

Rook released a breath and reached out. Her hand met his. The contact brought immediate comfort. "I had no idea. If I'd had the oath…" He broke away and flung out his hands. "This is exactly why I said it was worth having." He hurled a few choice swears at the situation and completed a tight circuit around the room. "I wonder if there's a way to get it back. We should ask Kieran. I…"

Lenore placed a gentle hand on his chest. His hands flew up to grasp hers, pressing it tighter against him. "I appreciate your concern more than I can say, but it's better this way."

"Better for whom? Lenore, had I known…"

"You can't always protect me, remember?"

Rook nodded, not wanting to believe it. He refocused. That was an issue for another time. "What did the lout want then?"

Oddly, Lenore's voice brightened. "He, um… He wants me to spy on you."

A smile made of pure mischief curled up Rook's cheeks. "Does he now? That's the first good idea he's had. How close exactly do we need to get? I can move in if you like. All for the cause, of course." Lenore's expression fell, and Rook furrowed his brow. "What is it, little bird?"

She mustered a smile. He saw how hard she was fighting to be strong.

Lenore pulled away from him. "That's a different conversation."

She recounted the previous night's events. Rook's face grew darker with every word. By the end, they faced each other on the flower-patterned sofa.

"He'll regret threatening you," Rook growled. "Have you at least told Kieran? It'll help to have him at your back."

"Neal and Mina have taken care of that. Kieran won't show himself here unless he has to, out of respect for Eamon. I told them in the cab home. Neal looked like his head might explode, but we didn't have much time to talk. Well, whisper. I'm meant to go over there tomorrow." Pain flashed in Lenore's eyes.

Rook studied her face. He pushed concern for whatever she was struggling with to the back of the queue in his brain but made a note to press the issue later. "That Vampyre is quite the enigma when it comes to what he will and won't do, even when protecting his family."

"He struggles with it. He's worried for his humanity, but he won't stand by and let us die either. To be honest, I don't like putting him in this position."

"That seems to be your theme tune." Rook smiled and playfully tapped Lenore's hand. She smiled back. "We can use Dempsey's request to our advantage, you know."

"Oh, definitely. I did try to turn things in our favor."

Rook smiled wider at her. "Clever little thing. So he's let the cat out of the bag about me still doing what I do. What a terrible shock it must have been for you."

Lenore cocked an eyebrow. "Any chance you'll tell me what exactly that is now?"

Rook made a face back. "That's very need-to-know. I still think it's better if you don't know. Plausible deniability and all that."

"But I can report it back to Dempsey."

"He works for the Reaper. If he doesn't already know, finding out won't help him since the Reaper definitely does."

"But it might convince him I'm doing a good job."

Rook grumbled. "You make a fair point. I'll consider considering it. In the meantime, I'll feed you some innocuous little snippets." He just hoped his old information didn't go out of date too quickly. He really was going to kill Dmitri. Lenore's agreement brought him back. "So what's got you in a tizzy?"

"Later," Lenore said. "I have something else for you."

Rook leaned back on the sofa. "Apparently, I should have blocked out my entire day."

Lenore raised concerned eyes to him. "Am I keeping you from something?"

"Not in the least. What else do you have for me?"

Lenore dithered, twisting a pillow tassel between thumb and forefinger. Rook's curiosity spiked. She didn't look so serious now, so he hoped for something at least amusing.

"Do you, by any chance, still communicate with your family?"

Rook's features flattened into decidedly unamused lines. "No. Never. And I don't intend to. Why are you asking me this?"

Lenore grimaced. "Beatrice told me that the Speaker of the magistrate council is your father, Lord Pendragon. She wanted to know if you might—"

"Little bird, as much as I care for you, whatever you're about to say, the answer is no."

"But you can talk to—"

"No." Rook got up and began to pace.

"You can ask him to throw support behind Neal, try and convince him to—"

"No. Absolutely not."

Lenore followed him. "Just have a conversation."

Rook spun on his heel; she nearly ran into him. "Lenore, I *can't*."

"Why not? It could help us change the Enforcers into something good. Don't you want that?"

Rook sighed and shook his head. "I haven't spoken to my parents in years. When I left, I left them well and truly behind. I don't want anything to do with them. Ever. I understand what my father's influence can do for you and Neal and Lady Katerina, but you have to understand I've burned those bridges."

"Could you not build new ones?" Lenore clasped her hands before her. "What would happen if you tried?"

Rook shrugged. "Probably nothing. I doubt they want me back any more than I want them."

"So what's there to lose?"

Rook leaned back, rocking on his heels. He rolled his head around his shoulders to stare at the ceiling.

You, he thought.

The night he'd confessed to Lenore about losing the oath, he'd been prepared to leave her. Her determination to keep him in her life had both shocked and elated him. He saw that chance flitting away again. After all, why should she keep him if there was nothing in it for her?

Rook groaned and rubbed his face. "You have no idea how insufferable they are."

He looked back down to find Lenore smirking at him. "I can't believe I finally found it, the thing that scares the mighty Rook. Talking to his family."

Rook fixed her with a challenging glare. "Is this really the game you want to play with me, little bird? I can see what you're doing."

"What would it take for you to knock on their door?"

"You have to come with me," he said. Lenore blanched. "That's what I thought."

She shook herself and curled her fingers around Rook's. "Fine. When shall we go?"

"I'm warning you, you're in for a truly abysmal time."

She leaned toward him. "You don't scare me. I've had to luncheon with the Jones family."

They traded a few dates before settling on one.

"*Now* will you tell me what has you so worked up?" Rook asked.

Lenore deflated and drifted into the nearest chair. The way she curled in on herself told Rook this would be the biggest blow of all, though he didn't know for whom.

13

~Cutting Ties~

Lenore tapped on the library's doorframe with her knuckles. They barely made a sound. Eamon, who was reading in an armchair with a drink beside him, didn't look up. She tried again, forcing herself to knock harder this time. Eamon still didn't look at her but spoke.

"Yes?"

"I need to speak with you." Her voice barely rose above a whisper.

He sipped his drink. "Speak then."

Lenore's features cinched together. "Eamon, this is important. Please look at me." She cursed the way her voice cracked.

"I'm listening, Lenore," he replied, unmoved.

She swallowed the growing lump in her throat. When she spoke, the words sounded like they came from someone else.

"I'm leaving." Eamon's eyes snapped to hers. "I'm moving back in with Neal and Mina. They've already agreed to the arrangement. Everything should be moved out within a fortnight."

Eamon stood, dropping his glass. It bounced off the chair's cushion and clattered onto the rug. Only after watching its contents spill everywhere did Lenore look back at him. Eamon's face had gone white, and his jaw hung slack. She waited for some other reaction, but none came.

Her next statement was harder than the previous one. "I leave it up to you how to divide our wedding gifts. I understand if you want to keep them all."

Eamon made a strangled noise and closed his mouth. Lenore waited while he tried to form words.

"I-I... Wedding gifts? Lenore, how... What?" He rubbed his hands along the sides of his head. "You're leaving?"

"Yes." She folded her hands before her, pleased that her voice hadn't cracked again.

"For how long? No, wait. Dividing up gifts. Are you... divorcing me?"

"I leave that up to you as well."

Eamon's face changed from white to red. "To me? You're leaving that humiliating business to *me*? How dare you?!"

"Because I don't really want to divorce you, Eamon."

"Then why the blazes are you leaving?"

"What is there for me here?"

"Everything!" Eamon gestured around the room. "Our marriage. Our future. Our entire life!"

Lenore fisted her hands into her skirts. "And what sort of life has that been of late? You don't speak to me. You wouldn't even look at me when I came in here."

"You lied to me, Lenore. You hid that Vampyre from me!"

"HIS NAME IS KIERAN! And I have endeavored every day to make it right. I report my every movement to you and never question where you disappear to."

Eamon bit off his words. "Nowhere but the club, work, or to see my family."

"And I am *tired*, Eamon. I'm exhausted from trying and getting nowhere."

"So you'll just throw away everything we have?"

Lenore gritted her teeth. "I said I don't want to divorce you, but what would you have me do? Continue to bear this hell until I die? You act as if I don't exist. I don't even know if you want to fix what's broken. You've given me nothing to hope for."

Silence fell heavy and thick between them, a rising fog of black pain. Lenore's anger ebbed as quickly as it had come, rushing out and leaving her empty. She turned and headed for her bedroom—the one he'd asked her to use after that night at the Halls of Justice.

Lenore hid there for the rest of the evening. She heard Eamon along the floor. It sounded angry at first. Doors slammed, and his tread stomped like lead. Her fury returned as she remembered his umbrage with her pronouncement. Surely he couldn't be blind to what had happened between them? Her anger soon settled into acceptance, however. What was done was done, and now he knew.

)(

Eamon ranged from room to room that evening. His mind jumped to a new idea every other breath. He considered sending a note to Neal, demanding to know if what Lenore had said was true. No. Eamon didn't believe Lenore had lied about that. By all appearances, she had been truthful with him since that night. Although, she could still be hiding things. She had told him about things that had happened between Rook and her. What could be worse than that? Eamon had questioned her further at the time, but she'd denied anything more.

Perhaps he should call Rook, the little wretch, and ask for himself. Eamon knew how to contact him. When they'd been briefly allied for Lenore's safety, she had shown Eamon Rook's symbol.

His shoulders tightened as he thought of the thief. Surely Rook had put this idea into Lenore's head. Would Neal and Mina have agreed if they thought it unwise, though? Despite what Eamon thought of their judgment regarding the Vampyre, they'd always otherwise been good and rational people. Yes, perhaps he would send something to them first. Then again, it was getting late. Maybe he should go himself.

Coat in hand, Eamon headed for the door. He stopped. Whether Neal and Mina truly knew about Lenore's plan, speaking to them meant facing the shame of it all. He replaced his coat. His anger was making him act rashly. He needed to slow down and think before he did something humiliating. Perhaps he ought to occupy his mind with something else while his emotions settled. Reading failed him, however, and he didn't keep cards in his house. It was too dark to go for a walk in the garden, so he made a few laps around the house. When he passed Lenore's door, he considered knocking. There was nothing to say, though, so he walked on.

With time, Lenore's words sank deeper. They burrowed beneath his skin and pulsed, *I'm leaving.*

He pushed the memory away. She wasn't serious. It was a scare tactic. For her or him, he wasn't certain. She'd back out. She wouldn't be able to bear the shame.

That's you, not her.

She came from middle class—divorce wouldn't be to her what it was to him. Well, she still wouldn't go through with it. She cared for him too much.

But she's already arranged things with Neal and Mina.

Eamon stopped. Lenore had begun to prepare. She'd owned up to failure. She had a plan for completing the operation.

Lenore was dead serious.

Eamon sank into the nearest chair. Throughout the rest of the night, he ruminated. Anger, fear, sorrow, hope, and desperation came and went. Paths like twisting vines unfurled in his mind, all of them unpleasant. Those that pointed toward reconciliation lay shrouded in mist, but those leading away from it came with gates that would lock behind him. He didn't want to travel any of the latter, but the former...

How was he to even begin navigating them?

)(

The next day at work, Lenore received a visit from Patrick, one of the Anthropology apprentices. He came to the Arc-Tech department to ask if Eamon was alright.

"He sent a note to say he's not feeling well," Patrick said. "That's not like him. I've seen him come in looking like death warmed over."

Lenore forced a sheepish smile. "Blame it on me."

She left it at that, and Patrick smiled like he understood. She was glad to have spared Eamon any shame in this case. Thinking of him tightened her throat, so she went to see what Ezra was up to.

When Lenore arrived home that evening, she was tempted to check on Eamon. She wondered what kind of state he was in. She hesitated outside of her room. The old Lenore would have cut ties and left him to himself. She had to admit that might be for the best.

Perhaps she should begin cataloging her things for packing instead. She could get a little done before going to spar with Rook. Heavens, a sparring match sounded good right about now. Then again, she cared for whatever was left of Eamon's and her relationship. It'd be good of her to at least look in on him.

When she knocked on his bedroom door—after having searched the rest of the house—there was no answer. Lenore tried the knob and found it locked. She sighed. Very well, she'd leave him alone. She left a note letting him know where she was going, though.

)(

An inordinate number of candles lit Kieran's room.

Lenore squared up to Rook for their sparring match. "I told Eamon I'm leaving."

Rook's eyebrows shot up. He opened his mouth to say something, but she struck out before he could utter a word. She was sloppy and knew it. She'd barely evade one blow before attacking again, and she left gaping holes in her defenses. Rook pressed his advantage. Lenore retaliated with more careless fury.

Without warning, something broke in her. A sob seared up her throat. Rook leapt back, and she turned away. From the corner of her eye, she saw Rook's hands grasp at the air. He was reaching for her and she was tempted, which made her cry harder.

Rook pulled back and looked at Kieran. The Vampyre was already there. Lenore buried her face in his shoulder as she wept.

Rook placed a hand on her shoulder. "It'll be alright."

"He's right," Kieran said. "It will."

The little door to his room sounded. They turned to see Neal squat-walk inside.

"I apologize for interrupting," he said gently. "Lenore, Eamon is here. I've asked him to wait upstairs. Do you wish to see him?"

Lenore nodded. She wiped her face and stuffed down her sorrow. Neal led her to the conservatory, where Eamon fretted with an embroidered sofa cushion.

"I'll be close if you need anything." Neal pointed his glare left of Eamon.

146

Lenore waited for Neal's footsteps to fade. She didn't sit but looked at Eamon with soft eyes. "You missed work today. I hope you weren't too bad off."

"I wasn't in a good place, to be honest," Eamon said. His breath rattled like dry autumn leaves. "More than anything, I wanted to think in peace."

Lenore nodded. She was impressed with how steadily she was holding Eamon in her gaze. He looked back at her, lines etching his face. Dark circles hung beneath his eyes. Even so, his hair and clothes were neat.

After a long silence, he said, "I don't want you to go."

"I can't continue on as we have, nor should I be asked to," Lenore said. "I have apologized, and I…"

She trailed off as Eamon raised his hands in surrender. "Yes, I know. You explained yourself perfectly last night. Can we not rehash everything, please?"

Lenore checked her indignation and locked it away. "Very well then. Why are you here?"

Eamon spread his hands, clasped them, and opened them once more. "I don't want you to leave. I'm still angry, but I want to stop this. Please, Lenore."

She was surprised to see his eyes glisten but shook her head slowly. Her own tears were returning. "It's already sorted, Eamon."

"Then un-sort it. Please. We can fix this. I locked you out, I admit that. I'm sorry. I…"

It appeared he wanted her to pick up the thread. She refused and waited for him to continue.

"I am learning, slowly and painfully, that this is not, in fact, the proper way to deal with conflict," he said. "And I know this is a repeated offense. That has no doubt undermined your faith in me." Lenore granted him a nod. "That is… difficult for me to swallow, but you're right. I haven't given you anything to hope for these last few weeks. My actions were intentional, to punish you. That's not conducive to maintaining a good relationship. I'm sorry."

"That's putting it lightly," Lenore snapped. "Do you have any idea how difficult it has been to try and try, only to have you spit on every attempt for peace? Fat lot of care you've shown about… about *anything* between us."

"Yes, and I should have known better. I'm sorry. I'm so sorry, Lenore. Please don't leave me. Please."

Lenore took a deep breath and looked away. She willed rationality to override her emotions.

"What can I do?" Eamon asked. Fear trembled in his voice. Had he only just realized she wasn't bluffing?

Lenore tried to be gentle again. "You have to understand how difficult it was for me to decide this in the first place. What it took to approach Mina and Neal. I wouldn't have done it unless I believed the spirit of our marriage well and truly dead." Something in Eamon's grey eyes splintered, like the top of a frozen lake cracking, revealing just how fragile the surface had been. "I can't go backward without careful consideration, which will take time."

"So you don't know if you believe I'm in earnest," Eamon whispered.

"I do, truly, but these are deep wounds. On both sides. I don't know how well either of us can recover."

"I want to try, and I think we have a better chance together."

Lenore swallowed hard. She saw his logic but also suspected there was harm in not taking time apart.

"I need time to decide," she said.

Eamon nodded. His eyes swept across the floor. They looked a little wild. "Is… is Kieran here?"

Hearing Eamon say Kieran's name threw Lenore. It was as inconceivable as Mina swearing off being a doctor. Lenore wasn't sure she'd heard correctly. "What?"

"Is Kieran here? He usually is, isn't he?"

Lenore still couldn't believe Eamon had asked after Kieran, by name no less. That Eamon had been listening when she'd explained that Kieran made his home with the Allens was only slightly less shocking.

"Yes," Lenore hesitated on the word. "He's in his room. Why?"

"I could meet him. Properly, I mean."

Lenore's heart broke at the desperation in Eamon's voice. "You don't have to—"

"I should," Eamon said. "He's your… friend. He's important to you."

Lenore glanced at the door of the butler's closet. "That's his choice. I'll ask."

When she opened the kitchen door, she spied Kieran's shadowy form waiting in a dusk-draped corner.

"Kieran," she said, "would you like to come in here and meet Eamon?"

"I would love to." Kieran spoke loud enough to be heard in the next room.

Lenore took his hand and returned. Eamon stood but held his ground as soon as the gaunt figure appeared.

Lenore didn't let go of Kieran's hand. "Kieran, meet Eamon, my…" Out of habit, she was going to say more, but her voice caught in her throat. She could tell Eamon caught her mistake by the way his throat bobbed.

Kieran inclined his head as if nothing had gone amiss. "This is an absolute pleasure. I sincerely hope we will become better acquainted."

Eamon didn't take his eyes off Kieran. "Yes. A-as do I."

"You are a man of discovery, are you not?" Kieran said.

"Indeed I am." Eamon sounded wary. "Why do you ask?"

"Have you ever wondered how an Old World creature like a Vampyre feeds? I could show you."

"Oh no, thank you. That's not nec—"

"On Rook."

Eamon's eyebrow twitched. Lenore almost glared at Kieran, but knowing his good intentions stopped her. She'd told him enough about Eamon for the Vampyre to know curiosity would conquer fear. And why not sweeten the deal by making Eamon's nemesis the test subject?

"It's his turn to, erm… donate, is it?" Eamon straightened his waistcoat. "I take it the deed has yet to be done this evening?"

"Correct," Kieran said. "I'm certain he won't mind. Shall I fetch him?"

"Um, Kieran," Lenore cut in. "There's… the rule to consider."

Eamon's eyebrows creased. "Rule?"

Kieran sighed. "Indeed. Miss Camilla has asked that Rook venture no farther than the kitchen."

"Huh. Why exactly? That hasn't always been the case."

"No," Lenore said. "After what happened to our mothers, she... Well, she blames Rook."

Eamon's mouth opened and closed several times. "I'm sorry. I didn't realize."

He looked at Lenore with an expression she didn't want to see, so she turned to Kieran again. "Let's move this to the kitchen, shall we?"

Kieran led them to the kitchen. Rook shrugged at the change of plans and said nothing to Eamon, who asked questions with growing courage about what he called "the procedure." Since Kieran was busy eating, Lenore answered what she could from what he'd told her in the past.

"It's difficult to switch between eating and talking without making a mess," she explained.

Eamon looked abashed. "I see. Apologies."

He waited until after Kieran was sated, which left them standing in silence. Rook busied himself with examining his nails and ignoring Eamon's occasional hateful glares. Kieran answered Eamon's questions after his meal.

Lenore asked Rook if he wanted to finish sparring.

"I can stay," Eamon said.

Lenore pushed away emotions she didn't have the energy to examine. "You don't have to. It's been quite a day."

"To be honest, I don't think I'm up for more practice tonight," Rook said. "Gadget has had me reorganizing her storeroom."

Eamon turned to Lenore. "Shall we head home together then?"

More feelings for Lenore to dissect later. They said little on their way to the townhouse. Once there, Lenore hurried for the stairs. She'd just mounted them when Eamon spoke.

"I didn't know Camilla blames Rook for what happened," Eamon said. Lenore gripped the banister. "Didn't Mrs. Hawkins offer your mother her place?"

"Yes, she did," Lenore whispered.

"What does Camilla say to that?"

"None of us have the heart to point it out."

"I see." Unspoken words weighed in Eamon's tone. "I'm sorry I haven't been there for you while you've been mourning your mother."

Lenore bit back a nasty retort. She thought carefully but couldn't conjure an honest response that wouldn't hurt. Instead, she simply nodded before continuing upstairs.

14

~The Scent of Rot~

The catacombs weren't as frightening this time around, but they were no less unpleasant. The wet cold seeped through every seam and gap in Camilla's clothing. It made her shiver and cough. Nightmare had met her at the entrance again. Due to Camilla's connections, they'd decided she should appear as if nothing had changed. She covered her time at the catacombs by telling her family she'd joined a new study group. The Reaper was waiting in the hazy sitting room. Incense hung thick in the air again. They interrogated Camilla to get a better understanding of her education, and she did her best to answer accurately yet succinctly. It took a long time before she received any indication of approval.

"I see I chose well," rattled the Reaper.

Camilla's cheeks warmed as she fought down a smile. She'd been eager to impress and gave a deferential nod. "Thank you."

They eventually moved into the laboratory. The Reaper explained in more detail than last time the purpose of every station. When they reached the table where the Reaper made their truth serum, Camilla's eyes lingered on the tiny vials of the strange potion.

"Is it detectable?" she asked. "If you mix it with something, I mean."

The Reaper turned hollow eyes onto her and tipped their head. The motion made them look more like a bird than the mask already did. They selected a vial, uncorked it, and held it under Camilla's nose.

"I can't smell anything," she said.

The Reaper held out the vial. "Consider it a gift."

With a new sense of awe for the preternatural being, Camilla couldn't help but smile. She reverently took the little bottle. "Thank you. You are very gracious."

The Reaper nodded and moved on with the tour.

)(

Lenore and the Allens, plus Eamon, Kieran, and Rook, gathered around the dining room table. Mina and Neal stood behind Lenore's chair, overseeing everything. Rook sat beside her. On her other side sat Eamon, who kept glancing at Kieran across the table. No one said a word about Lenore and Eamon's situation. They all knew about his request, which kept the tension ratcheted up. At least Camilla was busy with a new study group tonight, so she wasn't here to glare at Rook. They had temporarily lifted her rule since the kitchen wasn't conducive for the task at hand.

Lenore's first correspondence with Dempsey sat before her. A page of notes waited beside it. Given that Lenore's safety hung in the balance, everyone wanted to be involved. This made things tricky since Rook got surly about sharing with anyone besides her.

Neal scanned the notes. "You're not deathly allergic to fish."

Rook was leaning on the table with his head resting in his hand. He looked lazily to Neal. "No, it's just a horrible texture." He made a face. "If they want to try assassination by halibut, though, fine by me."

Mina asked, "Your agents use crossbows? I thought weapon sales were highly regulated."

"They are, which is why I'm a criminal." Rook sat up. "My source is a lie so the Reaper goes chasing a false lead. Ranged weaponry is the most regulated of all. Few places can, much less will, sell it or even ammunition. Better to have someone on your payroll who can fashion some from raw materials."

Lenore didn't look at Rook. Lowell had such skills. She wasn't certain she wanted to know how he employed them in his partnership with the crime lord, although, she was pretty sure she could guess.

Rook had helped create the list of tidbits before them, but he'd left out which ones were true.

"Should I know the difference between the false and real leads?" Lenore asked. "In case Dempsey wants more information."

"Surely he'll ask for it via letter?" Eamon's hand rested on the table, extended toward Lenore but not touching. She read it as a silent offer, one she declined just as quietly. "Dempsey has to know you're on your guard now. I can't believe he'd risk meeting you in person again."

"I'd like to agree," Neal said, "but there's no telling what that madman will do. He tried to have Lenore assassinated because he was jealous and thinks she's some kind of enchantress."

"Witch," Lenore corrected.

"Rook?" Kieran gave him a hard look. "What's the safest course of action?"

Rook's glare matched his tone. "You could take out some of the Reaper's people, night stalker. That would certainly make things safer for everyone."

Kieran growled, which made Eamon push back his chair. Mina barely jumped out of his way, loosing a sound of protest.

"You may see fit to throw around your humanity, but not all of us have the same luxury," Kieran said.

"Does anyone here actually know what happens when a Vampyre kills?" Rook looked around. "No one? Right, so maybe it's no different than when anyone else does."

"And you would happily let me be the test subject?"

"Rook," Mina snapped. "I think—"

The doorchime rang, and they froze. Kieran got up and headed to the kitchen. Lenore was inclined to follow—Rook had been harsh, and now Kieran was relegated to the back of the house like a dirty, little secret. She stood, thinking of things she might say to comfort him, but Rook placed a silent hand on her arm. Esther called from elsewhere in the house that she was on her way. Those in the dining room exchanged looks.

Shortly after, Esther appeared alone in the doorway. "It's Dmitri Sawyer, sir and madam. Shall I let him in?"

Before anyone else could answer, Rook asked, "Is he alone?"

Lenore's heart had calmed at hearing who it was, but the deadly edge in Rook's voice made her reconsider her relief.

"Yes, Master Pendragon," Esther said. "He was when I left him."

Rook's jaw worked. His hand still rested on Lenore's arm. She avoided looking at Eamon, not wishing to see his reaction.

At last, Rook said, "Let me go talk to him."

From her vantage point, Lenore could see Rook thumbing the handle of one of his daggers with his free hand. She swallowed hard.

Neal said what she was already thinking. "If there's danger—"

"You all stay here." Rook's tone brooked no argument. "That means you too, Esther."

Rook's hand remained on Lenore's arm until the last possible second. And that frightened her more than anything else.

)(

As Rook left the dining room, Eamon volunteered to join him. Rook just gave a dark laugh, while Esther *tsked* at the idea of a guest answering the door when she was perfectly capable. Rook preferred Esther over Eamon at his back any day, but the world couldn't bear to lose someone like her.

In the receiving hall, Rook threw the door wide open and stepped out of the way. Dmitri stood there, seemingly weaponless. Seeing him heaped fresh coals on the glowing embers of Rook's anger. He smiled like a shark. "And what are you doing bothering these nice people?"

"I could ask the same of you." Dmitri's tone was flat.

The coals within Rook caught and flared. "Oh, the little pup makes a joke! Stealing my act too, are you?"

"Is this really where you want to discuss this?"

Rook performed an exaggerated bow and beckoned Dmitri inside. His mouth quirked up as Dmitri glared. If the cretin had the gall to show his face, he'd have to endure every ounce of cheek Rook could muster.

Once the door was closed, Dmitri spoke as if addressing a troublesome child. "Rook, I'm not here to argue."

"Then what are you here for?"

"Officially, I'm here to call on Camilla."

"Tough luck, old bean. She's not here, so you can piss right off." Rook jerked a thumb at the door.

"Unofficially, I'm here to update you."

Rook clenched his fists against his sides. The coals' heat made it difficult for Rook to keep hold of his control. "You think you're some big dog now? That you can drop me scraps whenever—"

Someone cleared their throat. Neal stood at the parlor entrance, a severe expression on his face.

"Whatever this is about, gents, perhaps we could finish our previous business first?" He motioned them into the dining room.

Rook stomped back to his old seat, while Dmitri took up a spot next to Neal. Dmitri's eyes scanned the papers, making Rook bristle. Kieran reappeared, brooding off to the side of the room.

"What's all this?" Dmitri asked.

Everyone turned to Rook.

"He doesn't know?" Lenore asked. "I thought he worked for you now."

Rook's eyebrow hitched while he transformed his features into an impassive mask. Steepling his fingers before him, he looked at Dmitri and willed the man to keep his stupid mouth shut. Shockingly, Dmitri stared back in silence.

Rook said, "Ladies and gents, I apologize for this interruption, but I need a word with my... associate." He stood. Eamon began to protest, and Rook's control nearly slipped completely. "We won't be but a few minutes."

He stalked to the kitchen, down to the cellar, and into Kieran's room. Thank the stars Dmitri followed, because Rook really didn't want to have to drag the man after him. He waited barely a second after the door shut before catching Dmitri's jaw with a right hook. Dmitri stumbled back, rubbing his face.

"You little cur," Rook snarled, advancing. "I trusted you! I gave you a safe place, and this is how you repay me? By stealing my business out from under me?" Rook was roaring. Dmitri tried to speak—to object, by the looks of it—but Rook grabbed him by the throat and swept his legs out from under him. "Do you have any idea what I've had to do?!"

Dmitri landed hard on his back but scrabbled up before Rook could pounce on him. A shadow swept between them and solidified into Kieran. He held his hands out between them, baring his fangs and growling from deep inside his chest.

They carried on despite the warning.

"If you'd listen to me for one minute," Dmitri snapped back, "you'd know I haven't stolen anything."

"You've cut me out!"

"You put me in charge! I didn't ask for this, but now I have to make sure it doesn't fall apart. I have to make sure *you* don't ruin it."

"Me?" Rook tried to advance, but Kieran blocked his way.

"Your unwillingness to give up any measure of control would have bungled the whole operation. You have to trust me, Rook."

"And how do I know this isn't part of your plan?"

"I didn't have to come here. I could have carried on, but I don't want you gone. I can't do this alone."

Rook sneered at Dmitri. "And why not? Ermine, the little turncoat, seems to be doing just fine on his own."

"Because I'm not. I have no idea what I'm doing."

Rook's chest heaved, fists and feet still ready to fight. He looked for an opening, but Kieran was a solid wall between them.

"Prove it."

"Carver's recruiting extra people for us," Dmitri explained. "And Twigs has bribed some of the Collective's suppliers to send them corrupted materials. For those he can't convince, Nieva's working to lose those shipments, or at least delay them. The latter hurts their ice shipments most, which is hopefully throwing a wrench in the chop-shop side of things."

Rook stalked to the other side of the room. "Good. Hopefully that'll dry up the maniac's coffers. No money for new explosives."

"Does that mean you believe me?" Dmitri actually sounded hopeful.

"Not entirely. What's Prince doing?"

"He's funding a team of crusaders. They're drumming up support on the ground and in the magistrate council for Lady Katerina's proposal."

Rook's mouth flattened into a line. "Independently?" Dmitri nodded. "Get someone on that with him. I don't trust that spoiled ratbag not to shoehorn in his own agenda items." Dmitri and Kieran were looking at him with twin expressions. "What?"

"I think Dmitri might have a point," Kieran drawled.

"I'm only controlling because I know what I'm doing," Rook said. "And anyway, you said you needed help."

Dmitri gestured upstairs. "You haven't explained what all that is. Who are you feeding information?"

Rook and Kieran gave him the brief version of the events that had transpired with Dempsey.

"So she doesn't know you're not working anymore?" Dmitri asked.

Rook cut his eyes to Kieran. "No, and I'd like it to stay that way."

"And I'd like you to stop threatening the tenuous hold I have on my humanity, but perhaps neither of us will get what we want." The gaze Kieran returned was the same cats gave dogs.

Rook's mouth curled into a smooth smile. "So sorry about that. As you now know, I had reason to be on edge, but we're all better now." His smile tipped toward feral as he looked at Dmitri. "Aren't we, Dmitri?"

"If Lenore and Eamon do get divorced," Kieran said, "this development could benefit you. Your job prevented you from being together, did it not?"

"They're getting divorced?" Dmitri's jaw dropped, which made Rook chuckle. "Is this a result of…" Dmitri paused, straightened, and motioned upstairs again. "Not the time. I noticed you're surrendering the location of the pasty shop hideout. When were you planning on telling me?"

"Never, given the circumstances." A thread of anger still wove between Rook's words. "I have other places."

"Are you going to tell me about any of them?" Dmitri asked.

"No. If you need to contact me, send a note to the furniture shop. And use a code."

Dmitri glowered. "I know to use a code. I wasn't born yesterday."

"Can we please hurry this up?" Rook twirled his hand through the air. "I told them I'd only be a few min—" The door to the secret room opened again. Lenore walked through. "Speak of the angel."

She regarded Dmitri's bruised face. "Is everything alright? We thought we heard shouting, and then it got quiet."

"We're fine," Rook said. "Apologies for the delay. Dmitri and I were just going over some of the finer details. Let's get back up there and finish this, shall we?"

Lenore's expression told him she saw through his act, but she turned and left anyway.

As they returned to the kitchen, Lenore addressed Rook and Dmitri. "You both should know Camilla's home."

Rook regretted hitting Dmitri... slightly. Brawling certainly wouldn't help him get back into Camilla's good books. He'd be on his best behavior from now on and straightened his clothing.

They returned to the table—Camilla was changing upstairs—and Lenore started a new letter based on Dmitri's comments. A few curious looks went back and forth as Dmitri updated details, but no one interrupted. Finally, they deemed the letter sufficient, and Lenore prepared it for posting.

As they tidied the table, Eamon said, "I'd love a cup of chamomile tea before bed. Would you join me for one when we get home?"

Rook caught an annoyed twitch in the corner of Lenore's mouth. He couldn't blame her—the scumbag had cornered her in front her family.

Her face relaxed in surrender. "Yes, that sounds nice. Thank you."

Rook considered inviting himself to join them but decided against it. He'd started enough fights for one day.

)(

Rook left through the back while Dmitri stayed a little longer for appearances. Lenore burned with curiosity as to what their fight had been about. She doubted Rook would ever tell her, though.

As she and Eamon made their way out, Camilla met them at the stairs.

"I'm so sorry I missed you." Camilla kissed Lenore's cheeks. She turned away to cough and cleared her throat. "Apologies. I must be coming down with a little cold. We must get together soon."

"Absolutely." Lenore said. "Did you have fun at your study group?"

Camilla's eyes brightened. "Oh yes. It's a great help."

Lenore smiled. It had been a while since she'd seen joy like that on Camilla's face. "I'm glad you've found some classmates who aren't horrible."

Camilla nodded. They turned as Eamon approached. Camilla gave him a rather cold curtsey before folding her hands before her.

"I'd like to apologize," he said. "To begin, allow me to say again how sorry I am for what happened to your mother. Furthermore, I must make amends for my behavior that night. Had I known, I never would have addressed you or Lenore in that manner."

"It was a difficult night for all of us," Camilla said. "I think we're all due a bit of grace."

The tension in Eamon's features eased. "I'm glad to hear you say that, because I think you're being too hard on Rook."

Lenore's smile crashed to the floor. She tried to catch Eamon's eye, to signal danger, but he either didn't see her or paid her no mind.

"You know how I feel about the man," he continued, "but he wasn't the instrument of your mother's demise. She kindly and courageously gave…"

With every word, Camilla's expression darkened. Eamon faltered when her usually sky-blue eyes transformed into a stormy sea.

"You weren't there. You know *nothing* of which you speak."

Bewilderment suffused his face. "But she did."

"Eamon, stop," Lenore said. She wanted to take his arm, but she hadn't touched him in so long.

"Had she not offered Lenore's mother her place, Mrs. Hawkins might yet live. I—"

Thwack!

Eamon gawped as a red mark spread where Camilla had slapped him. She ran upstairs while he and Lenore watched. It took Lenore a moment to find her voice.

"That was very noble of you," she said, "but very ill-conceived." He turned back to her. "I am willing to share that cup of tea, but I should check on her first."

Eamon nodded, and Lenore hurried after her adoptive sister. On the way up, she spotted Dmitri hovering in the back hallway

160

and shook her head at him. He wisely retreated to bide his time elsewhere.

Upstairs, Lenore knocked on Camilla's door. Knocked again. Called her name.

"Leave me alone, Lenore." Camilla was sobbing. Lenore ignored the request and turned the handle. "I said I don't want to see you!"

The anger in Camilla's voice sent Lenore back a step. She laid her hand on the door. "I'm sorry, Camilla," she called. "I love you."

Camilla didn't return the sentiment, and Lenore went back to Eamon.

)(

Darkness enveloped Camilla and Kieran like a thin blanket. The barest glimmer of petrolsene light washed through the gloom. Dmitri had left soon after Lenore, and Mina and Neal had said goodnight. Once the house was quiet, Camilla had gone down to the kitchen in her housecoat and slippers to steal a leftover piece of Esther's latest cake. Camilla leaned against the counter, while Kieran did the same against the nearest worktable.

"Would you like to talk about it?" he asked.

She stabbed her fork into the cake. "I don't know what there is to talk about." Thank goodness for cake. Cake didn't ask prying questions, well meant as they were.

"Are you angry with Lenore as well as Eamon?"

Camilla didn't answer; she wasn't certain. Anger chomped on her heart like a dog on a bone. Things that had never bothered her now caused inordinate frustration. She knew Lenore continuing to try with Eamon was a good thing. Camilla wanted them to heal. So why was the thought of her sister making her so edgy?

"Would you like to talk about your mother?"

Camilla paused. Kieran did have some excellent stories about Adelle. He'd courted Mina, but he and Adelle had gotten on like a house on fire—once she'd decided he passed muster, of course.

"Does it still hurt for you to talk about Annabelle?"

Kieran sighed. "I feel these are two very different situations, but yes, it still hurts."

161

She nodded. True, their situations were very different. At least Kieran had always been able to keep tabs on Gadget. Well, not when she'd gone through her purging. He'd been a mess during that time, or so she'd heard, but understandably so. In any case, it didn't hearten her to know the pain would never leave.

"When was the last time you looked in on her?" Camilla's voice was softer than before.

"During Neal and Katerina's masquerade." Kieran chuckled. "A starfish. I have to admit, that's quite good."

Camilla managed a wan smile. Her hair, plaited at the side, slipped over her shoulder. She flipped it back. Kieran's nostrils flared. He leaned forward and sniffed the air between them.

She gave him a puzzled look. "Why are you making such a horrid face?"

"Because you smell of death and..." He sniffed again. "Something else. Something strange. I must say, I don't like it."

Camilla willed her heart to beat normally and gave Kieran a sheepish smile. "Apologies. I didn't realize how offensive the odor would be. My class went to the city crematorium today." It wasn't a lie, but it had been a quick field trip. She'd spend most of the afternoon and evening under the Reaper's tutelage.

Kieran nodded and leaned back again while Camilla took another bite of cake.

)(

Kieran looked into the night and pondered Camilla's words from earlier. He'd taken a similar field trip to the city crematorium when he'd been in medical school. It was a basic lesson. They'd seen a body go from the delivery door, through preparation, and into the fire in one morning. It was a speedy process if one didn't count the time waiting behind other bodies in the queue. Even that, however, was fairly fast. His brain hadn't worked the same way then as it did now. Kieran's sense of smell, for instance, was far sharper. It clung to memories better. He couldn't quite remember the crematorium's odor, but he didn't think it was the same as what he'd smelled on Camilla.

The crematorium had been sterile and efficient. Its technicians, with heavy rubber gloves and protective goggles, filled the bodies with an accelerant—not petrolsene but something like it, something even cheaper. Then the prepared bodies chuted into the enormous belching furnace. The scent that hung around Camilla was damp and long-lingering. The sort of scent where rot has had time to spread.

She'd always been an obedient, trustworthy girl, but grief could change a person more than most other forces in the world—Kieran had seen this with his own eyes—and Camilla was juggling a lot. When she'd told the family about Harding Smoke's suspicions, they'd discussed options. There was nothing to be done, though. Camilla had established her alibis. The family had set up what defenses they could. Now they could only wait and hope the lack of evidence would win out. Falcon wanted to return to work and monitor the situation, but his body wasn't ready.

Kieran didn't want to believe the voice niggling at the back of his head, but it refused to quiet no matter what arguments he threw at it. He believed Camilla had lied to him.

He sighed and ran his hand through a shadow. It clung to him like mist over cold ground. Kieran desired to protect her but had no wish to invade her privacy. She was family, one of the few people he had. The thought sent needles through him. He wouldn't have worried so much if it hadn't been for the smell. Wherever it came from, it promised nothing good.

Since being turned, Kieran had tried to note the differences between his old and new selves. He needed to be aware of and vigilant against Vampyre instincts—measuring everything as prey, self-preservation first, taking life. He'd pushed himself early on, tried to see how long he could go without eating. There'd been some close calls, but he needed to know his limits to keep those he loved safe. He suddenly saw the reasoning behind some of Neal's decisions, mostly those that had curbed Lenore's independence or betrayed her confidence in exchange for safety.

Would Camilla forgive Kieran if he took some of the same paths?

15

~Family Reunion~

Every noise grated against Rook's ears. That damnable bird over there had no right to be chirping. Weren't birds supposed to have flown south for the winter anyway? Idiot bird. Rook hoped it froze to death. Even the trees were annoying, all uniformly lining the drive and looking so proud to be a part of the vast, perfectly manicured grounds. The only bright spot was Lenore walking next to him up the ridiculously long drive. It was all for show, making guests trek absolute leagues just to get to the house. Boohoo, business had to be done in the city and they preferred a country house.

"Are you alright?" Lenore said. "You're looking incredibly sour."

Rook hunched deeper into his coat. "I feel incredibly sour."

"You catch more flies with honey than vinegar, you know." She softened the irritating adage with a quick brush of her fingers along his wrist, at the gap between his sleeve and glove.

Rook had given her a litany of highly specific instructions for what to do and not to do. One of them was no displays of affection. None. Her small rebellion smoothed his ruffled feathers into something like sensibility again.

He took a deep, calming breath but couldn't keep a grumble out of his voice. "I just hope you see how much your happiness means to me."

"I do. I really, really do." She gifted him a smile. Knowing her current turmoil, its brightness lightened his heart.

On the way here, they'd discussed Lenore's need to decide about moving out. Rook wished she would cut ties with Eamon, but her integrity was also one of the things he adored about her. At the sight of the first gardener—why did they even need gardeners in winter?—he'd let the conversation die. People here listened and talked more than in other places.

He and Lenore finally reached the front door. The butler who answered started at seeing Rook, who gave his best smug grin. "Hello, Whitby."

Whitby reassumed a dour expression. "Who may I say is calling?"

Rook ground his teeth, letting the smile fall from his face. "You know perfectly well who I am." The man didn't move. Rook's hackles rose, and he grit his teeth. "Varick Pendragon."

"And what is the nature of your business today, sir?"

"I need to speak with my father... please." The last word made Rook want to retch.

"About what, please? Master Pendragon is a very busy man."

Well, *that* certainly wasn't something Rook was about to go blabbing to the gossipy house staff. Not that it, or some version of it, wouldn't make it back to them anyway. "Whitby, I haven't been home for years. I think it's safe to say there are a good many things we could discuss."

The butler sniffed and bowed them inside. "Please wait here. I will see if you can be received today."

Whitby left.

Lenore turned to Rook. "Have we come to the right house?"

"Of course. You can tell by the snide comments and superior air."

She fidgeted with her gloves. "I think I'm going to owe you an apology by the end of this."

"I think you already do." Despite his words, he put a gentle hand on hers to reassure her and stop her fidgeting, which was one of the many items on the don't-do list.

Lenore grimaced. As they waited, house staff walked through the receiving hall. Some carried housewares, some cleaned, and all threw Rook sideways glances.

At last, Whitby returned and asked them to follow him. He led them past room after room wafting scents of flowers and food.

More paintings, tapestries, and statues than Rook remembered stuffed the hallways to just shy of the line from magnificent to gaudy.

The butler ended their journey through the impressive hallways in a small sitting room.

"Delightful," Rook said. "Mother's bumpkin basin." He turned to Lenore. "She says it's for keeping those guests who might leave questionable stains on the upholstery."

Somehow, Whitby made his bow contemptuous and left again.

Rook eyed the doorway. He'd stand for now. Lenore followed his lead and he motioned to the sofa. "You can sit."

Lenore's eyes darted to the doorway before she whispered, "Can I, though? I think it's worth more than my entire ensemble, and I wore my best." She looked him up and down. Rook smirked. "Speaking of which, are we underdressed?"

Rook's smile crept higher. "We look perfect."

He was wearing his usual attire, sans the dark makeup that usually outlined his eyes. He listened to the noises of the house: two sets of skittish footsteps scurrying down a hall, not a word passing between the owners; water tinkling into planters, blooming with flowers chosen and appreciated only for how impressive they looked; an overabundance of stiff silence. Memories rushed back. Each added another scale to his armor, hardening his skin against what he knew was coming.

Ten minutes passed, and Lenore began to wander around the room. She examined the heavy pepper-red curtains, the embossed wallpaper.

"Are they coming?" She circled back to Rook. "It's been an awfully long time."

"It's for appearances. They're showing us how much more important they are, or so they imagine."

Soon, the tapping of hard-soled shoes approached. A maid entered, carrying a silver tray with tea and cakes that looked too pretty to eat. Rook sized her up. Young, probably one of the latest hires. She likely hadn't been here long enough to cut her teeth on this world of glittering schemes. This might even be a test, set before her by Whitby or one of her other overlords. Rook considered flinging himself onto the sofa to run his own assessment. Then again, Lenore's request hung in the balance. He'd behave himself. For now.

He sat and Lenore followed. They thanked the young lady. She barely looked at them as she acknowledged the words. What kind of tales had she heard about him? He might have laughed if half of them hadn't likely come from his own family. She left without asking if they required anything else.

Rook served tea for Lenore and then himself.

"It's safe to eat?" she whispered.

"Of course. Heaven forbid anyone have any reason to accuse them of being poor hosts." He lowered his voice. "Besides, there's more than one way to destroy someone, and they don't deal in death. Their cruelty is far more subversive."

Whitby reappeared soon after to announce Lord Magnus and Lady Constance Pendragon. Rook made a derisive noise in his throat at his siblings' false titles. True, the Pendragons held more seats in the magistrate council than any other family, but far more Pendragons than positions existed. There was no telling who in the next generation would jockey themselves into those coveted spots. Although, Magnus and Constance had a better chance than most. Nevertheless, he stood as his older brother and sister entered.

)(

Lenore tried not to stare as she observed Magnus and Constance. They looked older than she, possibly Rook as well, though it was difficult to tell. Rook's life had hardened his features differently from theirs, but there was no mistaking the family resemblance. All slimly built with dark hair and eyes. All moved with an almost feline grace. It was uncanny to see the man who'd always set himself apart next to such similar strangers.

"Lenore, may I introduce my siblings, Magnus and Constance? Magnus, Constance, this is Lenore Blackbird-Lee."

"A pleasure to meet you." Lenore gave them a warm smile and a deep curtsey.

Magnus nodded. Constance smiled back, but Lenore read her in a second. Constance's smile was a practiced empty gesture, simply what one was supposed to do in these situations. There was no emotion, no sincerity, just muscles moving into place and back again.

"Mother wanted to give us a few minutes to catch up." Constance sat. Everyone followed her lead. "Tell us, Ricky, what have you been doing since your... return?"

It took every ounce of Lenore's willpower not to make a face at the nickname. A muscle in Rook's jaw twitched, but he gave no other indication of displeasure.

"I'm working for a furniture maker in Sand," Rook said.

"Oh, fancy yourself an artist now, do you?" Lenore swore she heard ridicule in Constance's voice.

Rook gave his sister a wry smile. "Nothing of the sort. I run deliveries, lift heavy things. Honest work."

"I see," Constance said. Lenore imagined Constance had strained something trying not to sneer. "And, Lenore, how did you and our little Varick meet?"

Lenore laughed without meaning to but turned it to her advantage. "It was just one of those things you never see coming. We just ran into each other one day and started talking."

Lenore gave Rook a playful nod, and he smirked back at her.

"You just... started talking?" Constance said. She looked like Lenore had suggested everyone should start walking on their hands.

"Yes."

Constance's face turned cold and inscrutable. It reminded Lenore eerily of Rook, right before he killed someone.

Constance turned to Magnus. "Don't you have something you'd like to say to our brother?"

Magnus glowered. "Nothing he wants to hear."

"So nothing much has changed then," Rook said. "You keeping up with your fencing?"

Magnus leaned back in his chair and crossed an ankle over his knee. "Not as well as I used to. Some of us have meaningful work to do, you know? I'd wager I can still make you lick my boots, though." He turned to Lenore, who didn't school her expression fast enough. "Just boys being boys, you understand."

"Apologies, but how does being male disqualify one from being decent?" Lenore set her mouth into a steely line and fired a glare dead into Magnus' eyes.

Magnus' lip curled, but he turned back to Rook. "What do you say? We can have a match, and the ladies can have the privilege of watching."

The tendons in Rook's hands tightened, and his eyes flashed. Lenore swallowed the rejoinder she'd been ready to deliver. Before anyone could say anything, however, a new voice interrupted.

"That won't be necessary. I don't expect Varick will be staying much longer."

Constance and Magnus shot to their feet and turned toward the speaker. Rook did as well, though he caught himself halfway and slowed. It was a clumsy, obvious move, and Lenore swallowed hard.

Through the doorway came a paunchy, older man with hair smooth and shining as a sheet of tin. Right on his heels followed a taller woman with dark eyes. Her hair, the color of a mourning dove's feathers, had been swept into a complicated up-do. Jeweled pins worth a small fortune glittered from the coiffure. She and the man walked with purpose but no hurry, as if they were owed every moment they wanted. Together, they looked Lenore and Rook up and down. Magnus and Constance came to stand on either side of them.

"You're dressed inappropriately, Varick," the woman said, "and your posture is sloppy."

"It's lovely to see you too, Mother," Rook replied flatly. He nodded at the man. "Father."

"Sarcasm is beneath you." His father narrowed his eyes. "It's *common*." He smacked his lips like the last word had left a bad taste in his mouth.

Rook ignored the barb. "Thank you for seeing us on such short notice. I have—"

"Did the purging rid you of your manners?" his mother cut in. "Introduce us to your companion."

"I'm sure he needed a good beating," Constance stage-whispered behind her hand to Magnus.

Magnus copied her. "Probably needs another one."

"*Enough.*" Their mother swatted Constance across the arm with her fan. She then opened it to cool herself, while her daughter rubbed the resulting angry red streak.

Rook almost spit the words, though Lenore could tell he was trying not to. "Lenore, my parents, Lord Henry and Victoria Pendragon. Father, Mother, meet Lenore Blackbird-Lee."

Lenore's chest tightened. Her legs shook as she curtseyed, but she managed to steady her hands by clutching her skirt extra tightly.

"I'm very pleased to meet you, Lord and Lady Pendragon." She wasn't sure if it was correct to assign Victoria a title. Mina didn't carry one, but Lenore understood she could do so honorarily if she wished. A perk of being married to a magistrate. Nevertheless, it seemed like a wise move just now.

"Indeed," Victoria said. "Blackbird isn't a noble name, is it, Varick?"

"Seeing as how the nobility was abolished along with magic, there's really no such thing anymore."

Constance and Magnus' matching looks of disdain were fairly epic.

"Nonsense," Victoria said. "Nobility is in the blood. You cannot simply wish it away." She returned her attention to Lenore. "You kept your maiden name when you wed?"

A lump formed in Lenore's throat. She nodded to give herself an extra moment. "Not officially, but my major accomplishments occurred before I married."

Victoria arched an eyebrow. "That certainly tells me everything I need to know, or at least as much as I care to."

"Yes, Mrs. Lee, about that," Henry said. "I understand you've made a bit of a name for yourself in the scientific community. You created an artificial bird or some such thing, did you not?"

Lenore's confidence crept back out. "Something to that effect. The experiment's original purpose was to figure out how an artifact we have might have flown like a bird. The project grew beyond that, and in the end, we—"

"I don't need a lesson." Henry practically barked the statement, making Lenore jump. Magnus, Constance, and Rook all tensed but otherwise restrained themselves. At a more normal level, he continued, "I suppose you're not a total loss, seeing as you've done something to rise above your station. Still, it is no replacement for lineage." Lenore opened her mouth to object, but

Henry started up again. "I understand your mentor is Lord Gwenael Allen. Is this correct?"

"Yes, sir." Lenore intertwined her fingers and squeezed them together before she started wearing holes in her gloves.

Henry looked back to Rook. "Does that have anything to do with why you've suddenly come swanning back into our lives? Looking for favors?"

"I'd hardly call it swanning, but yes," Rook said. "I came to ask if—"

"I am an impartial party, pup," Henry interrupted.

Rook's voice strained to remain civil. "You've thrown support to one side or the other when it benefitted you."

"You know nothing. I am the Speaker of the magistrate council—"

"So you love to tell everyone you meet." Rook rolled his eyes. "Look, give me five min—"

Whack! Henry backhanded him across the face.

Lenore's hands flew to her mouth. Rook stood frozen where he'd caught himself against the sofa, his back to her. Lenore stepped closer but didn't reach out. She looked back to the rest of the Pendragons, unable to keep a poisonous glare from her eyes, though she did manage an even tone.

"Well, this has been—"

"Listen, girl. I can tell you're the organ grinder here, so I'll be straight with you. A public apology from this runt might sway me to offer Lady Holmes and Lord Allen's agenda some support." Henry's calm, almost genial voice was still somehow condescending. "Tell anyone about this, however, and I'll deny every word. I'm only making you this offer because his actions—" He jabbed a finger at Rook. "—have marred the reputation of this house. People still associate him with us. I'll accept a public declaration that he's no longer a Pendragon. Get the mewling prick to do that, and I might consider it."

Lenore's mind buzzed with disbelief. She snapped her hanging mouth shut and looked at Rook. His muscles pulled tight along his back. His hands shook as they gripped the sofa.

"Okay. Thank you for your time. I think it's time we left. Varick, shall we?"

She bobbed a quick curtsey as Rook slowly turned around. She kept one eye on him, expecting one of his knives to flash into view and spray gouts of blood across the room. He kept his hands at his sides, however, and they left.

)(

"Rook, I'm so sorry. Please, say something."

Lenore and Rook stood outside the townhouse. They'd gotten a cab home. Rook had seethed silently while Lenore tried and failed to find words for what had just happened. She'd reached out to him within the safety of the cab, but he'd shrugged her off.

Rook took a deep breath. His voice came out as a low rumble. "I told you I didn't want to go, Lenore. Don't you think there's a reason I've always avoided talking about them?"

"I know. I'm sorry."

"You keep saying that."

"I don't know what else to say." She looked at the door. "Why don't you come inside? Esther sent over a nice pie. We can have some."

Rook turned away. "I'm not in the mood."

"I really am sorry, Rook. I... I shouldn't have asked you."

He paused, though he didn't turn back to her. "No, you shouldn't have."

Lenore watched him go, wishing for better words. She slunk into the house. Majesty came trotting up to her, tail wagging and eyes bright. Lenore stooped to pet the wolf and buried her face in Majesty's thick ruff. Eamon's step approached from farther in the house.

"Everything alright?" His voice sounded strained.

Lenore sighed and looked at him through Majesty's fur. He had ink smeared across his shirtsleeve. His tie hung loose around his neck. She guessed he'd been making notes for work. She stood, leaving Majesty looking bereft with the loss of attention.

"Would you... like to talk about it?" he asked.

Lenore barely had the energy to shrug. "I met Rook's family today. We were hoping to ask his father for support. It... did not go well, and Rook is very cross with me."

"I see." Eamon shifted from foot to foot.

Lenore waved at his appearance. "You look like you've been busy."

Eamon chuckled. "Yes. The Bone Port bodies have been fascinating to study. I'm beginning to agree with Oya, though— this would be much easier if we had records from back then. The BPHS has been asking the Arnavi questions and relaying the information to us. Did you know the Arnavi have never had magic?"

Lenore half-smiled. She'd heard some of this around the museum, but she hadn't joined as many of those conversations as she'd have liked. It was too close to the subject of Eamon, too possible for someone to sniff out what was going on between them. All of that combined with losing her mother had made the whole thing too painful to deal with.

Eamon's face had lit up with the telling, but he softened at Lenore's expression. "Maybe we should discuss your issue before we get into this. Perhaps over dinner?"

Lenore had no wish to betray Rook's trust. Then again, she also didn't want to appear as if she was hiding things from Eamon again.

"I don't know how much is mine to tell. Some of it is personal. Suffice it to say, it was… difficult for Rook. He was too kind to go with me in the first place."

"It's for a good cause, though, yes?" Eamon asked. He looked at Lenore's hands but didn't reach for her.

"Even so, it took a toll. Speaking of which, given our attempt at reconciliation, do you think you'll start accompanying me to any of Neal's support events?" Eamon started to make a face. "You don't have to. I understand I'm not the only one who hurt you."

Leaning back against the stairs' newel post, Eamon rubbed the back of his neck. "To be honest, I don't like involving myself in politics, at least not in that way. I haven't stopped my financial contributions to crusaders, though."

"Do you know if any of them are in contact with Katerina or Neal?"

"Katerina is more likely given how Neal feels about them. I can check."

Lenore leaned against the other newel post. "It's less direct, but I suppose it's something." Eamon looked away. Conflict pinched his features, and Lenore felt the chasm between them open again. "Whatever it is, just tell me."

He looked at her with concern. "I really am trying. I don't want you to think I'm not, but I'd prefer for my political leanings to remain a secret."

"Meaning you'd rather not attend Katerina and Neal's events."

"Yes. I'm sorry. I promise it has nothing to do with you. I've operated like this since before we met."

Lenore bit her lip. She had hoped for a different answer. Eamon was supposed to be bound in everlasting honesty to her—at least, he'd sworn an oath to be. His had never affected him like Rook's had affected the crime lord, though. They didn't know if Eamon's had taken root. Eamon had once claimed that he tried not to deceive people to begin with, save for lies of omission. Maybe that was why it had never been an issue. Then again, they knew so little about oaths. Perhaps he'd missed a trick and hadn't done it correctly. In any case, Lenore decided to believe him. If this endeavor to repair their relationship was to go anywhere, she had to risk it.

"I understand," she said. "I'd prefer for you to join me, but I see your point."

Eamon smiled awkwardly. "Thank you." He paused. "You are charming enough for the both of us. I mean, would the masquerade have gone any differently if I'd been there?"

"Maybe Dempsey wouldn't have shown up?"

Eamon's face hardened. Lenore winced as if he'd slapped her. She turned away, stopped, and forced her feet to stay still. She didn't want to walk out, but his look brought back the recent heartache that had festered between them. She felt tethered by a desire for reconciliation and pushed away by the impending scorn.

"I know the trouble that follows me isn't what you signed up for," she said, "but I…" She wasn't certain how to proceed.

Eamon sighed. "Let's just have dinner, shall we?"

So they made dinner—a simple meal of rolls, peas, and some leftover beef roast.

"To be honest, I wish I'd seen you dressed as a hedgehog," Eamon said as they grasped for topics. "I bet you make a cute hedgehog."

Lenore smiled. "Sebastian was a bull. Did I tell you he's engaged now?"

"Is he? That's wonderful."

Eamon sounded sincere, which gave Lenore hope; however, she felt like having left this out reflected badly on her.

"I'm sorry I forgot to tell you," she said. "It got lost in the shuffle behind more important issues."

"I'm pleased you still consider our marriage one of the more important issues." Eamon's voice was soft but genuine.

Lenore had decided to postpone the movers for now, but nothing more. It was easier to cancel than to move all her furniture only to move it again later.

She said, "It's something I'm willing to fight for."

Palm up, Eamon reached across the table. Lenore let only her fingertips brush his in return. When he tried to take her hand, she pulled back. Eamon did too.

"I'm sorry, but I'm not there yet," she whispered.

The threat of all this meant hung in the air.

Eamon nodded. "I apologize, but I want you to know I'm here for you."

Lenore summoned a small smile. "Thank you."

Silence fell between them, and they tucked into their meals. Sticky hopelessness picked at her, and she considered what they'd lost. While their physical relationship might never be the same, they could restore their friendship. Hadn't they built everything on that to begin with? The realization brought Lenore comfort, especially since they'd begun their marriage without physical intimacy.

She motioned her fork toward Eamon. "I'd like to hear more about your project. Will you tell me about it, please?"

Eamon looked less wounded and picked up where he'd left off. Lenore listened and asked questions. They soon managed to get a lively conversation going, and Lenore felt more hopeful than she had in a while.

16

~A Purple Hyacinth~

The furniture shop beyond the storeroom hummed with melding conversations. Where the rooms out there were arranged to show off each piece's best side, back here they were stacked atop one another under dim lights. Having been the one to recently reorganize it, Rook had taken the liberty of creating a cubbyhole for himself between stacks of chairs. Not really private, but a good vantage point and a wee bit of cover. The storeroom was clean and dry. It smelled of wood oil and lavender sachets. Rather soothing really, though he currently didn't feel soothed.

Rook gazed at the parcel like it might bite him. He slipped the tip of a dagger beneath the messily wrapped paper. The package had been delivered to the shop just a few minutes ago, addressed to Varick. The tag said it came from Lenore. It certainly looked like her work—crooked edges and enough twine to tie down a zeppelin—but with how his luck had gone lately, he wasn't about to trust it.

Rook retreated a step, flicked his wrist, and sliced the wrapping open. Pushing the paper away with his blade, he found a folded note atop a grease-stained box. He opened the former, and out fell a pressed flower. Like the packaging, it looked worse for wear, but Rook understood its meaning.

A purple hyacinth. *I'm sorry. Please forgive me.*

Sending messages via flowers was a common—and absurd, in Rook's mind—practice, but his family had twisted it into a merciless sport. Over the years, acres upon acres of flowers had been sacrificed for their passive-aggressive games. Not that Lenore knew that, which he preferred. Why couldn't flowers just be sent and appreciated because they were pretty? He scowled at the unfortunate-looking purple blooms and read the note.

~~My dear friend,~~
Rook,
I know I've said this ~~hundreds of~~ a lot, and I suspect you're tired of hearing it. Words can't fix what I broke. I ~~know~~ can't imagine what it took for you to see your family again. I was a ~~poor ghastly~~ ~~dreadful~~ terrible friend with my selfish, thoughtless, irresponsible request. What can I do to make things better? ~~I hope this~~ ~~I don't mean to sound~~ I miss you. ~~I know it's only been since yesterday since~~ I don't care how it sounds. I'm really, really bloody sorry and I feel horrible and I wish I could fix it. Included are some apology cookies I baked for you. Sorry for the slightly overdone ones, but I think I'm getting better. If you'd like more or even a full meal, just say the word.
~~Sinc~~
Much love and more sorries,
Lenore

P.S. Apologies for the poor presentation. I left in a hurry this morning and forgot my notepaper, so I've nicked one from the counter at the courier shop.
P.P.S. If you don't want a home-cooked dinner (and I completely understand if you don't. I'm no Esther, after all), I can just send more flowers and even some chocolates. Or all of the above. I'm rather lost here but open to suggestions.
P.P.P.S. If you'd rather never see me again, I'd understand that too.
P.P.P.P.S. Neal and Mrs. Holmes have asked to meet with you. I don't know what it's about. Otherwise, I'd tell you. I really would. He'd like you to send your card with your availability as soon as you can. Sorry you've had to hear it this way, but he knew I was writing to you, so he asked me to ask you. I'll make sure not to be there when you go so you don't have to see me.

Rook brushed the hyacinth petals against his cheek. His guts still boiled from yesterday's events while his skin prickled with cold. A bruise bloomed below his eye, darker than the flower. He'd been foolish, as he always was when it came to Lenore. He grumbled and let his head fall back. What did normal people do in this type of situation? He still cursed himself for agreeing to such an insane request. How hadn't he realized how soft she made him? A thought-beetle skittered into his head and refused to leave, no matter how many times he tried to swat it away.

There's no more oath.

He could sever ties. Did he really need another obstacle in his life? What a mess he'd been after he lost the oath. Over a single person, who, truth be told, had caused him more pain than most of his enemies. Even if it hadn't been her doing, the reality remained. Life would have been much easier without her and the attachments she came with.

Rook moved before he could think any more about it, before that pathetic person he'd been showed his face. He crumpled the note and threw it into the nearest waste bin. Followed by the hyacinth. Then he grabbed a sheet of paper and a pen from Gadget's desk and wrote the quickest reply he could manage.

I think it's best if I didn't see you again. —R

He addressed the letter and dropped it into Gadget's outgoing mail tray before returning to his parcel and taking one of the cookies.

As he chewed, Rowan strolled into the back. Eyes peering through chair legs, she spied the cookies. Another minute and she had traversed the path to his cubby and sidled up to the box. She looked at Rook, back at the box, back at Rook.

"Yes, you can have one."

"Cheers." She took one and pointed at the hyacinth in the waste bin. "What's that?"

"It's nothing." Another voice inside Rook tried to argue, but his anger kicked it into the background.

)(

Lenore's fingers twitched toward the neatly laid out tools. They'd not been selected for her but for Copper and Ezra.

They'd managed to make the Subaquatic Sloop prototype waterproof, as proven by yet another trip to the docks in the Cobalt quarter last week. It had been a brilliant achievement, one the museum felt confident publishing despite not knowing where this project might go. Heaven knew they needed as much good press as they could get. The black powder demonstration that had gone so wrong earlier that year still marred the museum's reputation as black as the stains the tragedy had left behind. Given the success of the wooden SS copy, Copper and Ezra had been given the go-ahead to make a sturdier version—one that might hold a person.

Lenore regretted handing over the project, even if it had been for a good cause. Though she had several ideas, she had yet to declare her next venture. The pressure of choosing made her want to work on anything else.

That, and she needed something to take her mind off Rook's letter. Tears came to her eyes, sharp as his daggers.

"I say, are we in the right place?" came a voice from the front of the workshop.

Lenore wiped her eyes and called, "Hello? We're back here."

Copper looked up from poring over Ezra's drawings with the artist himself. Footsteps approached, and a group appeared from between the parts shelves.

"Hullo." Copper walked toward them. "Engineer Cooper Richmond at your service. How can we help you?"

One of the men seemed vaguely familiar. He wore a signet ring that bore the surname Warren. It flashed like liquid gold as he pulled at his muttonchops and his curly-cue moustache with a broad smile. Magistrate Warren. He'd attended one of Katerina's support soirées.

The other two were strangers, a man and a woman. They had brown skin, burnt sienna and umber, and wore traditional Springhavian clothes, but an excessive number of rings decorated their fingers. She had an ebony waterfall of long, silky hair. His was coarse and twisted into short cords, which refused to be contained under his hat.

"Magistrate Dean Warren." The politician extended his hand with so much enthusiasm Lenore wondered if he'd pulled something in the process. "Very pleased to meet you, Engineer Richmond. And might I introduce Rumi and Saman, representatives of the Arnavi Nish?" He turned back to his two guests. "Did I pronounce everything correctly?"

His guests smiled and nodded.

Lenore stiffened. Nish—she'd heard that word before. It was the Arnavi word for leaders... or leadership... or government. It had never been totally clear. Or rather, she'd never had a chance to learn, given everything that happened in Bone Port when the Arnavi had arrived. Lenore was afraid to even move before these foreign government representatives.

Copper cleared his throat. Anyone who didn't know him might have thought he was preparing to speak, but Lenore knew he'd been both collecting himself and sending Ezra and her a message: best behavior, *now*.

"It's an honor to meet you," Copper said. Lenore was surprised when he executed a bow worthy of a grand ballroom.

They shook hands. Lenore performed the traditional Arnavi greeting Neal had taught her and the rest of their team in Bone Port. The motion made her feel like a one-legged pelican with an inner ear imbalance as she repeated Copper's sentiments. Had she mumbled her way through them?

Ezra bobbed quickly but respectfully. "Pleasure," was the only greeting he gave. It sounded better even in its brevity than hers.

"You know our traditional greeting?" Rumi asked.

He and Saman returned the gesture with fluid grace.

Lenore grasped for her voice. "Yes, thank you."

Thank you? What is that even for?

"I mean, I learned while I was in Bone Port. Our team went there on an expedition earlier this year."

"Ah, you were one of those we observed then," Saman said. "It's a pleasure to meet you. Lenore, was it?"

She nodded.

"Spectacular," Magistrate Warren said. "Miss Lenore and I have also met before. You see, we're all good friends here. And speaking of friends, is Magistrate Allen around?"

"'Fraid he's out," Copper said. "He's asked me to look after things while he's gone, though. Is there something I can assist with?"

"We were hoping to discuss building a partnership with your museum," Rumi explained. "As you may know, we've been working with the Bone Port Historical Society since we arrived. We're interested in a similar relationship with your museum."

"We had the pleasure of meeting Magistrate Allen when he visited our ship," Saman added, "but he didn't mention his position in your government."

Copper chuckled. "Magistrate Allen doesn't like to brag. Let me introduce you to Scholar Bates. He's our Head Curator, basically the man in charge."

"Splendid," Magistrate Warren said. They turned to leave. "He'll be eager to hear how our ideas will increase museum profits."

"I'm sure he will," Copper replied.

Lenore and Ezra watched them disappear into the shelving. Magistrate Warren was saying something about making mutually beneficial arrangements all around. The department door opening and closing echoed through the room. Ezra and Lenore looked at each other and released a collective breath.

"That was unexpected," Lenore said.

Ezra motioned at her arms. "Teach me that greeting?"

She apologized in advance for her poor tutelage. They spent the next fifteen minutes practicing with one ear open should their guests return.

)(

Rook sat in Neal's drawing room, drink in hand. With a low fire smoldering in the grate and the leather chair perfectly supporting him, this would have been an ideal evening if Neal and Katerina weren't looking at him like a rat and an exotic animal respectively. Beatrice sat at a small desk in the corner, scratching away with her pen as if none of them were there. Rook sipped his drink and waited. He was perfectly content not to say anything the entire evening if he could help it.

Katerina's words took any semblance of a nice time and throttled it. "We understand you recently paid your father a visit."

Rook gave her a sideways glance. "And how did you hear about that?"

"He was blustering about it in the magisterial lounge," Neal said. "He announced rather loudly how you had crawled in, begging for forgiveness."

Rook rested his gaze on Beatrice. On first glance, she appeared to be catching up on her correspondences, but her pen moved with urgency and scrawled a sort of shorthand unfamiliar to Rook. He puzzled over the code as he said, "Of course he did, the old prat." He gave up for the moment—he was too far away to really study the symbols, and without a key, they'd remain a mystery. He took another long sip. "So that's why you asked me here." He left the statement open for interpretation.

"I know perfectly well that you went," Neal said. "While I don't believe Lord Pendragon would outright lie about you going, I do believe he would... shall we say, alter some of the details to his advantage. I also understand Beatrice asked Lenore to ask you, so I inquired with Lenore. She said the visit went poorly but wouldn't go into details."

Rook put on his best show of lazy unconcern.

"Lenore didn't come right out and say you two had an argument," Neal went on, "but she's clearly upset about what happened. I gather she's left off that particular strategy?"

"It's fair to say the experience left a bad taste in both our mouths." Rook put down his drink and intertwined his fingers before him. He looked at Neal, then Katerina, and fixed each with a hard look. "To whom, if you don't mind my impatience, does this discussion pertain? Me or Lenore?"

He wouldn't put it past Neal to give him a dressing down for hurting Lenore, as Rook was certain his letter had done. If that was the case, however, why was Lady Katerina here?

"You," Neal said. "Let us be clear, Varick. Neither of us is here to be your friend."

"So good to know where I stand." Rook emptied his glass and stood.

Katerina's eyes followed him. Her face was calm, but her tone rang with authority. "Not so fast, Mister Pendragon. You haven't even heard our offer."

Rook met her eyes, looking just as relaxed. "I can't imagine what you might have to offer me."

Neal looked a mite annoyed. "Given his tale, I'm guessing your father wants some kind of humiliation from you. I won't pretend to think you'll help us from the goodness of your heart, even if it is for our city's welfare."

"Anyone ever tell you you're not much of a charmer, *Lord* Allen?" He smirked when Neal grimaced.

Katerina said, "Mister Pendragon, you work for the delightful Miss Annabelle Wilson, do you not? Do you enjoy your job? Because I can provide you with the means to work elsewhere, if you're so inclined." Rook turned back to her. "Here, let me get you a refill."

Without waiting for a response, Katerina got up, took his glass, and headed for Neal's globe. Rook noticed she didn't need to ask how to operate it. She poured as she spoke.

"I'm not saying Miss Wilson isn't a good employer. I'm sure she's wonderful, but it's a shame purged citizens are barred from so many opportunities. Just another reason our system needs to change. What incentive is there to turn oneself in anyway?" She handed Rook his drink. "Very few, I'm certain. A magistrate can grant a limited number of former criminals rights to own a business. Did you know that?"

Rook looked to Neal. "I'm guessing you used one of your chances on Gadget."

"I did," he said. "One of the best decisions I ever made."

Rook turned back to Katerina. "I take it, in exchange for me making nice with my father, you're offering me rights to start a business?"

"I am," Katerina said. "Rather, Neal is. I'm afraid I've used all of mine."

Rook smiled. He could absolutely see her making far more deals than Neal.

Rook turned falsely apologetic eyes onto Neal. "I'm sorry to disappoint you, but what my father has asked is impossible."

"And what is that?" Neal asked.

"He wants me to publicly declare myself no longer a Pendragon. Sever all ties and save them from the shame of association with me." Rook's voice dripped with scorn. "You see, I turned my back on them long ago. In my mind, I'm already quite happily, quite adamantly, *not* one of them."

"I see," Katerina said. "Very independent of you, certainly. I can't imagine what it took to turn your back on all that wealth and influence." Rook forced himself not to laugh. "But I'm certain a man as clever as you sees the issue."

"I'm not giving him what he wants."

"Did I mention capital as well as opportunity?" Katerina's rejoinder came quick as lightning. "I may not be able to give you the latter, but I can provide the former. I'm sure you'd turn the funds into a booming business in no time."

Some new cunning crept into Katerina's voice, and she smiled like a cat with a canary in its mouth. Rook felt very much like the canary just then.

He locked eyes with her. "Do you have any suggestions as to what kind of business I might start?"

"Anything you like, I imagine. General goods stores do very well—more flexibility with them. You could even include imported goods to add some variety to your stock."

Rook felt Neal watching them. Too close. Neal couldn't learn about the market because then Le... others might learn of it too. He'd thought he liked Katerina a moment ago, only to realize she was a match for him. Of course she had her fingers in pies she shouldn't. All good politicians did.

Rook leaned back in his seat, pretending to think. "I suppose that's quite a generous offer."

"I think so," Katerina said. "Do we have an accord? We can even turn your name change into an event, try to rub it in the old man's face."

Rook slid his eyes back to her. Maybe she wasn't all bad. "Very well. Let's separate me from my family for good." The words felt like lead on his tongue.

"Splendid." Katerina clapped. "We'll have to be careful, of course. Can't alienate the Speaker either, now can we? Beatrice will help sort the details. Neal? Anything you'd like to add?"

Neal shook his head, looking exhausted with the whole business.

17

~The Hot-Headed Queen~

The restaurant was mostly empty, given it was squarely between lunch and dinnertime. Camilla wished she'd eaten something earlier, but apprehension had stolen her appetite. Lack of food made her hands shake, or perhaps that was her nerves? The floor rocked gently with the tide below, and a long line of windows looked out over Cobalt Bay. A retired steamboat called The Hot-Headed Queen, or the HHQ to those familiar with it, served as the restaurant's base. The occasional waiter, dressed as a sailor, drifted by. Their wide-legged pants, knotted neckties, and hats made them look, in Camilla's opinion, rather ridiculous. She wasn't here to advise the restaurant on their dress code, however. The bold red carpet brought back memories she didn't want to deal with, so she stared at the sea-themed wall murals. Being in the Cobalt district and sporting a broad menu meant the establishment saw patrons of all types, but they had private booths for their more well-to-do diners.

"Are you sure about this, Milly?" Falcon's words hissed through an ornate ventilation grate that separated their booths. They'd opened a little flap between the two grates, which Beatrice, curiously, was perfectly familiar with operating.

Asking Falcon and Beatrice to accompany her on this strange outing had been less difficult than Camilla had expected. She didn't know when the idea to question Harding Smoke about her father had occurred to her, but once she'd become aware of it, she hadn't been able to shake it. Perhaps it had germinated when she'd learned about the Reaper's truth serum? In any case, once she had

186

the vial, it seemed the obvious choice. After all, what else would she do with such a potion? She hadn't told Falcon about it, of course, only asked that he come with her for support.

Beatrice had provided a way to drug Harding without notice. She'd joined Camilla one day to check in with Falcon. Though she suspected Beatrice had ulterior motives, Camilla was happy for the company. When she had made her request of Falcon, Beatrice leapt on the opportunity.

"I've got a better idea. Let us hide out in the booth next door and listen for anything we can use to help our mission." When Falcon had opened his mouth to object, she'd cut him off. "It's nothing untoward. Camilla will just ask a few additional questions of our combined creation to see if we can't gather some helpful intelligence. You want reform too, right?"

Falcon did, and Beatrice's powerful will had bent him to the plan.

Now it seemed unbelievable that Camilla was aboard the HHQ with a contaminated drink sitting across from her.

In response to Falcon's question, she whispered back, "Yes. Trust me, I know what I'm doing."

She really didn't. The Reaper had said the Verisap would force truth from even the most unwilling lips. Camilla believed them, but what if Harding sensed something amiss?

"Just relax, my dear," Beatrice said through the vent. "It's all about confidence."

"I *am* relaxed." Camilla didn't at all sound relaxed. "Hush now. I see him."

The booth's heavy, sound-absorbing curtain hung open, while Beatrice and Falcon had closed theirs. Camilla watched, heart in her throat, as Harding Smoke hobbled closer. He leaned heavily on his cane and swatted away the sailor-suited man offering his help. Camilla tried not to stare and tried even harder not to look at the glass. Instead, she looked down at her nails. When Harding's wheezing came within earshot, she looked back up and did her best to smile. She remembered what her mother had told her as they'd run through the Halls of Justice—Harding Smoke had threatened to tell First Iago about an affair between Camilla's father and First Iago's wife unless an arrangement involving Camilla's mother was made. It tugged the corners of Camilla's mouth back down. In the end, she managed to maintain a pleasant, if somewhat cool, expression.

She began to stand, but Harding waved her back down. "I haven't got enough time left to waste it on pleasantries."

He lurched into the seat opposite Camilla, still shooing away the waiter. After he'd gone, she undid the curtains to muffle her conversation.

"What's all this then?" Harding waved his cane at the curtains and looked Camilla up and down.

Camilla ignored the look and folded her hands. "I'm afraid what I'd like to discuss is of a very sensitive nature."

"Sensitive, eh?" Harding looked at the drink in front of him. "This meant to soften me up?"

Camilla gave him a sheepish smile. "I confess to having asked Falcon for suggestions. He said you took your brandy neat."

"That'd be a yes, then."

Harding lifted the glass to his nose and sniffed noisily. Camilla's heart raced. She hadn't smelled anything when she'd examined the little vial in private, but Harding might know what to look for. He took the barest of sips and smacked his lips. A long moment passed. Camilla forced herself to sip her water.

A knock outside almost made her jump, but she managed to only tense instead.

"Can I get you anything else?" The waiter's voice was quiet but still intelligible behind the curtain.

Camilla gave Harding an inquisitive look. He shook his head, glaring at her. Harding's default seemed to be glaring, so she wasn't certain if he was onto her.

"No, we're fine." She barely kept a tremor from her voice.

Camilla thought she heard the waiter move on to Beatrice and Falcon's booth. A bead of sweat rolled down her back. Beatrice had tipped the staff to give Falcon and her some privacy and given them a cheeky wink to go with it. Falcon and Camilla's cheeks had colored, but the staff seemed to know Beatrice and had just thanked her with a bow. Even so, Camilla worried one of her friends would be forced to answer and thereby spoil the plan. No sound came through, though, and Camilla looked back to Harding. He was still taking loud sniffs and tiny sips of his drink.

188

"Is everything alright?" She couldn't stand the suspense. "Is there something wrong with your drink?" Her stomach twisted and urged her to abandon the scheme. The words *We can get you a new one* pushed up her throat, but she kept her mouth shut.

Harding smacked his lips again. "I suppose not. Lots of people would like to see me dead, you know. They're threatened by my service record and pull with First Iago." Camilla swallowed a retort. "Let's get on with it then. What are your designs for my grandson?"

Camilla reeled back and blinked. "I beg your pardon?"

Harding took a long drink of his brandy. "I've looked into you, missy." He pointed a crooked finger at her. "I saw the meeting request you sent to your father the night of the attack. Marriage advice. That was what you wrote. You trying to get a piece of his inheritance?"

"No." Camilla said. She and Falcon had spoken enough to know they were nothing more than friends. "I'm not romantically interested in Falcon."

"Then who was it about?" Harding's tone was reminiscent of an interrogation.

"Sir, you forget yourself." Camilla's cheeks colored with indignation. "That is none of your business."

"It *is* my business when it concerns the safety of our city. You're a suspect, young lady, and I mean to find out what you were up to that night."

Camilla wasn't sure if this was the Verisap doing its job or just Harding's natural abrasiveness. Either way, this could benefit her, but she needed to control it. The curtain only soaked up so much sound.

"Second Smoke," she said gently, "I think we can help each other. So let's take this slow, shall we? I want to know more about the man my father was. You worked closely with him. Let's exchange information."

Harding took another drink, running his eyes over Camilla again. "You're hardly in a position to bargain. I've put cleverer people than you into the Halls on less evidence. As you're easy on the eyes, however, I'll humor you."

A lump formed in Camilla's throat. She wasn't sure if it was fear or revulsion, but she swallowed it back down. The truth serum seemed to be doing an excellent job. "I don't know if you know this, but I was never terribly close with my father. Did he, um... Did he ever talk about me?"

"Never, but we don't let unmanly types into the order. At least we didn't back in your father's and my days. You know the type—nancies. So he wasn't the type to whimper and mewl about his ungrateful daughter." Something like kindling snapped inside Camilla. She tamped it down. "Some say they saw a girl following Fourth Hawkins through the Halls that night. Did you follow him?"

"Of course not. That'd be insane." She paused to consider her next words. "How do you know so much about what happened that night? You weren't there."

Harding growled and leaned forward. "You watch your tone. Back in my day, you'd be getting a sharp lesson about holding your tongue. All these oversensitive types don't allow that sort of thing now."

Camilla strangled her napkin beneath the table. "My apologies, sir. I'm just trying to understand so I might clear my good name."

He sneered before a coughing fit overtook him. Camilla caught the sound of a life of too much smoking in his phlegmy gasps. She resisted the urge to advise remedies.

Harding fixed Camilla with an even harder scowl. "I still have a good many contacts in the order, little miss. Don't think I can't get any information I please. You hear me?"

"I hear you, sir." Camilla made herself nod deferentially. "Any information I can provide regarding this case, I'm happy to oblige."

"Don't think I don't see what you're doing. Your mother was the same. She was a pretty one, no denying that, but she was as prickly as they came. You tried sweet-talking her and she gave you venom in return. I nearly got her in the end, when I caught your father fornicating with First Iago's lady. He set her up to fall before I could seal the deal. The case had his fingerprints all over it, but you know how the order is. They weren't about to disgrace one of their own for an outsider." He slid around the booth, eyes on Camilla. "If this were really a private booth, I'd bend you over this table the way I—"

Smack!

Camilla held her dinner knife in one hand. The other stung from striking Harding across the face. She struggled to breathe. Red clouded her vision. Her voice came out low and threatening. "Second Smoke, I will thank you to remember you are a gentleman."

Harding chuckled. "You look like your father when I used to tell him about my exploits. He worked hard to shield our female prisoners. When the opportunity to advance came up, though, those protections fell by the wayside, didn't they?"

Camilla's face burned as hot as her anger. "You said you'd arrested cleverer people than me on less evidence. What did you mean?"

"People are easy to set up. You just need to find the chink in their armor. Like this one chap who barred me from his restaurant. I expect to be treated with proper respect, but he made me wait with the rest of the cattle. Every time. I called for an investigation of his finances. No business is perfect. Found a few accounting errors in his books. Next thing you know, he's embezzling money from the place, and away he goes. His wife wanted so badly to help him." He chuckled again. "Not that it helped, but I sure did let her try."

Camilla's stomach roiled. She heard a scuffle in the next booth over. She didn't want to hear another word, about her father or otherwise. And part of her wanted to see what would happen if she did nothing to stop whatever was happening next door. The other part, which barely surpassed the first, called for a slower revenge, a more satisfying fall for Harding, so she drummed her fingernails on the wall as if bored.

"Do you have any questions for me regarding your case?" She barely held back bile. "Anything I can do to put this matter behind us?"

Harding scooted closer, leering at her. "I can think of a few things. You let me call you Adelle and I'll let the whole thing drop."

He put a hand on Camilla's thigh. She shot up as if he'd bitten her and resisted the urge to drive her dinner knife into his face.

"I assure you, sir, that is *not* what I meant," she snarled. "I've done nothing illegal and I have people to vouch for me."

"That so? Then who are they?"

Camilla swallowed. She'd meant Lenore and Dmitri and Rook, maybe even Falcon, but their testimonies wouldn't carry weight. In Dmitri's case, it'd get her into even hotter water. Lenore might be in danger if they pressed her any harder. Camilla should have thought of a better alibi, but the time for that had passed.

"I've given my testimony, Second Smoke. Now, if you'll excuse me."

Camilla swept out of the booth, nearly knocked over a waiter standing next to the curtain, and left the restaurant.

)(

Beatrice's sitting room was one of the most well-appointed spaces Camilla had ever seen. It changed with every season, reflecting the latest styles and colors while remaining welcoming and cozy. Even in deep winter, when the curtains were shut against the cold, it remained bright. It was large enough to comfortably accommodate at least a dozen but created separate spaces for smaller groups. Tufted chairs and a settee dressed in deep jewel tones with curved backs grouped around the window. Armchairs and small console tables sat by the fireplace. A whist table with matching, easily moved seats clustered in the corner.

Falcon paced before the window. He gesticulated wildly but apparently couldn't find words. He garbled the beginning of one sentence—something about his grandfather—before trying to apologize to Camilla, which ended with mumbling, scarlet cheeks, and switching back to his first mode of non-communication. He'd kept his mouth clamped shut all the way home in Beatrice's private coach, only to explode once the doors to her sitting room were closed.

They'd snuck out after Camilla, tipped the restaurant staff again, and thanked them for their discretion. Then the three had shared an uncomfortable ride to the Holmes manor. When Falcon had started on his tear, however, she'd raised a hand to stop him. Beatrice had taken it in hers and shaken her head.

Let him get it out, her eyes had said. So the two sat in silence, allowing Falcon to talk circles around himself.

At last, he took a deep breath and leaned back against the windowsill. He covered his face with his hands and groaned into them in frustration. "Camilla, I am so, *so* sorry." His voice muffled into his hands. "Stars, I… I think I might be ill."

"The water closet is that way." Beatrice gestured to a door on the far wall.

Falcon didn't move. Camilla couldn't look at him for long. What if he looked up and their eyes met? To say nothing of actually speaking on the subject.

After a long, uncomfortable silence, Beatrice said, "I think we can all agree that was an utterly revolting display." Her words were clipped. "Falcon, we don't judge you by your grandfather's actions. Do we, Camilla?"

"Of course not." Camilla kept her eyes on Beatrice. "Falcon wouldn't…" She couldn't hold back a repulsed shudder. "Falcon's never behaved like that."

"Nor would I! I swear, Milly, Beatrice, I… *never*…" He circled his hand in the air to indicate the rest, apparently unable to speak the words.

"As for the rest of it…" Beatrice turned softer eyes on Camilla. "We'll make sure he's punished."

"How?" Camilla asked. "He was a Second, and he clearly still has a lot of influence with the Enforcers, not to mention his magisterial position."

"We are witnesses." Beatrice motioned at herself and Falcon.

Camilla finally raised her eyes to him. Her cheeks burned as their eyes met.

Falcon frowned and shook his head. "I can't publicly defame him."

"Why ever not?" It was one of the only times Camilla had seen Beatrice surprised.

"Because he will disinherit me." Camilla's jaw dropped. "I'm barely fit to rejoin the order. What else am I supposed to do? I don't have any other skills."

Camilla stood and balled her fists against her sides. The old argument between them flared bright and white-hot inside her. "He outright admitted to grossly abusing his power, and you're concerned about money?"

Falcon's eyebrows knitted so hard they twitched. "How did you even get him to tell you all those things anyway? Did you drug him? Can we even be certain it's true?"

"You can't discredit it because you don't like what you heard," Camilla snapped.

"I deplore what I heard, but—"

"My mother told us your grandfather tried to blackmail Fourth Hawkins, using her as the price. You heard her that night in the Halls as well as I did. Before she... she..." Camilla turned away, pressing a hand to her mouth to hold back her tears. Sobs clawed at her throat as memories burst bright before her eyes.

Beatrice stood and spoke gently. "With all due respect, Camilla dear, I don't want to know any more about whatever you're referring to. And, Falcon, consider how much stronger your testimony would be than mine. My mother is campaigning against Magistrate Smoke. They would see my account as biased. It might even undermine her credibility."

"And what would you have me do?" Falcon asked. "You're the mastermind behind all this."

"Marry rich." Beatrice suggested this like it was the most obvious solution. "I'm sure there's many a lady who wouldn't mind sharing her fortune with such a handsome—"

"No," Falcon said. "I'm done discussing this. Camilla, I'm sorry again for... for everything, but I can't be a part of this any longer." He paused, huffing. "I'll try to protect you from my grandfather's schemes where I can, but I can't make any promises."

With that, he strode out of the room. Hot tears traced down Camilla's face as she watched him go.

18

~*What's in a Name?*~

Newssheet and tabloid reporters comprised most of those within eye-line of the dull administrative building. Rook had noticed them as they hid behind papers and sipped drinks at a cafe across the road. They might have been inconspicuous if it hadn't been cold enough to see one's breath.

Rook firmly believed bureaucratic sites were designed to be difficult to find. It fit their goal to be so crushingly frustrating that people just gave up. Case in point, he'd almost passed the Citizen Information building on his way there. Its inside wasn't much better with its line of empty, utilitarian chairs and walls painted the color of bland.

Of all the things he'd seen Lady Katerina pull off, clearing out this municipal branch to streamline his name change had been the most impressive. He didn't like that she'd baited the vultures outside, though. Not that there was any proof to link it back to her—an "anonymous source" had tipped them off. The infamous ex-criminal offspring of Henry and Victoria Pendragon was officially breaking away from the family. Katerina couldn't be there, of course. What reason would she have for attending such an obscure and completely spontaneous event? Same for Neal. Thus, Rook was alone as he filled out the paperwork. Paperwork with which the clerk was suspiciously helpful.

And then they stamped it as official. That was it. The deed was done.

He turned toward the windows. The vultures were still there and no longer trying to hide. And they'd multiplied. They crowded around the base of the building's steps, greatcoat collars pulled up against the cold and pens poised to misconstrue every word. Katerina had given Rook a speech. He'd memorized it like any good little co-conspirator, but the words globbed in his throat as he faced the door.

He put one foot in front of the other and headed outside to face what he'd done. The sight of a familiar coach down the road stopped him. The seal on the door—a dragon breathing fire—was as repugnant to him as his father's face at the window. His mother sat on the other side, also looking down her nose at him even from this distance. Magnus and Constance's smug faces popped out from behind their parents. Four pairs of cold eyes, so much like Rook's, stared him down as the reporters shouted questions at him.

Rook tensed. New speeches formed in his head, each one more scathing than the last. Indecision over which his family would hate the most kept him from speaking. Slivers of ice ran through his veins. They cut him again and again as he remembered every reason he wanted to disgrace his family. Why he had left.

Green eyes caught his attention, a gaze he knew better than any other, and he hadn't even needed his oath to spot it amongst all the others. She excuse-me'ed her way to the front of the crowd and fixed her eyes on him. He read in her face how hard she fought to look at him, but she kept at it. Her eyes encouraged him and apologized. He remembered his letter, and something inside him crumbled.

The vultures still shouted at him like the desperate creatures they were. Rook cleared his throat. Silence descended.

"You want to know why I've come here to change my name, yes? The Pendragons are an illustrious and… noble family." Rook swallowed a bit of bile. "I have been fortunate to be a part of them." He suppressed a smirk as he decided on an addendum. He was supposed to be consumed by contrition, after all. "They made me what I am today. I am not what the Pendragon family aspires to be, however. As it is no longer a fitting name for me, I have cast it aside and claimed a new one for myself."

The reporters started to clamor again. They all asked the same question, as if they somehow wouldn't hear the answer together. "What new surname have you picked for yourself?"

"Hollow," Rook said.

The crowd paused. He looked back to Lenore. She smiled at him. A hesitant fragile thing, but it was there.

The vultures recovered.

"What's the significance of this name to you?"

"How did you decide on it?"

"Are you worried other members of the Hollow family will seek retribution?"

To this last one, Rook replied, "If there was anyone else with that surname, it wouldn't have been available."

He glanced back at the Pendragon coach. His parents were closing the curtains, blocking him from them. Something felt as if it shifted, though Rook couldn't examine it just now. Instead, as the reporters continued to pelt him with questions, he raised his hands and received quiet again.

"That's all I have to say on the subject." He skirted the crowd and headed for a cab waiting nearby.

The vultures circled and snapped at his heels, but he said nothing more. The cab knew where to go—the Allen manor, where he would report back to Neal. They followed a circuitous route to avoid detection.

Upon arriving, Rook was surprised Esther led him to the conservatory. Lenore sat there with red-rimmed eyes and a cup of tea before her. When he entered, she started. She clearly hadn't expected to see him.

"I-I'm sorry." She stood. "I'll go."

"Finish your tea, Miss Lenore." Command and comfort wound through Esther's tone. "Master Hollow, I'll come fetch you when Master Neal is ready for you."

The name sounded strange to Rook's ears, but he didn't dislike it. Esther left, shutting the conservatory door behind her.

"I'm sorry," Lenore said again. She looked at the kitchen door and picked up her teacup.

"Wait."

Lenore stopped but didn't look at him. Soft anger rumbled beneath Rook's thoughts. He paused, sifting through his words. "You read my letter?"

"I did," she whispered. Tears slipped from her eyes. She looked at the ceiling to drive them back. With a stronger voice, she said, "I didn't tell anyone about it. Not even Eamon. I swear. I don't know why Esther brought you back here."

Rook shook his head. "Sharp as her knives, that woman."

Lenore swallowed hard. "Would you like me to see if Neal is busy?"

Rook kept his gaze on Lenore, reminding himself of the reasons he'd written that letter in the first place. He envisioned himself agreeing, her leaving and removing yet another tether between them. He could cut it as cleanly as if he used one of his daggers.

She headed for the door.

"Don't." The word dropped from his mouth unbidden. They both stood like statues while he searched for something else to say.

"What are we doing here, Rook?" Lenore asked.

He hated how hard her voice sounded. He recognized that tone all too well—it was the sound of someone closing off their heart to avoid more pain.

"Please don't go." Rook leaned against the wall and crossed his arms. "I'm still angry, but I don't want you out of my life."

"Your letter said you didn't want to see me again." She still didn't look at him.

"You came today anyway," he said. "I saw you."

"I meant for you to see me. I didn't want you to be alone." She finally turned to face him. "For the record, I don't agree with Neal and Lady Katerina. They shouldn't have asked you to do that, just as I shouldn't have made my request."

"How much did they tell you of our arrangement?"

"Nothing. I asked them not to betray your trust in me any more than I already have."

"You still think there's hope for us, even after something like this?"

Lenore looked away again and rubbed her arms. From cold or discomfort, he couldn't tell. "I'm not trying to minimize what I did. I care about you, Rook. Deeply. I'm just trying to do better. I don't want you out of my life either, assuming…" Her voice dropped to a whisper. "Assuming you really do want me in yours. I'd understand if you don't."

"Little bird…"

A sob escaped her throat. She pressed a hand to her mouth.

"Little bird." He opened his arms.

She shook her head so hard her dark tresses swung back and forth. "I'm not trying to manipulate you." She scrubbed her tears away, only for more to follow. "Sorry."

"I believe you. And I do want you in my life, angry as I am."

Lenore hesitated. Arms still open, Rook wiggled his fingers. Her face crumpled, and she traipsed over to him. He folded her in his arms. "I'm not good at this friendship thing. This is all I know to do."

She nodded. "Thank you. I didn't want to lose you."

Thank you? Rook thought. He hadn't expected that, but it made him smile anyway.

They stood like that for several minutes. She leaned into him and cried.

"What is it?" he whispered.

Her answer smothered into his waistcoat. "I was terrified I'd lost you, Rook." A pause. "For what it's worth, I like your new name."

"Varick Hollow? I think it fits my public persona. 'Varick' stopped meaning anything to me a long time ago."

"It's pretty," Lenore said. "It sounds like a nice place to live."

Rook smiled again and held Lenore tighter. He shoved down the urge to kiss her, to show her what a lovely place the realm of Varick Hollow could be. She was trying to patch things up with Eamon, and Rook wanted to support her happiness, even if it wasn't his.

They eventually broke apart. Lenore led Rook back into the parlor. Neal was suddenly available, and Esther led Rook up to see him, all so Neal could tell him *good job*. Rook was grateful his black waistcoat hid the wet spots from Lenore's tears.

)(

Your reports have been passable, but you need to work harder to get information. I suggest utilizing some of your feminine wiles in addition to your witchcraft. I've asked around, and Rook/Varick isn't known to frequent any houses of ill repute. No one knows of anyone he's taken to his bed either, so he's probably desperate enough to take you. If you find his preferences lie elsewhere, let us know. I'm certain we could use that to our advantage. In any case, I hope you're not so thick as to need reminding what will happen should you fail to get results.

Lenore glowered at the letter as if trying to set fire to it with her eyes. Eamon and Neal looked disgusted, the latter shaking his head. Mina's expression was cool, save for a single arched eyebrow that promised evisceration if she ever got her hands on the author.

Rook considered suggesting that he could just slit Dempsey's throat, but he wasn't certain one of those gathered wouldn't accept the offer. It would be poor form if he couldn't make good on the threat, so he kept his mouth shut.

Lenore looked at him. He was surprised to see her blushing.

"Now that Dempsey's made such a wild suggestion," Eamon said, "there's nothing to stop him from assuming Lenore's actually gone through with it."

Rook's answering glare demanded, *What the blazes?*

Lenore gathered her dignity and sat straighter. "He believes I witched my way into success. I don't think there's a force on this earth that will stop him thinking whatever he likes."

"I agree," Mina said.

Kieran and Dmitri sat across the table. The Vampyre gave Lenore a questioning look, and she handed him the letter. Kieran wafted the paper beneath his nose before reading it. Rook looked away just as Kieran caught him watching.

"You could always tell Dempsey I prefer men," Rook said. "Or that I prefer no one at all. The first might make him think he has the upper hand, though."

"Does it make a difference in your world?" Mina asked.

Rook almost burst out laughing. It was clear from the look in their eyes that Eamon and Neal were curious too, but the upper class was too buttoned up about such things to ask. Except for the ever-pragmatic Doctor Allen, of course. At that level of society, some saw preferring the same gender as unmanly or unwomanly, Dempsey apparently being one of them. If one did their duty to bring legitimate heirs into the world and kept unseemly activities hushed, however, fewer knickers got in a twist. Lenore, Kieran, and Dmitri looked unfazed by the idea.

"No," Rook said. "All that matters is how good you are at your job." Carver and his success were proof of that.

Everyone made appreciative gestures, but nothing more was said on the matter.

"You could mention we're working to block up the Collective's charcoal shipments," Dmitri said. "Tell Dempsey we've got a plan to rob the next train coming into the city."

"Yes, grand. I'd forgotten about that." Rook made a mental note to ask Dmitri about the sulfur shipments they'd actually planned to interrupt. Perhaps this charcoal thing was a new, developing plan? Blazes, there was a lot to keep up with when one was outside of things. Rook bristled but stuffed it down and returned to the issue at hand.

)(

Camilla listened from the parlor. She hadn't spoken with Lenore, much less Eamon, since they'd all been here the last time. She also hadn't told Mina or Neal what had happened at the end of that evening. Given neither of them had asked, she guessed no one else had mentioned it either. They had, however, informed her of Lenore's situation. Camilla had acted appropriately stunned and appalled, but the information had paralyzed her for a while. The Reaper was powerful and magnificent. Why would they hire a cretin like Dempsey? Well, Neal had hired him once upon a time too. The ruffian probably had some talents. But had the Reaper known about her connection to Dempsey, tenuous though it was? If so, why had they not mentioned him?

Hearing Dmitri and Rook's plans for deceit pulled her heart in two directions. She could foil their scheme, whatever they were up to, by sharing what she'd heard with the Collective. It would help the Reaper, and maybe it would prove they could trust her more. But the danger to Lenore... Even though thinking of her still sent a strange tremor of pain through Camilla, they were sisters.

A sound like wind brushing across curtains shushed behind her. Camilla almost jumped and turned around.

"Kieran." She drew closer to speak without risk of being overheard. "I didn't hear you come in." She hadn't even heard him get up from the table.

"Is there a reason you're eavesdropping?" His nostrils flared.

Camilla wrung her hands. "I... I was thinking about having a word with Dmitri." It wasn't a lie, as an idea had just occurred to her. "It's just, um, a little awkward, you know, given our history."

Kieran's onyx eyes sharpened. "Do you mind if I ask what it's about?" Camilla gave him a look. "Between Dempsey's threat against Lenore and Harding Smoke's against you, it's a dangerous game we're playing. I feel compelled to ensure every member of this family remains safe."

"That's very nosy." She almost forgot to keep her voice down and considered questioning Kieran's right to ask such things.

Camilla, she scolded herself. *He is a member of this family. He has as much a right as you.* That the question had even occurred to her painted her cheeks with crimson shame.

Kieran continued to watch her, though his expression remained closed.

"When we separated Rook from his oath, Dmitri and I discussed trying to reconnect," she said. "I intend to make good on my word." Maybe he could help her situation with Harding Smoke—no telling what contacts he still had.

Kieran bobbed his head once before turning away. He must have known about her ignoble, secret objection. Had he read something in the blood of her blush? Camilla didn't know if Vampyres could do that. She couldn't remember Kieran mentioning something like it, nor could she recall reading such a thing, but Vampyres had so many strange abilities.

Fear tempted her to call after him, to ensure her dear friend wasn't hurt, but the desire to keep her secrets concealed stayed her.

)(

Kieran returned to the dining room via the back corridor. Rook and Neal gave him inquisitive looks, but he only nodded. Camilla had lied to him again. He knew it. He just didn't know about what. His patience was waning. How might he track her when she was already out? Granted, sunset came earlier during these cold months, but Camilla was usually out by the time he awoke. It wouldn't be the first time he found someone in the city.

He worried about what that smell coming off her meant. Dempsey's letter reeked of the same scent.

)(

Chrysalis ducked below the windowsill. She panted as her heart tried to break free of her ribcage. What the blazes was this family? The gaunt figure talking to the blonde girl, Camilla, what was wrong with him? She knew the woman of the house was a doctor. To have a patient living with them wasn't so surprising, but the poor man looked half dead. At least the one Lenore went to go see all the time—the brother of that harpy Rook had running his market for a while—was lively. Rook had told Chrysalis to leave while he met with the Allens, but curiosity had gotten the better of her. After all, she had a new sneak suit to test, and it was going well so far.

When she gathered her nerve to peek through the window again, the parlor was empty.

19

~Rally and Rage~

The winter wind nipped at fingers and noses, competing with the sun. The lawn stretched like a sea to the foot of the ivory mountain that was the Parliament building. Warm tendrils of light cut through the cold air and reflected off polished wooden planks. The stage had been erected overnight. Its dark wood reminded Lenore of other presentation days. She tried not to think about how the last one had gone tragically awry.

Turning her face toward the sun, she basked and pulled her jacket so it hugged her more tightly. The crowd around her murmured and huddled together toward the stage. Their combined body heat did wonders against the cold and for morale. Many wore all-white ensembles with red armbands, sashes, or hat ribbons. They weren't silent like the protesters from last summer had been, though many had been here then too. Energy hummed through this crowd.

Lenore stood on tippy-toes to see how far back they went, but her short height foiled her efforts. She debated trying to find Gadget, who was somewhere here. The craftswoman had agreed to share her experience on a smaller scale instead of making a public pronouncement against the Enforcers. Face to face with the protesters, Gadget could answer questions too, but this method had its own problems. Gabriel from the Raven's Tower had been recruited to escort Gadget, and Beatrice was helping orchestrate a few other pieces behind the scenes. Between them all, it would go smoothly… Hopefully.

As she searched, Lenore caught a mouth-watering whiff of something. Her stomach piped up, and she turned to locate the source. To the side of the stage stood several great, black iron smokers. A thin stream of smoke wafted from each one—sleeping dragons with low fires and livestock simmering in their bellies. Copper squatted at the firebox door of one, shuffling the fragrant wood pieces within.

Lenore wandered over and summoned a cheerful tone; things were still a mite strained between them. "Do you need any help?"

He gave her a crooked smile. "Aye. Could you hand me those chips over there? The cherry ones. Need a bit more to get the right blend."

She did and watched as Copper sprinkled them into the firebox, handful by handful.

"How're you doing with… everything?" he asked.

Lenore shrugged. For once, tears didn't burn in her eyes, but she still felt it. Grief, sitting beside her like an unwelcome presence.

"Sometimes, it leaves me alone," she said, knowing she wasn't making sense. "Like now. And sometimes, it tackles me to the ground."

To her surprise, Copper nodded. "I know the feeling, lass."

Lenore watched while he continued to work. He too had lost people.

"I understand if you don't want to talk about him," she said, "but I'm curious what your brother was like."

Chuckling, Copper closed his bag of chips and the firebox door. "Our mother called him a gentle spirit. He didn't eat meat because he didn't think animals should die in the prime of their lives for our enjoyment."

Lenore smiled at him. "You two must have argued a lot."

"Not so much. We debated, sure, all the time, but we respected one another. He lived with us. Great with the kids. Had wild ideas about the Old World, how they might have lived. We spent hours talking about it."

"My father and I did the same." Lenore kept her voice low. "And my mother would work on her sewing and listen."

Lenore and Copper traded stories in hushed tones while the crowd grew. Eventually, Katerina climbed the stage, stood before an amplification cone, and beamed a perfect smile over the audience. Neal stood behind her, hands clasped behind his back.

"Thank you, everyone, for coming out to join us today," Katerina said. "I realize it's a bit chilly, so we'll get to the food as quickly as possible." A chuckle went through the crowd. "Today is a day for strength and unity. Today is for standing up, not just for ourselves but for our loved ones as well. But today is also a day for peace." She paused and let her gaze roll over the crowd. "Let me repeat that: today is a day for peace.

"We do not wish to overturn the Enforcer order. Indeed, their job is dangerous and important. We should celebrate them for stepping up to do it."

Katerina began to applaud, as did Neal. Lenore and Copper exchanged a look and followed, though their claps sounded labored, like slapping shutters in a storm. The crowd seemed hesitant too, but mostly followed suit.

"Let me be clear, my friends. This support is not license for abuse. Our citizens have a right to legal representation. To fair trials and sentences. That is all Magistrate Allen and I are asking for, and you can help us." Someone *whoo*ed, and Katerina flashed her brilliant smile again. "That's right, my friends. You! *You* have the power. Write to Speaker Pendragon, to every single magistrate. Flood their offices with letters backing our requests. Leaflets are circulating, providing you with some suggested language so we can be unified in our message. And don't forget you have the power of impeachment. It hasn't happened in so long some of us might have forgotten about it, but there it is, in black and white, in Springhaven's bylaws."

As Katerina continued, Lenore spotted Beatrice at the edge of the crowd. She tried to give the socialite a little wave, but Beatrice's eyes were elsewhere. They followed a lone figure making their way through the crowd. Lenore knew a handful of Enforcers were running security for the event, though most didn't. Katerina had struck a deal—Enforcers assigned to police the event would dress in their street clothes so as not to cause alarm. The figure moving through the crowd wore the same uniform style as the Enforcers, but this one was black with red trim instead of the traditional grey and blue. It set Lenore's senses on high alert. Whether or not the figure was connected to the Enforcers, they were looking to cause trouble. Though they kept their head down, Lenore guessed it was a woman by the hairstyle. She had dark skin, darker than Neal's. Lenore walked over to Beatrice, who drew a fan out of her reticule. They exchanged a glance and refocused on the figure.

Katerina finished her speech, and Neal stepped up to the amplification cone. "I'll keep this brief. What she said."

A laugh burbled through the crowd. Neal waited for it to die down before speaking again.

A shriek ripped through the air. "LIARS! THIEVES! FALSE PROPHETS!"

Smothering silence followed. Every eye turned to the figure in the Enforcer-style uniform.

Lenore's heart seized inside her chest. Ebony. Lenore hadn't seen her face during the Halls of Justice attack, but she remembered that voice. The hate overflowing from every word brought back memories of their shoot-out, which had resulted in Fourth Hawkins' death. Lenore swallowed hard, remembering the short-sword-firearm combination Ebony had wielded. Without thinking, she reached into her bag and pulled out her curio. She held it close. If she wasn't careful, she'd electrocute members of the crowd.

Next to her, Beatrice opened her fan with a soft *shiiiiick*. The handle was a slender engraved dagger, while the spines were ornately etched and hinged blades, thin as razors. It was a work of deadly art.

Ebony glowered around her. "You're mindless sheep. All of you."

"Ma'am," rang a voice of silk and steel. Some, including Lenore, looked back at the stage. Katerina had joined Neal at the amplification cone. "Whatever your issue, I would be happy to discuss it, but now isn't—"

"Deceivers!" Ebony pointed at Katerina. The Collective member had painted her fingertips and palms crimson, bright and wet as if she'd dipped them in fresh blood. "You will lead these people to ruin. You who claim to be against the Enforcers—"

"That is not what we've said," Neal broke in.

"—have made deals with those devils. Even now, they close in on us."

Several men, their features hardened for impending battle, worked their way toward Ebony in the crowd's center. Lenore recognized Fifth Jones. The others might have been temporary reserve members, but it was impossible to tell while they wore their street clothes.

"We aim to bring about peaceful change," Katerina said.

"Fight!" Ebony spun to look at the entire crowd. "Use the sole language the Enforcers understand. Violence! It's the only way to save yourselves and your city."

Just as one of the Enforcers was mere yards from her, Ebony ran. She shoved people aside and left scarlet smears in her wake. Fifth Jones and his comrades pursued her. Ebony was nimbler and had less regard for the people in her way.

Lenore spotted another figure pop out from an alley in the distance. They beckoned with a wide sweep of their arm before disappearing again.

They hadn't faced Ebony when they made the gesture.

Lenore swiveled but saw no clues as to who it had been or what the motion meant. Meanwhile, Neal and Katerina were working to settle everyone. The crowd had begun to mumble, then chatter. The magistrates called for attention until the audience quieted and turned their attention back to the stage.

"Please, everyone, remain calm," Neal said. "This isn't the time to lose our heads."

"Maybe she's right," called a voice from the crowd. "Maybe we do need to show the Enforcers we mean business."

Agreement rumbled through the crowd. It quieted when Katerina spoke again.

"My friends, we are doing that very thing. Violence may seem more effective, like it will bring speedier results, but those results will not be what any of us want. Violence only breeds more violence. Remember the Halls of Justice." She pointed in that direction. "Remember what happened after. The Enforcer order is, as they should be, sworn to defend against threats. Violence is unequivocally a threat." Katerina paused and opened her arms to the people. Her voice remained confident but was gentler. "We are a powerful force, yes. So let us do the things that will get us what we want, because we will succeed when we stand together. Let us overwhelm our city's leaders with pressure for change. Bury them

208

in a sea of requests." She raised her hands. "We are a swelling tide. Gather your siblings, friends, lovers, parents, strangers off the street, and ask them to join our wave of peaceful revolution!"

Neal began to applaud behind Katerina. Beatrice and Lenore joined in as loud as they could. Others in the crowd followed. Lenore thought she spied Falcon leaning against a tree and clapping. The sound became a roar, crashing breakers against a cliff face. Katerina smiled at them like she was their proud mother hen.

"Now, I think we've all heard enough talk for one day, don't you?" An enthusiastic cheer rolled from the crowd again. "We've got some delicious food cooking over there for everyone. Sir Allen will explain the process for getting yourselves some."

Neal chuckled and pulled at his collar. "Engineer Allen is just fine, thank you." He then laid out the serving system Copper had devised.

Lenore looked back out. Had the figure from the alley been friend or foe?

Beatrice closed her fan with another *shiiiiick* and tucked it into her bag.

"That's unexpected." Lenore gestured at the harmless-looking, embroidered reticule hanging from Beatrice's arm.

"A lady must be able to protect herself." Beatrice nodded at Lenore's curio. "As you well know."

Lenore slipped the weapon back into her bag and merely bobbed her head before they both returned to their jobs.

)(

Dmitri slipped between buildings and leapt over fences. The frozen cobblestone streets tried to slip him up, but his shoes—leftovers from his Enforcer days—gripped like they too wanted to catch Ebony. Dark beams, greying plaster, and red brick flew past. A cat went yowling onto a windowsill to get out of his way.

His teammates' footsteps pounded nearby. The exhilaration of working in unison again rushed in Dmitri's ears. He'd signaled, they'd followed. So far, a seamless operation. He met up with Broody, one of Rook's—his now, he supposed—upper-level goons. Then Garrick. The old man could run faster than Dmitri had expected. Grunt was panting somewhere behind them. The first three turned a corner and surged into the shadows of a narrow alley, only to skid to a halt.

Ebony faced them from a dead end.

"Ermine." Her voice sizzled with rage.

"Ebony," Dmitri said, his tone flat.

The scrape of shoes echoed behind him. He half-turned to see two more Collective members dressed in street clothes. He couldn't remember their names, but he remembered their faces from the catacombs. They blocked the path out. Cold eyes locked on Dmitri and his two cohorts. Even odds now.

He wanted to call for calm, to tell them there was no need for bloodshed, except there were no other options. The Collective had killed Whistler, one of the market's people. Retribution was required.

Dmitri sized up his opponents. Ebony had bested him in fights before, but he hadn't been fighting for his life then. He'd killed Sphinx at the Halls of Justice because he'd had to, and would have killed Ebony too if he'd had the chance. Dmitri couldn't tell how the injury she'd sustained during that skirmish was affecting her now. The other two Collective members were just plain big, but none, thankfully, seemed to be carrying crossbows—the standard-sized ones were rather hard to conceal and extremely illegal.

Without a word, the Collective members at the end of the alley charged. Their silence was more unnerving than roars would have been. Only their heaving breaths echoed off the brick walls on either side.

Dmitri took up position with Broody and Garrick and waited for the attack, praying Grunt caught up soon. At the last moment, the latter two pulled out loaded miniature crossbows, courtesy of Lowell, and shot. Their cords twanged in the eerily quiet alley. The disadvantage of the smaller version was that they neither aimed well nor did much damage. Only one of the five-inch bolts found their mark in a bicep.

Dmitri turned to meet Ebony. As expected, she'd snuck up from behind during the charge on panther-silent feet. The meaty sounds of punches, the ring of weapons clashing, and grunts heaving back deathblows exploded behind him. Dmitri's shot went wide, but it made Ebony sidestep. She sprang forward, wielding her hooked blades. Dmitri raised his truncheon and blocked her strike as it descended toward his head.

He pushed her back. "Stabbing people while their backs are turned seems fitting for you." He dodged a kick between his legs.

He'd try to keep her alive. Perhaps he could extract some information from her. She hadn't been a Crypt-Keeper, but she had been vying for the position.

"It's better than you deserve, traitor!"

Dmitri did not miss the way she favored her injured side. He struck to disarm her; it earned him a fist to his ribs. Ebony got in two more jabs before Dmitri recovered and pushed her back again. He lashed out, only to pull back when Ebony reacted too slowly. Her injury hampered her. She took advantage of the opening and ripped one of her hooks across Dmitri's side. Fire scorched along the wound—shallow, but bloody painful. The metallic tang of blood invaded his nostrils. Her knives were inches from his throat, and he drove his anger into his next block. She shifted. His injury screamed as he maneuvered to defend himself. Her daggers flashed hungrily as they flew to make a killing blow.

A shadow interceded. Metal clanged against metal. Breaths rasped. Dmitri couldn't see the face, but he knew the movement of those arms. Rook. Solid black clad him from head to toe. He swept in for strike after strike, opportunistic and brutal. Ebony was hard-pressed to hold Rook back, doubly so when Dmitri jumped back into the fray.

A sound like a bull giving birth tore from the other end of the alley. Grunt had finally arrived and lifted one of the big Collective members above his head. The other retreated and snatched the miniature crossbow from Grunt's exposed belt. Grunt slammed his opponent onto the ground with a thud and a series of sickening cracks.

Garrick and Broody advanced. The other Collective member leveled the crossbow...

And sank a bolt into Garrick's chest at close range.

Garrick staggered back, one hand over a spreading red blotch beneath his left shoulder. Too late, Grunt grabbed the Collective member by the neck and yanked him away.

"No!" Rook shouted.

Rook spun, aimed his blades at Ebony's throat. Dmitri barely blocked the strike and used his momentum to kick Ebony out of the way.

"What the blazes are you doing?" Rook snarled. He disguised his voice to sound low and gravelly.

"I want her alive."

Ebony was just regaining her feet when Dmitri landed a direct hit behind her knees. Two more across the back sent her down. He pulled her hands behind her. Broody came and secured her. Blood ran down from a gash across his face. Rook faced them for a moment before running to Garrick, who lay on the ground and fought to keep himself propped up on one elbow.

Grunt held the other Collective member around the chest. Grunt's arms squeezed like a boa constrictor. "You want him alive too?"

Dmitri spared no more than a second on the captured thug. Not a major player, just dumb muscle. "Kill him. Broody, hang on to her."

Grunt held on with one arm while the Collective member spewed all manner of obscenities. A moment later, Grunt dammed the river of verbal bile. Dmitri didn't watch. Instead, he joined Rook at Garrick's side.

"Heh, I thought I'd outlive the lot of you," Garrick croaked.

Rook spoke softly enough that only Garrick and Dmitri could have heard him. "You were certainly salty enough to."

Garrick wheezed one last laugh before he fell back to the ground. Dead.

Dmitri looked back at Ebony. She'd stopped struggling, but hatred burned in her eyes.

"Get her to the market for questioning," he said.

"What about Garrick's body?" Grunt asked.

Dmitri looked at Rook, who almost imperceptibly shook his head. "We leave him here for someone to find, but we'll honor him tonight."

Rook stood and drifted back into the shadows.

"Ermine, who was that?" Grunt asked.

"Don't worry about it. He's on our side."

20

~ *"You've got a floppy fish hanging off you"* ~

Surrounded by the comforting smells of sawdust, oil, and tangy metal, Lenore leaned against the workbench and closed her eyes. The scent reminded her of her father's workshop from when she was growing up. It soothed her nerves after yesterday's almost-ruined rally. Thankfully, the barbecue had pacified the crowd. On balance, it had ended up a success. How much better it could have been would forever remain unknown. At least Lenore had been able to bring some leftover barbecue for Lowell and Felicia.

Though half-finished projects and diagrams of barely formed ideas cluttered his workshop, he had systematically organized his tools. The raven Lenore had seen in the conservatory perched on a nearby shelf, preening. The soothing quiet of morning washed through the room.

Lenore opened her sketchbook and searched for some of her latest drawings. She sketched ideas as they came to her, so going back always took a minute. Flicking page after page, one made her freeze. The handheld firearm looked innocent despite how large she'd drawn it. Outlined in short, erratic strokes of grey, she'd recreated it from memory as best as she could. She'd lost it in the Halls of Justice during their mad dash down an exploding stairwell. Black powder had powered it. She barely remembered her thoughts from when she'd sketched it. The days after the attack had been a constant tug of war between processing and repressing her feelings. She did, however, remember what she'd thought after the so-called accident at the museum. Even after her colleagues had lost life and limb, she hadn't wanted black powder research to stop. Why had it taken a disaster of this magnitude to change her mind? She wished they'd never found the wretched Old World books and their secrets in Bone Port.

"Found them yet?" Lowell asked from his workstation.

Lenore flipped more pages and located what she'd been looking for. "Yes. Did you receive the rest of the pieces?"

"The last box was delivered today." Lowell punctuated his statement with a clap, his gnarled hand thumping against the other.

They laid out their project on a large table and marked where the final attachments would go. Lowell and Lenore had designed the pieces together before he'd sent their designs off to have them fabricated. Now it was just a matter of assembling and testing. The latter began several sweaty hours later.

"There she is." Lowell motioned to the completed device with his wrench, which was attached to him and stuck out from his palm like a metal branch. He gave it a twist to release it from its fixture. Then Lenore helped him position the new augmented arm, but Lowell insisted on being the one who strapped it in place.

"It's a rather fussy process, you know?" he said while adjusting a buckle. "There's a fine line between just right and accidentally flinging the whole thing across the room."

Lenore giggled. "And how old were you when that happened?"

"Oh, pretty much every time I test a new arm. Can't make it too tight or you're half dead up to the shoulder, and then you've got a floppy fish hanging off you." Lowell flailed his arm around like an out-of-control mackerel.

Lenore laughed harder this time, and Lowell readjusted the prosthetic. It had gone *catawampus*, as he called it, during his demonstration.

"There we are." He fastened the last strap. "Are you ready, my tinker belle?"

Lenore lifted her pen above her head like a sword and held her clipboard out like a shield. "Ready!"

)(

Lowell beamed and slowly turned the new arm, feeling the weight of it. It was heavier than those he'd made before. Then again, none of those had the functionality he hoped this one would have.

Their testing ground was the back garden. Unlike their last work session out here, it was sunny, though it didn't do much against the cold. Lenore hopped in place. Her red-and-yellow scarf wound over her head and around her ears. Lowell rather liked the colors. If this new arm worked out, perhaps he'd paint it in the same shades. A bit flamboyant, to be sure, but what was life without some vibrancy? Would he decorate the leg the same, though, or would he be prismatic?

He decided to stop putting the cart before the horse. They were only testing one limb for now.

"Day one, test one, ferrousite arm. Bending." Though he wanted to assist his hand the most, they'd designed the shell of the new arm to attach at his shoulder. That gave him options for keeping extra bits and bobs on him. "The springs feel good." He shook the arm. "Holding securely." He marked the fastening places for future use. "Now for the real test."

Lowell bobbed his eyebrows at Lenore, one dancing above the line of his mask. He'd chosen an old favorite today, one painted in simple flesh tones. Felicia had helped him with it. She could paint fine details like eyelashes better than anyone he knew—not that she allowed him to know many people. Before Rook had come into their lives, the only other being besides Felicia he spent time with was the raven. She had followed them outside to watch their progress. Not even she was as protective as Felicia, though.

Lowell reached into a box of props they'd carried out with them. A wire sticking out of the false hand caught on the handle of a battered metal teakettle. He unhooked it, careful not to tug. They'd left some of the arm's casing off to make adjustments more easily. He looked at the little pads on either side of his elbow. Just how effective would Lenore's idea prove to be? Her explanation had excited him, even if he didn't understand it all.

The metal hand was filled with a combination of springs, ferrousites, and wires, which connected to the... What had that nice chap at the museum called them? Elec... Eleccorrodes? No, something like trombones. Lowell chuckled. He'd much rather give them a silly name until he knew it would work.

He waggled a finger at the little flaps stuck to his thick, crinkled skin—another reason he wasn't certain this would work. "If you prove yourself, I'll get your proper name and call you by that. Until then, you're electro-nubs. Is that rude? Oh dear, I shouldn't be unkind. Apologies, chaps. In any case, I'll find out."

Lenore crept over, looking from Lowell's face to his arm. "Everything alright? It doesn't hurt, does it?"

Lowell's heart fluttered. He still remembered a time when such kindness had been difficult to come by. He smiled and shook his head. "No, it doesn't hurt. Just giving the new gents a pep talk. Couldn't hurt, eh?" Lenore nodded but didn't back away. "Behind the safety line, please. We don't know what might happen, and I never want to have to stitch you up again."

She touched the scar by her lip where that scoundrel Dempsey had once begun to torture her.

After she'd retreated to the spot they'd designated, Lowell turned back to his arm and... Well, he wasn't certain how this part was supposed to work. He'd never had proper strength in his twiggy fingers. Should he try some movements? Lowell shrugged and let his arm hang. He wiggled his index finger. The hand of his new arm was essentially a glove with assistance. In theory, it would improve his withered hand's abilities. As he'd expected, one of the exposed rods moved and his finger curled.

"Well, that's a result." He tried again, and his other fingers moved. "Lenore! It's working!"

Lowell handed himself the teakettle with his other arm. He'd always been able to hold on to things, but this was different. He gripped and squeezed and kept going. The glove insulated his hand, which had always been light on nerves anyway, from the pressure. Releasing his grip, Lowell realized he'd crunched the teakettle's handle as easily as a slice of bread. Eyes goggling out of his head, he looked at Lenore. Her expression mirrored his own.

"That was unexpected," she said. "How do you feel?"

"This is… absolutely spiffing! I didn't mean to mangle the poor thing, but I'm jolly pleased I can."

Lenore took a step forward, hesitated, then rocked on her heels. "I really want to come see."

Lowell turned so his non-mechanized arm faced her and beckoned. She practically skipped over and goggled at the kettle. They grinned at each other like their birthdays had come on the same day.

"We *have* to see what else you can do," Lenore said.

They spent the rest of the day testing Lowell's newfound strength and learning control. He accidentally punched the lyrist statue's head off its shoulders, adding insult to injury after having lost its nose when they'd made their ferrousites. They also needed to see if the new arm gave him increased dexterity, but the power pack installed into the arm's casing gave out before they got that far.

Lenore extracted the power pack. "The constant need for an external power source rather takes the shine off, doesn't it?"

"Not in the least," Lowell said. "That's the universe keeping balance." When Lenore gave him a quizzical look, he dropped his voice to a conspiratorial whisper. "Can you imagine if this wonder were self-powered? I'd be unstoppable! After all, I was a marvel *before* today."

Lenore beamed. "Too right." She looked back at the power pack. "I think I know someone who can help us get more. My friend Iggy works at the museum as an Alchemy apprentice. If she can't help us, she'll know who can."

"Perhaps Felicia will allow me to go along this time."

Lenore had suggested they speak with some of her museum colleagues about the power pack and electro-nubs together. Felicia had wasted no time shutting the idea down, which left all the fun to Lenore.

"I'd never see you again," Felicia had half-joked. "Heaven knows you'll move in and only be back here for holidays and to do your laundry."

"That sounds rather like a university student," Lowell had said. "Another tempting option."

"You already know more than anyone at any university could teach you."

They'd batted semi-serious banter back and forth until Felicia put her foot down. To be fair, Lowell had pushed her rather hard, but Lenore's return stories did nothing to quell his itch to get out. For years, he and Felicia had worked to establish themselves in the criminal underworld, with Lowell secretly operating in the background. Now they'd built their small fortune. There'd been that harrowing episode when the little upstart, Spades, had kidnapped Felicia and tried to force her to share her secrets. In the end, it had clinched her place in that world, but the memory still shook Lowell to his core.

Their security was all well and good, even downright boring at times, but something niggled in his brain. Was this all he wanted to do with his life? Lenore had brought him such joy and curiosity. Her stories made him want to set out on his own explorations. He'd been tempted to go to the museum with her anyway, but the thought of losing his dear friend, which would undoubtedly be his punishment, was too frightening. Thus, he'd stayed home, daydreaming of what it would have been like to join his friend.

)(

Dmitri was well acquainted with Rook's interrogation process. Rook had designed his office so he could perform one at a moment's notice. Preparation required nothing more than moving a chair to the center. A small rolling table waited nearby. Various torture implements—nail puller, boning knife, clamps—lined its surface. When Grunt and Broody hauled Ebony from Rook's holding cells, Dmitri's stomach turned. The way they paraded her before the market, barefoot and bound in chains, harked uncomfortably close to his Enforcer days. He understood the point of the show, but this was the sort of thing Dmitri had been glad to leave behind. He'd never imagined running Rook's operation, much less having to fulfill the job's darker obligations. Guilt gnawed on his insides, and he searched for reasons why this wasn't as bad as what the Enforcers did. He came up wanting.

Ebony didn't fight as Broody led her on her iron leash. She didn't have her mask; she didn't need it for the market's patrons to know who she was. People packed the aisles below, craning their necks to see the display. One of the Reaper's Collective was here.

A prisoner. Some of the onlookers practically drooled as they looked up at Dmitri.

He stood a story above them at the top of the metal stairway that led to his office. They'd compare him to Rook. Already he'd heard the whispers—the fearsome Rook was still alive, still about town, yet Dmitri was here filling his shoes. The other crime lords hadn't broadcasted their plans, but people had eyes. They saw the changes. The absence of certainty fed the rumor mill like coal in a steam engine.

Dmitri took a deep breath, hoping to appear cold. His bowels had gone watery. One show of weakness, and Rook's empire would crumble. Just before Broody got to the top of the stairs, Dmitri locked eyes with Ebony. He sent her a frigid stare, turned away, and re-entered the office.

)(

Chrysalis peeked past the edge of her cloak to watch the procession. She wasn't the only person in the market who wore one, especially at this time of year, but she'd dressed in a disguise underneath just in case. Platform shoes beneath her trousers helped her see better. A curly black wig perched atop her head, paired with muttonchops and a connecting mustache. Around her, people jostled and pressed to get the best view of the prisoner. She widened her stance for better balance.

Rook had given Chrysalis some time off. He'd been doing that more often since Dmitri had taken over. Dmitri, on the other hand, hadn't issued her a single order since the transition. She'd kept a low profile, not trusting all these jiggery-pokey changes. She could tell Rook wasn't happy from how he acted, but he and Dmitri were still very much in cahoots. Rook had given her a short speech about how much he appreciated her "discretion during this tumultuous time." She'd been pleased he thought of her even as he dealt with whatever else had been happening.

The memory gave Chrysalis courage as she gazed at that familiar face. Ebony, she'd heard the prisoner called. The one who'd trapped Chrysalis in a cell during the attack on the Halls of Justice. Rook had rescued her, risked himself and the girl he was so clearly besotted with to do it—yet another speck of light against a black night. More courage. Chrysalis looked at Ebony despite how her innards trembled. Ebony was just a person, and she was caught now. Chrysalis kept her eyes locked on the prisoner until Ebony disappeared behind Rook's—now Dmitri's—office door.

)(

Dmitri motioned to the chair in the center of the room. Broody yanked the chain, and Ebony stumbled forward. Dmitri almost reprimanded him for unnecessary cruelty but caught himself at the last second. Didn't he need to be cruel now? He swallowed the bile creeping up his throat and stood before Ebony. Grunt tied her hands to the chair, his thick fingers fumbling with the rope. The resulting knots were messy but would do.

"Chains off," Dmitri said. "The people have seen what they need to."

He had Broody shut the curtains, which blocked the long window that took up most of one wall and looked down over the market. It made the room feel small and oppressive.

After Grunt finished with Ebony's ties, Dmitri brandished a sheet of paper at her.

"These are the questions I'm going to ask you," he said. "You can be straight with me, or we can force answers from you. Your choice."

This was a technique he'd borrowed from his Enforcer days. She spit on his sheet of questions. Dmitri's heart turned to lead, but he pushed the dread down.

This is necessary. His former C.O.s' voices saying the same words played in his head.

"Broody, her toes."

Broody grabbed a small piece of wood from the table. It resembled a tongue depressor, except it curved along its length and one end had been carved into a sharpened point.

Dmitri had thought it would be easier to order someone else to do the dirty work. Not so. More guilt piled on top of his dread and dropped iron slugs into his gut. If he couldn't be the one to do the deed, he had no right to ask anyone else. He forced himself to watch as Broody pushed the sharp end of the tool beneath one of

Ebony's toenails. It pulled a scream of agony from her throat. Her limbs strained against their bonds.

"Leave it at that," Dmitri shouted over Ebony's screams.

Broody backed off, and Dmitri waited. Ebony eventually grit her teeth and swallowed her screams. Blood dribbled from the injury.

Dmitri had once advised Rook on slowing blood loss in torture victims. He wondered if he should follow that same advice today. The weight of the decision pressed against his throat.

"Come on, Ebony," Dmitri said. He had a sudden appreciation for the fact that Rook did this too. He wasn't even smarmy about it. Dmitri knew him well enough to know the crime lord took no pleasure in violence, he was just hardened to it. Dmitri had imagined he might be a kinder leader. "Just give me one answer to start. Tell me anything you know about the Reaper or the Collective."

Sweat beading on her forehead, Ebony bared her teeth at him. "The Reaper will burn your heart out. They will destroy everything you hold dear."

Dmitri did his best to appear both impassive and respectful. "I admit, I left that open-ended. You did tell me something. Would you like some water for your pains?"

Ebony said nothing.

Dmitri looked back at his list. "Let's try an easy one. How many agents does the Reaper have, as far as you know?"

Ebony pressed her lips together and looked like she was trying to shoot acid from her eyes.

"We don't have to be enemies," Dmitri said. "I just want to make sure the Reaper doesn't hurt more people."

"Do whatever you like, scum. The Reaper will be our salvation," she snarled.

Dmitri sighed, though not as heavily as he felt. "Broody, again."

This went on for an hour. Dmitri tried again and again to get Ebony to talk. She gave him nothing. Eventually, blood puddled under her feet. She leaned forward in her chair, panting and hoarse. Dmitri turned away, his gut in knots. He motioned Grunt and Broody to the other side of the room with him. He needed to decide his next steps and hoped to engender some positive employee relations by soliciting their feedback. Something good needed to come of this. Out of Ebony's earshot and sight would be best too—who knew, maybe she could read lips. He wasn't taking any chances.

Someone would need to patch her up if Dmitri intended to hold on to her. Perhaps he could ransom her, but for what price? The Reaper wouldn't surrender the entire operation for one member. Dmitri suppressed the urge to slump; he really didn't want to deal with everything keeping her required.

While he and his goons traded ideas, the sound of a chair scraped across the floor. Dmitri turned to see Ebony, free of her bonds, racing across the room. Not in the direction he'd expected.

"Grab her," Dmitri yelled.

Ebony dove through the curtains and the glass behind. A *thump* followed. He heard the market patrons murmuring, but the shattering glass echoed louder in his head. One fear tried to bolt Dmitri's boots to the floor, but another shoved him forward.

Ebony's body lay on the market floor below. It bent at unnatural angles, none so extreme as the one in her neck. Blood seeped from slices in her skin. A swear whooshed past Dmitri's lips. He looked back to the chair. The messy knots had not, in fact, done.

21

~Trade-Off~

The restaurant prided itself on the best of everything—drinks, food, decor, and service. Fewer than a dozen tables scattered around the dining room, each topped with a tablecloth as white as fresh snow. They didn't need many patrons when only the most well-to-do citizens could afford to dine here. Even Neal balked when Katerina had told him the meeting's location. He hadn't wanted to order a drink, knowing it would probably cost him the same as a small parcel of land, but the others had, so he'd folded. He barely sipped it throughout dinner.

Katerina had been drinking slowly as well, likely to remain sharp. She was on her second, however. Speaker Pendragon and First Iago on either side of Neal had been downing them like water. He hoped Katerina planned on footing their bills since she'd been the one to arrange this meeting. Neal regretted passing up the opportunity to do so, even if it had temporarily made his life easier.

The four made stilted conversation at first, replaced by the sounds of eating when the first course arrived. As the meal wound down, Katerina folded her hands before her—a sign that she was about to dig into the meat of the issue.

"Thank you again, gentlemen, for joining us tonight." She turned to Speaker Pendragon. "And thank you for bringing First Iago along. It's so helpful to hear other viewpoints."

Neal resisted the urge to make a face—that certainly wasn't what she'd said when she first heard that the Enforcer leader would be joining them.

"You mean bring the two sides together." First Iago swirled a piece of duck in its cherry-red wine sauce. Given his enormous stature, it looked as if he could easily polish off six more of the birds.

"I do not mean that," Katerina said, "for I don't believe we're on opposing sides. We both want safety for this city. Our views on the best way to do that just differ."

First Iago pointed his fork at her. "You'd have us all out of a job if it were up to you."

"Not in the least. You can ask anyone, even Speaker Pendragon. I have always praised your order for the brave work you do."

First Iago looked at Speaker Pendragon. "Henry?"

The familiar way he said the man's name rankled Neal, doubly so when Speaker Pendragon smiled back like they were old friends, which they were.

"She's correct," Speaker Pendragon said. "Lady Holmes has always supported the Enforcer order, just not their methods."

Neal internally grumbled to himself over how slimily Speaker Pendragon had made himself seem unbiased. Nothing could be further from the truth.

First Iago turned back to Katerina. "Let me tell you why your initiative is—"

"Allow me to save you some time," she said. Neal stifled a smile as First Iago's neck bulged. "Perhaps we should do some tests before anyone makes any overarching decisions. It will be a good opportunity for your order and will paint *you* in a very appealing light."

Speaker Pendragon leaned back in his chair and folded his arms over his rotund belly.

First Iago narrowed his eyes at Katerina. "What kind of test?"

Katerina gestured to Neal with her glass. "Lord Allen is better with these sorts of technical details."

First Iago whipped his head around. Neal got the impression the First was trying to use his eyes to pin Neal to his chair like a butterfly to a display. Neal looked steadily back at the man as he slotted facts into his quiver, ready to deliver a volley.

"Lady Holmes has assembled a team to survey citizens about how they feel about Springhaven's policing practices. Trials were the number one item people wanted. Fair trials overseen by elected judges and a jury of the defendant's peers. If you agree to run trials on a, well, a trial basis—pardon the pun." Only Katerina cracked a smile, and an indulgent one at that. "Ahem. As I was saying, we are prepared to tell the populace this was your idea."

"Your pitch would be better if you weren't a known fraternizer with several former criminals," First Iago said.

"You mean like the newly monikered Varick Hollow?" Neal asked.

At that, Speaker Pendragon cleared his throat, leaned forward again, and addressed First Iago. "I think this is a good maneuver for all of us. My magistrates have begun receiving letters, lots of them, and I expect more will follow."

"Because of them!" First Iago jabbed a finger at Katerina and Neal.

In his periphery, Neal saw several nearby diners stare from the corners of their eyes or behind fans.

"Come now, old friend," Speaker Pendragon said. "The people have spoken. If they call for impeachment, I may not be able to protect us both. And when the council holds their vote, it might take this decision out of your hands anyway. Perhaps it would be better to save some face beforehand."

First Iago's eyes bulged. Neal worried the top of his head might blow like a poorly regulated boiler. His next words sounded like rocks grinding against each other. "No trials."

"Then what is your counter-offer?" Katerina asked, sipping at her drink.

Before he could answer, Neal said, "Crisis responders." The others' eyes turned to him. None were sharper than Katerina's. Something like anger glinted in her gaze, but it was cold and well-restrained. "Think back to the Halls of Justice attack."

"What about it?" First Iago growled.

"Your order was wholly unprepared for the resulting injuries." Neal's voice gained force as First Iago's hackles rose. "Sir, I was in my wife's clinic as Enforcers were brought in. Your people didn't know how to staunch the wounds. No triage measures whatsoever. You might not have lost as many men if that hadn't been the case."

"Irrelevant. There won't be another situation like that."

"It's not just about your headquarters. Arresting criminals isn't the only way to serve our city. What if there's a different kind of disaster? A natural one? Are you going to beat back nature with truncheons?" Neal stopped short of mentioning how useless the Enforcers had been after the black powder accident.

Speaker Pendragon chuckled. "Trying to put your wife out of a job?"

Neal didn't dignify that with a response. "First Iago, even just basic skills would have made a difference."

"Of course, proving the efficacy of this requires misfortune," Katerina said.

"It's something," Neal said. "Better to have it in place and not need it than the other way around." He also made it a point not to mention the protesters and turned back to Speaker Pendragon. "If First Iago won't budge on trials, then perhaps training a small emergency response team is an option." To First Iago, he added, "Though I still think trials are a better choice."

"I agree," Katerina said. Neal caught the undercurrent of disapproval in her voice.

First Iago crossed his arms. "And if I were to agree, how might we execute such a plan? Who, for instance, would provide training?"

After much more discussion, they reached an agreement. Neal and Katerina would oversee the new emergency response team. Even so, Neal didn't feel he'd achieved a victory. He felt exhausted and defeated. Katerina said not a word to him as he escorted her to her coach, and he couldn't blame her. They were now responsible for an initiative he'd tossed into the conversation without discussing it with her first—and its failure could ruin everything they were working for.

22

~Prices Paid~

Camilla tried to keep one eye on her work, but the soft chirping behind her, before her, and flying above her head snagged her attention and frayed her patience like a run in her stockings. A Collective member, some underling eager to impress the Reaper, was running around like a kitten after a fly, except in this case the fly was a bat that had managed to sneak into the operating theatre.

Camilla's hands shook. The cold damp settling into her bones and her constant fear of the flying rat getting tangled in her hair made steadiness impossible, not to mention the low rasp of the Reaper breathing over her shoulder. She was beyond pleased to study under such a knowledgeable being, but what if she did something wrong? Camilla had dressed as warmly as possible, but these catacombs seemed determined to freeze her into a solid block. The cadaver beneath her radiated almost as much cold as the floor.

She turned her head to cough into the crook of her elbow again. A slight but growing headache accompanied it—yet another problem, but she at least knew how to deal with it. She'd go by Thyme's Apothecary for a treatment if it got any worse.

Camilla wondered if the Reaper had ever honored Dmitri in such a way. Given he'd broken away from the Collective so easily, he'd probably never even been close to the Reaper. A vague niggle knocked on the back of her skull. Thinking of Dmitri's appearance in the garden that night, dressed in the Collective's black leather uniform, reminded her that the Reaper had orchestrated the Halls of Justice attack, which had resulted in her mother's death. Camilla shook the misgiving away. That had been the Enforcers' fault for being so awful.

"Focus, Camilla," the Reaper hissed behind her.

Camilla pursed her lips, attempting to hone her concentration as sharp as her scalpel. She leaned closer to her work. The Reaper had tasked her with detaching the complex network of veins, arteries, muscles, and other fibers that connected her dead patient's kidney to the rest of its body. The bat swooped by her ear. She tensed but kept a steady hand. No harm done; she breathed a sigh of relief.

Something heavy slammed into her, sending her scalpel slicing clean through the organ. Camilla caught herself on the operating table. The Reaper caught themself too, then spun to lash out at the recruit. The Collective member was babbling apologies and backing away from the Reaper.

"I-I didn't mean to touch you, y-your grace. Please, I'm so sorry." He sounded barely older than a child.

A new kind of cold drenched Camilla as she looked at the Reaper. She'd been told to never touch them. Never ever.

The crooked quarterstaff Camilla had seen in the Reaper's sitting room hung from their back. Slowly, they pulled it from its holster. The staff's edge caught the light and flashed. Camilla hadn't noticed this feature before—a notched, curved blade as dark as the staff sat folded against the wood. The Reaper snapped the weapon open, and it reverberated off the walls like a death knell.

A scythe.

A fringe of slender, jagged blades spread around the hinge. Clawed fingers reaching for victims.

"No," Camilla said. "It was an accident. He—" She coughed.

The Reaper swung the scythe and sliced off the lad's head. It made a sickening *slurp*, as if the weapon drank his death.

She covered her mouth, heedless of the gore covering her hands. The stench shot into her nostrils. She took her hands away and hung on to the table. Camilla fought back the contents of her stomach.

Then she realized she too had touched the Reaper, though through no fault of her own.

Camilla lifted her eyes back to the shadow-shrouded figure. They wiped blood from their blade, liquid jewels of bright red dripping from the malicious tip. Just beyond, the recruit's head rocked on the floor. His mask had slipped, revealing his face. His eyes gaped in an expression of pure terror.

Camilla's resolve slipped. Her stomach emptied itself onto the floor, slapping against the hard stone. She wiped her mouth and looked back up to see the bird-like, empty-eyed mask staring at her. The Reaper came closer and reached for her. Camilla trembled, half stood, and closed her eyes. A presence cupped her face, though there was no physical contact. A scent like carnations and lilies surrounded her and soothed her fears.

"Camilla," the Reaper whispered. "Look at me."

She opened her eyes. She was calmer than before, but fear that she was about to die still shouted at the back of her mind. The Reaper's hands hovered on either side of her head, just shy of touching her. Their mask's long beak tipped down between them. Camilla imagined she saw a light behind the glass orbs gazing at her.

"The world is hard," they said. "You know this. We must do what is necessary to protect ourselves. Do you understand?"

Camilla nodded, though her thoughts jumbled and bumped against each other like dizzy moths. The boy had broken the rules. But it had been a mistake. He should have been more careful.

The Reaper took in a deep, rasping breath and released it over Camilla—more of that lovely scent. They then drew away like a wraith on the wind. Camilla leaned against the operating table. Gratitude washed through her. She was alive.

She and the Reaper salvaged what they could from the cadaver. They'd use the fat to make candles and study the other organs. Other Collective members appeared and took away their comrade's body. It too would be prepared for use.

As people moved in and out of the room, Nightmare's voice floated in from the hallway. She was ordering people out of her way. She limped inside with Beetle, his arm covered in blood. Neither wore their masks.

"You ran into trouble," the Reaper said.

Nightmare nodded. "He's pretty bad off."

The Reaper motioned for them to come through to the laboratory, where the two Crypt-Keepers settled on stools. The Reaper examined their injuries. Camilla followed and fell into the familiar but urgent routine of patching up new patients. Strips of flesh hung from Beetle's arm, and blood smeared all the way to his shoulder. Nightmare had a single deep bite on her leg, which looked like it had come from a large dog.

"Thank you for your dedication," the Reaper said to Beetle. "You are a faithful servant. Camilla, what are your thoughts?"

They probably wouldn't have to amputate, but the limb would never be the same. The Reaper let her take over. She stitched what she could and cut away what was unsalvageable.

Nightmare spoke in low tones, while the Reaper attended to her leg. "The Verisap didn't work."

"That's two formulas that have failed us," replied the Reaper. "Contact our suppliers, and press Sunspot harder for answers."

"He's protested he's not an alchemist," Nightmare said. "I don't think he understands how the formulas work."

The Reaper swept a double-gloved hand around Nightmare's head as if caressing her face, though they never actually touched her. "I believe in you, my dear. I know you can convince him to figure it out."

Nightmare smiled even through her pain. "Of course, your grace."

Camilla suffered another coughing fit. Pressure stung at her temples. She wanted to ask about what they were discussing. Were they planning another attack? Another voice in her head cooed that it would all be fine, that there was a reason for everything. Despite this, she couldn't shake the fear shuddering in her core.

)(

As hooves clip-clopped outside Beatrice's private coach, Lenore recalled the lovely morning she'd spent with Eamon. She smiled. They'd had breakfast together, and he'd surprised her with a small bouquet of snowdrops.

"Could I weave them into your hair?" he'd asked. "Like we used to do?"

Lenore had been all too happy to oblige. Beatrice raved about the look when she'd collected Lenore later that day for a shopping trip.

"I think you've earned yourself a little treat, good sir," Beatrice had said. "I'll make sure Lenore picks out something equally fetching."

"That's not necessary," Eamon replied.

Beatrice had given an easy wave of her hand. "Nonsense. It's just a little positive reinforcement."

Not knowing if Beatrice had puzzled out that something was amiss between them, Lenore had decided to try smoothing things over just in case. "I'm happy to find something."

Eamon had flashed a genuine smile. In a voice too soft for Beatrice to hear, he'd said, "I want you to be happy. You know that, don't you?"

Lenore's heart swelled as she remembered it. They'd made real progress of late. A few times had felt almost normal. His promised gift—a new pair of cufflinks and a matching pocket square—sat in her lap as she and Beatrice rode back to the townhouse.

"It's so nice to get out and relax once in a while, isn't it?" Beatrice said. "Thank you again, Lenore, for all your help recently."

"Of course," Lenore said, "though you still spent a good deal of time catching up with that Pendragon magistrate and his son."

"His *Enforcer* son," Beatrice said. "I can't pass up an opportunity when it arises. Leopold and his father have been softening to our cause."

Lenore's lips curled up mischievously. "And have your charms done the softening?"

"Not in the least, darling. I'm not his type. Leopold prefers a more masculine touch, though it probably helped that I introduced him to his current paramour. And the one before that, come to think of it."

Beatrice asked to use the ladies' room at the townhome and disappeared toward the out-of-the-way part of the house.

Lenore bounced a little as she held Eamon's gift in her hands. He hadn't mentioned any plans to go out. That could have changed, but no note waited for her near the door. She headed to the library—always a good guess. When she entered, she spied the back of his head peeking over the top of his favorite reading chair.

"Eamon," she sang. "I've got a surprise for you." She rounded the chair, held up the little box…

And dropped it with a scream.

Eamon slumped in the seat, his head leaning against the back of the chair and his hands limp on the armrests. Empty, bloody sockets stared where his eyes should have been. Over his mouth in a crisscross pattern, thick metallic thread had been stitched along his lips like a metal grate. Deep scratches marred the chair's leather arms under Eamon's fingers.

"BEATRICE!" Lenore shrieked.

Quaking seconds, or perhaps minutes, later, her friend burst through the door.

"Get Mina! *Now*! *Right bloody now!*"

Beatrice was out the door before Lenore finished. Lenore felt for Eamon's wrist for a pulse, but her fingers trembled. She couldn't make out whether she felt any rhythm beneath his skin.

Her breath came ragged and shallow. "Eamon. Eamon?" She gripped his shoulders. "Oh, stars, please. *Eamon*."

He didn't move. Lenore wracked her brain for anything she could do to help him but came up empty.

Failing that, she searched the house. She found no intruders, but Majesty lay unconscious in the conservatory. Bitsy sat beside her in a congealed pool of blood and looked at Lenore with sad eyes. Lenore pressed a blanket to the wounds marring Majesty's magnificent ruff before hurrying back to Eamon.

Mina arrived, and Beatrice held Lenore as the doctor worked. Not a minute passed before Mina looked at Lenore with glistening eyes full of pain and shock.

"I'm so sorry, my darling." Mina said.

Lenore shook her head. She tried to pull herself from Beatrice's grasp. "No. No, no, no, no. Eamon, he… can't be…"

"I'm so sorry," Mina repeated.

Lenore collapsed to her knees, still in Beatrice's arms. She wailed as Mina wrapped her arms around them. She sobbed and swore, crawled over to Eamon's knee and took his cold hands in hers, begging him to come back.

The Enforcers were called. Statements were taken. They would simultaneously inform the rest of the Lee family and question them. Lenore watched as they took Eamon's body away. He'd be cremated, as was custom, after an autopsy. Someone from the museum came and collected Majesty so she could be treated.

Lenore went home with the Allens that night, a new hole carved into her chest.

)(

It was after midnight when Rook was finally able to do his rounds. He swung by the dark townhouse and then the Allen manor. From atop the courtyard wall, he spotted his mark drawn on the ground beneath a familiar hosta. Its leaves hung brown and withered. Before heading inside, he checked in with Chrysalis, who crouched behind a bare, twiggy bush.

"Something's off," she said, "but I don't know what."

Rook almost told her to stay back—after losing Garrick, the thought of putting Chrysalis in danger chilled him. Then again, he might need the backup, so he swallowed the coddling command.

"Be ready if I call?" he asked. "I don't have too many people left, you know." Chrysalis gave him a determined bob of her head. "Cheers. I knew I could count on you."

Rook practically felt her beaming through her sneak suit. Then he prepared for an ambush and slipped through the kitchen door.

Esther stood at the counter. She dabbed her face with a tea towel, her shoulders shaking.

"Esther." Rook waited for her to turn. "What's happened?"

"Oh, Master Hollow. Something dreadful."

Rook swallowed hard and approached slowly. "What's wrong?"

"It's Eamon. He's—" Esther's voice broke.

Rook found himself reaching for her and wrapped his arms around her shoulders.

Bloody blazes, he thought to himself.

Esther collected herself and motioned toward the rest of the house. "Miss Lenore is in the dining room. She can't sleep, so I'm fixing up some tea. I'll be out shortly."

The air moved like molasses around him as he crossed from the butler's pantry, through the conservatory, and into the dining room. Lenore sat at the table with her head in her hands. Mina sat beside her, rubbing her back.

"Lenore?" Rook breathed.

Tears streaked Mina's face. Her eyes were red and puffy, her usually straight spine bowed. Lenore didn't stir, but Mina's eyes spoke volumes. Whatever had happened, it had been horrible indeed.

Rook lowered himself into the chair on Lenore's other side. He placed his hand on one of her arms. "Lenore?"

She turned to Mina. "Can you excuse us for a moment, please?"

Mina looked between Rook and Lenore. "I don't mind being here with you."

"Thank you, but I need to talk to Rook alone." Lenore's voice was a shuddering whisper.

Mina nodded and looked at Rook. *Take care of her,* her gaze said. *Or else.*

Rook watched as Mina left. Another moment passed before Lenore finally looked at him. His heart cracked when he saw her face. Lenore's eyes were raw and sharp and shone with fury. Her mouth was set in the same line Rook's took before he made a killing blow.

He'd never seen such hate in her.

"I want them dead," she whispered. "Every single one of them. I don't care how you do it, but I want it to *hurt*."

Lenore's anger snapped like ice, and she crumbled into weeping. Rook gathered her into his arms and stroked her hair.

"Oh, little bird," he said. "Tell me what happened."

Through hiccups and sobs, Lenore told Rook what she'd found that afternoon.

"It's my fault," she said. "If I... I should have... Eamon, he... I never considered..." Lenore's words disintegrated into choking tears. After a few more minutes, she said, "No. Me. I want to do it. I want to kill the Reaper. I want to kill Dempsey and the Reaper and anyone else I can get my hands on."

Lenore lifted her head to look at him again. Her eyes matched the manic fire in her voice. "Take me to them, Rook. Capture them and let me kill them. Tell me you'll come get me when you've got them."

"It may not be as easy as that," Rook replied gently. "I—"

"Then take me with you." Lenore bared her teeth. "They murdered my friend. I want to cut out their hearts."

Rook breathed an internal sigh of relief when Esther's footsteps tapped across the floor toward them. Lenore broke away from him, and the housekeeper appeared a moment later. The scent of lavender and chamomile wafted over as Esther set her tray down.

"Come now, my darling," Esther said. "Let's have a cup."

Lenore wiped her eyes. "Thank you, Esther."

They drank their tea in silence. Mina reappeared soon after and sat with them. She eventually convinced Lenore to go to bed, to rest, if not sleep. Rook watched Lenore disappear through the doorway as he helped Esther clear the tea things away.

"Just set it over there, dear," Esther said once they were back in the kitchen.

"Can I do anything else to help?" Rook asked. "Shall I wash up?"

Esther patted Rook's arm. "No, Master Hollow, but thank you. You just keep Miss Lenore in the light."

She fixed him with a sad look. Rook nodded, uncertain how much the old woman knew.

)(

Camilla paced in her room. Mina's voice burbled through the wall as she tucked Lenore into bed next door.

You should go to her, said a voice in Camilla's mind. *She needs you.* Another argued, *She brought it on herself. She fraternizes with criminals. There's good reason for this.*

Camilla had nearly decided when a new argument arose. *Eamon was innocent. Why should he have paid for Lenore's sins?*

A dart of pain whistled through Camilla's heart. It took advantage of her weakness. *Who else will suffer like Eamon?*

She shook her head. *No. Eamon conspired with them against the Reaper.*

When thoughts crept forward to explore *who else* had worked with Lenore to thwart the Reaper, Camilla's mind scrabbled for arguments. For one, the Reaper had spared her life despite the no-touching rule. Why? Because the Reaper loved their Collective. She'd also seen that in the care they'd shown Nightmare and Beetle that day. The boy who'd chased the bat had disobeyed, which required discipline. This was war, and war brought casualties. The Reaper wanted to take down the Enforcers. Enforcers like Camilla's father, who had framed her mother and condemned her to a life of prison and torture. Enforcers like the deplorable Harding Smoke and that coward, Falcon.

The embers of Camilla's anger heated and glowed. The Reaper was laboring to bring the same mercy they'd shown her to the rest of Springhaven.

Mina's voice still murmured through the wall. It sounded like Lenore was crying again. Camilla remained in her room and stewed in her bitterness.

)(

Dmitri stared at the door before him. Bright mid-morning sunlight struggled to shine through a greasy window at the end of the hall. These ramshackle Agate district flats weren't far from his family's home. Every minute he stood in the hallway increased his chances of being recognized. His fine but plain black suit wouldn't help avoid attention either. People loved to gossip, no matter what level of society they came from. Dmitri hadn't seen his family in months, though he still left them money in secret, and he really didn't want them to see him dressed like this.

This could be a trap. Rook had sent him an urgent coded message in the small hours of last night. It contained nothing but a sharp order to follow the included directions as soon as possible. Dmitri knew nothing about this hideaway. That didn't surprise him, but it also didn't fill him with confidence.

Hearing another door in the hall open drove him to act. He knocked on the one before him as the note had instructed. The door swung open, seemingly on its own. Dmitri knew whoever had opened it was waiting behind. He stepped inside and turned in one swift movement, truncheon out.

The door closed slowly, revealing Rook with daggers drawn. He looked almost as bad as he had when Dmitri learned he no longer had the oath.

"Problem?" Dmitri raised an eyebrow at Rook's disheveled appearance.

"Yes," Rook snapped. "I thought things would be clearer this morning, but I'm only seeing more tangles. Too many pieces. Too much risk." Rook spun and hurled one of his smaller blades at the wall. He hurled two more for good measure and spit some choice swears, all the while Dmitri watched him coolly. Finally, Rook took and released a deep breath. "Eamon's dead."

Dmitri jerked back. "When?"

"Yesterday. Lenore came home to find him murdered."

"How do you kn—"

"Because his eyes were carved out and his mouth was stitched up like those lunatics' idiotic masks."

"Bugger me." Dmitri wondered if the kill was over Ebony. "What are the Allens doing?"

"They called the Enforcers. Heaven knows they won't get anywhere. I went by the townhouse myself. There's nothing useful. Majesty apparently took a piece of them, but no evidence of a kill. Lenore found her locked in the back with some stab wounds and blood on her muzzle." He paused. "First Garrick, now Eamon. They need to pay for this, Dmitri."

Dmitri crossed his arms. "He's not one of ours."

"I don't care." Rook stalked over and extracted his knives from the wall. "They know Lenore is part of my circle. They did this to get to her. Blasted shame they didn't know what the marriage really was."

"I assume she's taking it hard?"

"Of course she is. She blames herself." Rook looked to Dmitri. "She wants to be the one to kill them, and I'm tempted to grant her wish."

Dmitri shook his head. "You'd only be pulling her deeper into this game. That's not good for anyone."

"It's not my place to deny her vengeance," Rook said, "but you're right."

Dmitri released some of the stern composure he usually maintained. Leaning against the doorframe, he took care with his next words. Rook wasn't heartless, but life had hardened him in a way Dmitri didn't always understand.

"Are you at all glad he's dead?"

"No." Rook jammed his knives back into their respective homes around his person. It was a wonder he didn't stab himself in the process. "Not like this. He was a preening peacock, but he didn't deserve this."

A long pause stretched between them.

"Do you really want me to rally our fighters?" Dmitri asked. "We'd lose a lot of good people. I'm not even sure we'd win. Those catacombs are like a fortress."

Rook rubbed a hand over his face. Exhaustion stretched his features. "Blazes, I don't know. Get me a map drawn up. List everything you remember about them, even what seems insignificant. Use the other code I taught you and hide it under the trick drawer in my desk. I'll decide later, but we need to be ready no matter what."

"Yes, sir," Dmitri said. He tried to sound confident for both their sakes. Rook's war-weary countenance was a first, and it frightened Dmitri.

23

~Finding Happiness~

Dear Oya,
You may have already heard from our Anthropology
department, but Eamon passed away.

Lenore looked at the words she'd just written and hated them to the very depths of her soul. *Passed away*. What an unfair and sugarcoated description. When she lifted her pen to write "was brutally murdered," her hand shook. A sob rose in her throat. Telling Oya made it too real, too final, which was why she'd put it off for so long. Three weeks had passed since the abominable event.

When Lenore had mourned her parents the first time, after they'd been arrested, she'd been alone. She'd heard that grief made you feel alone, but she really had been. When her parents had truly died, the circle had been mercifully small. Now, with Eamon's death, she had to share her pain again and again with *everyone*, only to receive the same well-meant condolences over and over. Lenore felt just as alone as she had before.

She left the sentence as it was.

The museum's halls were quiet at this hour. She'd decided to come in early on this first day back from her bereavement leave. The cloying scent of flowers from the condolence-wishers had made her want to return sooner, but Neal hadn't allowed it. Only three weeks, but it felt like months.

Thank the stars for Lowell. He'd let her stay late and come over early, urging her to work on whatever she liked, no questions asked. Not even when she'd begun to sketch and fabricate weapons.

Well, he'd asked one question. "Would you like my help with anything, my tinker belle?"

Lenore had refused each time and thanked him at every opportunity. She truly believed she might have gone mad without him.

Leaving her letter to Oya for now, Lenore penned another. One she could do without thinking, to avoid a whole different type of pain. Within minutes, she'd written an invitation for midday tea to Eloise and Elizabeth, two of Eamon's sisters. It was the second one she'd written. They'd rejected the first due to a scheduling conflict. Lenore expected this one to be similarly rebuffed and tried not to be angry. Mrs. Lee hadn't held anyone connected to Mina in high regard since the Halls of Justice attack. Mina had ordered Mrs. Lee out of the clinic while her daughter, Emily Lee, assisted with patients against the furious mother's wishes. Lenore's presence would no doubt cause the grieving family pain despite not knowing her connection to Eamon's killers. Emily would have accepted. Lenore regretted not getting to know the girl better. She'd returned from boarding school for the funeral, but Lenore hadn't gotten much of a chance to speak with her.

I should write her. Perhaps being away will allow her to correspond more freely.

Emily too might reject Lenore's attempts to connect, but she could at least try. After writing a quick letter and eager for a distraction from painful subjects, she looked around the empty Arc-Tech department for an easy task. Lenore had officially declared her independent Journeyman project but didn't have the energy to tackle it just now.

Neal's desk. Perfect.

She dove in. It wasn't as disorganized as when she'd first begun working at the museum, but it had gotten cluttered since she'd last seen it. She sorted through his correspondence, paperwork, and notes. One letter bearing the words "Arnavi," "Bone Port," and "Copper" caught her attention. She read it, and her stomach dropped. She set it aside to address later but found herself picking it up again and again to reread. Maybe she'd misunderstood the words the first time. And the second. And the third.

When Copper arrived an hour later, she accosted him before he'd even had time to hang up his coat. "You're leaving?" She'd meant to sound angry, but her voice cracked instead.

Copper looked at the letter scrunched in her hand and then to Lenore. His eyes softened. "Oh, lass, I'm sorry. I didn't want you to find out like this. Not after… everything."

"You're leaving?" she said again. At least she managed to sound a little demanding this time.

Copper shoved his hands into his pockets, shoulders apologetically rolling forward. "You remember those Arnavi folks who came in here a few weeks back?" Having read the letter, Lenore knew where this was going but nodded anyway. "They want me to come work in Bone Port. Scholar Simra's approved it and everything."

Her head drooped. She felt as if someone had scooped out her insides and left her empty.

"I'm sorry, Nori," Copper said. "It's a good opportunity. I'll be in charge of my own team, and this city… It's got a lot of memories. If our places were switched, I'd tell you to take the job."

"I understand." Her senses finally seeped back. "It's hot there. Absurdly hot."

Copper rubbed his beard. "Aye. I've been advised to shave."

Lenore chuckled before tears stampeded in to crush her. "Everyone's leaving me." Copper took her hands. Lenore turned the gesture into a hug. "I'll miss you so much."

"Me too, lass. You'll have to come visit."

"I will. I promise."

Lenore let herself cry for a while. Copper sat with her, a silent understanding presence. Eamon would have encouraged her, told her she needed to focus on her career—at least, that's what she liked to think. They'd been on their way back, had been in a good place. That last morning she'd seen him alive, he'd said he wanted her to be happy. Lenore wanted to honor that, but heavens, anything like happiness felt so far away sometimes. She could grasp tendrils of it in moments like this, though. When she was with the people she cared about.

Things improved when Ezra came in. Lenore had stopped crying, and her face was almost back to normal. He didn't say much, of course, but he put a bolstering hand on her shoulder. "Help me with the SS?"

"Sure," she said.

It felt surprisingly good to be back with the old girl in that it led Lenore to think about her Journeyman project. With Copper's encouragement, she'd decided to try to make a travel contraption. The dirigible she'd used as inspiration for her mechanical bird project covered air, and the SS prototype covered water. So why not try land? Bicycles and other velocipedes were a popular option with couriers. Lenore's plan was to improve on that framework. She nattered on about her ideas, while Ezra listened. He piped up with something beyond "uh huh" only when he had something substantial to add.

That afternoon, as Lenore lay under the SS copy, another familiar voice said her name. She slid out from under the hulking machine and smiled.

"Hello, Iggy." Memories of time spent in Bone Port with the alchemy apprentice and Eamon flooded back. Remembering what she'd decided earlier that day aided Lenore in driving back another barrage of tears.

She leaned against the body of the SS, while Iggy sat on the floor next to her. Continuing to work, Ezra's legs stuck out between the two ladies from under the bulbous machine. The sight coaxed a smile from Lenore.

"I hope I'm not interrupting," Iggy said. Lenore was grateful for the alchemy apprentice's soft-timbred voice; at least she sounded the same as ever. "I heard you were back and thought you might want these." Iggy held out a small box. Within it sat... Well, Lenore wasn't certain what they were. "Volta piles." Lenore blinked blankly at her. "They're the improved power packs you requested. I made some enhancements of my own."

Lenore nodded as realization dawned on her. "They last longer than the others?"

"Hours longer." Iggy paused and said more quietly, "They also provide more power than the others with no loss of time."

Lenore's brows bobbed. Iggy had a severe disinclination to toot her own horn. Just how much better would these Volta piles prove to be? Lenore beamed when she imagined how Lowell would react to the news.

"Thank you so much, Iggy. This is splendid. What do I owe you?"

Iggy shook her head. "Don't worry about it. I enjoyed the process. Although…" She rubbed her arm.

"Yes?"

"I wouldn't mind seeing how they perform on your friend's appendages."

Lenore's smile faltered as she thought of Felicia's disapproving glare.

"I'll see what I can do," Lenore said. "He's a bit of a hermit." It wasn't precisely a lie.

)(

Dutiful but distant. This was the only thing that pacified the opposite pulls of Camilla's heart. Tonight, she'd retreated to the Allens' library to distract herself with a novel. One of her only respites nowadays. Curled up in the corner of a sofa, she imagined herself on an island, isolated from the thorny complications of life that hounded her days and stole her sleep at night. Despite her thoughts the night Eamon died, misgivings she'd believed buried had revived and snapped at her with rotting teeth no matter what arguments she made. To appease these corrupted qualms, she did the bare minimum of what was expected of her at home, at school, and at the catacombs.

Thankfully, everyone from the first group was so consumed with supporting Lenore they didn't notice Camilla's retreat. Lenore was understandably shattered, but she agitated Camilla's misgivings. Just seeing her housemate's face or hearing her voice dredged up thoughts of Camilla's mother, of how things *should* have gone in the Halls. The pain burned as hot as a cauterizing rod. Her cough hadn't abated either, so neither that nor the accompanying headaches were helping her mood.

Now, when Lenore walked into the library, Camilla's irritation swelled and heated like an infected wound.

"Do you mind if I join you?" Lenore asked.

She almost sounded like herself, which poked Camilla's annoyance harder. It seemed shallow, and burdening Camilla with her presence was selfish.

"I'm reading."

"I know, and I'm sorry to interrupt." Lenore sat next to Camilla on the sofa. "It's just that we haven't spent much time together of late. I miss you."

Lenore's green eyes beseeched Camilla even more than her words. The two quarreling forces inside her grew loud again.

She's your sister. She needs you right now.

She's not, in fact, and she brought this on herself.

"No, thank you." Camilla's voice came out harsher than she'd meant for it to.

Hurt swam in those green eyes. "I... I really am sorry for interrupting."

"You've interrupted my whole *life*!" Camilla slammed her book shut. "Do you ever consider, for even a moment, how your actions affect others?"

Lenore shrank back. "Camilla, I'm sor—"

Camilla shot out of her seat. "That's all you ever say! But you never do anything about it, do you?" She coughed. Pain spiked in her head. Her anger flared, and every thought that had been swirling since Eamon's death came spewing out. "You're still friends with Rook, despite the fact he's probably the one who killed Eamon." Lenore reeled back as if Camilla had slapped her. "We all know what he is. That Dempsey has you collecting dirt on him is proof Rook is terrible and needs to be stopped, but you're too weak—"

"That is enough, Camilla!" Lenore stood too and balled her hands at her sides. "I know Rook never stopped being a criminal, that he does questionable things, but he is my friend. He's saved my life m—"

"Because he had to. The oath gave him no choice."

"What's wrong with you? Why are you being this way?"

Camilla speared a finger at Lenore. "Because if it hadn't been for you and your mother, mine would still be alive."

Lenore pressed her lips together so hard they went pale. The softer voice inside Camilla urged her to apologize, but she ground it beneath her heel. Lenore opened her mouth, shut it again, and shook her head. She stormed out of the library without saying another word.

Camilla flung herself back onto the couch, exhausted. Her anger still simmered, but venting her thoughts had lowered its fire to almost nothing and left a cold wind gusting through her. Well, that was done at least. Lenore knew where she stood.

That was very poorly done, the soft voice inside her said. Camilla ignored it. Thank goodness everyone else was out tonight, so no one would lecture her until tomorrow.

)(

Lenore sat on her bed, knees drawn to her chest. Since Eamon's death, her furniture and other possessions had been moved back to the Allens' manor. Mina and Neal had been good enough to store most everything left to her elsewhere. So far, Lenore had only gotten through bits of it. She was glad the Lees took ownership of everything else, including housewares, linens, and the townhome.

Bitsy snuggled into the crook beneath Lenore's legs. Since the horrific event, the little ringcat had barely left Lenore's bedroom, and never without her.

The window whispered open and closed. The mattress sank beneath Rook's weight as he pulled her into his arms. Bitsy chittered his displeasure, but they paid him no heed.

"Little bird, I'm so sorry." Rook nuzzled his nose into her hair. "I heard what Camilla said. It's not your fault."

Lenore had thought through everything. Her coming to the Allens, Dempsey ordering the hit on her, and the Halls of Justice attack had all happened independently of Rook. Who knew where they'd be without him? She understood Camilla was grieving, but Lenore hadn't recognized the woman spitting venom in the library. She worried the strain of everything had irreparably damaged their relationship. One more example of how her loved ones didn't need to die for her to lose them. It hollowed out another piece of her heart.

In response to Rook's words, she whispered, "I know."

"Neither was Eamon's death," he said.

Lenore sighed. "I know that too. That's down to the Reaper, along with so many other things. Even so, I shouldn't have married him."

Rook gave her a squeeze. "You did what you thought was best for everyone." His familiar scent wrapped around her and gave her strength.

"Everyone but myself. I'm not saying I wasn't happy, but it was the type of happiness where you make the best of things. Eamon knew I didn't love him, and he did his best anyway. For the most part."

"He worried," Rook said. "About different things than you, but it was genuine."

Lenore nodded, though her thoughts dwelled elsewhere. "He wanted me to succeed, to be happy. I've been thinking about that." Minutes passed before she found the energy for more words. Rook held her the whole time. "Are you planning on staying?"

Rook's hold tightened. "I'd love nothing more than to sit here with you all night, but I have a prior engagement. I'll stay as long as I can, though. Okay?"

Lenore nodded and leaned into him. She breathed in his comforting scent, while he stroked her hair. Even Bitsy settled. They sat together until Rook had to leave about an hour later. After he'd gone, Lenore considered changing into her nightgown and trying to sleep, but her mind was buzzing. She needed to take her mind off Camilla's odd behavior.

Lenore threw on her boots and left a note by the door.

)(

Lenore lifted the catamount door knocker again as another gust of frigid air whipped around her skirts. The thick hedges at the front of the property swayed and shushed in the cold night breeze. Just as she was about to knock a third time, Felicia opened the door.

"Lenore?"

"I'm so sorry to bother you." The lunacy of Lenore's idea crashed down on her, soaking her with clammy humiliation. "I, um… Well, I was thinking, and now I realize…"

Why had she thought she could just show up in the middle of the night? So what if Lowell had said she could? He obviously hadn't meant literally. What, suddenly the world owed her something because of what she'd lost? Stupid, weak Lenore.

"Why don't you come inside, pet?" Felicia's voice was gentler than Lenore had ever heard it.

Lenore shook her head, her cheeks on fire. "No, I'm sorry. I shouldn't have…" Just then, it clicked that Felicia was dressed as finely as ever. "What time is it?"

"Nearly half past eleven. Come now. I've just taken some bread out of the oven."

With the offer of bread and the way Felicia herded her inside, Lenore couldn't resist.

As Felicia shut the door behind them, another woman appeared. "Felicia, dear, is everythi—Oh, hello. Are you alright?" She was about Lenore's age, with a skin tone similar to Neal's.

"Yes, I'm fine. Thank you." Lenore couldn't bring herself to care that it was the most transparent lie in history. "I came to see Lowell."

"Ah, I see. You must be Lenore. He's told me all about you. I'm Calandra, and very pleased to make your acquaintance." Calandra smiled as warm as sticky buns in front of a crackling fire on a cold night. Her raven-dark curls bounced as she walked to the corridor and called, "Lowell, my love. Lenore's here."

Who is this woman? Lenore thought.

Neither Felicia nor Lowell had ever mentioned anyone else in their lives, but Calandra seemed on close terms with them. Felicia guided Lenore into the sitting room and armed her with fresh bread, jam, clotted cream, and hot apple cider. Lowell joined them and refilled Lenore's plate and cup every few minutes.

Lenore's wonder grew with each passing moment. "What are you all doing up at this hour?"

One side of Felicia's mouth curled up in amusement. Her eyebrow on the other side arched with incredulity. Lenore guessed what she was thinking and couldn't blame her—who was she to ask, given her own unorthodox visiting hours?

Lenore shifted her gaze to Calandra. "I remember where I've heard your name. Do you run the Raven's Tower?"

Calandra bobbed her head. "I do."

"Ah." Lenore was about to say more when she realized her private thoughts might be considered rude—she'd always pictured Calandra, well, older. Much older. So she switched tack. "It's one of my mentor's favorite haunts."

"Who is your mentor?" Calandra asked.

"Engineer Neal Allen."

Calandra smiled as she sipped her cider. "Yes, I know him. He's a wonderful person."

Silence descended on the room with an almost audible *fwump*. Lenore was grateful for Felicia and Calandra. They were so kind, but—

Felicia rose. "Well, I am sorry to leave you, my lamb, but as you pointed out, it is very late."

"It was lovely meeting you," Calandra said.

The two ladies left without another word.

Lenore stared at the space they'd filled. "Was it something I did?"

"Not at all, rose petal," Lowell said. "It's clear you don't want to socialize."

Lenore flopped back into the sofa. She closed her eyes to hold back tears. The way the cushions moved next to her told her Lowell had joined her in her slumping.

"I'm sorry for invading," she said. "I just need a place to breathe."

"Take as many breaths as you need."

Lenore rolled her head to the side and opened her eyes again. Lowell looked back at her, his uncovered eye pink with coming tears.

"I know I keep saying this, but I'm so sorry, my tinker belle."

Lenore's resolve crumpled. "I know. Thank you."

She leaned into Lowell and hooked her arm with his. They wept together for a while. When they'd both stilled, Lenore looked back at her friend.

"You've lost people too, haven't you?"

Lowell nodded. "I'm afraid the story isn't just mine to tell, but yes."

"How did you get through it?"

He pressed his shoulder against hers. "Felicia and I leaned on each other."

"And here I am, leaning on you." Lenore gave him a watery smile. "I can't tell you how much you mean to me. How much I appreciate everything you've done."

Lowell tapped the tip of her nose with one of his crooked fingers. "That's what friends do, if I'm not mistaken."

Her smile grew brighter.

)(

Lenore awoke to sunshine and birdsong streaming in through the sitting room's large windows. Cold radiated from them too, but it only touched her nose and ears since someone had covered her with a blanket. Lowell was gone, and Lenore heard movement elsewhere in the house. She stood. Her muscles complained after having been in the same position for so many hours. Following the sound to the kitchen, the smell of frying bacon, stewing beans, and brewing tea greeted her before she reached the door. Hearing her name, however, stopped her before she actually went in.

"But do you think Lenore would be interested?" Worry coated Lowell's tone. "She's been through so much. Yes, I know she feels suffocated there, but they're her family. Th—Oh! Lenore, is that you?"

She peeked into the kitchen and forced a smile. "Apologies, I wasn't trying to eavesdrop. How did you know I was there?" She regretted asking, unsure the answer would comfort her. After spending so much time around the siblings, she knew there was something… different about them.

"We heard you, darling." Felicia nodded to her boots. "It must have been terribly uncomfortable sleeping in those. Feel free to remove them. No need to stand on ceremony with us."

Lenore's toes did pinch, and the warm kitchen was a great relief after waking up in such a chilly room. She looked at the twins. Lowell was immaculately dressed in a different outfit from last night, but Felicia wore a housecoat over a long nightgown with rabbit fur slippers. Lenore decided to give her feet some relief.

"I apologize again for invading your house like this."

"Nonsense," Lowell said. "I've told you before, you're welcome anytime, day or night."

Lenore smiled. "Can I help with anything?"

"Just need a few more bits and pieces," Felicia said as she slid a tray of potato scones from the oven. Lenore had seen them during some of her ladies' brunches but had never tried one.

Lenore fetched jam jars, butter, plates, and whatever else they asked for. Questions about what she'd overheard plucked at her like violin strings. She kept her mouth shut, though. Guilt over listening in and even just being here played next to curiosity.

They sat down for breakfast in the dining room. The house was so quiet. She heard the wind blowing outside and branches scraping against the house. The fire crackled in the grate, and silverware against dishes reigned as the loudest noise in the house. Curious as she was, Lenore was grateful for the quiet and indulged in it. Felicia opened a newssheet and read while she ate. Lowell sketched in a book next to him. Only when Lenore had begun mopping up her egg yolk with her toast did anyone speak.

"Lenore, dear," Felicia began. "How would you feel about running some errands with me today?"

Lenore, mouth full of eggy bread, made a muffled inquisitive noise and looked between the siblings.

"To see how you might like living here," Lowell said in a stage whisper behind his hand and giggled.

Still chewing, Lenore cocked her head and made the same noise again, only louder. Felicia sighed and let her newssheet fall.

"Lowell, honestly, you have no finesse," she said. While Felicia folded the newssheet and set it aside, Lenore swallowed and straightened up. "We understand you've had a difficult time of late." Lowell made a face at Felicia. "Understatement of the year, yes, I am aware. No offense taken if you're not interested, but I am in need of a lady's companion. You're welcome to live here, have your own space—"

"Full access to the workshop," Lowell cut in. "In fact, you could have your own. Oh, that would be absolutely spiffing!"

"Yes." Felicia talked over Lowell and he quieted. "There are many options."

Lenore blinked at them. "I, em… I'm not certain what to say. I mean, thank you. That's such a generous offer. If you don't mind me asking, though, why me?"

Felicia chuckled. "It's no secret we keep our circle rather small. We have done very well over the years, but things are changing." She sighed. "Calandra, who is our dearest acquaintance, is making plans to move to Duskwood. Without her, I'm afraid I have no ladies with whom I am close, and even I must admit I've become accustomed to a little company. You are the ideal choice given your friendship with Lowell and knowledge of some of our other contacts."

Lenore turned back to her plate, biting her lip.

"You don't have to decide right now of course," Lowell hurried to add.

"Indeed, take some time to think about it."

Felicia returned to her newssheet and Lowell to his sketching.

The prospect was tempting. Moving back into the Allens' manor, while necessary, had felt like a step back. After her quarrel with Camilla, Lenore couldn't help but wonder if her adopted sister would prefer for Lenore not to return. Maybe it was too much togetherness, or perhaps the sight of Lenore reminded her too much of what had happened to Adelle. On the other hand, the idea of moving again exhausted Lenore. She chewed the last bit of her bacon as she thought. It'd be nice to assist Felicia after she'd permitted Lenore to come over and eat their food all the time. And who knew? Perhaps she'd get to know the enigmatic woman better.

"I will have to think on it," Lenore said at last, "but I would love to join you today, Felicia."

Felicia looked away from her paper and gifted Lenore a smile. "That sounds lovely. Thank you."

A broad smile stretched across Lowell's face. Lenore smiled too.

24

~Cold Clarity~

Lenore found Felicia's life surprisingly pedestrian, or this piece of it anyway. They went grocery shopping. Felicia took the same care with choosing her ingredients as her brother did with his building materials, turning the experience into a full-blown event. They spent most of the trip in companionable silence. When they did chat, they talked about nothing of consequence. It allowed Lenore to sort her thoughts, while Felicia considered the ripeness of winter squash and beetroot.

Lenore didn't think too long about the Reaper or revenge. That would come when Rook accomplished his part. For now, she ruminated on next steps. She balanced Felicia and Lowell's offer against her responsibilities at the museum. The role of a lady's companion entailed conversation and companionship—essentially a hired friend—but it also included attending social events together. Lenore wasn't certain what type of events Felicia attended or how much of her time Felicia would require. It'd be best to get an idea of Felicia's expectations first. Yes, good. A pre-decision list of priorities was coming together.

Lenore thought about Neal and Mina and even Camilla. The first two would worry about her, but Lenore had already decided she needed to do what was best for her. She'd do her best to soften the blow should it come. As for Camilla...

Lenore sighed as she thought about Camilla's outburst. Her pain must have rooted far deeper than Lenore had realized. She hoped the resulting scar wouldn't create a permanent rift between them.

When she and Felicia returned to the Thorne manor that afternoon, they were both surprised to find Lowell gone and Rook puttering around in the kitchen.

Felicia looked down her nose at him. "What are you doing?"

"I'm hungry." Rook shrugged. "Can I help put groceries away in exchange for food?"

Felicia shooed him away. "You'll only disrupt my system. Go somewhere that will keep you out from under my feet."

Rook sat in a chair against the wall, while Lenore did her best to make herself useful.

"I was hoping to get some sparring in this evening," he said. "Only if you're willing, of course. Felicia, is there a place you'd be willing to lend us?"

"There's an empty drawing room near Lowell's workshop. Just don't damage anything. In fact, Lenore, why don't you go now and get him out of my hair?"

"Much obliged, as always." Rook mimed tipping a hat to her.

Felicia waved him away. "Yes, yes."

"Are you sure you wouldn't like me to stay and help?" Lenore asked. She hadn't sparred since before Eamon's death and realized she missed it. Repaying Felicia for her generosity was a higher priority, though. Then again, so was not annoying the woman.

Felicia didn't look at them. "Not just now, thank you."

Once they were out of the kitchen, Rook took Lenore by the hand and trotted down the hall. He looked back at her, a cheeky grin on his face.

They found the room without difficulty. White dust sheets covered the furniture like snow. Rook swept one off a loveseat with an illusionist's flair. Lenore cocked her head, confusion crinkling her forehead.

"We don't have to spar," Rook said. "I thought you might like a little time to yourself."

Lenore gave him a crooked half-smile. "Wouldn't that mean without you?"

He flopped onto the loveseat, arms stretched across the back. "But I make for such excellent company." His shameless grin faded into something more tender. "Unless you really would like to be alone. I'd understand."

Lenore shook her head. She'd have some alone time when she went to bed, assuming Felicia and Lowell let her spend the night. She should send a note to update Neal and Mina. Lenore flicked her hands as if shaking off her thoughts like water droplets. Her brain and heart felt a bit mushy after everything, but her limbs itched to expend energy.

"I'd appreciate a good sparring match, actually," Lenore said.

Rook's brows creased. She couldn't tell if his eyes were assessing her or himself. "Are you sure that's what you want? We can sit if you like. Talk?"

"Blazes, no. That sounds exhausting. Everyone's been treating me like glass. I understand, bless them, but I don't want to be coddled. I want…" She fisted her hands into her skirt to stave off lurking sorrow. "I want a bit of normalcy."

Rook's eyes shone with sympathy for a moment before a smirk tugged at his lips. Whether it was an intentional shift for her sake or sincere feelings, Lenore felt encouraged.

"I'd best take care then, lest you bash me into a pulp."

Lenore laughed at the absurdity of the idea. It made her feel lighter than anything else had recently, and she was especially pleased she didn't feel guilty over it. Though Eamon had never liked Rook, she hoped he'd be pleased for these precious moments his old nemesis gave her.

"I might be rubbish against you," she said, "but you don't have to rub it in my face."

Rook winked. "You're getting better."

He removed his jacket and rolled up his sleeves before they pushed the furniture against the walls. Just as he finished, Lenore took advantage of the opening and jabbed his side.

"Ow!" Rook grinned as he sprang back. "You might warn me if you're going to play rough."

Lenore adjusted her position. "Sorry. Antsy."

He chuckled. "I can see that."

To no one's shock, Rook bested Lenore within minutes. When they almost tripped over an end table, he called for a break to move it. Lenore leapt forward and struck while his back was turned. Her punch landed against his ribs. She celebrated for a split second before Rook turned on her. He transformed into a panther, all instinct, strength, and grace. Lenore dodged, but he was quicker. He grabbed her hands and spun her toward the nearest piece of furniture—an armchair. She tripped and landed in it with a soft *oof.*

Rook planted a knee in the seat next to her and his hands on either side of her head. "That's very bad form, little bird." His voice thrummed low, rumbling from deep inside his chest.

Feelings she'd squelched for the sake of her situation surged in her, but the dust cloth cooling her sweaty neck gave her clarity. She was a guest in Felicia and Lowell's home.

Lenore steered the feelings toward stubbornness. "Just how easy have you been going on me?" She held Rook's dark gaze in hers.

He didn't move. His voice, sound and breath in equal measures, brushed against her face. "You know I don't want to hurt you."

"I want you to push me harder."

"Do you?" Rook inched closer.

Lenore felt the heat coming off his body and swallowed hard. Despite reminding herself she was in another's home, she grazed the tip of her nose against Rook's. "I won't get better otherwise."

Rook returned the gesture and whispered, "How hard *exactly* would you like me to push you?"

The sound of Lowell clomping down the corridor reverberated through the closed door. Rook pulled away. Relief and regret washed through Lenore.

Probably for the best. She reminded herself of all the reasons they'd never courted in the first place. *Yes, for the best.*

So why did she want to reach out and pull him back?

Rook leaned against the chair at a more acceptable distance and rested an arm across its back. Lenore was acutely aware of his warmth right above her head.

Lowell opened the door without knocking.

Lenore gave him an inquisitive look. "Why are you dressed like that?"

He wore what could only be described as beggar's rags, walked on a crutch, and wore no attachments on his arm. "Just doing a bit of work today," he said as if that explained everything. "I heard you two were fighting. Jolly exciting. Might I have a go?"

Rook's eyebrows bobbed. "You want to fight? Like that?"

Lowell waved a dismissive hand. "Oh no, don't be silly. With my latest improved limbs. Lenore has been helping me ever so much, and it's time they went through a proper test. I'm sure you're just the tough old chap to help me, hm, shall we say, regulate the new equipment."

"That reminds me." Lenore jumped up. "I have gifts for you. I… With things… It's the power packs. I haven't had them long, I promise."

Lowell shook his head. "Think nothing of it, my tinker belle. Do you think I could have the next go against Rook next?"

Lenore shook her head. "You can have all the next goes." She looked at Rook, and her heart beat a little faster. "I think I'm done sparring for the day."

)(

A wind as sharp as knives and cold as stone blew through the buildings and tugged on Camilla's hood. The sun setting over the horizon reminded her of an enormous floating pumpkin.

A pumpkin? she thought. *Perhaps I'm more ill than I realized.*

As Camilla tried to open the door to Thyme's Apothecary, an angry gust fought against her. A coughing fit overtook her, and she doubled over. The doorframe caught her before she realized she'd begun to sway. She pushed herself upright and took up the battle with the door again.

She'd thought she was getting better, but the day's early spring mildness had turned cold again. The sudden temperature change exacerbated whatever had brewed in her chest these last few weeks.

Lenore hadn't returned to the manor, so there'd been no one to tattle on Camilla. Even if Lenore had, though, Mina and Neal had been busy. Mina was helping Neal organize and train the new crisis responder unit. Kieran, of course, had spent the day sleeping in his cellar hideaway.

As soon as Thyme laid eyes on Camilla pushing through the door, the apothecarist came around the counter like a harried mother hen. "Oh my stars, look at you. Darling, come in from the cold." Thyme rubbed some heat into Camilla's arms. "You're like an icicle."

Foxglove Oran appeared through the doorway to the back. "Who's like an icicle? Oh, dearie me." She swept around to Camilla's other side and repeated Thyme's motions. It made Camilla feel like the middle of a well-meaning sandwich. "Let's get you into the back."

"Thank you," Camilla croaked before another coughing fit overtook her.

Thyme clicked her tongue. "You should have come to me sooner."

The Oran ladies herded Camilla into the little kitchen at the back of the shop. Mint and Ginger were there putting away canisters and vials of ingredients for the day. Before they could say anything, Thyme handed out assignments. She reminded Camilla of Mina in that moment. No wonder the two got on so well.

Foxglove ushered Camilla into a seat at the table and wrapped a blanket around her. Meanwhile, Thyme dropped a thick handful of dried herbs and spices into the smallest of the hot-water pots they kept topped up and going throughout the day. In their line of work, one never knew when they'd need hot water fast.

"Mother and I have to go back up front," Thyme said, "but the twins will take care of you." She turned to her daughters. "When this is ready, make sure she drinks the whole lot. And don't forget to replace the water."

"We won't, Mama," Mint said.

With that, Thyme and Foxglove returned to the shop. If pressed—and if healthy—Camilla could have assisted. There'd been enough crossover between the clinic and the apothecary shop throughout the years that each side was familiar with the other's practices.

The shop's back room was small but well-lit and comfortable. Like the storeroom across the hall and the shop up front, everything had been neatly arranged and labeled. It was more crowded than usual at the moment, since the kitchen served as a winter home to many of the Orans' plants.

Camilla blew her nose into her embroidered handkerchief with an ungainly *honk*. Ginger didn't strain the water into one of the usual delicate porcelain cups but into a thick ceramic jar. It oozed glorious heat into Camilla's hands as she held it against the spot where brambles chafed her airway. Warmth seeped through her as she breathed in steam from the cup.

"Drink up," Ginger said. "You heard Mama. You're to finish every drop while it's still hot."

That meant gulping. Camilla's sophisticated upbringing balked against the idea. She swatted the objection away, wanting to rid herself of this infernal cold as quickly as possible. She emptied half the mug before she had to take a breath and was pleased she didn't start hacking like her lungs wanted to escape. She finished the rest, and Ginger emptied the pot into her cup.

As Camilla drank her second serving, Ginger donned a special pair of spectacles with several lenses, which made her eyes appear huge. While Mint handed Ginger ingredients, Ginger dripped them into what Camilla thought might be the world's tiniest measuring cup. It was the size of a thimble and had miniaturized markings on the side. That's where the spectacles came in, so Ginger could read the tiny writing.

"This treatment is so lovely," Mint said. "It'll clear up that nasty cough of yours in no time."

The twins added powders to their liquid compound and emptied the resulting slurry into the top portion of a contraption called a nebulizer. They filled a reservoir at the bottom with water and lit a flame underneath. When the water boiled, steam would travel up a tube to where the medicine waited. Growing pressure carried the steam-medicine mixture to the mouthpiece, which Mint was busy attaching.

The smell of peppermint, along with something Camilla couldn't identify, wafted toward her.

"You'll need to breathe deeply," Mint said. "It'll feel strange. Very cold, in fact, but not to worry. That's perfectly normal."

Camilla was all too familiar with the process. She'd used nebulizers many times since chest infections had ailed her every winter as a child. It had gotten so bad one year that Mina procured a portable one with a squeeze pump, a bit like a perfume bottle. Thank heavens the issue had abated as she got older.

She thought Mint was exaggerating but lowered her face to the mouthpiece without comment and took in an entire lungful of air. Camilla nearly coughed again, though this time from surprise.

The mixture was far stronger than anything she'd been treated with before. It felt as if ice sheathed her throat, bringing her instant relief. The sore scratchiness melted away with each inhalation.

When the steam lulled, indicating only the scantest bit of water remained in the reservoir, Camilla lifted her head. "What did you add?"

Ginger exchanged a mischievous look with her sister. "It's a new recipe from Bone Port. Those Arnavi folks have traded a bit. Mama got her hands on some bottles of a new oil. Isn't it wonderful?"

"We can't sell it yet, though," Mint said. "Don't want to prescribe something we can't keep giving people, you know?"

Camilla nodded and took another deep breath. The effect was already fading, but the relief remained.

"Could I possibly take a bit with me? I'd like some for my—" Revulsion gripped her with slimy hands as she thought of going back to the catacombs. Back to the Reaper. She barely croaked out, "study group" a moment later.

The awe she'd felt for the Reaper had sizzled away like water in a hot pan. The thought of returning to those horrendous halls made her want to vomit. What had addled her brain so badly that she'd wanted to work for the Reaper?

"It sounds like we'd best give you a whole bottle." Ginger removed a vial the size of her pinkie from a cabinet. "That froggy voice tells me it'll take a bit more for you to shake this thing off. Now, a little goes a long way, so this might even last you into next winter."

Camilla took the vial, and the twins packed everything into a bag for her.

"I've included a new portable nebulizer too," Ginger said.

Camilla took her things and bid the twins goodbye before hurrying home. Her feet knew the way after so many years, leaving Camilla to think. She saw herself in her memories like another person, sleepwalking through a nightmare.

"Are you alright?"

Camilla looked around to find herself in the second-floor corridor. Kieran stood before her, rubbing his eyes. He must have just gotten up.

He leaned toward her and sniffed. "You smell minty. Is this a new perfume?"

Without thinking, she grabbed the Vampyre's hand, dragged him into her room, and shut the door behind them. As was proper, Kieran made a beeline for the sitting area but didn't sit. Camilla wrung her hands, debating with herself as she paced. They'd killed Eamon. Oh heavens, Beetle and Nightmare's injuries... Majesty's wounds... Nothing would stop them from killing someone else if she disobeyed. They'd kill her if she returned and was found out.

Think, Camilla. Who can help? Rook. Of course! And maybe even Dmitri too. But why would either of them help me? Rook is Dmitri's employer now, so he could simply order Dmitri to help me. And Lenore could help me convince Rook.

"Where's Lenore?" Camilla asked, her mind still whirling.

Kieran hesitated. "She sent a note to say she's still at the Thorne residence."

Was that mistrust in Kieran's voice? Had Lenore told him about their quarrel? Not that it mattered; Camilla's heart was beating like a hummingbird's wings. He had to know something was wrong.

Camilla covered her face with her hands. Stars, she'd forgotten. What a horrible fight they'd had. No wonder Lenore hadn't come back.

Camilla stopped pacing and pushed the Vampyre's suspicious gaze to the back of her mind. "You don't happen to know where that is, do you? No, of course you wouldn't. Apologies."

"Camilla, what is going on?" The timbre of Kieran's voice made her think he suspected her insane. Fair enough, given how she'd behaved lately.

Her vision swam. "Kieran, I said the most dreadful things to Lenore. We had a fight, and I... Oh, I was absolutely monstrous."

"I'm sure you can apologize when she returns." Kieran sat on the sofa.

Camilla still felt his eyes on her. *There's no time for that. How long do I have? Two days before I'm meant to go back.*

Her heart finally slowed. Two days was a good amount of time to figure something out. Yes, she could do this. She just had to get Rook here. She'd send a note for him to the Thorne residence. If he wasn't there—unlikely, since the man never strayed far from Lenore—then Lenore could get it to him. Camilla would send a second message to her and ask her to return with Rook in tow, just in case. If the latter happened, she'd ask for a private word with him.

"Are you sure everything is alright?" Kieran didn't veil the suspicion in his voice this time.

Camilla considered telling him the rest—he could protect the family—but when she opened her mouth to speak, a vision of him rearing back in disgust floated before her eyes. And why shouldn't he be revolted with her? She couldn't tell Kieran, who cherished humanity and fought so hard to maintain his, that she'd worked for a monster, a mastermind of chaos and suffering. Instead, she mustered every ounce of acting skill within her and gave him her best contrite smile.

"I'm sorry," she said. "What a mess I must appear. I lashed out at Lenore. I suppose with Eamon's death…" She swallowed a lump in her throat. "I'm frightened for our little family, and here I am, driving one of them away. You'll watch over us, won't you?"

Kieran softened and rose from the sofa. Taking her hands in his, he nodded gravely. "Of course. I will protect you all to the best of my ability."

)(

Kieran breathed a sigh of relief as he left Camilla's room. He didn't know what had changed, but she seemed back to her old self. Recently, in the dead of night, he'd tracked her scent to the Cobalt quarter only to lose it around the catacombs. The cemetery's smell of loam and decay was similar to what he'd smelled on her, though not exactly the same. It had made him wonder more than worry.

A knot of tightly coiled fear unwound itself in his stomach. He'd been afraid of what else he might have to do if he continued down that road.

25

~*"Just sit tight and trust me"*~

"You should have seen it, Felly!" Lowell crowed. "I sent Rook flying like a rag doll." Lowell mimicked Rook's flailing arms, nearly knocking over his water glass.

Rook didn't remember the experience being that dramatic, but his hosts were happy, so he didn't argue.

He, Lowell, Lenore, and Fetch sat around the Thornes' dining room table and were enjoying the delicious dinner Fetch had put together. Lenore wore an amused half-smile as Lowell told his tale, and Fetch kept throwing smug looks Rook's way. Rook smirked back as he tucked into his second Duskwood pudding—a buttery poof of baked batter with mixed-in herbs and covered in gravy.

He'd been rather impressed with Lowell during their match. It had been a long time since anyone had bested him one-on-one. Oya might have been the last one. Rook rotated the shoulder on which he'd landed during said event. The uncovered loveseat had caught him. Even so, he suspected he'd be sore for days to come. He chuckled at the memory of Lowell tossing him around with that new mechanical arm.

Someone knocking at the front door echoed through the house.

Fetch's expression soured. "We are eating *dinner*," she said, as if the knocker knew this and had plowed ahead anyway.

"Not to worry. I'll get it." Rook dabbed at his mouth with his napkin. "You sit back and relax."

Fetch smiled and turned back to hear the rest of Lowell's retelling. Rook opened the door to a courier, who handed him two notes in the same handwriting. One bore Rook's public name and the other Lenore's. He was tempted to tip the man a little extra and send his regards to Nieva—her business logo shone from the courier's coat—but that was Dmitri's job now. Rook didn't want to appear like he was overstepping his bounds. He had another rendezvous scheduled with the sourpuss soon anyway and would remind him of such things then.

Dmitri was upset about the debacle with Ebony. "I can't wait for you to take back over," his encoded letter had said. Rook had imagined him muttering it.

Too bad he'd had to tell Dmitri that he hadn't yet thought of a way to make that happen without the entire criminal underworld turning on them. Prince's ultimatum had left them between a larger rock and a harder place than Rook had calculated. He'd figure something out. He always did. Secretly, there were times he was glad for the "holiday", as he referred to it. It gave him more time to spend with Lenore, give Chrysalis breaks in her duties, and see how a legitimate business was run at Gadget's shop.

Closing the door behind him, Rook looked at the two notes from Camilla. Her delicate penmanship stared back at him. He opened the one addressed to him—she'd marked the inside with nothing but his symbol, the one they drew in the garden to summon him. Alarm bells rang in his head and, without another thought, he opened Lenore's as well.

Dearest Lenore,

Please accept my deepest apologies for what I said last night. I was absolutely horrid. I am so sorry for the pain I'm certain I've caused you during this difficult time. Please come home so I can repeat these sentiments in person. To show you how sorry I am, bring Rook. I know he's a source of comfort for you, and I want to make things better between us again.

Sincerely yours,
Your loving sister Camilla

Lost in thought, Rook flapped the notes against his other hand. Lenore's might have seemed innocuous if he hadn't read his first. He tucked both into his pocket; he'd look into the matter alone first.

When he sat back down at the table, Fetch turned the searching gaze she so often wore onto him. "Who was at the door?"

Rook smiled. "A courier. He got a bit turned around."

Keep Lenore here tonight, he mentally added, willing whatever strange ability Fetch possessed to receive the message.

She held his gaze for a moment before turning away. Rook went back to his meal and looked for an opening in the conversation. Thankfully, Lowell was just wrapping up his story.

"Rook, you missed the part about my incredible donkey kick," Lowell said.

"I was there." Rook chuckled, rubbing his bruised thigh. "I assure you, I recall it quite clearly."

Lowell laughed and proudly bobbled his head. "Yes, of course, old bean." He sipped his wine, still glowing with self-satisfaction.

Rook took his opportunity. "I apologize, but I will have to eat and run. Business never stops moving, you know?"

"Would you like to take a cab together?" Lenore asked. "I should be getting back to the Allens."

Blazes, yes. After their little encounter that afternoon, he'd have loved nothing more than to cozy up with her in a dimly lit cab, even just for a few minutes. Whatever Camilla had called on him about had better be bloody important.

"Why don't you stay another night?" Fetch asked Lenore. "We love having you here. The house gets so dull with just the two of us, and I have a New Year's menu to start crafting."

"Felicia makes the best New Year's feasts," Lowell said. "Oh, do stay, Lenore. It'll be ever so much fun."

Lenore looked so happy Rook considered staying, just to see what other joys they could rouse in her that evening.

"Well, it's hard to refuse when you put it that way," Lenore said. "I'll just need to send another note home—" Her voice wobbled over the word. "—to let them know where I am."

"I have a little extra time in my schedule tonight," Rook said. "I'll deliver it for you." He'd give her the one from Camilla when he returned tomorrow. It'd tie everything up nicely and get him an extra visit with the deal.

)(

Within the Allens' grounds, Rook scuttled over the courtyard wall. He prepared to land on feet soft as a cat's, but the icy stone had other plans. His arms pinwheeled as he slid on touchdown, and he landed on his back, knocking the wind out of him. He coughed, sat up, and flicked his eyes across the garden.

Did anyone see that?

His search stopped on a figure wrapped in a fur-trimmed cloak. The darkened cowl stared at him.

Rook stood and sauntered over as if the incident hadn't happened. He made out golden tresses beneath the cloak's hood, as well as her eyes. They looked haunted.

"Already here?" he said. "Were you really willing to wait out here all night? What impressive dedication. I'm touched." The harsh line of Camilla's mouth grew grimmer. Time to try a different angle. "You're the last person I expected to send for me."

"I know," replied Camilla.

He waited, but she didn't elaborate. "Are we going to stand in the cold for hours, or will you tell me why you asked me to come?" Rook flashed a cheeky smile. "Or maybe you just missed me?"

Camilla scowled. "Don't flatter yourself. I need your help."

"Are you sure we can't discuss this inside? It's a mite nippy."

"Worried you might fall over again?"

Some of the warmth leached from his smile. "You're not exactly getting on my good side. Whatever you're offering me had better be good."

Camilla lifted her chin. "You won't hurt me."

"No, I'm sure the night stalker has your back." Rook's eyes roved over the garden. "Hello, Kieran."

"You're right, but that's not why. Lenore's too important to you."

"That's hitting below the belt, don't you think?" Camilla's scowl deepened, and he bowed his head. "Apologies. I didn't mean that how it sounded. It is rather unfair, though, don't you think?"

"I'm sorry, but it's important. She can't know about this. No one can."

"Except Kieran."

Camilla said nothing.

Rook folded his hands behind his back. "You keep driving up the price, and I haven't even heard what you want. Do you mind terribly hurrying this along?"

She took a deep breath. "I've infiltrated the Collective. And you're going to help me get out."

Throwing back his head, he laughed until his sides hurt and tears ran down his face.

"Are you quite done?" Camilla demanded.

Rook commended himself. He hadn't even meant to annoy her that time.

He quelled his laughter to a chortle. "Hoo! Powderpuff, you're hilarious. Why did you really call me here?"

"I'm serious, Rook." She stamped her foot. "I... They deceived me somehow. I think I must have been drugged. I've been studying under the Reaper. They're teaching me how to do organ transplants."

Belief dragged itself over him—the mention of organ transplants had done it. He studied Camilla as if she'd transformed into a different person. "You? You of all people have been visiting that freak? In the catacombs? On purpose?"

"I can't explain it. My mind was completely befuddled. I actually thought..." She made a disgusted noise. "I thought the Reaper was awe-inspiring, like a divine being."

Rubbing his chin, Rook began to pace. "And you're in the Collective's confidence now?"

Camilla's eyes grew wide. "You don't honestly think I can go back? They'll kill me."

Rook sized her up. "No, I don't suppose you can. And my best mimic can't fake your skills or knowledge. I suspect you really will have to stay away."

"That's not enough," Camilla said. "I need you and Dmitri to stop them."

"We're working on it, but these things take time."

"Work on it faster! This is my family we're talking about. Their lives are at risk."

Rook said, "I'm all too aware of the danger. Believe me, I want your family to remain safe as much as you do, but I have to stay my current course." He turned to walk away. "I'll keep your secret, Camilla. Make it easier for you to repair some of those bridges you've tried to torch. Just lay low and—"

A delicate hand clamped onto his arm. Slowly, Rook turned to see her glaring at him, her jaw set. His eyes traveled down to where her fingernails dug into his coat.

"I've removed people's digits for less," he said, his voice low.

"Don't brush me off. They will find me. They will get to one of us. You know what they did to Eamon."

Rook shook her off, but she grabbed him again. He wrenched her hand off him with just enough strength to do the job and more than enough care to ensure he didn't hurt her. "I'll thank you to not touch me again."

Camilla took a step back.

Scanning the garden again, he said, "Kieran's not here. He doesn't know about this little scrape of yours, does he?"

She rubbed her wrist and kept her head down. "No. I thought about telling him, but I can't face him."

"But you said you didn't know what you were doing. You think he'll blame you anyway?"

At last, Camilla raised her head and looked at Rook. "You really have killed people? In more than self-defense, I mean."

"How do you think I got to where I am? And Kieran still seems to like me well enough."

She looked despondent. Rook's voice grew gentler when he spoke.

"I will do everything I can to ensure your family's safety. Now, goodnight." He stalked off.

"Rook, I'm sorry," Camilla called after him. "Please, I truly need your help."

"No."

"Then at least give me a weapon!" Her voice tightened and cracked. "I can't just sit around and wait. At least then I'd have some way of defending myself. I could even kill the Reaper."

He turned back. "Don't be stupid, Camilla. Lenore's lost enough people, and you're one of her most important."

"Then help me!"

He walked on.

"I can give you money," she said.

"I don't need it."

"I'll call off the restriction."

Rook paused before spinning on his heel to face her again. "And?"

Camilla pinched her features together, eyes wild. "And what?"

"What else? No one holds Lenore's keys but her. The restriction is merely an inconvenience."

"More people are going to suffer. Give me something to work with."

His eyes hardened. "The Reaper will fall, I'll make sure of it, but that world is no place for you. It kills whatever light it can, so stay far, far away."

"Help me, Rook!"

"I'd prefer for you to live. I'm sorry, Camilla. Just sit tight and trust me. You have to let Dmitri and me do what we're good at."

With that, Rook sauntered off. Perhaps he would get Camilla a weapon, but he had to think about the right one.

)(

Chrysalis hunched against the tree trunk, nothing more than another shadow in the cold night air. She watched Rook go. Camilla's shoulders hunched as she began to weep. Chrysalis's chest ached for the girl who looked so forlorn, but she couldn't blame Rook and was plenty grateful he'd decided against having her pose as Camilla. She shuddered at the idea of going anywhere near those creepy catacombs.

Seeing Rook and then Dmitri struggle as they had of late had made Chrysalis worry for her own place in their organization. She had nowhere else to go, nowhere else she could make her way as she had there, so she too could only sit back and trust they would succeed. Her heart went out to Camilla as she cried alone in the garden. Chrysalis had been where Camilla was now. Back then, she'd had only herself to depend on.

The similarity between their situations almost tempted Chrysalis out of hiding. She didn't, of course—her mission was to remain unseen. She wouldn't risk the assignment for sentimentality. Nevertheless, she pondered what she could do to help.

26

~Letting Go~

Lenore awoke in the Thorne residence to sunshine, a puffy coverlet, and the smell of breakfast cooking downstairs. She'd have to go home today, especially given this was the third day of wearing the same clothes. Felicia had given her a nightgown several sizes too big but comfortable nonetheless. During their New Year's feast planning last night, Felicia had also offered to order something simple.

"I know several excellent tailors," she'd said. "We just need to provide your dimensions and they'll courier over a new ensemble first thing."

"Thank you, but I've intruded upon your hospitality more than enough," Lenore replied.

"Nonsense, we love having you," Lowell had said. "I'll let Felicia handle the order, however. It wouldn't do for me to be privy to such personal information. No indeed."

Lenore had given a playful head wobble. "And you are nothing if not a gentleman."

Lowell had preened at that. She'd won in the end, despite a few more tries by the twins.

Now, as Lenore looked around her borrowed room, she wondered what her reception at the Allens' manor would look like. She'd avoid Camilla. Yes, that would be best. Although, maybe she'd leave a note under Camilla's door to say "I love you." Losing so many people had made her realize the importance of sharing the sentiment.

Lenore got out of bed and donned an exceptionally soft dressing gown. She probably should have dressed first, but she worried she was already running late. That, and she wasn't keen to step back into her grimy clothes.

Downstairs in the kitchen, she nearly bumped into Rook as he played assistant to Lowell and Felicia.

"Good morning," Lowell said. "Don't you look bright-eyed and bushy-tailed."

Lenore didn't think that was the least bit true but smiled anyway.

"This came for you." Rook handed her a note. Her name looped across the front in Camilla's handwriting. "I admit to opening it. I was curious after what happened the other night."

Lenore gave him a scolding look. "Please don't read my mail."

"My apologies." He actually looked sincere about it.

As Lenore read the letter, a smile bloomed on her face. She pressed it to her chest. "Oh, thank goodness!"

Felicia piled several trays with breakfast food. "Good news then?"

"Extremely. I'm afraid I must go at once."

Lowell's face fell. "But we made breakfast."

Lenore stopped in the doorway. "Oh. Oh yes, you're absolutely right. I apologize. I just got so excited. Thank you both for everything. I really must leave after breakfast, though."

"Of course, pet." Felicia handed Rook one of the trays. "We understand."

Breakfast was a quieter affair than dinner the night before. Felicia read her newspaper, while Lenore and Lowell batted project ideas back and forth. Rook hummed and flipped through Lowell's sketchbook when Lowell wasn't occupied with it.

"You looking for something in particular?" Lowell asked.

"Something small but powerful. Easily hidden."

"I might have just the thing. There's a prototype in my workshop if you'd like to look at it after breakfast?"

"Perhaps later," Rook said. "I have a prior engagement, haven't I, Lenore?"

He gave her a cheeky grin, and she indulged him with a smile. She couldn't be happier Camilla was extending such an impressive olive branch to Rook. Lenore would have been pleased even without it. Maybe things were settling. Now she just needed to wait for Rook's plan to catch the Reaper, whatever that was. She'd ask about it after she made up with Camilla.

)(

The Allens' manor was empty when they arrived. A note for Lenore from Neal and Mina sat in the receiving hall. They'd gone to do more crisis responder training, and Camilla had her own errands to run that day. They hoped to see her that evening, however, and said they missed and loved her.

"That's very sweet," Rook said.

"I suppose we can stay and wait," Lenore said. "Unless you have somewhere else you need to be?"

The warmth of his gaze made her heart somersault. "Not at all, but I have a different idea. Would you like a surprise?"

"What's the surprise?"

He smirked and leaned toward her. "It wouldn't be a surprise if I told you, now would it?"

A line of worry remained between her brows. "I don't suppose so, but I do need to speak with Camilla today."

"I promise to have you back at a perfectly decent time." Rook took her hand and swept a kiss along her knuckles.

Lenore smiled and nodded as a gentle warmth glided over her cheeks.

Not long after, they arrived in the Cobalt quarter via cab. Rook led her past shops and fishmongers, bakeries and gaming clubs. They doubled back, him always checking over his shoulder, and finally skirted around the side of a restaurant near the docks. He pressed a finger to his lips as they climbed the backstairs. A salmon-colored door greeted them on the fourth or fifth floor— Lenore hadn't counted on the way up. Once they were through, she was surprised to see no fewer than seven locks on the other side. Rook took great care to secure each one.

"When you have as many enemies as I do," he said, "and you have an actual door, you have to take precautions."

Lenore nodded, surprised Rook had anyplace that actually appeared as a place.

He pointed at the windows. "Escapes are there."

She smiled, appreciating his thoughtfulness.

One room and the water closet comprised the entire abode. The faint sounds of boats in the nearby bay, along with gull cries and other harbor noises, drifted through the broad windows. The furniture was simple but functional. A few pieces bore Gadget's logo. In one corner sat an assortment of items Lenore didn't understand, so, naturally, she approached. A horizontal bar fixed to the wall hovered a few feet above her. Nearby sat a contraption with a handle attached to a thin cable, which was connected to a wheel inside a cylinder of water. A seat and spots for someone to place their feet on either side had been affixed to the other end.

Rook sauntered over. "A rowing machine. It's for building strength."

"Did you design this?" she asked. Rook shook his head. "Lowell?"

"No, though I reckon he could make some improvements. I commissioned this after seeing some folks with their canoes in Bone Port."

Lenore let her eyes linger on the clever machine before turning back to Rook. "You said Lowell could make some improvements. So he hasn't ever seen it?"

A slow smile drew across Rook's face.

She smiled back. "That means he's not been here before." Rook shook his head. "Who else knows about this place?"

"No one except you." Rook's voice crooned low and soft. "You'll understand if I ask you not to come here without me. This place needs to remain a secret."

Lenore cocked her head at him. "Why show me?"

He took a step closer, so close their bodies nearly touched. "I know you found some solace with Fetch and Lowell. I thought I might be able to give you a bit too."

"But only when you're here as well." Lenore smirked at him and was surprised when he didn't return the expression.

"I'll leave if you'd like to be alone. We'll just need to coordinate when I can come back for you. Or, if you don't want to stay, if you'd rather go back to the Allens', that's fine too."

Lenore's features melted into incandescent gratitude. She placed a hand on his arm. "That's very generous. You're always so patient with me."

He shrugged. "You're patient with all the secrets I keep from you." Then his lips tilted into a lopsided smile. "Besides, someone taught me that's what you do when you love someone."

Lenore's heart fluttered against her ribcage. The look in Rook's eyes fed something she'd starved for so long. She gave it free reign now, drank in the look, and suddenly couldn't find her voice. A heavy, silent beat passed between them. She saw the moment Rook began reading her, in the way his eyes flicked from one feature to the next.

His gaze fell on her lips last and lingered there. She swallowed, trying to find her voice.

Rook broke out of her grasp and stepped back. "I'm sorry. I didn't mean to—"

"Please, don't."

She reached for him again. Her hand hung in the air. Rook looked to it, to her, and raised his own hand to meet it. Their fingers brushed and entwined. They took half a step toward each other.

The way he'd taken such deliberate steps to ensure she felt safe and comfortable despite the desires smoldering in his eyes brewed a new type of trust in Lenore. That he'd leave her here if she asked, that he'd distance himself with a word from her and get her a cab home, drew her to him.

"I've spent so much time and energy doing the *right* things," she said. "I played pretend, and all it's done is hurt everyone. I'm sick of pretending." She locked eyes with him. "It's time I focused on what I want, but…"

He released her hand to curl his fingers around her face, brushed his thumb over her blushing cheek. "What do you want? Ask anything of me."

"Rook, I love you too." A relieved laugh followed her confession; pressure eased off Lenore's heart as if it had released her from a vise. "I have for so long, but secrets do damage. There's so much you haven't told me."

His eyes danced and his jaw hung slack, as if he couldn't believe what he'd just heard. It drew a quiet giggle from Lenore.

Rook grinned back for a moment, then grew serious again. The light in his eyes remained, however, as he tucked a lock of her hair behind her ear. "My secrets are to keep you safe."

Lenore took his hand in hers again. "I know, but there's greater safety in knowledge. Otherwise, I'm walking blind. Please, Rook. I'm not saying tell me everything here and now. I just want to start knocking down the walls."

While his eyes stared down, his mouth ticked up. "Knocking down walls, eh?" His throat bobbed in a silent chuckle. He played his free fingers through loose tresses of her hair. "I did say ask me anything, didn't I?" Rook took a deep breath and murmured, "Safety in knowledge." When his expression hardened, she knew he'd made a choice. "What if I told you I run the underground market? Or rather, I did."

Lenore blinked at him, not quite sure she'd heard him right. "Are you serious? I used to go there, before I met the Allens."

"Did you?" He didn't sound interested in the story just now. Rather, his voice rumbled low and husky. His hand swept through her dark locks, curling them around his slender fingers. "I also kept Camilla's note from you yesterday evening." He raised his eyes to meet hers again. Real fear shone in them. "Truly, I was only concerned for your well-being. Can you forgive me?"

Rook's hand brushed past her throat as it played with her hair. She bent her neck toward the touch before realizing the distraction. Lenore tilted her head in the opposite direction. He paused, and she fixed him with a stern look.

"That sort of thing needs to stop. Immediately." Then she held his hand to her lips, laying a kiss along each knuckle. "And yes, I forgive you." He hadn't kept it secret long; she'd see Camilla this evening, so no harm done.

He beamed. His gaze burned with the intensity of blue fire. It warmed something inside Lenore. "You have my word." He pressed a soft kiss to her forehead. "We are partners, after all." Another kiss. "I apologize for not treating you as such."

Lenore lifted her face for the last kiss. Rook cupped her head in his hands and brushed his nose against hers. Then he closed in. One kiss became two. Rook wrapped his arm around her waist and pulled her close as two flowed into three. Lenore ran her fingers along the back of his neck. A sound of appreciation thrummed in his chest, so she did it again. He thrummed louder and walked her back a few paces to the wall.

Pressed between it and him, a laugh bubbled up from her throat. Rook retreated a few inches, but his fingers never stopped stroking the nape of her neck, nor did his other hand move from her hip.

"What?" he asked.

"This is how we met." She laughed again.

Rook laughed too and kissed her neck. Muffled between kisses, he said, "This is *not* how we met. I would remember that."

Lenore wanted to explain the wall and—Oh, but who cared right now? Rook gently bit the spot where her neck met her shoulder, and a small moan escaped her throat.

"Can I hear you say it again?" he asked.

"Say what?" Lenore squeezed Rook's shoulders as another kiss sent a shudder through her.

He hissed and pulled back. "Sorry. Sore from sparring." Lenore kissed his shoulder. "Can I hear you say the thing again? About how you feel about me?"

She placed her hand over his heart and smiled as it drummed against her palm. "I love you, Rook." She felt joy pour into him as he released a shaky breath. "I love y—"

Rook's mouth consumed hers. He dragged the tip of his tongue across her lips. Lenore had forgotten how good he tasted. She wanted to remain here in this secret place forever with their hearts crashing against each another.

Disappointment rushed in when he pulled his lips away. He bent close to her ear and nuzzled the side of her face. His breath blew hot against her skin, making her shiver with pleasure.

"I love you, Lenore. And I have a whole *list* of ways to show you how much." His fingertips stroked the column of her neck. "Will you have me?"

"Stars, yes," she breathed.

Rook's every movement slowed to an exquisite pace. Not a second went unsavored. Still kissing her, he gently guided her to the bed. His grip remained loose enough for her to pull away, but Lenore pressed herself against him as she followed. The luxurious mattress sank beneath Rook as he sat and pulled her into his lap. Lenore sighed as he ran his nose along the line of her jaw. He swept her hair aside, his dexterous fingers tangled and twined within her locks. His palms massaged her neck while he played. Lenore giggled, feeling Rook smile against her as she unbuttoned his waistcoat, his shirt, and ran her hands over the solid planes of his chest. He rumbled his approval, vibrating against her fingertips. The musky scent of him clouded around them, and Lenore took deep draughts. Rook traced the shell of her ear with the tip of his tongue, nibbled down her throat and along her collarbones.

He hummed against her shoulder, nosing the edge of her sleeve off. "You taste like honey and sunshine."

"You feel like safety," Lenore whispered. "And home."

Rook released a ragged breath, and his mouth claimed hers again, fervent but tender. As Lenore smoothed her hands under his shirt and pushed it off him, his heartbeat hammered against her. She ran her hands over his back, raked her fingernails across each rigid muscle. Rook groaned. His lips, teeth, and tongue scraped against the sensitive skin of her throat, slow and delicious. His hands rippled down to Lenore's waist, fingers dragged along her thighs. She purred and rolled her hips into his, melting beneath every touch. Slowing his attentions, he lowered himself onto the mattress.

"I'm yours, little bird," he said, dark eyes alight.

Lenore sank atop him. Rook's skin tasted salty as she kissed his lips, his neck, his chest. His sinewy muscles pulled taut beneath her palms as he caressed the length of her, across her ribs, and around her back. His hands slid along her spine. With a soft moan, Lenore arched beneath his nimble fingers as he loosened her corset laces. Layer by layer, with reverent care, they divested each other of the rest of their clothing.

Wherever Rook's skin touched, Lenore's ignited. He traversed every inch of her, dropping kisses and nips into hollows and curves. His calloused hands gently scraped over delicate flesh. Lenore examined the constellation of scars peppered across Rook's body. Stripes and gouges, nicks and dots. She kissed each one, lingering on those she knew he'd received for her, and thrilled at the sounds of pleasure this elicited. Rook returned her affections with enthusiasm, seemingly determined to tick every item on the promised list. Using every tool at his disposal—fingers, voice, lips, tongue, and more—he experienced every part of her.

Little by little, Lenore felt him let go of the carefully controlled desire she knew he'd held in check all this time.

27

~Chocolate and Sage~

Camilla had to stop herself from drumming her fingers against the table. Dmitri wasn't late yet, but arriving early had made it feel like he was.

The chocolate house was bustling with patrons. Dishes and silverware clinked. Every sound grated against her patience. Steam rose from cups and long-handled chocolate pots, making the room feel stuffy. Camilla dearly wished to curl up on the colorful brocade-and-walnut sofa with a steaming cup of hot cocoa like some of the other ladies in the place had done, but it wouldn't have been proper. Not indecorous, but certainly not what was expected of a lady of her station. And she had no wish to attract anyone's attention.

The chocolate house served dual purposes. It was a casual meeting spot as well as noisy enough to cover her conversation. Camilla sipped her hot chocolate, appreciating its warmth and depth of complex flavors. Thick, molten, and nutty with a twist of orange—a lavish addition imported from Bone Port.

Is this the last cup I'll ever enjoy? she wondered.

Rook had given her nothing, and she'd begun to despair that Dmitri would follow suit. Rook was slippery. He might see Dmitri as an exception to keeping her secret since they worked together. A plan had begun to form in Camilla's mind, but she needed to exhaust all her other options before she could bring herself to enact it.

"There you are."

Camilla jumped, sloshing her hot chocolate. At least she'd drunk enough to avoid spilling any.

The man standing next to her sofa held himself in a familiar stance—formal, wooden even, with his hands behind his back. He wore a simple black suit.

"Dmitri?" she whispered.

Behind a face that wasn't his, she recognized his eyes and neat haircut. Dmitri's cheeks were fuller, his skin a few shades darker. His nose and chin, both meatier, jutted out. His eyebrows frizzed twice as thick as normal, a pair of angry caterpillars.

He bobbed once in assent. She motioned for him to sit and looked around to make sure he hadn't attracted any attention.

Satisfied, she asked, "What on earth do you have on your face?"

"A disguise," he said. "I disappeared from the Enforcer order, if you recall."

Camilla did, but she hadn't thought about what that meant. Could Dmitri never risk going out as himself again? If Magistrate Smoke had his way, was she doomed to the same life? She hadn't heard anything since she'd drugged his drink, nor had she heard from Falcon since their argument. No Enforcers had bothered her again. She hadn't seen any watching her either. Surprising, as she'd expected some kind of surveillance. Or was that paranoia talking? She sent those thoughts to the back of her mind. Now wasn't the time, which frustrated her even more—it was still a pressing issue.

"Thank you for meeting me," she said.

A waiter came by, and Camilla ordered for Dmitri even though he hadn't asked for anything. A basic hot cocoa seemed the perfect choice. Dmitri wasn't a man of frills, after all.

After the waiter left, she said, "This is on me."

"Thank you." Dmitri sat up straight and stiff on the pretty couch. "I appreciate you being open to exploring our friendship again."

She gave him a smile that felt tighter than she'd intended. She resisted the urge to look around again. Dmitri's ramrod bearing had to look odd to their fellow guests.

"Please, relax," Camilla said. "We used to be far more at ease with each other."

Dmitri's eyes flicked over her own guarded posture. Camilla forced herself to assume a more casual attitude by leaning back on the sofa. He followed, though she suspected they still looked rather stilted.

"How have you been?" she asked.

The waiter returned with a fresh pot of plain hot chocolate. Camilla thanked him as he served Dmitri's drink and topped up hers from her pot. Primroses danced across the delicate porcelain cups and saucers. The design was far too cheerful for her mood.

Alone again, she said, "How's working for our mutual friend then? Is it very different from the other positions you've held?"

Amusement twinkled in Dmitri's eye as he sipped. "Friend? That's very funny. And you make it sound like I've worked for a handful of banks."

Camilla's head waggle said, *Well, it's not like I can say what you've really done.*

Dmitri nodded. "It's fine."

"And you're... happy?" She looked for any sign that Rook had shared her secret.

Dmitri shrugged, which soothed her—he never shrugged unless he was truly comfortable. "It's the only job that provides protection. That has to be enough."

"Ah." Well, that was rather... dour. "I daresay it's better than your last one." She gave him a meaningful look over her cup.

"Indubitably."

Camilla leaned forward and did her best to dredge up some measure of care for him. Surprisingly, she found a good bit of genuine concern. She'd meant it when she offered to try rekindling their friendship, but she must have missed him more than she'd realized. That, or desperation was taking over.

"I'm curious," she said. "How did you ever survive working for that... individual? I can only imagine how horrendous it must have been."

"I laid low." Dmitri looked around before whispering, "The Reaper tolerated me. He handpicks his followers; I volunteered to join. He didn't kill me, but he also didn't care about me. I did my job and stayed as far away from the rest as I could."

Camilla didn't address Dmitri's incorrect pronoun use. It would be too revealing. His assumptions, however, prickled her.

She set her annoyance to the side. An issue for another time. Instead, she rolled Dmitri's words over in her head. No wonder he hadn't fallen victim to the Reaper's spell. It gave her an idea, one that brightened the haze of gloom and fear that had followed her since Thyme's Apothecary.

"I'm sorry you ever had to be involved with them. How is your family keeping?"

Dmitri had worked to help support them since adolescence, but he hadn't been the one to tell her. She'd learned about it during a visit to their house when they had been courting. His father had mentioned what a good son Dmitri was for doing it. Camilla had thought Dmitri might die of mortification right then and there.

"They're well, thank you," Dmitri said. "And how are you with... everything?"

His eyes shone softly, full of unspoken meaning and sympathy. It poked at tender places in her heart with a sharp stick.

She smiled. "I..." She intended to say she was well, managing, fine—any of the throwaway answers people gave—but the words stuck in her throat. Anger sluiced along her vocal cords and shot from her mouth. "The more I learn about my father, the more I wonder how my mother ever married the wretch." Dmitri's eyes widened, and Camilla slapped a hand over her mouth. "Goodness, I am so sorry. I don't know where that came from."

Dmitri paused. "He certainly was a complicated man."

"Complicated?" Camilla forgot to keep her voice down. She looked around; no one was looking their way. The usual din buzzed in the air, which had probably muddled her outburst. She poured herself another cup of hot chocolate and sipped the comforting concoction. "We both know what he did. 'Complicated' is too generous a word."

Dmitri dipped his head in apology. "You're right. And having known your mother the little that I did, I don't know how she could have married him either."

"Sometimes I think I should just take Mina and Neal's surname, be done with him entirely, but then I'd lose my mother's name, Husselbee."

"Didn't you once tell me you embroidered the two initials onto a handkerchief?" Dmitri asked.

Camilla smiled weakly and reached into her bag. She produced a lace-edged handkerchief and showed him the corner. A much younger her had messily embroidered an H and an A on either side of a larger C in bright pink. "I've been carrying this around with me of late. It brings me comfort." Her voice softened. "Would you mind telling me about your experience with her? Just the good bits, please. Nothing dark."

Dmitri shifted in his seat. His expression changed to something one might wear if they'd been told to wrangle a dozen cats into their pocket. "I'm not sure how much I have, but I'll do my best."

Camilla listened, savoring each word as she savored her drink. As Dmitri shared, she saw the brave, strong woman Adelle had been in a new light.

It gave Camilla courage for what she had to do.

)(

As Rook and Lenore shared a cab back to the Allens' manor that afternoon, a cloud rolled in to darken their otherwise extremely enjoyable journey. At the earliest opportunity, he had closed the curtains, pulled Lenore against him, and kissed her like it was the first time. He was gobsmacked at how right everything felt with her. Elation trilled inside him as scenes of what they'd shared replayed in his head. After everything they'd been through, this gift didn't feel real. Even if he'd wanted to, he didn't think he could shake the ridiculous grin stretching across his face.

Too soon, Lenore pulled away from him and asked, "What's your plan to capture the Reaper? I meant to ask before but got... distracted."

"A delightful distraction, if I may be so bold." He kissed the tip of her nose.

She grinned, green eyes alight with joy. "Undeniably. Still..."

Her voice faded as Rook trailed kisses below her ear. "Are you really interested in that right now? I can't do this and strategize at the same time." She made a purring noise he rather liked. "Your choice."

It took a moment, but she collected herself and pulled away. "Yes, please tell me."

There wasn't much to tell. She vaguely knew about his and Dmitri's machinations to crumble the Reaper's operation. Back at the flat, Rook had told her about being out of his own organization. As far as catching the Reaper and delivering them to Lenore, it would require an all-out assault on the catacombs. As Dmitri had said, they were a fortress unto themselves. Rook still didn't like the idea of Lenore taking on the burden of killing the Reaper herself, but she was determined.

Rook had considered tipping off the Enforcers as to the Collective's whereabouts, but ratting out an entire syndicate was one of the worst crimes in the underworld. Even with the other crime lords in on the scheme, a move like that would get him killed. Even just sending an anonymous letter carried risk and little chance of being taken seriously.

He said, "I'm still working on it. The Reaper rarely leaves their base. It'll be a big job."

"But you *are* working on it?" Lenore asked.

"Yes, I am. That maniac needs to be stopped."

"Thank you."

He'd been about to say more—nothing of real consequence—when Lenore pressed her lips to his. He was glad no one was home when they arrived at the manor. Except Esther, of course. Rook grinned as she herded him into the kitchen.

"I'll take good care of him." Esther shooed Lenore up the stairs. "You go get yourself freshened up, my dear."

This was definitely the best day of his life. Esther sat Rook down in an out-of-the-way corner of the kitchen. She set some leftover cold meat, rolls, cheese, butter, and jam in front of him and returned to prepping dinner. Rook chatted idly, asking after her children and grandchildren, while he ate and reflected.

Lenore, dressed in clean clothes, joined them soon after. She was tucking into her first roll when Camilla's voice rang out from the receiving hall. Mouth full, Lenore leapt from her seat and returned a muffled response. In a fashion so unlike her usual graceful self that even Esther looked surprised, Camilla dashed into the kitchen and threw her arms around her adopted sister, nearly bowling Lenore over in the process.

284

"Lenore, I'm so sorry. I was perfectly awful. Can you ever forgive me?" Tears were already running down Camilla's face.

Lenore hugged her back. "Are you alright? I was so worried."

The girls talked over each other as they exchanged apologies and heartfelt words for the next minute. Rook exchanged a smile with Esther. Camilla seemed in a much better place than last night. Well, maybe—while Esther turned away to fetch a mixing spoon, Camilla shot him a glare over Lenore's shoulder that could have seared flesh.

She assumed a mask of congeniality. "I did say bring Rook along, didn't I?"

"I hope it's alright he came today," Lenore said. "I didn't mean to spring him on you, but he is feeding Kieran tonight."

"Of course." Camilla's voice was warm, but her eyes were icy chips when she turned them on Rook. They melted again when she faced Lenore. "You know I love you, don't you? Are you sure you forgive me? Even after my abominable behavior?"

"Of course," Lenore said. "I love you too. We're sisters, after all."

Camilla's shoulders relaxed, and she squeezed Lenore in another hug. "Thank you."

Rook remained quiet while the ladies caught up, content to stuff himself on Esther's cooking and observe the happy scene. It reminded him of his and Lenore's reconciliation after the fight that had followed their meeting with the Pendragons.

Thank the stars for that. To think he'd nearly left her. How many wonderful future experiences would he have thrown away? He wanted to draw her into his arms and kiss her, not caring a whit who saw, but he didn't. There would be opportunity for that later. This was Lenore's time to reconnect with her family, and Rook had no wish to put a damper on that.

)(

Falcon took in the crowd of protesters. Hundreds of them. They spread over the rolling lawn of the Parliament building like whitecaps on the sea. The Old World palace rose like an island behind him. Bare, scraggly branches reached into the sky like supplicants. He imagined them asking for peace.

The protesters' ranks had grown since Neal and Katerina's rally, which meant the number of Enforcers assigned to monitor them had too. Falcon gripped his cane more tightly, while his uniform coat flapped in the wind. His cheeks stung under its bitter chill. The weight of responsibility pressed down on him as he rubbed a new patch on his sleeve. Three sage leaves in the shape of a shield—the new crisis responder team's symbol. The cane, a gift from his grandfather, was identical to the eagle-topped one in every way save one: Falcon's had a falcon instead. He'd smiled and thanked Harding, done all the right things, but his insides twisted at the gift.

Mina had cleared Falcon for light duty. He'd gotten a commission as squad leader for the Enforcer's newly created emergency response unit. "Due to his outstanding record of duty and sacrifice to the order," or so said the Enforcer Third who'd come to his house to deliver the news. The Third also happened to be a friend of Harding's.

Falcon hadn't felt up to such a task, not while he was still recovering. He'd almost turned the offer down when Harding had pulled him aside for a private word.

"I think this new *initiative*—" Harding had donned a mocking tone for the word. "—is bullocks too—"

"That's not what I said," Falcon replied.

"—but this is a promotion. And straight back from leave? I've never known anyone to get that. This is your chance to move up the ranks."

"I have concerns about taking up duty again while other issues occupy my mind."

Harding had blustered. "What concerns?"

Falcon, who'd never had much in the way of acting skills, had done his best to look awkward. "Perhaps it'd be better if I focused on assisting with your investigation."

Harding had narrowed his eyes at his grandson. "Are you telling me that little trollop is distracting you?"

Falcon hadn't trusted his already stretched deception skills. Instead, he'd focused on the bits of truth he did have. "Grandfather, Camilla is a dear friend." His heart had panged as he thought of how he'd left her. He couldn't bring himself to face her again, but the sentiment had been sincere nonetheless. "I don't believe she's done anything against the order or this city. It was utter chaos that night. We had more than a few blonde females in custody, including Adelle Hawkins."

"*Hrmph.*" Harding had worked his jaw as if literally chewing over the words. "You accept this commission and make me proud, I'll see about wrapping up the inquiry on your little strumpet."

"Please don't call her that." Falcon's words had come out angrier than he'd meant for them to.

Harding had shot him an unimpressed look but said nothing more.

Now Falcon was back on duty with over twenty reserve members under his command. Magistrates Allen and Holmes had been displeased that temporary recruits comprised most of the new team, but neither they nor Doctor Allen had shown any indication of knowing what Harding had said to Camilla. The powers that be had decided the new crisis responders should police the protesters, given the violence of last spring's riots. Ironic, considering many from the new unit had itchy fingers on their truncheons.

Falcon didn't like his team members much. Likewise, most of his men didn't seem to like him. Not that he blamed them— support staff never loved rich boys with connections being put in charge. He'd delivered his instructions with authority, however, and was grateful First Iago didn't want another incident like what had happened last spring.

Leaning on his cane for support, Falcon began a slow circuit around the group. His legs still weren't as strong as they had been. Doctor Allen suspected his spine had suffered some damage from the fall.

A figure in an all-white cloak skirted the edge of the group. Given the cold weather and the protesters' chosen garb, the cloak itself wasn't the issue. It was the exposed trouser cuffs. He'd seen the agitator at the last support rally, and these cuffs matched the ones she'd worn—black with red trim.

Falcon tried to be casual as he made his way toward them. It was difficult to be both stealthy and quick with his labored gait. The figure glanced at him, shed the cloak, and revealed the same black Enforcer uniform.

"REPRESS THE REBELLION!" A man this time, with light skin and dark hair. He darted into the crowd. "KILL THEM ALL!"

The protesters cried out and scattered like flushed birds. Some turned to the Enforcers circling the assembly.

"Make way!" Falcon called. "Enforcers, self-defense only!"

He struggled to keep his eyes on his target and took a blow as he made his way through the maddening crowd. And then another. Shouting at the top of his lungs, he repeated his orders and used his cane to carefully sweep a path.

The false Enforcer looked back. With a hateful scowl torn across his face, he raised a metal canister above his head. He yanked a pin out of the top and tossed it farther into the crowd, then took off in the opposite direction.

"Ledbetter, Carew, after the one in black!" Someone kicked Falcon in the back of the knee. His cane was the only thing that saved him from going down. He couldn't see through the throng if any of his team suffered similar attacks. Just in case, he shouted, "Only the one in black. *That* is your target, men."

Smoke as red as blood rose in a thick, choking cloud. The protestors around it screamed, gripping their faces and running blindly. Some stumbled, tripping more of their fellows. The panicked crowd ran over them, battering bodies beneath their feet. A few stooped, shrieking and petrified.

Falcon pushed past a growing pain in his legs and back. "Get to safety!" While pulling the fallen he could reach to their feet, he called more orders to his squad, directing them to protect the protestors. Trampling would take more lives than anything else. He still couldn't see any members of his team and therefore didn't know if his efforts were having an effect.

The air rang with screams as people panicked. His eyes and throat began to burn like millions of red-hot needles were stabbing it. He was so close to the canister now. The plume of scarlet harm billowed, barely outlined against the cloud around it. The needles grew worse, as if they'd begun to rip out the soft tissue inside his face. His eyes and nose streamed, and Falcon wondered if it was blood. He gripped his cane so hard his hand ached, to remain on his feet as yowling protesters stumbled into him and to keep himself from turning and hurtling in the opposite direction like every sense was telling him to do.

Keep going. Protect the people. Don't let anyone else die on your watch. Keep going.

The pain roared when he found the device. He wanted to howl and scratch out his eyes, but he couldn't add to the panic. The cylinder burned his hand with frigid fire. He ran, shoving past the pain. He called again for people to make way, but his voice came out as a strangled rasp. Acid seared along his windpipe.

Just a little farther.

Finally, he was beyond the main throng. Nearly blind, he hurled the spewing canister into a fuzzy green mass in the distance. The people were loud, white blurs around him as his eyelids swelled and his eyeballs streamed. Falcon's legs were trembling. He leaned on his cane heavier than ever as he summoned the courage to cry out for peace and order again, to once more endure that feeling of pouring flaming petrolsene down his throat.

Before he managed it, someone took his arm. "Dawkins here, sir."

"Protect the protestors," Falcon croaked. The pain was more bearable when he didn't try to shout. "Keep order."

Dawkins held on to him and repeated what Falcon had said, doling out orders as they came. Falcon could only hope his efforts were enough.

)(

As the distant sounds of early morning in the Cobalt district clanked, thumped, and creaked, the weight of Camilla's full nebulizer soothed her. She'd taken a leaf from Lenore's book and sewn pockets into her skirt. That's where her nebulizer hid now. Clever, though marring the lovely fabric had pained Camilla.

While she waited for Nightmare to let her into the catacombs, Camilla took a deep breath through her nose. She'd mixed a bit of her medicine with an inert jelly compound and had swabbed the inside of her nose with it. The medicinal concoction coated her airways with cold. A small tin of the stuff stashed inside Camilla's glove pressed against her palm. The sharp, cool scent lingered like a benevolent ghost as her breath fogged in the air. Mist snaked around her feet and warred against the watery sunlight trying to squeeze through the clouds.

Camilla patted her other pocket where Lenore's curio, nicked in the middle of last night, was waiting for her. She imagined using it on the Reaper to ready herself for the deed.

Inside the catacombs, her heart pounded so loud she was surprised she didn't hear it echoing off the damp walls. By the time they reached the laboratory, she'd managed to calm it to a dull thudding.

Until she saw the Reaper.

The abhorrent being stood in the operating theater with yet another cadaver. It lay under a blanket, but it didn't look quite right. Realization washed over Camilla like someone had dumped a bucket of icy water on her.

The body lacked a head.

She leaned against the doorway for support. The recruit lad. He was her subject today. Fresh horror churned in her as she remembered him losing his head.

This was a mistake. Fear seized her, and she broke out in a cold sweat. They'd discover her. And then they'd kill her.

Get out! screamed a voice in her head.

"Are you unwell?" The Reaper's crackling voice broke through Camilla's thoughts.

She dared not meet their eyes and placed a hand over her stomach. "I'm afraid so. I think I need to go home."

She didn't wait for an answer and turned. *Just get away.*

"Stop."

Camilla forced her feet to stay put, though everything inside her urged her to run. She looked at the door, her escape, while the Reaper's robes whispered over the floor. Their presence pressed against her as they cupped the air beneath her chin, herded her gaze up. Camilla's heart was hammering. Her mouth went dry, and her breath caught in her throat. That familiar heady scent assaulted her senses. Mixed with the medication in her nose, it smelled noxious and cloying, like rot and wilted flowers.

The Reaper examined her with their empty gaze for a long moment. Camilla did her best not to breathe in the putrid scent, but her need for air won. She coughed...

Onto the beak of the Reaper's bird mask. They started back.

Camilla gasped and turned her head away. "A-apologies."

It took a while for the coughing spell to abate. The Reaper didn't move, but it gave Camilla time to think. No one else was here, and the Reaper stood within arm's reach. She could do it.

She could also die.

Camilla thought of her mother, of Falcon and Eamon and Twila and all those who had suffered at this creature's hands. She could also do as Rook had said and trust him.

Camilla gulped in air. "I really must go. I'll return when I'm well again."

"You will stay."

Camilla kept walking. "I-I can't."

"You. Will. *Stay*." The Reaper's voice, rasping like a bone saw, echoed off the walls.

The sound awoke a primal fear in Camilla. She ran. In the corridor, a Collective member blocked her way. Camilla struck out with Lenore's curio and hit the figure in the shoulder. The ensuing flash was blinding in the catacomb's dusky light. Camilla staggered back as a man's cry of pain clanged in her ears. She saw spots, stumbled forward. Two strong hands grabbed her. She struck with the curio again but closed her eyes this time. She saw the flash's brightness even with her eyes closed. The hands let go. She took off, but her vision still blurred. Her feet got in their own way; she went sprawling. The curio flew from her hands and slid into the darkness.

Where did it go? Wherediditgo?!

Someone grabbed her hair and hauled her to her feet. She cried out, clawed at the massive hands holding her. It did no good. Her captor spun her and clamped her shoulders in their meaty vises. She found herself staring into the hideous bird mask again.

"I'm sorry," she whispered, voice trembling. "I got scared. I really am unwell. Please, I didn't mean—"

"Enough." The Reaper's voice was the sharp slam of a coffin lid. "Lock her away."

Camilla begged and apologized. The Reaper's goon dragged her down the dark passages to whatever hell they kept their prisoners in.

28

~An Embroidered Threat~

Dmitri sat at the table in Rook's entertaining corner and forced himself to smile. His face felt ready to crack as he and a few of the market's bigger vendors shared drinks and talked. That was all they did—talk. About nothing.

Not having any better ideas, Dmitri had kept Rook's recurring appointments. Twice weekly vendor entertainment was one of them. Since he hadn't assigned Garrick's replacement, Dmitri had to figure out who to treat next.

Someone told a joke. *Laugh,* his brain said. Dmitri went through the motions while screaming inside his skull.

"Just pick someone you trust not to double-cross you." That had been Rook's advice when Dmitri sought advice on how to pick a new right hand. Fat lot of help that was.

"I'd sooner have you back." He'd immediately regretted saying it.

That idiotic smile had stretched across Rook's face. "Aw, I miss you too, mate. Sadly, your buddies say no."

"They're not my buddies."

Rook had laughed, but bitterness had tinged his voice. Now Dmitri sat here hating everything and pretending like he was having a grand old time.

Finally, their time came to an end. He led his guests out, patting shoulders and wishing them well. As soon as the door closed, he rubbed his hands over his face. Blazes, he had to think of a way to get Rook back.

A heavy knock rattled the door. Dmitri had to take a monumentally deep breath before he found the strength to open it again.

"Someone here for you, boss," Grunt said.

"Who is it?"

"Uh..." Grunt's eyes darted around as he realized his mistake.

Dmitri waved a hand at him. "Never mind. Go ahead and let them up."

Maybe they'll kill me and put me out of my misery.

By the time Grunt returned a few minutes later, Dmitri had seated himself at the desk. At least here he felt comfortable.

The figure who entered wasn't at all what he'd expected. With cool confidence, in walked a young woman wearing a pleasant smile and a practical high-low-skirt-and-trouser ensemble. Her hazel eyes sparkled at him.

With the warmth of old friends reuniting, she said, "Hello, Ermine."

The voice tolled every alarm bell in Dmitri's head. He shot to his feet. "Nightmare. What the blazes are you doing here?"

She looked him up and down, seeming genuinely surprised. "Are you quite alright? I've never seen you so rattled. What happened to the silent sentry I liked so much?"

He glowered at her. "Why are you here?"

She smiled again. "Well, you never were very charming. I have something for you. Or perhaps it's for Rook? Word on the street is he's not been around, that you've taken over, but that doesn't really add up." She opened a side pouch slung around her hips and withdrew a small black box. Nightmare held it out to Dmitri. He made no move to take it. She set it between them on the desk, waited, and pushed it toward him. "You'll want to open that sooner rather than later."

"Why?" he asked.

She gave him a sympathetic grimace. "It'll be worse for someone if you wait."

Dmitri's heart leapt into his throat. "What are you playing at, Nightmare?"

"I really think you ought to open it."

Steeling himself, he weighed the small parcel in his hand. Lightweight, so probably nothing dangerous… hopefully. He held his breath and opened the lid toward Nightmare. Nothing happened, so he tipped it toward himself.

A lock of blond hair, ripped out by the roots, sat on a lace-edged handkerchief spattered with blood. The letters HCA had been embroidered in pink in the corner. He swallowed thickly and raised his eyes to Nightmare.

"What have you done?" he growled.

Nightmare's countenance hardened. "I'm telling you this because I like Camilla. I don't want to see her hurt any more than necessary." Dmitri clenched his fists but kept his mouth shut. "She turned on you. The Reaper didn't even have to use Verisap. We know what you and Rook have been doing to foil our operations. The full moon is in two days. If you two don't abandon your schemes by then, we'll begin removing whole pieces from her."

"I don't kno—"

"Ermine, save it. For her sake, shut it down."

Dmitri pressed his fist into the desk. He searched his screaming thoughts for something helpful. Nothing.

Through clenched teeth, he said, "Can you be more specific, please? I want to be certain I understand the terms in their entirety."

Nightmare circled a finger in the air. "All of this. The market, your plans to stop us, everything. The Reaper wants it gone."

"And what if I just killed you right now? Or held you for ransom?"

She shook her head. "We are willing to die for the cause. It would be a loss, but for the greater good. The Collective would continue." She almost chanted the words, which sent a chill down Dmitri's spine.

"Don't hurt her anymore. Please. I'll figure something out."

"You have heard the terms."

"I know!" Dmitri punched the desk so hard his hand throbbed. He took a deep breath. "I know. I…" He looked at Nightmare. He knew his eyes were begging her, and he didn't care. "You said you like Camilla, yes?"

"Very much. She's a kind and accomplished young woman. It would be a shame if the world lost her."

The passive phrasing made Dmitri's hackles rise again. "Then don't let it." Nightmare opened her mouth, but he cut her off. "I'm asking you to look after her. If you value her worth, then do what you can to protect her. Please."

"You have two days."

With that, Nightmare turned and left.

Blood roared in Dmitri's ears. What could he do? What?! He opened the hidden compartment in Rook's desk drawer. Inside laid the plans, maps, and details he'd written out for Rook—maps of the catacombs, the Reaper's organizational structure, the suppliers Dmitri remembered. Every scrap of information he'd dredged up from his memory stared up at him. He could sneak in, try to rescue Camilla. Probably suicide on his own. And what if he failed without telling anyone she was there? He needed to get help.

Leaving everything as it was, he closed the compartment again and hurried out. The Char quarter's grave-like silence did nothing to hearten him.

)(

The stars scattered above Rook like diamond dust. He smiled at them. Perhaps, when it was warmer, he could treat Lenore to something outdoors. A picnic here in the museum gardens would be lovely, though he didn't want to remind her of Eamon. Those two had made up after their first fight during such an occasion. The memory would be bittersweet for her. He could plan something, but it would require care.

"Where the blazes have you been?"

Rook turned slowly. Though the voice was familiar, it took him a few seconds to realize the disheveled young man standing there was Dmitri. His hair frizzed and stuck out in odd places. Even his eyebrows, quivering above bloodshot eyes, looked askew. Rook's brows slid up as he searched for words.

"I've been searching all over this bloody city for you!"

"Mate, calm down," Rook said. "I—"

"The Reaper has Camilla."

Rook's insides went as cold as the air around him. "Bugger." He motioned for Dmitri to follow him. They headed to a remote section of the gardens with decent sight lines. A small stand of birches nearby provided a bit of cover. After checking to make sure no one was around, Rook said, "Explain."

"Nightmare, a Crypt-Keeper, delivered this to me." Dmitri pulled a small black box from his pocket and shoved it at Rook.

Rook examined the contents in silence.

"It's Camilla's." Dmitri said. "I've already checked in at the Allen residence. She's been gone all day."

The lock of hair looked right, but there was no way to be certain. "What are these letters?"

Dmitri pointed at each one. "Camilla. Husselbee. Allen. Husselbee was her mother's maiden name." Rook's features twisted as he tried to find holes in the story. "I'm telling you, Rook, it's hers. She showed me this just yesterday. She wouldn't have given it up without a fight."

Rook took a slow breath. "What else do we know?" Dmitri relayed what Nightmare had told him. Rook's expression darkened with every word. "Blazes, this is bad. When Camilla told me, I should have—"

Dmitri punched Rook in the face, knocking him back into one of the birch trees. The pain spiked before ebbing into a low pulse.

Rook rubbed his jaw. "Fair enough. I deserved that."

"You knew what she was doing?" Dmitri snarled. "And you kept it to yourself? You bloody imbecile!"

Rook motioned for him to lower his voice. "Shhh. I thought I had it under control." He stepped forward, only for another punch to land where the last one had. Rook stumbled again but remained upright. The pain burrowed deeper this time. It wasn't the worst beating he'd ever gotten, but it was getting bloody annoying.

"You can't control everything! Camilla might die thanks to you!"

Rook reined in his impulse to hit back. Had their places been switched and it was Lenore in danger, he'd be doing a lot worse than punching.

"Let's stop wasting time and work on a solution, shall we?"

"I know a back way in," Dmitri said. "It's closer to their holding cells than the front entrance."

"How much closer?"

"I'm not entirely certain."

Rook fixed Dmitri with a hard glare. "You want to mount a rescue operation on incomplete information?"

"I only went to the holding cells once, and I'm fairly certain I remember the way. The front entrance is a death trap."

Rook shook his head, worked his aching jaw.

"Rook, trust me. I wouldn't suggest it if I didn't think we had a chance."

Heading into the Reaper's stronghold looked like suicide from every angle. Then again, giving up the business and their plans against the Reaper wasn't an option either. There had to be an alternative, one that wouldn't get him killed. Unfortunately, nothing came to mind.

And they had less than two days until those lunatics started cutting bits off Camilla.

If word reached Lenore, she'd march right up to the doors and demand Camilla's release. And if Rook abandoned Camilla, Lenore would never speak to him again.

He took a slow breath through his nose and released it through his mouth. "Are you sure we can pull it off? I mean, really sure? You're not letting how you feel about Camilla cloud your judgment?"

Dmitri shook his head. "Camilla's just a friend. She's made it clear she doesn't want to pursue a romantic relationship with me again."

"The question still stands."

Dmitri looked surprised but nodded. "Yes. I have a plan. I believe this can work."

Rook heaved a sigh, thinking of Lenore again. He looked to the sprawling museum where he'd planned to surprise her with a visit. He'd planned to meet Chrysalis here for a report too, but that would have to wait.

"I really hope we don't die."

)(

Chrysalis, one with the dark in her sneak suit, squatted inside a rhododendron. The plant had retained its thick leaves this season. On more than one occasion, it had provided her with cover during

297

her surveillance assignment. Her mouth hung open as she listened to Rook and Dmitri argue.

They were going to the catacombs?!

She'd heard tales about the mysterious Reaper and their cult of fanatic followers, each one stranger and more harrowing than the last. Eyes that saw into your soul. Dark nights of bloody worship. Removing organs from living people and switching them around like a game of chess.

Uncertainty rooted Chrysalis to the spot. She wanted to fly out from her hiding spot, beg them not to go, but that would be weak. One of them—whoever was in charge now—might even kick her out of the organization for such cowardice. She liked to think she and Rook had a rapport by now, but Dmitri had always been a tougher nut to crack. Stern and distant, she'd never been able to get a read on him.

Then again, they'd be killed if they went. Gutted alive and made to watch as their entrails were hung up like streamers for a New Year's party.

Chrysalis looked at the museum, rising like a city unto itself. Could anyone there help? Lenore was precious to Rook. Chrysalis couldn't endanger her, but her mentor, Magistrate Allen... He had power. Although, from what Chrysalis had seen, he was neither keen to exercise it nor a huge fan of Rook.

Rook and Dmitri had left while she deliberated. Blast it all, she had to do something.

29

~Secrets in Journaling~

L
enore checked her belongings as she prepared to leave work. She carried a suitcase and had sent Neal and Mina a reminder note about her plans to stay at Lowell and Felicia's house overnight. It probably wasn't necessary—she'd discussed her plans with the family last night—but she didn't want to cause any undue concern. Mina had been protective since losing Adelle and had yet to meet the Thornes. Lenore was running out of ways to squirm out of dinner party offers.

Copper came up beside her. "Heading out? I'll walk you."

Ezra joined them. Lenore asked how Copper's preparations for his move to Bone Port were going. Moving a family as large as his was a big job, and the paperwork was going slowly. Magistrate Warren was his sponsor, however, and that helped cut through some of the red tape.

"Still haven't found a replacement for me, though." Copper grimaced. "Scholar Bates is talking about absorbing Arc-Tech into Anthropology if we shrink any more."

Ezra made a grumbling noise.

Lenore smiled. "We'll find someone. Not a replacement, but someone good. And the council vote is coming up, so Neal can get back to work here."

It was Copper's turn to grumble. The peaceful protests had grown despite the incident with what reports were calling "pepper gas." Tension thrummed louder than ever. People had been injured that day, but thankfully, there hadn't been any deaths. The newssheets had commended Falcon as a hero. There was even talk of him being promoted again. It made Neal and Katerina's crisis responder experiment look good too.

The incident also meant Enforcers patrolled the protest grounds in higher numbers than ever. More troublemakers were appearing. They didn't wear the same uniform as the others had, but they called for violence all the same. Peaceful voices were winning so far and no more pepper gas attacks had occurred, but it was only a matter of time before violence erupted again—or so everyone was saying. Lenore didn't think this general consensus was helping. It felt defeatist, if not downright permissive.

At least the protests weren't the only way Springhaven's denizens were showing up. Neal said the magistrates were drowning in letters. In the end, however, the final decision would fall to the council.

Lenore and her friends parted ways, and she took a hansom to the Thorne residence in the Rose quarter. She hoped to see Rook during her visit, though her focus was on her plans with Lowell and Felicia. She'd made it clear she had every intention of respecting their hospitality, and that meant certain activities were off limits while she was their guest.

Felicia was dressed to go out when she answered the door. "Hello, dear. I apologize for being such a poor hostess, but I'm running quite behind. You and Lowell will have to fend for yourselves tonight in regard to dinner."

Lenore assured her that was perfectly fine and followed Felicia into a sitting room she'd not been in before. It was smaller than any Lenore had seen in the house. A fire crackled in the grate, and four armchairs circled before it. Tiny gems no bigger than pinheads studded the wallpaper and made the evergreen walls look like a pine forest covered in frost.

Felicia looked at Lenore as they walked in. "Was there something you needed?"

Lenore fidgeted with her nails. "Um, I thought you were taking me to Lowell."

Felicia chuckled. "No, pet, though that's very polite of you. You're free to wander the house as you like. Just please respect closed doors."

"Oh. Why, thank you. That's incredibly... hospitable." Lenore stopped just short of saying *trusting*. It was, though, especially given how secretive the Thornes were.

"Honestly, we might need to think about getting you a key. While I have you, do you mind sending Lowell my way? We have a little tradition every evening and, as I said, I am running behind schedule."

The authority in Felicia's voice told Lenore it hadn't been a true request. Nevertheless, she was happy to oblige. She found Lowell, unsurprisingly, in his workshop.

He wasn't wearing a mask.

Lenore had briefly seen him without one before, but that had been during a fight. One she'd lost and had been carted off from to be questioned prior to being assassinated. Now that she had a moment to see his face, she wondered why he wore a mask at all. One eye wasn't like the other—it bulged larger than its twin and was covered in a milky film—but neither was his arm. It was just different.

"Lowell."

He looked up. A smile bloomed on his face, but it wilted as realization dawned. He turned away. "Oh, pardon me." He grabbed a mask from a nearby table.

"You don't have to wear that if you don't want to." She registered her mistake. "I mean, of course, if you do, by all means. Whatever you prefer, really." Another realization. "I should have knocked. I'm sorry for intruding."

Lowell held the mask in his hands and looked sideways at Lenore. "You don't mind me not having it on?"

She shrugged. "I like seeing your face. It's entirely up to you, though. If you're happy, I'm happy."

Lowell turned to her. His beaming smile put sunshine into Lenore's heart. "Perhaps I'll leave it off then, yes? It can get ever so stuffy inside."

Lenore smiled back. "Whatever you like." He set the mask back down. "Felicia asked me to fetch you, by the way. She says you two have a tradition, and she's in a hurry."

"Jolly good. You make yourself at home. I'll come find you once we're done." As he passed, he leaned toward Lenore and said

301

in a stage whisper, "There are freshly baked jammy shortbreads in the kitchen."

Lenore gasped, mouth already watering. "Yes, please!"

)(

Lowell headed to Felicia's personal sitting room. She looked surprised when he entered without his mask. He smiled in return, and she said nothing about it. A familiar leather-bound book sat before her on a small table. Pens sat waiting in a gold cup on the mantle within arm's reach. Lowell took the chair next to her as he always did and looked at her face. It helped him focus just as journaling helped her, though he didn't know why.

Felicia remained quiet as she began to write out a detailed account of her day. Each hour and event, conversations and inner monologues, descriptions of what she'd seen in others' heads. As she did, images and words, some fragmented, flowed through Lowell's mind.

Neither of them understood the mechanics of their abilities, though they'd often compared notes. It was like hearing music, except the music was thoughts and came with pictures. Felicia's accounts were meticulous, which made the memories roll slower. This helped Lowell to understand and absorb what he saw.

His eyes drifted to Felicia's elegant handwriting. The words provided more structure to what he saw in his mind. People's secrets poured onto the page and into Lowell. Not only that, but also information Felicia had traded that day like currency—and some of it *for* currency too.

Later, he'd write a few indexing notes. Those got stored separately from the book in a card catalog system of their own design. Mountains of other books like this one, filled throughout the years, were hidden behind a false wall in Felicia's room. A forest of information, all of which had value to someone somewhere.

As Felicia wrote, a picture of someone Lowell knew passed by. It was distorted, Felicia's memory of someone else's memory, but there was no mistaking the golden hair and bright blue eyes. The cherubic face, streaked with tears and begging, though the words were garbled. That tended to happen once memories layered. Emotions came with it too. Cruel triumph. His stomach roiled, and he focused hard on the images. Masks of brass and black leather. A dark room where Camilla was. And... *horror!* With glee, they ripped out a lock of the poor girl's hair. A small black box. And then they traversed corridors, pushed her into a cage. Out again. Into the sunshine through a grate.

"Lowell, are you quite alright?"

The images dissipated like ripples across water. Felicia focused on him, which usually comforted Lowell—he sensed her care for him in these moments—but not now. He wanted her to start journaling again, to focus on what she'd gleaned from the person who'd hurt Camilla. He didn't dare say so, however, and thanked the heavens their connection didn't go both ways. Ideas were already forming in his head.

Concern creased Felicia's brow. "You're pale."

"I shouldn't have skipped lunch." Lowell gave her a shaky smile. "I am utterly famished." In truth, he was glad his stomach was empty; otherwise, the contents might have made a rather spectacular re-entrance to the outside world.

He sensed satisfaction in his sister.

"I'll finish this up, and then you and Miss Lenore have some dinner straightaway. And be safe tonight. I don't want you two doing any work outside. With this cold spell that's just come down, you'd catch your deaths."

Lowell nodded, silently urging her to get back to her work.

He learned little else about Camilla or her predicament. He saw gravestones before the memories moved on to something else. When Felicia finished, she bade Lowell goodbye and hurried off to the Raven's Tower for a game night.

"I'll give Calandra your love," she called before she left.

When the door shut behind her, fear unfurled itself in Lowell's chest. He had to tell Lenore what he'd seen.

Lowell found her, as expected, in the kitchen. She was munching on one of the thumbprint cookies.

"I've only had three!" Then her face fell. "Lowell, what's wrong?"

His throat had gone dry. "I... I'm afraid I have some terrible news, petal." She came close, and he took her hands in his. "Something's happened to Camilla."

Lenore's mouth dropped. "What? How do you know? When? Sorry. How?" She shook her head. "Help me understand."

"It will take too long to explain. Suffice it to say that Felicia knows how to extract secrets from people, and she tells me those secrets. She's never met Camilla, so she doesn't know, but I saw her." Nausea gripped him again as he remembered the dark glee from the memories. "They've done awful things to her."

Lenore's face froze in disbelief. When she found her voice again, it was soft but certain. "I have to find her. Please, tell me what you know."

"Lenore, these are very dangerous people." Fear gripped him, stealing strength from his words. He hadn't considered what she'd do when she found out, yet her reaction didn't surprise him.

She tightened her grip on his hands, pain shining in her eyes. "I'm sorry, but I can't lose anyone else."

A new emotion surged forward to replace Lowell's fear. He remembered his own losses, the pain. A fierce desire to prevent his friend from experiencing more burned in him. "No, indeed. We'll need to be prepared." He turned on his heel. "Follow me."

A moment passed before Lenore's footsteps trailed after him. "Lowell, what are you doing?"

"We're going to get your sister back."

Lenore drew even with him as they made their way to his workshop. "I... Alright, but how? We don't have any weapons."

Lowell tipped his head toward her. A smile made of mischief curled up his face. "For once, my tinker belle, you are mistaken. We have my new limbs, of course, and something else. Rather, several somethings."

Entering his workshop, he headed for the wall where most of his tools hung. He notched a wrench around the large brass nut decorating a wall sconce's base. The others had the same frippery, but this one had an extra function. The wall split down the middle, making the tools shudder on their hooks. Lowell pushed the doors apart, and they rolled to the sides on hidden casters. The already shaking tools swung wildly.

"You're brilliant," Lenore said. "I mean, I knew that already, but *goodness*." She stared at the doors in awe. When she saw what lay behind, her eyes grew as big as saucers. "What is all this?"

Lowell chuckled and rubbed the back of his neck. "Well, you see, Rook and I have an arrangement. He pays me to—"

"Design weapons for him."

"Precisely."

They smiled at each other before turning back to the small arsenal inside the secret room. There were crossbows of various sizes and a complex bow with miniature arrows loaded into a pair of rotating barrels. There was also a stave armed on each end with an explosion of spikes. Handles attached to chains that, in turn, attached to wickedly spiny metal ends. A razor-sharp metal circle split into halves with grips on the interior crossbeam.

Lenore studied each piece. "I couldn't find my curio this morning. Do you have anything like it?"

"I'm afraid not, but we'll find you something. Don't forget about those lovelies you've made for yourself. Then I'm afraid we have one more stop to make. We need to go to Rook's office and see if we can't recruit the man himself."

"Rook's office?" Lenore repeated, as if naming a legendary land of myth. "If we tell him… No, you're right. We need all the help we can get, though he will probably try to stop me."

"I expect so, but we both know the likelihood of you not going." Lowell gave her an encouraging nudge. "And we'll need something to eat too. I fear it's going to be a long night."

Lowell saw the impatience in Lenore's eyes, but she set her jaw and nodded.

He left a note for Felicia. When she returned home to find him gone, she'd feel like he'd felt when Spades had kidnapped her years ago.

Felly,

Please don't be cross. Lenore's sister is in danger, so we're off to the catacombs to rescue her. I have my new limbs, and we're going to gather reinforcements. She'd do no less for me if you were in danger again.

Try not to worry,
Lowell

)(

Given the increased security, Chrysalis had to use every ounce of stealth, guile, and skill she possessed to break into Rook's office. Dmitri not having assigned a new number two had hindered her—Garrick had known she was one of the few with permission to go in. She missed that old grump. The memory of Ebony flying through the now boarded-up window made Chrysalis feel like the universe occasionally tried to maintain balance. Not very often, but every once and again.

Dressed in her sneak suit, she crept through Rook's office. She knew he and Dmitri had been plotting against the Reaper, but she didn't know many details, only what she'd gleaned while eavesdropping. A bowl, marred by fire, sat empty on the desk. Nothing but liquor bottles and glasses in the entertaining corner. Reports covered in names and numbers laid on the desk, but she couldn't make heads or tails of it.

Climbing feet reverberated on the stairs outside. She scurried over to the sofa against the wall and scrabbled under it. Like a rabbit, she waited.

"I am permitted entry," rasped a ghostly voice outside the door. "And she is with me."

"Um, remind me who you are?" Grunt sounded confused but stern.

"Wraith." The hissed word slid through the broken window like cold. "Check your list and stop trifling with me."

Grunt mumbled a few incoherent thinking words before presumably finding the name on whatever list he kept. Head on the floor, Chrysalis watched through her ink-black hood and measured her breath. Grunt opened the door and turned the petrolsene lights on low. A dark figure trailed behind, hooded and dressed in layers of tattered black robes. Followed by someone, also hooded, in a long cloak, which they pulled tightly around themselves. The cloak turned in place, probably taking in the shadowy office. Grunt left them and closed the door. The cloak's hood came down and there stood Lenore, the very person Chrysalis was supposed to be keeping an eye on.

Lenore whispered, "So this is where Rook runs his business."

The specter pushed his hood back too, revealing her friend Lowell. Chrysalis' jaw dropped. *That* silly dandy-man was the fearsome Wraith?

"It is." Lowell flicked through the papers on Rook's desk. "You truly didn't know what he did until recently?"

Lenore shook her head. "For my protection. I understand better now, but I'd rather know."

"Indubitably." The two exchanged a look, but Chrysalis couldn't read what passed between them. Lowell returned to his work. "He is jolly difficult to keep track of, though. I'd hoped Ermine would be here to assist."

"Ermine? Wait, isn't that Dmitri?"

Lowell cocked his head. "Yes, I believe that's his proper name. Without him, I'm afraid we'll have to look for clues to both their whereabouts."

Lenore joined Lowell in the search, though it was clear she had no idea what she was looking for. Thankfully, some kind of urgency hurried them. Chrysalis' heart beat faster as they gazed over the couch, but neither noticed her. Nor did they spot the false panel in the desk drawer, through which Chrysalis used to pass encoded notes to Rook. They soon discovered that Dmitri, like Rook before him, kept the office neat as a pin.

"There's nothing here," Lenore said. Her eyes were on a clock on the wall. "And Camilla is still out there." Worry and pain carved lines into her face, and her thumb fidgeted against her other hand.

Lowell's eyes roved over the room again. He sighed. "I know. I don't like having lied to Felicia, but I think we'll have to do this alone."

"Do you really think we can rescue Camilla?"

"I saw the path. If we can avoid being noticed, we stand a chance."

"And if we are noticed?"

Lowell strode over to Lenore. His gait had improved considerably since Chrysalis had last seen him. He reached past Lenore's cloak, beyond where Chrysalis could see. With the *shiiiick* of metal sliding against leather, he pulled out a short sword. It had a curved tip, which would increase its damage radius, plus a guard with its own bladed outer edge and a spiked pommel. It even looked lightweight. She wouldn't have minded a weapon like that. Smaller, of course.

"If we are noticed," he said, "then we'll be ready to defend ourselves."

Lenore gave him a wobbly smile and flicked a finger against her stomach. It made a noise that told Chrysalis something besides whalebone reinforced her corset.

"Just so long as we're careful. Last time I did something like this…" Her smile faltered. "Not everyone made it."

"We will be careful, sweet pea." Lowell squeezed her hand.

They replaced the sword, raised their hoods again, and headed out. Chrysalis goggled from her place beneath the sofa.

Has everyone gone mad? Why were they all risking their lives for one person?

She slowed. Rook had risked time to get her out of that Halls of Justice cell. It had scared the daylights out of her, but it had also cemented her trust in him. That had to be what these people had between them too.

Dreck! Lenore and Lowell didn't know Rook and Dmitri had set off to do the same thing they were.

Chrysalis mimed pounding her fists against the floor. Quiet as breath, she scuttled back to the desk and slid open the drawer she knew so well. She popped open the secret panel, uncertain what she might find, and removed the whole lot. It took her a few moments to decode the characters scrawled across the top sheet and discern this wasn't for her. Jealousy plucked a string in her. Why did someone else have access to the code and secret spot? Chrysalis didn't have time to indulge the thought. She needed to make decoded copies, which would eat precious minutes.

30

~Into the Grave~

Rook ground his teeth as he and Dmitri slipped past moonlight-soaked graves like ghosts. Well, he a somewhat hindered and poorly dressed ghost. They'd stopped at Dmitri's flat for supplies. There, Dmitri had given Rook Ebony's old uniform to change into. It wasn't the wearing of a dead woman's clothing that bothered him. Rather, it was how poorly the ensemble fit him. The hips—too large—and the shoulders—too small—were the worst in the ridiculous leather getup. It also lacked the modifications for hiding knives Rook's usual attire had. He'd managed to conceal two small blades in the skintight sleeves, but the rest hung in plain sight. At least the mask, donned once they'd entered the Cobalt district's less inhabited part, was adjustable. A crazed part of his brain looked for humor in this mad plan, and he wondered if this counted as cross-dressing.

Cold seeped through the gaps in his outfit and chilled the sweat collecting beneath the unbreathing material. The gravestones and their shadows jutted toward them like broken teeth, hungry for a meal. Pale wisps of mist—languid carrion fish—swirled over the ground.

Dmitri, seeming far more comfortable in his old Collective uniform, occasionally motioned directions. He never uttered so much as a whisper.

No one guarded the back entrance—a grate across a large sewer pipe. Thick, filthy water dribbled from it into a shallow pool. No lock secured the entryway. And why would such a thing have been necessary, given the horrific smell? Rook's gut lurched.

Dmitri waved him forward. Forcing nausea back, Rook steeled himself for the onslaught of putridity.

The sewer pipe opened into a larger space. A well of stinking water—at least, Rook preferred to think of it as water—yawned before them, draining past their feet. They used hooks attached to the wall as handholds and skirted around the pit on a narrow ledge of crumbling stone. The barbs on the end of each hook were rusted and covered with dark, brown grime. What these hooks were used for didn't bear thinking about, but Rook had never been more thankful for his gloves. He made the mistake of looking down into the foul soup and spotted an eyeball floating in it.

"What is this place?" His voice hissed more breath than sound.

"Deterrent," was Dmitri's only reply.

Conditions improved once they were past the fetid reservoir. The smell abated, and the ground dried up.

They'd entered the catacombs.

Spectral light cast by the blue and green lichen on the walls suffused everything with a hazy appearance, as if they were walking underwater. Rook had to take even more care as he moved—even the smallest noise echoed off the tunnel walls.

He tapped Dmitri on the shoulder. He mimed with his hands and mouthed, *How much farther?*

Dmitri looked around, and Rook tensed. Was Dmitri trying to figure out where they were or how to communicate his response?

Dmitri finally mime-mouthed back, *Two tunnels and three rooms.*

That didn't really tell Rook how far, but at least he had milestones to count down.

Noise behind them reflected off the walls. Syllables scrabbled over the rough stone and distorted the words. A small half-excavated room stood off to the side farther down. Rook and Dmitri ducked into it. Whoever was behind them seldom spoke and moved slowly. Perhaps someone had seen them and was trying to get the drop on them.

As he and Dmitri peered around the hideaway's entrance, skulls gathered in recesses around the room bored holes into Rook's back with lifeless eyes. He ignored the idea that some of the strange echoes came from them, and he refocused on the approaching danger.

Jerky shadows flitted over the walls. Rook made out two distinct figures, but more scratching footsteps came from the opposite direction. Three to two, at least. He drew one of his daggers. This would get nasty if someone found them.

Two Collective members appeared around the tunnel's curve farther in. They quietly debated some game they'd recently played. Hissed disagreement scraped against the walls like a blade over a whetstone. Rook and Dmitri withdrew farther into their hole. The Collective members passed without seeing them, and Rook released a tense breath.

The clang of metal against metal ripped through the air. Grunts and the thick sound of pummeled meat followed.

Some of those grunts sounded familiar.

Rook slipped out of his hiding spot, his heart in his throat. Around the bend, one of the Collective members slumped against the wall. His partner lay unconscious on the ground as a pool of blood grew under him. It glowed eerily in the lichen light.

Rook willed his eyes to see something else, but Lenore and Lowell remained before him. She wore a cloak and held a rather impressive sword edged with blood. A strange bow slung across her back. An odd miniature catapult laid flat against Lowell's false arm, which stuck out of his Wraith garb. Both their hoods had fallen back. Rook noted Lowell wore the new, powerful arm, but that thought was already leaving him.

He shook his head. "No. No, no, no, no, no."

Lenore's eyes flicked to him. She advanced, her sword dripping blood like a drooling fang. Rook held his ground. She kept coming.

Bugger. Mask.

He whipped it off. "Don't stab me!"

Lenore stopped, the tip of her sword less than two feet from Rook's belly. Behind him, Dmitri removed his mask too. They stared at one another for a long moment.

"I didn't know you were coming after the Reaper tonight." In this strange place, Lenore's words rustled like wind over grass. She wiped her blade clean and sheathed it.

Rook began to agree, but remembered their conversation in his flat and faltered. "We're here for Camilla. There wasn't time to tell you. I'm sorry."

"We're here for Camilla too," Lenore said.

Dmitri eyed the other two like a massive inconvenience.

Rook scowled at Lowell. "This is your doing. I know it is." He turned back to Lenore and took her hands in his. "Please go home. It isn't safe for you here."

"They took my mother, they took my friend, and now they're trying to take my sister. It's not safe for *them*." Jade fire burned in Lenore's eyes. "I'll do whatever it takes to get her back. Are you going to help us or not?"

"Little bird…"

Drag her out of here if you have to. Protect her. His heart hurt as it beat out each command, but he pushed them away. Rook drank in the sight of the incredible, brave person he cherished so dearly and nodded.

"We need to strip these bodies and dump them in the cesspit back there," he said. "You two will do better in disguise."

Rook had hoped one of the dead men was his size, but no luck.

As they peeled garments off bleeding corpses, Dmitri whispered to Rook, "You must feel very confident in yourself."

"No," Rook replied, though he provided no other explanation.

)(

Lenore fit well enough into her borrowed uniform, but the lingering warmth from its former occupant made her skin crawl. Lowell's situation was more difficult. His mechanical limbs, which everyone agreed were too helpful to do without, didn't fit inside the supple sleeves and trousers. In the end, they cut off those pieces and hoped they could pretend he was a new recruit.

Dmitri said to let him do the talking. The fewer interactions they had, though, the better. He also gave Lenore and Lowell a crash course on the Reaper's Collective. Their weapons could stay out, as every Collective member was always armed. He also explained how to pick out a Crypt-Keeper from the rest of the pack, plus any other useful tidbits he could cram in between stripping the uniforms and dumping the bodies.

They whispered, always listening for more people coming down the tunnel. Lowell especially had gone quiet; Lenore checked in with him while Rook and Dmitri disposed of the corpses.

"This is a very dark business," he whispered. Phantoms flitted in his eyes.

She reached out to him. "You don't have to come. We'd understand."

He put on a brave smile. "No, we're stronger together. And besides, perhaps after this Felicia will see I'm not as fragile as she thinks."

Lenore managed to smile back. "Thank you. I appreciate everything you've done."

Rook and Dmitri returned, and they started down the hall again.

Lenore's mask was uncomfortable and humid. It reeked of sweat and dried beef.

Lowell echoed her thoughts. "I say, these getups are a bit much, aren't they?"

Dmitri motioned for silence. Lenore, suspecting Lowell had been trying to take the edge off his fear, wanted to clap back. Dmitri was right, though, so she settled for pulling a face before letting it go.

They made their way out of the tunnel and through a storage room. Crates, some half open and still more nailed shut, clustered in groups. A few stank of rotten eggs—sulfur, a component used for making black powder. Lenore swallowed hard and hoped Rook and Dmitri had stopped the Collective from making more. A Collective member leaned against the wall next to a makeshift desk of empty crates and a board. A supplies clerk, if Lenore had to guess. Dmitri nodded at him. He nodded back, though his eyes lingered on Lowell's false leg and arm.

Through another tunnel, past more masked clones, and into a common area. About a dozen Collective members milled around. Some wore their masks as they chatted, sparred, and generally killed time. Lenore's heart clattered inside her ribcage. She watched her periphery, thankful for the mask.

"Hey!"

Dmitri kept walking, so the rest of the group did too. The call came again. Lenore felt eyes turning to them one by one. Dmitri finally turned and looked at a Collective member stalking toward them. It was a middle-aged man, pale and blond. A scar ran down the side of his face.

"Who's the gimp then?"

"Gimp?" Dmitri changed his voice to a deep timbre.

"Yeah, the gimp." Blondie spit at Lowell's feet.

Lowell stepped forward. "I don't see a gimp." He sounded how Lenore imagined a dragon might, if they weren't extinct and could talk. Lowell made a rude gesture. "Piss off." His growl suggested he'd just found the man on the bottom of his boot.

Where did he learn that?

Blondie squared up to Lowell. "Make me."

"We've got work to do," Dmitri said, sounding entirely relaxed, "but I don't mind waiting a minute to see him flatten you."

Lenore's eyes boggled behind her mask. Was he crazy? A fight was the last thing they needed, but it was too late—Lowell had taken his cue and pushed Blondie. The man stomped forward and drew his fist back. Even without his enhanced limb, Lowell was faster and stronger. He clocked Blondie so hard he pirouetted under the blow and dropped like a sack of potatoes.

Dmitri motioned them onward. "Not even gonna be late."

No one moved to help their fellow or stop Lowell. They all just went back to their respective activities. Lenore's wonder at how anyone in the Collective had been willing to carry out the acts they had faded.

They made it through a smaller and emptier room. Lenore ticked another marker off their journey.

Just one more room and another tunnel to go, then it was back out as fast as possible.

Lenore hoped the last room would be a filing office, a place for processing prisoners manned by a meek, bookish attendant. Not likely. She remained attentive and sharp but kept hoping anyway.

In the final tunnel, voices approached from the other direction. Dmitri swore quietly. His head swiveled, and he motioned everyone into another little tomb off to the side. Lenore had seen plenty of these alcoves as they walked, but it had done

314

nothing to make them less creepy. Some even had sarcophagi in them. She felt like the skull decorations were spying on them, ready to report back to their dark sovereign.

"I recognize that voice," Dmitri said. "It's Beetle, one of the Crypt-Keepers. He'll question us for sure. We need to hide."

They looked around, but only bare walls and empty eye sockets stared back at them.

"Lenore, with me," Rook said. "You two, into the corner. Sit on the floor. Lowell, face your add-ons toward the wall. Pretend to play marbles or dice or something."

"We don't have any…" Dmitri began.

Lowell produced a handful of small, round projectiles from his side pouch—ammunition for what he called his "wrist rocket"—and Dmitri snapped his mouth shut. They got into position. Lenore was pleased with how well the tomb's low light disguised Lowell's limbs.

Rook gently pressed her into the other corner, second farthest from the entrance.

"What are we going to do?" she whispered.

"This." Rook lifted her mask just enough to press his lips to hers. He'd either lost his mind or they were about to die.

She wasn't ready to give up and pressed against his chest. It was like trying to move a statue. His fingers curled into her hair, hands sliding along the sides of her throat, and kept her close. "Keep kissing me," he whispered.

Lenore realized what he was doing and dove in. Rook's warmth seeped into her skin as the footsteps came closer and entered the tomb. She poured her fear and desperation into the kiss to avoid tensing up, and Rook reciprocated.

"Ahem."

Rook retreated, blocking Lenore's face from view and keeping his own turned away while their masks slipped back into place. He looked back and altered his voice. "Yes, Crypt-Keeper?"

"Take it elsewhere."

Rook inclined his head. "Sorry."

The squat Crypt-Keeper cast a glance at Dmitri and Lowell, who nodded, before walking away. Messy stitches crisscrossed Beetle's exposed arm. Lenore trembled and tried not to think about what he'd done to incur such an ugly injury. Rook's hands tightened around her. No one moved until Beetle's and his companion's footsteps had faded down the corridor.

Dmitri looked at her and Rook. She couldn't see Dmitri's face, but she felt his censure. Lowell, however, mimed applauding them.

He leaned over. "It's about time. Can't blame you one bit. Have you seen how scandalously he fills those gas-pipes he wears?" Lowell fanned himself.

Lenore suppressed a giggle but allowed herself to think of the tight trousers Rook often wore. For a moment, she could forget they might be walking inside their own graves.

The last room wasn't, as Lenore had hoped, a filing closet. It was a training room complete with targets, shoddy practice weapons, and posters on the walls. These last items featured current organization objectives and encouraging messages about how the Reaper was their great, dark savior.

At the opposite end of the room sat cages. They weren't proper cells, just bars that encircled holes in the floor. There was a ledge around each crater for a prisoner to sit, but they'd have to hold on to the bars. The way some of the Collective members leaned against the cages, Lenore got the distinct impression that it might be safer inside the cavity.

A crown of golden hair hovered above the edge of one. Lenore's heart leapt. Camilla was the only prisoner. Lenore could only see her mussed hair and hanging head from this angle, but there was no mistaking her.

"Bugger me," Rook said under his breath.

Lenore felt the heat of the glare Rook turned on Dmitri. She agreed with the fury rolling off him. This would have been nice to know about.

Dmitri ignored their animosity. "Lenore, you have to do the talking. The Crypt-Keeper next to Camilla's cage? That's Nightmare. She knows my voice, and she might know Rook's too."

Lenore nodded. She stuffed down her hesitation and marched forward.

You're meant to be here. You are in charge.

Lenore strode up to Nightmare like an army leader. "The prisoner's wanted. We're here to collect her."

Nightmare didn't wear her mask. How calmly she met Lenore's dead stare was, frankly, shocking. "What is she wanted for?" She sounded almost uninterested.

"That engineer prick has questions for her."

Nightmare laughed, a pleasant sound that was odd in their surroundings. "Ugh, what does Sunspot want now? Is he looking to pin his failures on her?"

Lenore choked down a hysterical laugh. Sunspot? Was that really the code name Dempsey had picked for himself? Of course it was. Arrogant git.

Rook coughed, and Nightmare turned to him. "Got a cold? Our lost lamb here has an excellent cure for that. Camilla, would you please bring your little perfume bottle over?"

Camilla stopped pacing. She'd stiffened when Lenore had spoken but betrayed nothing else. She narrowed her eyes and shook her head.

"Come on, darling. Be a good girl." A thinly veiled threat purred beneath Nightmare's words.

Camilla walked up the spiral steps around the hole's rim and approached Nightmare. "I need it back, unless you want this cough of mine to develop into pneumonia and kill me."

Bruises darkened Camilla's skin. Lenore wanted to hug Camilla for her courage and strangle Nightmare.

"I promise to give it back." Nightmare sounded sincere as she extended her hand.

Camilla pulled a portable nebulizer from her pocket. Her hand shook as she gave it to Nightmare.

The Crypt-Keeper said, "I haven't tried it yet, but I think you do something like—*kack*!" Nightmare had squeezed the pump, delivering a strong dose into her face. Some nearby Collective members turned to see what the fuss was about, but Nightmare was already laughing about her mistake. Her chortles seemed to put them off their curiosity. "Just like that, you see? My, that is strong stuff. Want some?"

Rook shook his head. Nightmare shrugged and passed the bottle back to Camilla. She reclaimed it with the dignity of royalty.

"The prisoner?" Lenore did her best to sound bored.

"Mmhm." Nightmare pulled a keyring from her belt and opened the door. Her eyes were elsewhere, as if she'd forgotten something. Her gaze roved over the room and landed on Lowell's mechanical appendages. "Sorry, who are you?"

"Sparky," Lowell grumbled in the same fake voice as before.

"No." Nightmare shook her head, looking confused. "I know every new recruit. I would remember you."

The comment drew more attention than her earlier outburst.

Lenore grabbed Camilla's arm. "We're late already. Good day."

"Hang on," Nightmare said.

Lenore ignored her and turned toward the exit with Camilla. Two Collective members approached. Trying to appear confident, Lenore strode forward. She didn't know how successful she was but was certain the mask helped. Her attention split, however, as the gathering Collective members focused on Lowell. Rook and Dmitri remained by his side.

Fear gripped Lenore's throat. By risking themselves, they created a path out for her and Camilla.

She kept going, but her heart reached back. Was she sending her friends to their deaths? Did Lowell think she was abandoning him? Did she and Camilla stand a chance by themselves? She reminded herself that Rook, Dmitri, and Lowell were armed and experienced with the criminal underworld. It was the only thing that kept her moving forward. She prayed to the stars that they'd be right behind her.

Someone cried out. She risked looking back and saw Rook, Dmitri, and Lowell flying into action. Dmitri's mask hung from a Collective member's hands. Lowell kicked the nearest person with his false leg, sending them sailing and skidding along the floor. Rook flung his mask into the closest hostile's face. Nightmare backed against Camilla's cell, holding her head.

"Bloody blazes," Lenore said. "Camilla, we can't leave them. Take this." Lenore tore the bow from her back and shoved it at Camilla. She then ripped off her own mask for fear of being mistaken for the enemy.

Camilla held the bow like she might a scorpion. "What am I supposed to do with this?"

"Aim, pull the string, and release."

Lenore drew her sword and charged the nearest Collective member. She drove the jagged blade straight through them. Her conscience rebelled; if they survived this, she'd think about the life she'd just snuffed out.

More Collective members trickled into the training room, likely drawn by the noise. They wielded a variety of weapons, though short blades were the most popular.

Between the skills and weapons in Lenore's group—especially Lowell's wrist rocket and other ranged armaments—they inched toward the exit. Camilla found the bow's sight, though her aim suffered from inexperience. Lenore stayed close and finished off any targets that came within reach of her blade.

A boulder-shaped man came roaring at Lenore, caring nothing for the dart Camilla shot into his back as he barreled past. He knocked the sword from Lenore's hand with a thick gauntleted arm. She stumbled, and the man reached for her with dinner-plate-sized hands. Another figure leapt between her and the behemoth. They blocked the incoming blow and bowed beneath it but didn't break.

"Not my tinker belle, you malodorous brute!" Lowell sounded perfectly scandalized. He'd lost his usual mask as well as the stolen one.

With a heave, Lowell pushed the hulk back with his false arm and punched. The boulder-man bounced back unfazed and leapt at Lowell. Linked blades like teeth whipped toward the goon; Lenore hung on to the weapon's handle like a fishing reel. The blades wrapped around his neck and bit in, opening tiny streams of blood. He pulled at the weapon, cut his hands and smeared crimson. Lowell took advantage and finished him off. While Lenore unwound her whip-sword from the brute's throat, it recompressed into a solid blade bound by a slender cable. She caught Camilla looking at her waist where, only minutes ago, Lenore'd had a belt.

"Backup weapon." Lenore wrapped it around her and reclaimed her sword.

Rook and Dmitri fought like a single unit. One bashed, the other sliced; deadly dancers supporting one another. Rook flew around Dmitri's well-ordered movements, filling in injuries wherever he could.

Despite their victories, Collective members trickled in faster than they went down and squeezed the interlopers into a shrinking circle. Lenore, pressed back to back with Dmitri, prayed for an intervention.

"*Stop!*" The voice rattled like wind through dead leaves yet carried crushing authority.

Every Collective member froze. Some fell to incoming blows before Lenore's party had a chance to regroup and look at the owner of that chilling voice. At no more than a slow, sweeping hand gesture, the Collective members moved aside and bowed their heads, creating a channel straight to the figure.

The creature with the beaked Old World death-speaker mask and whole-body black shrouds could be none other than the Reaper. Fury rose in Lenore like steam, building pressure. The Enforcer order's growth. Copper nearly dying. Her lost colleagues. The Halls, her mother, Camilla, Adelle, Falcon, Majesty, Eamon. This creature spread poison, the deadly source of a corrupted spring. Its taint would kill everything if allowed to continue.

Lenore took off toward the Reaper, heedless of the flanking Crypt-Keepers and the long scythe in their hand.

31

~The Shepherd~

Lenore envisioned driving her sword into the Reaper's heart, ripping off their mask, and screeching into the creature's withered, monstrous face. She'd speak the names of everyone that devil's deeds had harmed.

A hand grabbed her arm and yanked her back. Lenore's limbs whiplashed out and back again. She'd have stumbled if the iron grip hadn't also steadied her. Lenore spun, ready to loose curses on whoever had stopped her, but shock shattered the words out of existence.

Camilla hung on to Lenore so hard she might have left fingerprints on Lenore's bones. Her eyes were wide with terror, and her hair shuddered as she shook her head. "No, Lenore. The Reaper would kill you without a thought. I've seen it happen."

"Come," the Reaper rasped. Lenore and Camilla turned to them. The Reaper pointed at Lenore and beckoned like death itself. "Stay your anger and follow me. My children, into a cage with the rest. Do not harm them, however."

The Collective members swelled around the group like lemmings, swarming and fearless. The horde separated Lenore from her friends and disarmed them. She reached through the throng, shouting their names. With a gale of dread howling through her ears, she heard her name as if from across a chasm. Her fingertips touched Camilla's before the Collective members pulled them apart. But her eyes remained on Lowell as they ripped off his mechanical limbs.

Lenore redoubled her efforts, shrieking to a fever pitch.

"Wait," said the Reaper.

The Collective froze and awaited further orders.

The Reaper examined Lowell with their empty eyes, turned from him to his separated limbs and back. "Him as well."

The Collective pushed Lowell forward like a tide. They had to hold him up since he now lacked his other leg. Lenore offered her shoulder, which he accepted with a stern countenance. Tremors, however, shook him as he leaned on her. They watched as the Collective members herded Camilla, Dmitri, and Rook into Camilla's cage. Nightmare stood a little way off from the crowd, her eyes trained on the prisoners. Lenore swallowed hard as she fought down visions of what revenge the Crypt-Keeper would take for their attempted jailbreak.

When the Reaper spoke again, their voice wheezed surprisingly gentle. "I am not without mercy. If you have words to share with your companions, you may do so now."

Lenore and Lowell tromped to the cell.

Lowell shifted his weight to lean against the bars. "Well, ladies and chaps, this is quite the sticky wicket." His voice cracked, and Lenore squeezed his arm against her.

"We'll think of something," she whispered.

Rook opened his mouth, but Camilla reached through the bars, took Lenore's face in her hands, and wiped at tears that weren't there. "Lenore, I am so sorry." Rook and Dmitri flanked her, closing their little circle. Camilla switched to Lowell and repeated the action. "Please, friends, forgive me."

Lenore barely managed not to choke as cold invaded her airways—with deft hands, Camilla had swiped her thumbs over Lenore's nostrils, depositing some kind of goo.

Tears ran down Camilla's face. "I love you."

"I love you too." Lenore swallowed her sorrow and fear. She looked at Rook. "And you. I should have told you such a long time ago."

He gave her a weak facsimile of his usual smirk. "I've always known." He turned to Lowell. "You've always been the best, mate. Chin up."

Lowell's throat bobbed, but his nod was firm. He bowed his head to Camilla. "My lady, I am honored to have fought at your side."

They looked at Dmitri together. All three shared a knowing look before facing the room again. The Reaper waited motionlessly beyond. Leaning on one another, Lowell and Lenore started forward.

The Reaper, flanked before and behind by Crypt-Keeper pairs, led them down a winding path. Lenore tried to memorize the route, though the dim stone corridors blended into one another. The Reaper's scythe tapping on the floor reminded her of a ticking clock. She thanked the stars her whip-sword seemed to have been overlooked and felt the weight of possibility around her waist.

At the end of the corridor, they entered a large circular room. Worktables lined the walls like the desks in the Arc-Tech department. A testing area with targets and dummies stood off to one side, while a small manufactory took up a fair bit of the other. What grabbed Lenore's attention the most, however, was Dempsey. Though pale and haggard, his face lit up like it was New Year's morning.

He bowed low. "Welcome, my liege. To what do I owe this most auspicious visit?" He regarded Lenore with a malicious glint in his eye.

The Reaper addressed Lenore and Lowell. "You may think of me like a shepherd. I take in those who are vulnerable to the world and give them a place to hide." They turned back to Dempsey, who silently gloated behind. "You told me of this witch's powers, yes?"

"I did indeed."

"For the last bloody time, I am not a witch!" Lenore looked at the Reaper. "He just can't believe I'm capable of achieving anything without guile."

"You will hold your tongue in the presence of your superiors, or I will remove it for you," Dempsey snapped. "In fact, with your permission, my lord, I recommend we silence this pernicious quim."

"I say!" Lowell shot back with enough condescension to make Felicia glow with pride. "That is *not* how you speak to, of, or before a lady. What sort of ill-bred, uneducated boor are you?"

Dempsey's face turned beetroot red. "You worthless cripple. I am a hundred times the man you could ever hope to be, if indeed you can call yourself a man at all."

The Reaper pounded the end of their scythe against the floor, stilling them all.

"Lenore." Claws skittered over her skin at hearing her name from those lips. "This one recommended you betray your friends to me. It was he who devised punishment for the loss of one of my flock, the death of your husband. Didn't you, Sunspot?"

"With great pleasure," he said.

Lenore's throat tightened. As Dempsey smiled victoriously at her with his perfect white teeth, she imagined setting fire to him with her glare.

"You will not touch her," the Reaper said. Dempsey opened his mouth—an objection, by the look on his face—but the Reaper made a sort of rattle-hiss, like bones clicking together. Dempsey fell silent. They turned to Lenore again and spoke gently. "Before you think I have poorly judged this one, know that he merely served a purpose. One which you will now fulfill." They looked to Lowell, while Dempsey flapped his mouth in silent disbelief. "What are you called, my friend?"

"Sparky," Lowell said.

Dempsey shook off his stupor. "No. *No*. Not again!"

He grabbed a wrench from the nearest table. The Crypt-Keepers, who'd been standing back like dark sentinels, rushed him before he could do anything more. They forced him to his knees, while he spit curses at Lenore.

The Reaper motioned to Dempsey. "He has injured you both. Please, I implore you to take your vengeance."

Ice filled Lenore from her toes to her scalp. She had killed in self-defense and to rescue people, but this was different. Her memories bled pain into the ice, hardening it. This vile man, who had paid to have her killed, had tried to torture her, had disparaged her and her friends… Lenore wanted to pour her pain into him. To make him feel every indignity and harm tenfold.

Lowell shook his head, but she didn't move.

Care etched into Lowell's features. "Lenore." Her name sounded like butterfly wings in summer.

"He's taken so much from me," she whispered.

"I know. And no matter what, I am with you."

Lenore took a deep breath and looked back at Dempsey. His mouth had twisted into a snarl.

"Do not fall prey to her wiles," he said to the Reaper. "She is a demoness. Men like us must stick together. We are under attack! Be strong, my brother. Do—"

With a hit from the flat end of the Reaper's scythe, Dempsey's head flew back. "Do not presume to address me so, cur." Danger wound a garrote around every syllable.

Blood ran from Dempsey's crushed nose and his chin where the scythe's edge had cut deep. The sight slashed through the ice within Lenore. A small inner voice cried out from beneath the splintered surface—a heart, twisted and vile though it was, beat inside Dempsey. What would it make her if she stopped it?

The Reaper motioned for Lenore to continue.

Her voice trembled as she said, "Whatever you thought about killing Eamon, everything you think about me, it's all wrong."

"Eamon was—"

"Shut it! You don't get to say his name. I hope whenever you meet your end, you're forgotten quickly and without concern. I certainly won't waste another minute of my life thinking about you. A sad, ignorant, egotistic child like you isn't worth the energy." Lowell held her hand. She was shaking but didn't cry. "I'm done."

Skepticism rolled off the Reaper. "Are you certain?"

Lenore nodded, not trusting herself to speak again. The Reaper nodded back and leaned down to Dempsey's ear. Lenore heard the faintest hiss of air, like steam escaping a pipe. Eyes boggling, he opened his mouth. Dark metal flashed as the Reaper buried the scythe's spined end in Dempsey's throat. Blood filled his mouth, spilled over his lips as he choked on his unspoken words. Lenore and Lowell jolted back, but the other two Crypt-Keepers barred them from bolting.

Dempsey's head folded forward. The two Crypt-Keepers holding him dragged the body away, leaving a shiny trail of blood along the floor. The Reaper wiped their scythe clean and placed it into a holster on their back.

Lenore forced herself to stay put instead of scrabbling backward the way her mind screamed at her to do.

The Reaper approached and cupped the air below her face. "His body will not go to waste."

The sickly sweet scent of dying flowers and moldering bodies assailed Lenore's nose. She gagged, pulled her head back, and coughed. The Reaper's dead eyes stared at her while she caught her breath. They turned to Lowell and rattled a long, heavy breath over him. He too coughed, and his eyes watered; the irregular one turned almost completely pink.

The Reaper folded their hands, which disappeared into the folds of their sleeves. "We will discuss your responsibilities later." They rasped at the remaining two black-clad officers. "Come. Let us turn our attention to Ermine and his handler."

Lenore cried out. "You said you wouldn't harm them!" She and Lowell traded a terrified glance.

The Reaper didn't look back at her. "They will serve as examples to those who would stand against us."

Rage and fear tumbled in Lenore's stomach. "You claim to oppose the Enforcers, but you're no different!"

The Reaper walked on. Their Crypt-Keepers closed in on Lenore and Lowell, postures threatening trouble at the slightest show of resistance.

Careful, a voice in Lenore's head said. *You can't help Rook and Dmitri if you're dead.*

One look at Lowell told her he was fighting the same battle. At least Lenore still had her whip-sword, but they were outnumbered. They shared a glance and followed.

More identical corridors, all awash in the same eerie lichen light. The occasional brazier sent their shadows jumping. They entered a large room. At the back sat a wooden throne. Braziers lined the walls every few feet and bathed the room in light and heat. If it hadn't been for the relentless damp, Lenore suspected the lichen would have ignited.

Not many Collective members were gathered here. An image captor had been set up, which explained the need for the sweltering light.

Camilla stood nearby with a Crypt-Keeper at her back. Lenore met her eyes, exchanging silent concern. She wondered why none of them had their hands tied. Then again, they were outmatched. Sweat trickled down her back. Lenore scanned the room for Rook and Dmitri, but they weren't there. The Reaper had said an example would be made; Dmitri and Rook's absence was more frightening than their presence would have been.

While Lenore looked and wondered, the Reaper settled onto the throne.

Lowell, still leaning on Lenore, whispered into her ear, "If I had my limb enhancements, we'd be in much better shape. I'm sorry."

"You have no reason to be," Lenore said.

"You might have stood a chance if it weren't for me, though."

Given their close proximity, Lenore could inject force into her voice without adding volume. "All this time, I've been leaning on you. The strength you've given me has nothing to do with your limbs. You are a marvel even without them, remember?"

Lowell's smile lit up his face. It disappeared when one of the Crypt-Keepers behind them growled.

At the back of the room, an ancient stone door opened. Six Collective members led Rook and Dmitri through it. Both had a noose around their necks, held at the other end by one of the Collective members. Their hands were tied behind their backs. Fresh fear pounced on her heart—rafters ran across the ceiling.

A Crypt-Keeper entered through the back, bearing a cat-o'-nine-tails before them like a holy offering. Beetle, the one with the mangled arm, followed. In the same fashion as the first, he held a long, thin knife like what Esther used to bone fish. A third carried a bone saw. They stopped behind Rook and Dmitri.

Lenore scrambled to think of something she could do, but every option ended in disaster.

"Please don't do this." She didn't care a whit for her dignity, but Rook's sad smile only broke her more.

The Reaper's eyes followed Rook and Dmitri.

"They're working to take down the Enforcers," Lenore said. "If you kill them, you jeopardize that." Her fear and anger shot to white-hot levels as the Collective members tossed the ropes over a central rafter. "I suppose you're happy to let the Enforcers run roughshod over our city. Swelling their numbers. Abusing people. Seems you enjoy seeing them hurt innocent people. Otherwise, why would you beat the hornet's nest like you do?"

Slowly, like an Old World automaton, the Reaper turned just their head toward her.

"Little bird, stop," Rook said, his voice strong.

The nickname poured acid over the fissures in her heart. She thought of never hearing him say it again, and the fissures split wide open.

"You aren't as bad as the Enforcers, Reaper," she snarled. "You're *worse!*"

"You are new here, but you will learn I do not tolerate insubordination." The Reaper turned back to the Collective members around Rook and Dmitri. "One hundred lashes before the flaying."

The Crypt-Keeper gripping the cat-o'-nine-tails stepped forward. Their brass mask and compression caused by the tight leather uniform made it impossible to tell whether this was a man or a woman, but the shoulders didn't seem wide enough for a man. They leaned toward Rook and Dmitri. Lenore imagined what horrible descriptions of the encroaching torment they were dripping into her friends' ears. The Collective member holding the ropes pulled just enough to make Rook and Dmitri stand straight lest the nooses strangle them.

The first lash made Rook arch and groan. Lenore screamed. The noose tightened around his neck. He gasped, pulled back, and coughed, while the cat-o'-nine-tail's bearer waited. Could Rook survive a hundred lashes? Rivulets of blood ran from his back, over tears in his stolen uniform. Rook's reaction made Lenore think the weapon had to be coated with something awful, something to increase the pain. She'd seen him get stabbed and react less violently.

Lenore grit her teeth. Four more lashes. Dmitri and Rook choked as they rocked beneath the blows.

The Reaper raised a hand. "Rest. I want them to live through this."

Desperation tightened around Lenore's throat as if she too wore a noose. Behind Rook and Dmitri, Beetle's slender blade glinted, a thirsty fang.

The Reaper meant for this to take hours.

Lenore clutched the handle of her whip-sword as if she were just hanging on to her belt. She could do a little damage before they disarmed her. Camilla and Lowell would likely suffer for her actions, but this useless nothing she was doing chomped at her innards.

Lenore leaned into Lowell. "Please, trust me." She shoved him away from her and yelled, "Stop hanging off me already!"

Lowell tipped to the side, windmilled his arms, and sprawled onto the floor. Lenore stared at him. At least the pain stitched into her features was sincere.

She threw all her fury behind the act. "You said you wouldn't be a burden, but look where we are!"

"Lenore!" Camilla gawped, her brows quivering in shock.

"Not a word from you," Lenore said. "You're the reason we're in this mess to begin with."

Rook and Dmitri's breathing wheezed painfully loud, but a surreptitious glance told Lenore more than half the room's eyes were on her. They followed as she marched to Camilla.

Lowell wailed. "She's broken me!"

The eyes shifted to him as he began to flail like he was suffering a fit. Some of the Collective members moved closer to him. Their glances looked as uncertain as any static clone-faces could.

Near Camilla, Lenore spun toward the Reaper. She yanked the belt from her waist and hurled it toward their head. The shot went too high; the teeth of her whip-sword bit into the throne's top rail above their head. The Reaper's dead eyes locked onto her. They rose from the throne, their robes flowing out from them like a billowing cloud of dark fury. Lenore's stomach dropped. She tugged at her weapon, but it refused to budge. Keeping a hold of the grip, she circled away from the Reaper.

Shouts erupted elsewhere in the catacombs. They reverberated off the walls as a dull hum at first but quickly grew louder. Lowell's cries and thrashing got worse. Rook and Dmitri cried out and writhed, though Lenore hadn't heard the cat-o'-nine-tail's crack. The room's attention splintered like fracturing glass. The Reaper raised a hand to claim the fight with Lenore and advanced on her. They opened the scythe with a hideous *schnick*.

Behind her, Camilla cried out. Lenore half-turned and saw her spray the nebulizer into her guard's face. The guard coughed and staggered back. In Lenore's periphery, the Crypt-Keeper with the cat-o'-nine-tails pulled a small knife from their belt.

"Look out!" Lenore wasn't certain who exactly needed the warning.

Lowell was up and hopping, but she couldn't spare a moment to see where he was headed—the Reaper was no more than a few yards away now. If she continued to circle, she'd start to wrap her precious weapon around the throne. The Collective members that weren't distracted by the growing shouts from the tunnels watched their leader. Their masks' glass eyes glowed orange in the brazier light. The scythe's blade flashed as the Reaper raised it.

"No!"

Rook's voice didn't come from where Lenore had expected. She was already in position, whip-sword raised above her head, when she caught him from the corner of her eye. He was running toward her, no longer tied or noosed and wielding two slim daggers. As the scythe came down onto the cable serving as the sword's spine, Lenore's elbows bent but didn't buckle. The force of the blow dislodged the sword from the throne. The Reaper barely dodged as its recompressing teeth shot back to Lenore. Rook flew in and kicked them in the side. The Reaper stumbled but steadied themself by driving the scythe's tip into the floor. Lenore and Rook jumped out of the blade's reach.

Lowell leaned on Camilla as they spritzed anything that came near with the nebulizer. The Collective members that came too close coughed, shook their heads, and looked around, seemingly dazed. Others headed down the tunnels in the direction of the growing commotion.

Lenore heard the words "Enforcers" and "breached," though she didn't have time to consider what that meant—a pair of Crypt-Keepers had rushed in to defend their leader. Rook was fighting them off and had just stabbed one in the gut.

Dmitri, free like Rook, rushed into the fray. Another Crypt-Keeper followed on his heels. Lenore turned to keep him from being stabbed in the back, but his tail skidded to a halt and ripped off the Crypt-Keeper mask.

It was Nightmare.

"Not me!" Nightmare pointed at the ancient door in the back of the room. "Get the Reaper!"

The Reaper fled through it. Without thinking, Lenore followed.

32

~The Brightest Star~

The Reaper was quick. Lenore found the sight of them running uncanny, as if it went against nature. Lenore was fast too, though. Another wooden door led them into a laboratory of some kind. Judging by the anatomical drawings on a blackboard, she guessed medical. The Reaper headed for a heavy wooden cabinet in the back of the room and pulled a key out of their robes. To remain outside that wicked scythe's range, Lenore flung the whip-sword at the Reaper. They ducked as the shot went wide and returned to her.

The Reaper hurried to unlock the doors and swung them wide. Metal panels reinforced the cabinet's doors and walls—this was a protected area. All manner of strange objects stuffed the space within, orderly but crowded. Lenore felt as if spiders crawled up the back of her neck. What did the Reaper want to protect?

She launched another strike. This time, the sword's teeth sank into the mask's long beak and ripped it off. The Reaper's hood flew back with it. Lenore froze.

"Phoebe," she whispered.

They snapped clover-green eyes to Lenore and sneered. The wild, bright ginger curls Lenore had seen in Mina's image-still had been clipped close to their skull. The freckles sprinkled across their pale face made them appear younger than Lenore had expected.

"Don't you say that name," the Reaper grated. "You have no right."

"Everyone thinks you're dead," Lenore said. "Phoebe—"

"You know so little. Phoebe *is* dead!"

"Then how are you standing here? I saw you in an image-still. Do you really think faking your own death makes you a different person? That no one would find out?"

"Phoebe was my sister, you ignorant wretch!"

Lenore snapped her jaws shut.

The Reaper's chest heaved. Fury blazed in their eyes. "Phoebe was the brightest star to grace this miserable city, and those cockroaches stamped every bit of light out of her. What do you suppose the Enforcers did when I asked for justice? *Nothing.* They said Phoebe's choice was her own. They said it's not their job to police some little girl's hurt feelings like a nursery school."

Lenore flapped her lips. Something crashed elsewhere in the catacombs, followed by screams, and she snapped back to her senses.

The Reaper returned to the cabinet, hurling books and tools and horrendous jarred curiosities to the floor. Lenore cast her whip again, but the Reaper was ready and used the cabinet's door as a shield. They pulled the scythe from their back.

Lenore retreated toward the worktables. *I need a better weapon.*

Flasks, vials, beakers, and test tubes scattered across every surface. Lamps burning low shrouded the room in faint shadows. Lenore could start flinging glassware and its contents, but she had no idea what it contained or if it'd do any good. Another scan of the room gave her an answer.

Every newssheet had shown pictures of the pepper gas canister after the protestor attack. Similar canisters stood on a nearby worktable. Their tops had nozzles, which the others hadn't. She didn't know if these contained the same agent, but she understood their potential.

Lenore grabbed one, aimed, and averted her face—she'd read about the gas' effect on the protestors. Where she'd expected a thick cloud of crimson, a thin stream of spray ejected. It shot across a lit Reedsen burner and ignited. She dropped the canister, and the flame died.

Discarded objects and broken glass clustered around the Reaper's feet as they dug through the cabinet, one eye on Lenore. The smell from the shattered jars reeked of chemicals and death, their contents splashed in every direction. The Reaper pulled a worn leather satchel from the cabinet, faced Lenore, and looped the strap over their shoulder. They didn't need to say anything for her to understand: *stay away or die*.

Lenore homed in on the satchel. It had to be important and was likely dangerous. She needed to get a hold of it or destroy it. After everything they'd been through, she didn't care either way.

"It sounds like your people have run into trouble," she said. "Shouldn't you be out there, helping them?"

"My flock will die for me." The redhead edged along the side of the room, their eyes on Lenore's whip-sword. "Their sacrifices serve a greater purpose."

Indignation reared up in her and shrieked like a wild animal. "I suppose you'd say the same thing about all those innocents in the Halls of Justice?"

"All for the cause."

Lenore grabbed a beaker from a nearby table and hurled it at the Reaper. They dodged.

"One of them was my mother! You murdered Eamon and put all of us in more peril. You are nothing more than a petty killer, knifing people in dark alleys."

"Do not presume to question me. I will lead us to a better life."

"You are a merchant of death!"

Lenore slung the whip-sword so hard her shoulder flared with pain. One of its teeth caught the satchel's shoulder strap and pulled but didn't tear through the thick leather. Lenore yanked, and the Reaper grasped the handle for dear life. They shook the shoulder strap free and jammed it back into place. With her free hand, Lenore picked up another canister. She sprayed and set it alight. A fiery plume licked toward the Reaper, who sidestepped around the edge of the room. Lenore focused on damage and keeping the Reaper away from the exit, but they were playing their own game, weaving around workstations and flinging whatever came to hand. They abandoned their scythe on a worktable, which made Lenore want the satchel more.

The Reaper stopped at a table where a gulf of nothing stood between glowing lamps and filled glassware. As they hurled a flask of clear liquid at Lenore, she released the pressure on her canister nozzle...

Not fast enough. Glass and fire exploded. Lenore dodged to the side, but the whip-sword flew from her hand. Liquid heat and glass bit into her uniform, burned through the leather, and left sizzling holes behind.

When she looked back, the Reaper was making a break for the door.

She relit her canister stream and followed. More glassware careened her way, anything the Reaper got their hands on. Lenore evaded what she could and shielded herself when she couldn't. A beaker shattered against her head; warmth trickled down her face.

The Reaper was nearly there.

Darkness roiled in the doorway. A shadow gathered form and substance and rippled waves of terror through the air. Lenore recognized the presence, though something primal in her still quailed. Her feet refused to move, and her hand relaxed on the canister unbidden. The Reaper stopped too, something besides fear working on their face.

"Kieran?" they said together.

33

~Seeing Red~

Kieran's heart didn't beat like a human's, but he felt it stop all the same. Lenore's eyes traced the blood spattered across him. The path he'd carved through human lives painted his hands.

He'd become a monster to save Lenore and Camilla. He wished to shrink to nothing under Lenore's gaze, but he needed to keep blocking the doorway because of who was staring at him with shock and rage.

"Zoe." Sadness as thick as the blood staining his clothes soaked his voice.

The Reaper's—Zoe's—eyes raked over Kieran's face. His fangs. His solid black eyes. Feral lines had sharpened his features since they'd last met, when Phoebe had introduced her family. Zoe had been barely more than a child, full of joy and bright hope.

Their voice rang hollow with disbelief. "I thought you died. What happened?" Kieran couldn't bring himself to answer, and Zoe's face twisted with rage. "Phoebe trusted you. You could have helped her!"

Kieran dropped his eyes. His voice shook. "I'm sorry."

Lenore's expression wilted with pity. It didn't deter her from her effort, though. While Zoe was glaring at Kieran, Lenore inched closer from behind, eyes on the satchel hanging from Zoe's shoulder. Lenore carried a canister Kieran recognized from pictures in the newssheets. Thankfully, she held it quiet and still.

Zoe shook, green eyes burning into him.

Kieran adjusted his timbre to that which he'd once used to soothe Lenore's nightmares. With his words, he pushed his will into the air. "Zoe, I regret the loss of your sister every day. Phoebe was a precious soul. Do you think she would have wanted this?"

Lenore and Zoe's gazes dimmed. The creases between brows grew shallower. Though dulled, so much anger remained, fighting against his voice's soporific influence. Lenore's previous exposure to Kieran's power gave her a measure of resistance. Once, she had likened it to morphine addiction. She hadn't been far off. Her movements slowed but didn't stop. Kieran feared what she intended but dared not endanger her.

Zoe seemed to realize something was happening and shook their head. Sweat beaded on their forehead as they grit their teeth and held on to their anger. They balled their hands into fists at their sides. "Phoebe's life taught me one cannot be a woman and hold power in this world, and I refuse to be a man. So I have become an icon."

Lenore's lips pressed into a thin line, damming whatever response she might have had. Close enough now, she snatched the satchel from Zoe's shoulder.

Zoe spun on her, and Kieran felt the tether of his control snap. It dazed him the way a punch would. While he gathered his wits, Lenore staggered back, bowing under the weight of her prize.

"You aren't worthy of such secrets." Zoe marched toward Lenore. "Perhaps you could have been, but—" Zoe yelped as Kieran grabbed them from behind and locked his arms around them.

The world slowed for Kieran. Lenore's opportunity for revenge hung before her.

And he was helping facilitate it.

Lenore's eyes bored into Zoe's, rage and pain sparking in both. Yet she wavered. Kieran suspected he knew something of her struggle—this wasn't the same as defending oneself or others. Kieran wanted to intervene, to prevent further bloodshed, but his friend's pain was valid.

Lenore seemed to be collecting herself. She took a deep breath. "Keep a tight hold on her, Kieran. I—"

"Not *her*," Zoe snapped. "I've left those distinctions behind."

Kieran exchanged a look with Lenore, and both nodded. "Don't let them go no matter what, please." Still clutching her canister, Lenore looped the shoulder strap over her head so it hung across her body. She stared down, gripping the satchel's handle so hard her knuckles turned white.

"Lenore."

She raised a hand. Kieran didn't know what he would have said anyway, just something to help. Lenore had lost much, but so had Zoe.

"You are not so different." Kieran delivered the words gently but without emotion—he couldn't bring himself to condemn or condone his friend's intentions.

Lenore's features pinched. Empathy and ire melded in her voice, cracking her words. "I'm so, so sorry about your sister, Zoe, but hurting people isn't the answer. We can reject the limits people try to put on us and support one another."

"Except they don't!" Zoe struggled against Kieran's grip. Holding Zoe's arms against their sides while they wriggled and kicked took barely any effort. As much as possible, they turned their face to him. "Your spoiled sweetheart did nothing as Phoebe suffered."

The words jammed needles into Kieran's heart, for all their losses. A part of him wanted to object, to use his own pain as a shield—he'd lost his whole life in one night *and* had to live with the consequences.

But he was still here, and Phoebe wasn't.

Focusing on Zoe's tragedy didn't undermine his. He reformed his pain into sympathy. "I know. Mina knows too."

"And she's sorry," Lenore said. "She told me herself when there was nothing to gain. She still regrets not doing more."

"And there's nothing left to lose either," Zoe said.

Zoe spit at Lenore, drove their feet into the floor, and thrust their fists at Kieran's throat. Two blades each shot from Zoe's sleeves.

They pierced Kieran's throat in four places.

His hands flew to his throat. As lightning ripped along his nerves, he stumbled against the wall. Cold followed the lightning, an odd numbness that turned out to be a mercy. The blades must have been coated with some kind of anesthetic. Zoe zipped away from him as quickly as a fleeing bird. Part of his brain shouted at him to follow, that Lenore would die, but his body wasn't listening. Blood so dark it appeared almost black poured over his hands.

The last time he'd seen this much of his own blood was the night he'd been turned.

Zoe tried to kill you, hissed a voice in his mind. The cold cruelty of it slapped him in the face. *Rip them apart. It will be easy, like pulling wings off a fly.*

"KIERAN!" Lenore shrieked.

She won't blame you, the voice said. *She wants Zoe dead as much as you do.*

The terror in Lenore's scream had restored some clarity to his mind, however. Her fear for him, echoing off the walls, existed because he'd worked hard to make amends after attacking her. She'd been so kind to forgive him.

He couldn't lose the person he was.

Shoving the voice to the back of his mind, Kieran spat at it, *Their name is Zoe*. He forced himself to look away from the blood pouring down his front—fear and dark memories made it easier—and searched for Lenore.

Farther into the room, Zoe lunged at her. Lenore scuttled back, clutching the satchel. Zoe's blades were dark with blood in the low light. The scent of Lenore's panic reeked so strong it burned Kieran's nostrils and made his mouth water.

You know the flavor of terror, that it tastes sweetest, the unwelcome voice said. With clammy hands, it gripped his throat.

Lenore had held his hand when Eamon had asked to meet him properly.

Neal and Mina had made a home for him in theirs. They'd forgiven him after he'd fallen prey to his darker nature and endangered Lenore.

Each memory landed a kick against the voice and drove it back.

Lenore lifted her canister and pressed the trigger.

Hands still trying to stem the flow of blood from his throat, half folded against the wall, Kieran thought, *Yes, my friend. Fight.* Another strike against his Vampyre instincts.

The canister's liquid stream hit Zoe in the face. She reeled back and spewed a blue streak of swears. Lenore retreated a few steps and flicked her gaze to Kieran. The gouges in his throat were slowly closing as his healing abilities worked, but the effort weakened him. While the bleeding slowed, his thirst gained strength.

Eyes streaming, Zoe advanced again. Lenore looked back just as one of Zoe's blades sank into her upper arm. Kieran tried to cry out but could only wheeze while his larynx was mending.

The smell of blood slammed into his senses. He pressed his back harder against the wall to keep himself from flying toward the wound and drinking from the ready-made holes. His thirst clawed at his parched throat and stole breath from his lungs.

You could leave, the darkness living inside him said. It crawled over his hunched form, fetid blood-scented breath blowing over his face, while Kieran gasped for clean air. *Feed on one of the spares out there, come back, and help.*

Kieran grit his teeth. No, he couldn't leave Lenore—he wasn't sure he would come back—and Zoe looked ready to kill. Their eyes had gone completely bloodshot. Lips pulled back in a hideous grimace, Zoe twisted the blade. Lenore screamed.

So much like that night he'd attacked her.

Guilt shot adrenaline into Kieran's veins. He'd almost killed her that night; he couldn't let her die here. Kieran pushed himself off the wall, temptation still clinging to him like a parasitic worm, and hobbled forward a step. It felt like a mile. His weakness pummeled him to his knees.

Lenore bashed the canister against Zoe's head. Zoe buckled and withdrew to a worktable directly in Lenore's path out. Lenore aimed again and pressed the nozzle, but the damaged weapon only emitted a soft whistle.

Stooped over the table, heaving, Zoe said, "We're after the same things."

Kieran assumed Zoe meant to sound entreating, but it was hard to believe given how manic they looked. Blood streamed from their head. His thirst hammered against him, surging with the scent of new blood in the air. His fangs ached like abscessed teeth.

You could break open this murderer's head wound. Gorge yourself. You will heal faster, save Lenore, and take vengeance all at once.

It raised his head, forced him to stare at the spot flowing so freely with scarlet nectar. Kieran tensed every muscle, fighting to remain motionless. He didn't trust himself not to lose control and hated himself for his weakness.

Their name is Zoe, Phoebe's sibling. He repeated it again and again. It kept him from launching himself at them.

Zoe's red eyes bugged from their skull. Their voice had changed from a rasp to a croak. "Give me what's mine, and I will leave you be."

Lenore risked another look at Kieran. He knew how terrible he must look. Not even he knew what it took to kill a Vampyre, but enough blood had gushed from the wound to soak the front of his shirt and waistcoat.

Lenore's uninjured arm pushed the satchel behind her. She backed away and shook her head. For whatever reason, she didn't want Zoe to get it back.

Zoe's face transformed into a raging war mask. Zoe charged with a roar, blades straight out. Lenore leapt and tripped over her own feet. She caught herself on a table but dropped her canister. Zoe reached to reclaim the bag. Lenore gripped its handle against a table leg, fingers straining to encircle both. Her other hand searched behind her. Lenore grimaced as her wound stretched and more blood streamed from it.

Kieran fashioned the countless tidbits that made Lenore unique into a pry bar. He used it to free himself from the urges coiling around his neck and beat them back with it.

Lenore's fingertips met a long, thin handle—the rest was obscured from this angle—just as Zoe struck again. The blades gouged her shoulder, left of her heart, and she shrieked. Kieran wheezed, tried to push himself up, only to choke and double over. Her cry cut short as Zoe grabbed Lenore around the throat with their other hand.

Kieran knew how close to Lenore's heart Zoe's blades were resting, how close to dying Lenore had come. He knew because of his medical training. He'd once dreamed of being a doctor.

341

That dream is dead. The voice slithered through Kieran's mind, fogging his brain with a numbing miasma. *And from its death,* you *are reborn. You're not one of these cattle anymore. You're better—stronger, faster, more powerful. You deserve to feed on them.*

Zoe examined the spot where their blades tore ragged holes into Lenore's shoulder.

Through the fog, Kieran remembered stitching up that same shoulder. A scar had formed where Lenore had been shot by a miniature crossbow. She'd come straight to him for aid. He'd attended her wounds after the Halls of Justice attack too—not just hers, though. Camilla's, Dmitri's, Rook's, and Falcon's.

The dream hadn't died. Kieran still could—still did—help people.

Disappointment flickered in Zoe's eyes as they looked over Lenore's wound. They pulled out the blades, slick with both Lenore and Kieran's blood.

Kieran gagged on the fresh, heady scent. The ache in his fangs had transformed into a pulse, radiating through his jaw and down his spine like jabs. Salivating, his thirst asked, *What do think it tastes like, having marinated in fear all this time?* He could almost imagine the taste, when all thoughts of feeding fled.

Zoe repositioned their blades over Lenore's heart.

Lenore was still gripping the handle behind her. As she struggled to lift it, her arm shook and agony rippled across her face. Zoe stiffened, eyes emptying as dull and lifeless as those in their mask. They began to press the blades into Lenore's chest.

An image of Lenore, dead in a pool of her own blood, appeared in Kieran's mind. His knee-jerk reaction was to sit and wait for this meal. Then grief split his heart at the thought of losing this dear friend, who'd risked her marriage and even her life in his defense. With whom he'd shared adventures and quiet nights.

Disgusted with his base thoughts, bile rose in his throat.

With a surge of effort, he gathered the scores of shadows around him and disassembled into them. As night made corporeal, he rose behind Zoe and flowed back into his physical form. His wounds still oozed dark blood, but barely. Dry, thirsty veins scratched in his black eyes. He knew they glowed scarlet in the murk, saw their crimson gleam against Zoe's blades. Kieran grabbed Zoe by the shoulder and wrenched them away from Lenore, putting a few feet between them and his friend.

Zoe drove the blow meant for Lenore into his ribs.

Lenore screeched; her heartrate screamed terror. She hauled up the weapon inch by inch. Zoe pushed Kieran away and extracted the blades from his ribs, leaving first fire and then ice in their wake. He snarled and pressed his bloody hands to his side. The torture of Lenore's effort gleamed on her brow. Arm shaking, she swung what she'd found at Zoe, who spun toward her again, bladed arms aimed at Lenore's head. Dark metal glinted in the room's dusky light.

Anger and love and fear and pain roared from Kieran's lungs. He shoved Zoe from behind. Their body hurtled forward. Lenore's trembling arm came around.

A long, curving blade sliced through Zoe's chest as easily as through lace. Zoe gagged. Blood spluttered over their lips as they looked down. The bladed hinge sat just under their chin.

Zoe didn't lift their head again.

Lenore's arm began to shudder more violently while Zoe slumped over their own scythe. She gasped in pain and dropped it. Kieran's eyes followed the descent. The crash stirred his heart, but it was difficult to hear over his thirst. It strained against him, tried to pull him to his knees to lick up the spoils. One realization froze him in place.

I killed them. After all that, I failed.

What was the point in fighting? He forced himself to look at Zoe as he stewed in his defeat.

Sliding tentacles over his skin, his thirst purred, *Don't let it go to waste or you'll have to feed off Lenore instead. What if you kill her too? Does it even matter? You've already killed so many tonight.*

He was still too stunned to move. *Their lives mattered,* he replied. *All these lives I've taken...*

So you see, there's no use in trying to resist what you are. There is no coming back from this.

"Kieran..."

He looked at Lenore. She stared at his eyes, which still burned like sand ran through his veins. He saw their crimson glow reflected in hers. He'd attacked her once, had almost killed her, and had come back from it. He remembered the early days, after he'd been turned. He'd killed then too, by accident. Guilt and desperation had driven him to learn control. He'd forced himself to go days without feeding, then a week, then longer. Those long and painful nights, he'd staved off his appetites by telling his thirst to wait, imagining it leashed. And he held the leash.

You don't control me.

The thirst snapped at him and latched sharp teeth onto his wounds.

Kieran looked back at Zoe. *They are more than food.* He'd met them, known their sister, and mourned Phoebe's death. He would mourn Zoe's too.

His thirst growled and curled away.

Later. And we will *make amends for tonight's deaths.*

Like a wolf that'd challenged its pack leader for dominance and lost, it released its grip but prowled not far off.

Kieran turned back to Lenore. They'd stood in silence for a whole minute. She stared at him, pressing the satchel to her chest, and extended her fingers to him—a feeble half wave, half query. He locked eyes with her, acutely aware of the blood flowing from her wounds. It was *her* life. Not his to take. He yanked his thirst's leash again. They would make it home, and he would feed it there.

Finally, he allowed himself to relax. "Lenore, my friend, I am still me."

She gave him a tentative nod.

Turning his attention to her medical needs drove his thirst further back. He ripped off one of his shirtsleeves, wadded it up, and pressed it to Lenore's shoulder. She groaned and tears welled in her eyes, but at least she hadn't flinched from him. He secured it in place with his belt.

"Apologies," Kieran said, "but we need to leave. Now."

34

~The Tower and the Truth~

As Kieran led them out of the catacombs, they had to avoid Enforcers and Collective members. He was too weak to disguise them, even bathed in darkness as they were, and led them through back passages that wound away from the fighting.

All the while, the satchel hung like a millstone at Lenore's side. She hadn't looked inside yet. Urgency, injuries, and fear had prevented her.

Kieran shared snatches of information when no one was about. "The others are safe, I believe. They were when I left them, in any case." The last of his wounds closed as they crept onward. "I will need to feed soon."

Questions flitted like moths in Lenore's mind, but she didn't dare ask for fear of being heard. Enforcers were here, but how? What had happened to Camilla and the others? Kieran wouldn't have abandoned them, but what if he'd had no choice? Lenore's arm pulsed, though the pain had transformed into numbness. It hung dead by her side. Was that normal? Perhaps Zoe had irrevocably damaged it, or perhaps the blades had been laced with something. Thoughts about whether she might lose it snaked in and out of her other wonderings. Kieran was moving fine. Then again, he was a Vampyre. She reminded herself she knew someone who could help if such a dire end befell her limb, assuming Lowell had escaped.

Rook too kept popping up in her thoughts. He'd gone to the end of the continent for her but hadn't appeared with Kieran. What did that signify?

They emerged from the catacombs like living corpses—up a narrow, crumbling tunnel and out of a sarcophagus. It led into a small mausoleum with a rusty iron gate, which had broken off its hinges. The outside air had never smelled so sweet, though the cold night air bit at their wounds as Lenore and Kieran made their way across the darkened city. Dead leaves crunching beneath their feet and Lenore's ragged breathing sounded as loud as sirens.

It was late enough now that the petrolsene lights had burned out, sheathing every building and lane in darkness. Lenore followed Kieran and tried not to think about how long it would take to get home on foot or everything else nipping at her brain.

She was surprised when he led them to a building that was far taller than wide. It squashed between one of Cobalt's twisting alleyways and a broad avenue in Sand, right on the line separating the two districts.

Lenore gave Neal's favorite drinking establishment a quizzical look. "The Raven's Tower?" she whispered. "Why are we here?"

"It's closer than home." Kieran beckoned her to the door. He slipped inside and locked it after them. "I hope everyone else has made it out safely."

Lenore swallowed hard. She did too. To distract herself, she looked around. She'd never been to the Raven's Tower before; it had always felt very much like Neal's place. "Kieran, I don't understand."

"Hush," he whispered.

She crept upstairs after him, laboring to step as silently as he. The stairs spiraled around the building's inside edge like wing nut threads, up and around for at least three stories. Lenore lost count as her head began to swim.

"Kieran." As dark spots danced at the edges of her vision, her feet went out from under her.

He caught her and supported her on his shoulder. Together, they came to a door at the top of the building. Kieran opened it without knocking, and Lenore failed to understand what met her on the other side.

"There you are!" Calandra, the woman Lenore had met at Lowell and Felicia's house, approached Kieran with the familiarity of an old friend. "What's this then? Right, get her into the sitting room. We have an infirmary set up in there."

Lenore knew she was unsteady but didn't believe she was hallucinating just yet. How could Calandra know Kieran, much less be on such familiar terms with him?

She gripped the satchel in her working hand. She hadn't let go of the handle once, despite it hanging across her body.

"Is that... Lenore!" Rook. Lenore's heart leapt. Her vision still dimmed, but she saw well enough to make out walls made of bright fabrics sprinting away on rollers. Then Rook was there, pulling her into his arms. "Thank the stars." Lenore melted as he kissed her like she was air and he a drowning man. He pulled back to kiss her shoulder above where Zoe had stabbed her. "I'm so sorry. Kieran said he'd find you, that the rest of us needed to get out—"

"And so he did," came Camilla's voice, tired but firm. "Over here, please. Let's not have her swoon from blood loss."

Lenore passed into Camilla's care. Rook stuck close and snuck in the occasional kiss or touch. Camilla led her to a sofa, while Kieran and Dmitri pulled back the fabric walls to make more room in the cozy flat. The satchel remained beside Lenore. She felt safe enough now to release the handle, but the shoulder strap remained. Camilla cut away Lenore's sleeve, cleaned her wounds and stitched them up.

"I didn't mean what I said, Camilla." Lenore was glad for the distraction. Rook was holding her lifeless arm where her sister needed it; she felt the pressure of his fingers but nothing more. "It was just for the diversion."

"I know that." Camilla didn't look away from her work. "Like you would ever misuse Lowell so. You weren't wrong about me, though."

"No, I—"

"Did someone say my name? I—My tinker belle!" Lowell placed a tray of food precariously on a small table and hobbled over. He wore a beat-up, false leg that Lenore didn't remember seeing before, but it served well enough for the moment. Lowell flung himself onto the sofa with a *fwump* and took Lenore's other hand. "I was positively beside myself. Mister Wilson said he was going to fetch you, but Rook and I were firmly aboard the SS

Fretful. I was in no shape to follow, but Rook would have if our sharp-toothed hero hadn't taken off so quickly."

Lenore had trouble following. That explained why Rook hadn't shown up, but who was Mister Wilson? Sharp-toothed hero? Only when Kieran gave her a nod did she realize the name belonged to him. But that meant…

"As Miss Camilla said, he is as good as his word." Felicia's voice came from the same direction Lowell's had. She rescued the precariously balanced tray and set it on a console table in the room's center. "I wouldn't have asked him to go if I hadn't thought him capable."

Kieran made a noise that said that wasn't the whole story. The rest of the tale came out in pieces. Camilla and Lowell had stayed together, fighting off Collective members with the clarity spray, as Lowell called it. It undid whatever influence the Reaper had cast. It took time, however, and at first only caused disorientation. Rook and Dmitri had fought, as had Nightmare, who Camilla explained was also called Aisling. She'd disappeared when the Enforcer horde had shown up, and no one knew where she'd gotten to.

"Oh yes, the reinforcements," Lowell said. "Jolly good bit of luck that was."

Felicia explained that she'd taken steps to have the crisis response team deployed, though she didn't provide details about what those steps had been. More than two-dozen Enforcers had shown up.

An irritated twitch appeared between Felicia's eyes. "I do hope no one disobeyed my instructions." She traded a look with Calandra, who stared back. Felicia's attitude shifted after this exchange, but she said nothing else on the matter.

"Once the Enforcers broke through the front doors," Dmitri said, "the Collective only cared about defending the base. We scarpered before any Enforcers saw us."

Tension eased as the night wore on. Lenore practically inhaled a bacon sandwich. Her arm, clean and stitched but still numb, rested against Rook. Kieran said he'd experienced the same issue, but it had healed with his wounds. His eyes had returned to their usual all-black color after feeding on a rather disdainful looking Felicia. She had been the only one not directly involved in the battle. Even Calandra had shown up. She sported an impressive slash across her face but refused stitches. Lenore had yet to find out how the bar owner fit into all this, but other queries came first.

"Falcon was there," Dmitri said. "I heard them call him. From the little I could gather, he took charge after the squad's C.O. went down early. It sounded like they knew their way around pretty well too." He fixed his eyes on Camilla.

"Do you honestly think if I'd told Falcon anything, he wouldn't have marched me straight to Neal and Mina?" she said.

Dmitri relented. "Fair point."

"Always watchful, Dmitri." Rook offered Lenore another bacon sandwich, which she gladly accepted. "That's why I like you."

Dmitri and Camilla made disgusted noises, then they smirked at each other. Rook smirked too.

"You're all welcome to stay here tonight," Calandra said, "but I expect some of you need to get back to your families." She shot a look at Lenore and Camilla. "I believe I saw Doctor Allen in the cemetery with medical supplies. She's undoubtedly worried."

"If we leave now, I can ensure they make it home safely," Kieran said.

"I'll come." Rook's tone made it clear he wasn't asking for permission.

The thought of being at home was the only thing that gave Lenore the will to drag herself off the sofa and back out into the cold night.

)(

Light barely touched the sky when Rook, Camilla, Lenore, and Kieran walked through the kitchen door of the Allens' manor. Rook took up the rearguard and breathed an inward sigh of relief once they were inside.

"I'm afraid I must retire," Kieran said. Haggard lines carved across his face.

"Can I have a word, please?" Lenore asked. "It won't take but a moment."

"I'll go find Mina and Neal, or Esther." Camilla said. She left before anyone could object.

349

Lenore and Kieran looked at Rook, who leaned against a worktable with his arms crossed over his chest. "You're mad if you think I'm letting her out of my sight anytime soon."

Kieran waved a tired hand at him and turned back to Lenore. "Is this about Zoe's death?"

"Yes. I... I wanted to be the one to kill the Reaper. For my mother and Eamon. I'm sorry you ended up involved."

Rook made a mental note to carefully address this with Lenore later. He'd been where she was. It was a hard thing to accept, and he hoped to help her through the emotions and wonderings that would likely come later.

"I hope you don't feel I took anything from you," Kieran said. "I truly didn't mean to."

Lenore shook her head as she looked to the floor. "No, but... do you think me horrible for wanting that?"

"Of course not." Kieran tipped his head to look at her face. "Why would you think that?"

Her voice was so soft Rook could barely hear it. "Because of how much you despise taking life."

"I am not your judge."

"I know. I just... Your good opinion matters to me."

Kieran looked at his hands. Rook remembered how they'd dripped with blood earlier that night as the Vampyre tore into anyone standing in his way. Kieran had since washed them, but Rook knew the feeling of it still coating one's skin.

"I killed tonight, to defend the people I love," Kieran said. He glanced at Rook, who gave him an encouraging head bob. "I regret tonight's losses. It's never insignificant when a life leaves this world, but I don't regret coming to your aid." He threw a half-smile at Rook. "Any of your aid."

Rook grinned back. "My hero."

Kieran returned his attention to Lenore. "My dear friend." She lifted her head to look at him again. "You were offered the chance to kill Dempsey, and you didn't take it." She nodded. "You had the opportunity to kill Zoe but didn't. I daresay we are not so different in this."

She hugged him, the satchel still hanging at her side. Rook yearned to know what it contained but would wait. His people were safe. That was enough for now.

Lenore and Kieran held on a moment longer than usual. "Forgive me, but I am about to collapse," Kieran said. "If you hear a thump, please drag me into my coffin."

Kieran headed downstairs. Lenore, and therefore Rook, trailed behind to make sure he made it to his bed.

When they were back in the kitchen, Rook caught Lenore around the waist and pulled her to him.

"Little bird." He breathed into her hair, against her ear, as he peppered her with kisses.

Their lips met with fire. A few hours ago, he'd thought he'd never feel her, smell her, hear her again. Every second was a prayer of thanks to each star in the sky that they'd made it out alive. They poured comfort into each other as their tongues collided and fingers skimmed over skin.

Too soon, approaching footsteps pulled them apart.

Camilla traipsed into the kitchen. "No one's here."

Lenore approached her sister, hands extended. "Mina's probably holed up in some room with Neal while they handle the fallout."

Camilla didn't look convinced. They'd both heard what Calandra had said about seeing Mina at the cemetery.

To kill time, they washed and got changed. Camilla and Lenore found some items Neal wouldn't miss in the back of his wardrobe and gave them to Rook. As Rook scratched where the tweed collar rested, he decided Neal needed a serious lesson in fashion. He listened at Camilla's door while she helped Lenore around her injuries. Lenore tried engaging her sister in conversation, but Camilla remained quiet.

Downstairs, the front door opened and closed, followed by Mina calling for the girls.

"Up here," Rook called. He vaguely wondered if Mina would scold him for being upstairs before deciding he didn't bloody care at this point.

Lenore and Camilla emerged, clean and dressed in nightgowns and housecoats, just as Mina flew up the stairs. Rust-brown bloodstains smeared her dress and skin. Locks of hair had fallen loose from her bun, but her eyes were steely.

"Lenore! Camilla! Goodness, there you are. With me, please. I want you both where I can see you. You as well, Rook, if you must be here."

He counted it as a victory that she hadn't pitched him out of the house. Mina ushered them into the conservatory. When they were settled on the couch, she dropped into a chair and buried her face in her hands. She allowed herself only a moment of this, however, before straightening back up.

"What am I to do with you two?" Mina said. "I've been half mad with worry all night, while you're off disappearing with friends or cult members and lying to me."

"Mina, I'm sorry," Camilla said.

"It was for a good reason," Lenore added. "We didn't skip into danger for jollies."

Mina stood and began to pace. "That doesn't change the fact that you two could have been killed tonight. Again! Don't you realize you're the only children I have?"

"It's my fault," Camilla said. "If you're going to be angry with anyone, be angry with me."

"Is this the sort of tripe they drill into you in those crypts?" Rook asked. "You told me yourself the Reaper drugged you."

Lenore jolted back in her seat. "Drugged you?" She had yet to hear exactly how they'd all gotten into this mess in the first place. At least, Rook hadn't told her, nor had it come out at the Tower. "You can't be held responsible for that."

Mina motioned for attention. "I think it's time you all explained exactly what happened."

Camilla began, tears running down her face, and interrupted herself to apologize. Rook picked it up. He left out quite a few pieces but covered the highlights. Lenore too put in a few gaps—mostly the darker details that would only worry Mina more. Mina wavered between horror and indignation. She sat and put a hand on her head.

"I really am sorry, Mina," Camilla said for the dozenth or so time. "If I had known, I never would have gone."

"Of course you wouldn't, darling," Mina said. "And I believe your sister is correct. You cannot be blamed for falling under the Reaper's influence. It sounds to me as if they used a powerful mind-altering substance combined with a tranquilizer." She sighed.

"None of this answers the question of what to do now. I rather feel I understand why Mrs. Lee sent Emily to boarding school."

"Mina," Lenore said. "Camilla was in trouble. I had to do something."

The doctor narrowed her eyes at Rook. "I think much of the blame falls on you, Mister Hollow. I should bar you from our lives altogether."

"No, that's entirely unfair." Something in Lenore's voice made Rook's heart leap. It outdid itself with a somersault when she took his hand in hers. "And besides, I love him. He's a part of my life and I'm not letting go."

Was he glowing? Rook felt like he was glowing. He certainly couldn't stop grinning like an imbecile.

Camilla grimaced. Mina blinked at Lenore and asked, "But what about Eamon?"

Lenore flinched, but her voice remained steady. "Eamon was an excellent friend. I'll never forget him. Rook and I, though…"

She looked to him. His cheeks hurt from all the smiling, but he didn't care.

"You two have always had a connection," Camilla said. "I'm not terribly surprised, despite how much I might wish otherwise."

Rook smirked at her. "Always a charmer, you."

Mina's lips flattened into a pale line, and she folded her hands in her lap. The very picture of sophisticated anger. "It seems I have no say in either of your lives."

"Mina, that's not true." Camilla's voice rose with emotion. "We love you and deeply respect…"

Mina waved her hand. "Perhaps that was a touch dramatic. Let's leave it at this then: no more secrets between us. Do you hear me? None." Her gaze rolled over the three and speared into Rook.

Perhaps it was exhaustion, or perhaps Lenore's words had emboldened him. In any case, he merely stared languidly back.

"None whatsoever?" Lenore asked.

Mina raised an eyebrow. "What else don't I know?"

Lenore twisted her hands in her lap. "Would you rather hear it from me or Kieran?"

"Let's have it now."

"The Reaper was Phoebe's sibling, Zoe."

Mina's mouth hung open in delicate shock. She closed it when Lenore explained, with false starts and pauses, how the death of Mina's sweet former classmate had driven Zoe to become the Reaper. Mina crumbled with every word.

Lenore knelt at her feet, holding her hands. "I'm so sorry, Mina."

Mina looked away and covered her mouth with her hand. Her eyes glistened, but she didn't weep. Camilla joined Lenore. Mina stood, pulling the girls to their feet. She hugged them and finally let herself cry.

The scene touched something in Rook's heart. He'd never had a family like this. Did this sort of kinship wait in his future? He hoped so. The thought would have made him smile if he hadn't felt so completely awkward, very much like the odd wheel. Unsure what to do, he willed himself to become invisible on the sofa.

The kitchen door opening and closing resonated. Esther was singing a little tune, which wafted through the conservatory door.

Thank goodness! Rook shot to his feet and mumbled something about helping her. In the kitchen, he greeted Esther quietly so as not to disturb what was happening in the next room over. He helped her unload her morning shop while sounds of sorrow floated to them.

"Seems like a round of tea is in order," Esther whispered.

Not long after, Mina entered the kitchen, eyes puffy and tears staining her face. Esther was just arranging the last of the tea accouterments on a platter.

"I'll take it in here, Esther." Mina's voice trembled soft and tired. "Thank you."

Esther produced a shawl from some hidden corner and wrapped it around Mina's shoulders. "Long night, my lady?"

Rook believed Esther had secret cubbies of comfort items scattered all over the house.

Mina nodded. "The girls have gone to bed. I'll stay up until Neal gets home."

"Very good, ma'am."

"Varick, I'd like a word, please." Mina beckoned him with a finger.

He followed, mind jumping between guesses as to what was coming. Her voice told him this promised to be a serious talk indeed.

In the dining room, Mina fixed him with a hard stare. "First, it seems I owe you an apology. These events are more complex than I initially surmised."

Rook suspected she also saw him as an easy scapegoat. To be fair, he did have his fingers in some rather unscrupulous pies. He kept his thoughts to himself and tipped his head. "Thank you, Doctor."

Her features hardened. "Second, as much as I wish for more influence in guiding Lenore's steps..." Mina took a steadying breath. "She makes her own decisions. I neither know the details of your career, nor do I wish to. If you are to be her beau, however, I suggest you consider how much your work endangers her and indeed us all." Rook opened his mouth to reply, but Mina wasn't finished. "And it goes without saying if you hurt her, I am well acquainted with human anatomy and amputations. Do I make myself clear?"

Rook gave her a sideways smile. "Crystal, ma'am."

She scowled and swept out of the room. "Come along then. We don't want Esther's tea getting cold."

35

~Casting Votes~

The Parliament building hadn't been this packed in decades, possibly centuries. The walkways inside and out had been roped off to allow the magistrates and other officials to pass without being mobbed. Anxious protesters in white, their red accessories like flags, waited alongside hungry reporters. Springhavians carried placards calling for one result or another. They spilled out of the Parliament building and onto the lawns. Candyfloss clouds dotted the sky's pure robin's-egg-blue.

Lenore sat with Camilla and Mina inside the council hall's gallery. Her arm rested in a sling. Mina had prescribed a physiotherapy regimen to ensure she didn't lose mobility, though. Camilla gripped her embroidered handkerchief; Dmitri had come by the other day to return it. She hadn't asked him to stay, nor had he pushed for it, but they'd exchanged a few warm pleasantries.

The gallery was usually empty. Family members enjoyed special viewing permissions only during major votes such as this one. Lenore tried not to fidget as she looked down at the assembled decision-makers. She'd already picked out Neal, who was reviewing his notes. Katerina's seat was on the other side of the aisle. She chatted as if they were about to watch a midday orchestral performance followed by a scrumptious lunch. Speaker Pendragon sat in his ornate chair at the front of the room.

The Pendragons had been monarchs over the continent of Invarnis before the War of Light. Henry Pendragon's ancestors had sat in that very spot, also in their own special chair, and had exercised great power. Granted, the Speaker's position was nothing like a king's, but it was still an uncanny tableau. That Rook descended from royalty did nothing to quell the strangeness.

First Iago sat on the other side of the speaking podium, dressed in the blue-and-grey livery of his office. Even though it was close to two years since she'd been a thief, Lenore wanted to hide. She reminded herself again and again how different she looked now.

Speaker Pendragon approached the podium. He welcomed the assembly in a serious but congenial voice, thanked everyone in advance for their patience—the day promised to be a long one—and laid out the council's agenda.

More than just the Enforcer issue was up for vote. Lenore had heard bits of how Neal, Katerina, and others traded support for this item or that like currency. Education reform was up again, as were tariffs and other boring tax-related items. Trade options with the Arnavi were on the table as well. Each side would have an opportunity to argue their propositions before the voting and moving on to the next item. Any changes required a two-thirds majority.

They began with an option to levy taxes against Dogwood Lane lumber coming into Springhaven from Bone Port's side of the line.

Never had Lenore been more convinced she could actually die of boredom. Even Camilla, who could listen with perfect grace as patient after patient shared every symptom of every ailment, looked as if her eyes were about to roll back into her head. They remained upright, however, as the magistrates debated and cast their votes. Lenore found most of her entertainment in watching the council stenographer, a stooped man with wild white hair and long fingers that zoomed over his typewriter. He looked like a maestro conducting a miniature orchestra. A handful of council artists sat in the same corner and created sketches of the magistrates in action. Many of these drawings would go to the newssheets to supplement the few image-stills they'd be able to take.

Finally, the Arnavi trade options came up. Even Magistrate Warren's muttonchops looked excited as he led the charge. He waxed poetic about the opportunities commerce with their friends across the sea would bring. Like a carnival barker, he showcased exotic items his emissary friends had lent him. Some were new foodstuffs, samples of which he passed around.

"And more like these wonders are on offer," he said with a blinding smile. "So vote yes, my friends, unless you'd like Bone Port to make the money we could be earning."

The opposition was less impressive. Their representative mostly pontificated about the dangers foreigners brought. Money talked louder than fear, and the motion passed with votes to spare.

A million questions sprouted in Lenore's mind. What new opportunities would this open for Springhaven? Travel, perhaps? As soon as she got home, she'd write to Oya with instructions to get answers from any Arnavi she could corner. Lenore would have to give Copper a list too.

Education reform passed as well, though not as enthusiastically. Neal had mentioned a more robust bill, but the price of politics had whittled it down.

They broke for lunch. The din of shouts from outside nearly deafened them as they searched for a place that wasn't packed. More Enforcers than Lenore had ever seen prowled the crowds, telling off anyone who appeared too rowdy. She swallowed hard. The tension had ratcheted up since that morning.

Lenore looked for Falcon but couldn't find him amongst the seething mass. He was probably still recuperating from the catacombs raid. From what she'd gathered—sensationalized by the newssheets—it had been chaos. Lots of injuries, an impressive number of arrests, and enough damage to cave in a few tunnels. Again, they had touted Falcon as a hero. An unnamed, high-ranking officer working off confidential intelligence had called for a large assault team. Not only had Falcon taken charge when the team needed him, but he had led them to take down the entire nightmarish syndicate. The newssheets and readers gobbled up the story like candy.

Lenore thought back to the satchel she'd retrieved that night. She and Camilla had gone through it. The contents could have far-reaching effects, both positive and negative. She was still considering how to handle them. Gratitude that it hadn't fallen into Enforcer hands ran all the way down to her toes. It currently lay hidden inside a concealed compartment under her bed, which she'd discovered after losing Bitsy yet again.

The Zoology department had pressed Lenore more than once to let Majesty, who was recovering well, stay on as a mascot and educational animal. Lenore's heart twisted as she considered the request. Majesty was a good companion and faithful protector, but some of the options for Lenore's future didn't have room for a dog—well, regal wolf. That was a decision for another time, though.

After lunch, the room seemed more packed than before. Leaden silence hung over the spectators as Speaker Pendragon took the podium again.

"The next and, thank the stars, last item on today's agenda is a motion to reform the Enforcer order—introduce courts, trials, community-elected judges and barristers in defensive and prosecutorial roles, and corrective sentencing options for convicted criminals—as well as institute emergency response training and a reserve corps. In exchange, the Enforcer order will receive increased funding. Just a small item then, yes?"

Lenore scowled when most of the crowd chuckled. She fumed at seeing that smarmy act slide off Speaker Pendragon like slime.

"This motion has been proposed by Lord Gwenael Allen and Lady Katerina Holmes." The Speaker motioned them forward.

Most of their opening comments repeated what Lenore had heard before—a diplomatic outline of what needed to change and why, while gracefully dancing around outright insulting the Enforcers. More magistrates spoke in favor, citing the deluge of letters calling for the change. To exhibit the force of the papery outcry, one advocate had wire carts brimming with said letters rolled into the council hall.

The opposition wielded plenty of ammunition as well. The Halls of Justice attack and the raid earlier that week showed how necessary and effective the Enforcers' measures were. They even claimed Gadget as an example, once a criminal and now a reformed and productive member of society. Lenore clenched her teeth. What utter poppycock. She'd have rubbed the truth in the Enforcers' faces if it wouldn't have gotten Gadget re-imprisoned.

Speaker Pendragon couldn't weigh in on the debate. First Iago also refrained from doing so, but the way his face darkened during the discourse made Lenore think he regretted his choice. A smile like a snake's slithered across his face when Magistrate Smoke hobbled to the podium and glared at the assembly with rheumy eyes.

"You should all be ashamed of yourselves," Magistrate Smoke said. "It's bad enough you've passed the motion to let foreigners make money off us. Now you want to cripple what little protection we have? Who will defend us when their criminals come over here? And they will. They'll come in droves, looking for easy targets. If you want to protect this city, you'll reject this proposal."

More followed in his wake. Magistrate Warren joined Neal and Katerina's cause, defending the Arnavi in his rebuttal.

Both sides traded verbal salvos for over an hour. When their arguments began to circle like a dog after its tail, Speaker Pendragon called for the vote.

Lenore could recite the numbers in her sleep by now. There were one hundred magistrates, which meant they needed sixty-seven votes to pass. Camilla reached over and squeezed her hand before doing the same to Mina on her other side.

"All those in favor, please raise your hand."

Lenore held her breath as she counted, and then again as her heart pounded against her ribs.

Perhaps she'd gotten it wrong.

"Sixty-six in favor," Speaker Pendragon announced. "The motion does not pass."

Lenore's heart sank into her stomach. In the sea of churning disappointment, the Speaker's gavel reverberated like a ship snapped in half by a mighty kraken. It didn't matter. Nothing had changed. All that effort and hope and organization had been for nothing.

Tears stung her eyes. She leaned into Camilla as Mina hugged them.

With the last slam of his gavel, Speaker Pendragon said, "With that, I pronounce this magisterial session officially cl—"

"I have an emergency proposition."

The crowd's silence deepened. Katerina Holmes stood, staring Speaker Pendragon down with a look that could smelt iron. Lenore leaned forward. If anyone had an ace up their sleeve, it was Katerina. Hope dared to spark in Lenore.

"Magistrate Holmes, we are all very tired." Annoyance edged Speaker Pendragon's tone. "Can't this wait until our next session?"

"If we've learned anything today, it's that people desire safety," Katerina said. "This is very much in the interest of public safety. And it shouldn't take terribly long." She gave her most charming smile.

Speaker Pendragon looked around, eyeing the newssheet reporters. Their held pens and notebooks poised for action. "Very well. In the interest of public safety, let's hear this emergency proposition."

Katerina tilted her head. "Thank you, your lordship." She turned to her peers. "I move to strip Magistrate Harding Smoke of his title and powers."

Lenore's jaw dropped. A collective gasp whooshed from the spectators and swelled to excited chatter.

"On what grounds, you conniving harpy?" spluttered Magistrate Smoke.

Speaker Pendragon held up a hand to call for peace. "That's quite an extreme proposal, Magistrate Holmes. As your fellow has asked, on what grounds do you base this?"

"He has abused his power and acted in a manner unfit for a magistrate and an Enforcer."

"How dare you?" Magistrate Smoke pointed a gnarled finger at Katerina. "This is nothing more than petty mudslinging. She's just put out because her motion failed."

Katerina removed a sheaf of folded papers from her bag and held it aloft. "I have statements from witnesses who heard Magistrate Smoke confess to his own crimes."

Reporters and onlookers pushed forward for the slightest chance to read the documents. Lenore leaned farther in her seat, just as eager. Why hadn't Neal mentioned this? She assumed he knew, but a glance at Mina's goggling face told her, if Neal did, he hadn't mentioned it to her either.

The Enforcers working inside shouted for the crowd to calm down and step back. Speaker Pendragon banged his gavel and called for order. That did more than anything the Enforcers had done, but the room's appetite remained palpable.

Katerina walked to the podium and handed her evidence to Speaker Pendragon. "In the interest of transparency, one of the witnesses is my daughter, Beatrice."

"Isn't that convenient?" Magistrate Harding said. "Let me guess, the other witness is your husband?"

"The other witness is an impartial third party. A waiter who, beyond that, wishes to remain anonymous." Katerina turned back to Speaker Pendragon. "His details are included for you, Lord Speaker."

Lenore twisted her gloves and craned her neck to look at Henry Pendragon. His eyes glided over the ink, his expression unreadable.

From his seat, First Iago put in, "If I may, I can personally vouch for Magistrate Smoke's conduct." He hadn't moved most of the day. Now, however, he sidled right up to Speaker Pendragon.

The Speaker's eyes flicked over the audience. They leaned forward, hanging on every word and movement. He curled the documents away from First Iago. "Can you now?"

"Most assuredly." First Iago grinned with all the confidence of an apex predator.

"Hm. Have a seat while I deliberate, please."

Surprise flashed across First Iago's face. Thinly veiled anger trailed it. He retreated to his chair and sat like a pageant child who'd come onstage before their cue.

Please accept the statements, Lenore thought.

Next to her, Camilla was green and pale. Lenore didn't dare ask why with so many attentive ears around.

Katerina returned to her seat. Being invested parties, neither she nor Harding Smoke would be questioned. The witness testimonies would have to do all the work. Harding practically vibrated with outrage and looked ready to spring all the way to the podium. Occasionally, he shook his cane as if acting out an argument within his head.

From Lenore's vantage point, one of the sheets looked like a work schedule or time card. If so, it likely proved the waiter had been at work during the confession in question.

After many long minutes, Speaker Pendragon folded the papers. "Due to her connection to Lady Katerina, I must declare Beatrice Holmes' statement as inadmissible. As for the other—"

"Pardon the interruption, Speaker, but I have a statement to add."

Every head snapped toward the new voice. Lenore nearly fell out of her seat.

Falcon stood in the center of the aisle in his dress uniform.

Harding chortled. "Good man! Ladies and gentlemen, Falcon Smoke—a top member of the Enforcer order and my grandson." He swept a hand toward Falcon as if presenting royalty.

Falcon kept his eyes on Speaker Pendragon. "I know it's highly unorthodox, sir, but might I speak?"

The Speaker rubbed his chin. "As you say, it is unorthodox. And I did dismiss Miss Holmes' statement on the basis of her connection."

"But Squad Leader Smoke has something Miss Holmes lacks," First Iago said from his chair in the corner. "He has proven himself the people's faithful servant time and again. You'll recall he protected dozens, if not hundreds, of our citizens during the recent protestor attack."

"Not to mention his part in the raid last week." Magistrate Smoke pounded his cane for emphasis.

Speaker Pendragon nodded. "I suppose, given your service record and position, I can allow it." He bid Falcon to the podium. "Please."

Falcon thanked him and strode forward. With eyes as wide as morning glories, Camilla squeezed Lenore's hand.

Falcon tentatively raised his eyes to the crowd and took a deep breath. "Ladies and gentlemen, Lady Katerina's claim is true." Murmurings sparked, and Harding Smoke's eyes nearly popped out of his head. "Harding Smoke, former Enforcer Second, has disgraced his post with unseemly and abusive behavior. He has framed innocent people, condemning them to a life in prison, and committed other atrocities too depraved to mention here in polite company. Speaker Pendragon, if you'd like me to corroborate my account with what you have in your hand, I will provide details in private."

The Speaker gave one sharp bob of his head and ushered Falcon to a closeted corner of the room.

Harding furiously shambled to the floor. "Now wait just a moment, you traitorous scamp!"

First Iago claimed the podium while Falcon and Speaker Pendragon convened.

"Second Smoke, you will remain in your seat," First Iago barked. He even had the gall to shake his head, as if he'd suspected Harding of having been a bad egg all along. Harding hesitated, glaring pure hate at First Iago. "That's a direct order."

Falcon's words had chummed the water. The reporters shouted questions, tossing out wilder and wilder speculations about the undescribed atrocities. First Iago called for order. The Enforcers pushed the crowd back. Lenore looked at Camilla, who returned a fearful glance. Mina leaned forward, eyes on the crowd. Concern tightened her features.

Under her breath, she said, "This is liable to turn dangerous."

Thankfully, Speaker Pendragon returned to the podium and called for silence. Falcon stood behind him, hands behind his back. He stared at a blank spot below the gallery railing.

"I have heard Squad Leader Smoke's statement," the Speaker said. "It supports the provided testimonies down to the minutest details. Therefore, as Speaker of this council, I hereby strip Magistrate Smoke of his position and powers." The audience began to burble again, but a sharp, "Furthermore!" silenced them again. "Furthermore, as former Magistrate Smoke no longer has influence in this council, his votes today are void. Regarding our most recent vote, that brings the count to sixty-six of ninety-nine in favor. The motion passes."

Speaker Pendragon hammered his gavel more forcefully than before, but the sound was lost in the cheer that spread from the council hall like a wave. Mina, Camilla, and Lenore leaned into one another, laughing and hugging. A great deal of work remained, but they had overcome the first and largest hurdle.

36

~New Beginnings ~

Every light in the Allen manor burned brighter than usual, but they couldn't compare to the light inside Camilla. The family toasted Neal and Katerina again and again. A fire roared in the grate. Beatrice and John Holmes beamed, while Mina played the perfect hostess and topped up everyone's glasses. Lenore and Camilla stuck close to each other and exchanged bittersweet glances as they sipped their wine and took turns being the strong one.

It was a grand victory indeed, but it had come so late. Over a century too late, Neal had said at one point, but at least it had come. The ladies smiled at each other. Yes, there was joy to be found, and they would cling to it. Esther bustled in and out of the room, conspiring with Mina's efforts and making sure no one looked the least bit hungry.

John Holmes speculated how they might help those currently imprisoned recuperate and return to society. Nuance was vital when it came to life-altering decisions that would affect so many. Camilla had borne the weight of such a sensitive discussion with consummate aplomb, but her stamina was flagging.

Thank heavens the doorchime rang. Probably another courier with a note of congratulations for Neal—they'd been arriving all night. Camilla excused herself to answer it.

She wasn't prepared for who she saw when she opened the door. "Falcon."

His hair was mussed, and a fresh bruise bloomed on his face. He was leaning on a cane, but not the one he'd been pictured with in the newssheets. He smiled, though it didn't reach his eyes.

"Hello, Milly," he said. "May I... May I come in, please?" He sounded like he hadn't slept in a hundred years.

"Of course. Please." She closed the door after him slowly, giving herself extra time to find gentle words. "If you don't mind my asking..."

"My face?" he asked. "My grandfather got the jump on me after today's session. Just the one hit. I suppose it's the least I deserve."

"Falcon." Compassion colored her voice in warm shades. She looked down. Emptiness left behind by their last meeting blew through her. "I can't tell you how much what you did today means to us, to so many." Her voice softened. "I'm sure you know that, though. Apologies. I'm not trying to be condescending, I just mean..." She looked at him with tears glimmering in her eyes. "Thank you. I know what you risked."

"What I lost." His voice was low.

"What you lost," she agreed. "I'm sorry. How did your family react?"

Falcon gave a helpless shrug. "They're upset. They can't decide if they want to know more or not. My parents did thank me for not completely disgracing my grandfather."

"And therefore them."

"Yes."

"That was very decent of you."

"Was it? Is that fair to... to the people he hurt?"

The gathering tears slipped from Camilla's eyes, and she pressed a hand to her mouth. Glimpsing herself in a mirror, she realized she looked quite a lot like Mina in that moment.

She shook her head. "I don't know. I don't think so."

"I'm so sorry, Milly. For everything."

Falcon offered his hand. Camilla hugged him instead, and he enfolded her in his arms. They stood like that for a long time. If anyone came to check on her, they were quiet enough not to be noticed and let them be.

"What will you do now?" Camilla pulled away and tried to shake off her melancholy.

Falcon sighed. "Well, First Iago said he'd like me to head up the reserves. All of them. It means a pay increase, so at least I won't have to live in a rubbish bin on the street." Camilla managed a smile. More seriously, Falcon said, "I think he wants to use me to make himself look better."

"Maybe that's a good thing. You can take the Enforcers in a new direction. Neal and Katerina would probably love the help since they're responsible for enacting the new changes. They'll be working closely with First Iago."

"And how does Magistrate Allen feel about these new responsibilities?" The barest hint of a smile played on Falcon's lips.

Camilla giggled. "Neal won't ever play the game like Katerina. He'll organize a team and delegate. After how badly today's education reform bill got picked apart, though, he's talking about drafting his own."

"Maybe he'll be elected as one of the new judges."

"He'd have to agree to run first. I wager Katerina might try, though."

"It'll certainly be interesting to see."

A contented pause settled over them.

Falcon smiled properly. "First Iago gave me some other good news."

"Why, this is a red-letter day. What is it?"

"All my grandfather's inquiries have been shut down."

It took Camilla a moment to process what this meant. When she did, her face lit up. "You mean the one on me…"

"All closed up. He didn't really have anything solid considering the chaos that night, but it's done."

"Oh Falcon, that's wonderful!" Fears of Harding Smoke taking out his humiliation on her via the investigation had crossed her mind. She hugged Falcon again. "I can't wait to tell the others. Later, though, when it's just my family. Is there anything I can do to thank you?"

Falcon rubbed the back of his neck. "If you know of somewhere with a room to let, I'd appreciate the tip. I think my family and I need a little space, and it's not much fun being the golden-boy-slash-tattletale in the Enforcer barracks."

"Of course," Camilla said. "We'll find you something. Beatrice can probably suggest two or three places off the top of her head."

Falcon sagged but smiled again. "Thank you."

Camilla nodded, and the light inside her surged to incandescent levels.

)(

The Bonny Botanist gin club buzzed with patrons. Everyone was talking about the magistrate council session, and most people here were celebrating. Rook assumed those who wished to drown their sorrows had chosen a less jubilant place. Dmitri sat beside him, making a face at his glass. If his disguise itched in the over-warm room, he was doing a magnificent job of hiding it. Rook hoped Dmitri would be able to re-enter society soon, maybe once the Enforcer order completed their impending overhaul.

Wooden tables gleamed under the glow of artfully designed oil lamp centerpieces. Red and green garlands snaked around dark rafters for the upcoming New Year's holiday. The rafters reminded Rook of the room where they'd almost died not long ago, though the creamy walls and boisterous crowd cheerfully disintegrated the resemblance.

"I don't like gin," Dmitri muttered. "Why are we here?"

"Because I like the atmosphere." Rook sipped his drink. Not his favorite, but he could see why Lenore liked it. Thinking of her, he grinned. They needed to catch up after such an eventful week and planned to escape to his flat tomorrow.

"You like the noise," Dmitri said.

Rook grinned wider. The crowd's din swallowed their conversation quite effectively. "You know me so well. Besides, I have yet to figure out where I stand at the Raven's Tower. Lots of unanswered questions there."

Dmitri made a noise of begrudging agreement. When they'd discussed the matter, even Dmitri hadn't been able to deny the curiosity of Calandra being close to Kieran.

Rook took another sip of his drink and decided to rip off a certain bandage sooner rather than later. "So Prince is buying the market then?" Dmitri nodded, bearing his herbaceous drink with an impressive measure of dignity. "Of course he is." Rook leaned back and sighed. "I'm going to miss the old place."

"Things would have gotten ugly if you'd tried to double-cross them."

"Yes, I know. I thought I could finagle something."

"You gambled and lost."

Rook smirked. He thought of Lenore again, and of some of his recent conversations. "Not so badly."

A dapper young man dressed in raspberry and goldenrod finery sauntered over to their table. Rook had to admit it was one of Chrysalis' best disguises yet. The perfectly applied pencil moustache and enhanced cheekbones really completed the look. If they hadn't established what he should look for, using notes written in a brand-new code, Rook would have missed her.

Chrysalis sat without invitation and rested her elbows on the table. She motioned to Dmitri's drink. "Did you order one for me too?"

Dmitri slid it to her without a word.

"Evening, Chrys." Rook tipped his glass to her.

She nodded back. Her eyes searched his face before switching to Dmitri. Her mouth ticked down disapprovingly as she examined his disguise.

"Relax," Dmitri said in a not-at-all-relaxed tone.

"Only good things tonight." Rook gave her a warm smile.

Chrysalis sipped her drink and traced the table's woodgrain patterns with a finger—a sure sign she was at ease. After a minute, Dmitri shot him an impatient look. He opened his mouth to say something, but Rook raised a finger. His smile crept higher. Dmitri scowled but waited.

"So what did you want?" Chrysalis asked at last.

"You did us a favor, didn't you?" Rook said.

"Don't know what you're talking about."

Rook cocked his head. "Come on, Chrys, admit it. You were worried about us."

She shrugged. "I didn't want you dead."

Dmitri leaned toward her. Her eyes clicked to his, hardening with the close proximity. He backed off. "Sorry. Some habits die hard." She looked back at the table, and he picked up again in a quieter voice. "You disguised yourself as an Enforcer officer and tipped them off about the Collective's location."

Chrysalis raised her eyes, looking every bit like a petulant adolescent. "Yeah. And?"

Dmitri smiled, warm and sincere. It nearly gave Rook a heart attack. "Thank you. That was quite the risk you took for us."

"It wasn't really." She shrugged again, though Rook caught a whisper of a smile.

Dmitri looked baffled. "You know the penalty for ratting anyone out to them."

Chrysalis grinned. "Disguise makes me anyone and no one."

Dmitri slouched, and Rook saw the implications wash over him. If nobody could identify you, did you exist? Dmitri touched his false face in thought.

"Now you see why she's so great." Rook jerked a thumb at Chrysalis. He looked at her. "Not just because you saved our skins, though."

Chrysalis beamed so bright she nearly glowed. Rook's answering smile was genuine. Her expression faded a moment later, though, and she shifted in her seat.

"Yes?" Rook asked.

"Word on the street says you're selling."

"Word on the street is correct." Her joy deflated out of her. Rook tapped the tabletop, waited, and tapped again. She looked at him, barely managing to conceal her sadness behind hard edges. "We're starting a new business."

Like a sprout, Chrysalis lifted back up. "Can you do that? Without getting offed?"

Rook chuckled. "The good Lord Gwenael Allen has granted this repentant soul a permit to start a business. And her ladyship Holmes is providing us some much-needed start-up funds." He practically heard Dmitri roll his eyes, but the hope in Chrysalis' was too priceless to break away. "Can you guess what kind of business?"

"Cheesemongering? Horse-drawn carriage rides? Haberdashery?"

Rook gave her a quizzical look, glanced at Dmitri, and back to Chrysalis. "Are any of those particular passions of yours?"

Chrysalis waved him off. "Don't care, really, just so long as I'm working." She shot Rook a searching glance.

"Well, you're not far off with that last one," Rook said. "Guess again."

"Oh, for goodness sake, you're taking forever!" Dmitri huffed. "We're starting a clothing shop. Fine wear for gentlemen and a small section for women. We need an assistant and would like to offer you the position." He glared at Rook. "Is that so hard, getting right to the point?"

Rook's chuckle grew into an all-out laugh as he remembered a conversation he and Chrysalis had once shared in a tree. Addressing her, he said, "It can be a family business, with us as your new dads." With a shameless grin at Dmitri, he added, "I'm definitely the fun one."

"I get to keep working for you?" Chrysalis asked.

"Of course," Rook replied. "We'll figure out where you'll best fit in later. Does this mean you accept?"

She gave an enthusiastic nod. Rook held out his hand. She shook it, followed by Dmitri, and they spent the next few hours discussing plans.

)(

Kieran paced the kitchen. He'd asked for this. Even though his heart no longer worked the same as before his turning, he felt it was trying to escape through his ribs.

Esther, with flour patterned over her apron, placed a calming hand on him. "It'll be alright, my dear."

He willed himself to believe that. Doubts crowded inside his head anyway. One shouted louder than all the others:

I've waited too long.

The doorchime echoed too loud through the manor. Distant voices murmured at the front of the house. He made out the words—common pleasantries—and gulped. They moved farther inside. He knew which room they occupied by the sound. Mina's voice pulled him out of the kitchen, through the butler's pantry, and into the conservatory. Too close? Probably, but he didn't want to miss a word.

"Thank you for coming," Mina was saying.

Only Mina. As few people as possible were involved, just in case. Neal had wanted it to be him. He had his own reasons, but circumstances and social dynamics made that the trickier option. Mina was the better choice.

"Of course. We don't get together enough, but I suppose that's the lot of working women like us." The voice, so close and raw like sandpaper, tilted the world for Kieran.

Mina continued the conversation, edging toward the goal of this evening. When she reached the subject of tonight's true purpose, breath left his lungs.

"About that," Mina said, segueing from the subject of Rowan and family. "There's something you should know. You're likely going to be angry. I should have... Well, it's not my decision, but I was involved in the deception nonetheless."

"Mina, what in the world are you talking about?"

"I think it's best if we get straight to it." She cleared her throat. "Please come in here."

Kieran's feet fell like lead as he forced himself forward. Every instinct urged him to dissipate, to become a shadow and sneak in, but he wasn't sure he had the courage to rematerialize if he did. So he walked through the doorway, into the dining room, and forced himself to raise his eyes.

A single eye, wide and disbelieving, stared back at him. An eye patch covered the other.

"Annabelle," he whispered, the name like knives in his throat.

Gadget slowly rose from her chair, mouth gaping. Her natural hand clenched into a fist, while the metal one hung by her side.

"I'm sorry," Kieran said. Still nothing but that thunderstruck expression. "I'm not dead." Gadget barely nodded. Another long pause. "Please, say something."

Gadget snapped her mouth shut, apparently collecting herself. In a move that reminded him all too painfully of a much younger version of her, she stomped her foot. "Kieran Wilson! Why the blazes are you alive?" She didn't shed a single tear, but her face twisted into a snarl. "You should *not* be alive, because that would mean you've been around for... for... how many years?" He opened his mouth to speak, but she snapped, "Don't answer that. I don't actually care. How dare you bloody well be alive?"

"I'm sorry." He scuffed his foot against the floor and fidgeted with his hands. "I should have come to you sooner. I... I..."

"You what?" She waved her hands at him. "You're embarrassed about this... whatever's wrong with you?" She turned to Mina. "What's this affliction called?"

"Vampyrism," Mina replied gently.

Gadget's brows bobbed. "Vampyrism? Oh, so you're a Vampyre now. Well, that changes things."

Mina blinked. "Does it? I—"

"Of course it bloody doesn't! You and I will have it out later." Mina actually looked frightened. Gadget turned back to Kieran and took a deep breath. In a level tone, she continued, "Very well. You're alive. And you're a Vampyre. You'll have to explain later what exactly that means, besides the obvious."

"You're still angry, aren't you?" Kieran asked.

"Of course I'm still angry. Expect me to be angry for a good long time." She paused. "But I'm also... indescribably grateful. I have my little brother back. I'm going to hug you now."

Kieran laughed and opened his arms. Gadget squeezed him as hard as she could, which felt like a silk shawl brushing against him. When she pulled away, she punched him in the shoulder.

"I know you're sorry, so we don't need to waste time and hear it five thousand more times. Got it?"

Kieran swallowed the words. "I'll do my best."

Gadget crossed her arms. "Good. Now let's hear the whole story. Sit. Mina, you as well. You both owe me explanations. Immediately."

Kieran stopped himself from laughing—it'd be cruel to Gadget's feelings—but he felt indescribably light.

As soon as they sat down, Esther appeared with some nighttime nibbles.

Kieran couldn't believe this was happening. He'd imagined what coming clean to his sister would be like, but he'd never dreamed it would go this well. At best, he'd suspected she would stomp off, never to speak to him again. He now dared to hope that the future held much better than he'd dreamed.

)(

Lowell followed Lenore into the Archeotechnologics department. His head was practically spinning, trying to look in every direction at once. He spotted her keeping one eye on him, and they smiled at each other. Neal walked behind them.

Lowell shut his gawping mouth. He was supposed to be professional, whatever that meant. What he'd always imagined it meant—dour and taciturn—certainly wasn't possible for him on a regular basis, much less with enthusiasm bubbling out of him.

"You get to work here?" he asked. "Every day?"

"I do." Pride colored Lenore's voice. In a very Camilla-like move, she even lifted her chin a little.

"Anything you're particularly interested in?" Neal asked.

Lowell twirled to face his new mentor, proud of his new enhanced leg. "Simply everything." He raised his arms to the Arc-Tech workshop—that's how Lenore referred to it, anyway. The abbreviation felt very daring, though, so he wouldn't use it in front of Neal just yet. He wanted to impress the old bean first. That's why Lowell had chosen to wear only his arm's accessory add-on for his first day. Lenore had been rather impressed with it when she'd first seen it, and he hoped the rest of their coworkers would be too.

Lenore giggled, and Lowell counted it as a good sign. She'd promised to warn him off any bad behavior, even if it was due to over-eagerness.

Another gent, stouter than Neal with somewhat patchy muttonchops, trotted up. He wore a welding mask pushed up his face. "This must be our new recruit. About time we had some fresh blood around here." He thrust an enthusiastic hand forward, which Lowell shook with gusto. "Call me Copper."

In his periphery, Lowell saw Neal grin. "Lowell, this is Engineer Richmond Cooper."

"Did Lord Gwenael Allen tell you I'm leaving?" Neal made a face at the title, and Copper chortled. "It's a real shame. I've heard impressive things about you, lad."

"Spiffing to work together while we can, though." Little did Copper know, Lenore had told Lowell great stories of their exploits plus a few vague, sad ones, but she'd said they'd made up now. Lowell planned on learning as much as possibly from the legendary man.

Lenore introduced Ezra and gave Lowell the full tour. When they were alone, behind the Arc-Tech loading dock, he took her hands and spun her around.

"Oh, my belle, I am positively elated. Thank you again for helping me get this job."

Lenore laughed. "You got the job yourself, *and* you convinced Felicia. Frankly, the latter seems more difficult."

Lowell laughed nervously. He'd been petrified when he'd interviewed with the impressive Scholar Bates, and he'd been in a tizzy every moment after until the decision came, delivered with flowers and bubbly by Lenore herself. The whole idea had caused such row with Felicia, he didn't know how he could have borne failure.

But he didn't want to stain Lenore's impression of his sister. "To be honest, I didn't really give her a choice." He released Lenore's hands to perform a dramatic re-enactment, glossing over the more personal bits. "'Felly,' I said, 'you can't keep me under your wing forever. I know you want to protect me, but it's time I got out into the world.'" He switched sides to play Felicia's part, and made his voice higher and his motions far more dramatic than hers had ever been. If the theatric arts weren't the place for exaggerated storytelling, then what was? "'Lowell, the world is hard! You know this! How we've struggled! They will devour you in their mighty jaws of dooooooom!'" He switched again. "'I've fought villains and won, reinvented myself multiple times over—literally—and made friends. You can't shelter me forever.'" He switched one last time and shrugged blithely. "'Oh, alright.'"

They'd made up, as they always did, but her thoughts had been broadcasting concern ever since. Lowell was determined to do such a good job he wouldn't have anything but good stories to bring back. And if he didn't have only good stories, then he'd make the best of them. Either way, he'd make himself proud and assuage her fears all at once.

Lenore was laughing so hard she doubled over. Between giggles, she said, "I have every notion the conversation went nothing like that."

Lowell bobbled his head. "I may have left out a detail or two." He returned to his usual manner. "Have you thought about our offer? We have a room ready for you and everything." He twiddled his fingers at her. "Think of all the mischief we could get up to."

Lenore swayed. "Does Felicia still want me around? I assumed she'd written me off as a bad influence."

Lowell chuckled but didn't share how Felicia had thrown around that very claim during their argument. He had defended Lenore, and Felicia had admitted in the end that she had taken her fears out on Lenore. In fairness, Felicia had been scared out of her wits that Lowell might die that night in the catacombs.

"And anyway, would it be good for us?" Lenore asked. "Me taking the lady's companion position? To live and work together? Might it be too much togetherness and all that?"

Lowell linked his arm with hers. "No need to rush. There's plenty of time to decide. Perhaps us working together and visiting is a good test." He mimed gingerly stepping into a pool. "Testing the waters, as it were. And speaking of, are you coming over today? I have a few more adjustments to make to my replacement arm."

She shook her head. "I'm sorry, but I have plans with Rook. With everything that's been happening, we haven't spent much time together."

Lowell nudged her side. "Ooh, very romantic. Tomorrow then?"

"Absolutely," she said. "Oh! I have yet to show you the Baby Blackbird exhibit. Come on."

They trotted back to the Arc-Tech door. Lowell was having a smashing time breaking in his new enhanced leg, and Lenore cheered him on. He wondered what exciting new things they'd accomplish in this new arena of their lives.

)(

Lenore sat on Rook's sofa with the Reaper's satchel beside her. Rook stood behind the sofa and leaned against the back. His hand was warm and encouraging on her uninjured shoulder. His eyes, though, were on the satchel like it was a venomous serpent.

"You're certain you want to do this?" he asked. "Our country does have a bad history of destroying information."

"I know." Lenore drew strength from Rook's hand. She didn't love her decision. Given the potential consequences, though, she believed this was the best path. "The museum still has the black powder formulas under lock and key. The information won't be gone, just under responsible protection."

"Hmm," Rook muttered.

She understood his concerns; they'd discussed them previously. Safes could be cracked. Every organization, even her beloved museum, could be corrupted, and the Enforcers had collected the Reaper's weapons cache. How long before they started reproducing and augmenting the pepper gas canisters? What else had they discovered? She didn't want to follow in her father's weapon-design footsteps, much less selling said designs, nor did she want to risk anyone else doing it, so she had to put her faith somewhere.

"And Camilla's taken what she wants from this?" he asked.

Lenore nodded. "Zoe's work on organ replacements and blood composition was apparently revolutionary. Camilla and Mina say it can save lots of lives."

Rook hesitated. "Are you sure we can't keep the Verisap formula?" His voice was only half-joking.

Lenore gave him a wry look. "Are you planning on getting back into the crime game?" She was teasing. He'd said he was out, and she trusted him.

Plopping a kiss on her forehead, he returned the jest. "No. And I suppose there's no reason why I'd need to pull secrets from my new clients."

Lenore wished she could laugh, but the gravity of the truth prevented it. Once their task was done, she'd focus on happier things.

"People know how to make Verisap too, just not in a laboratory. Someone will figure it out if they're really determined."

"You could say the same thing about black powder."

Lenore leaned back and stared at the battered satchel. Rook rested his chin on her head. She reached up and stroked his neck. The contact gave her comfort.

"I know, but I can't control that." The last magistrate council session had taught her that citizens did have power. She could and would make her voice heard if she saw things going in a dangerous direction.

Rook kissed her head. "Are you ready?"

Lenore took a deep breath and carried the satchel to the fireplace. A large rug stretched before it. She'd been through the bag's contents several times but wanted to take care with them, to ensure she didn't burn something she'd accidentally missed.

They started with the black powder formula. Lenore thought she recognized Copper's handwriting on a few of the pages but pushed the suspicion away. She wanted to look forward. Checking each sheet one last time, front and back, she fed them into Rook's fire.

Camilla had taken about two-thirds of the documents. Medical diagrams and intricate instructions, spread throughout journals and binders and wads of paper clipped together, explained everything she'd been meant to learn under the Reaper. A few of those pieces had Phoebe's name written on them, though it was impossible to tell where Zoe had taken over.

Once the hungry flames had gobbled up the black powder papers, Lenore moved on to the Verisap formulas. When she reached the bottom of the satchel, she hesitated. She couldn't believe it was over. Rook had sat next to her the entire time, but he slipped behind her now. Wrapping his arms around her waist, he rested his head on her good shoulder, careful to avoid the bad one. He said nothing, offering silent encouragement through his touch.

Lenore let the last sheet drop into the fire.

With the job done, Rook kissed her shoulder, behind her ear. Lenore leaned into him and let her head fall back. Her gaze drifted to the mantle, where Rook had hung some festive pine boughs for New Year's. It made her smile, as did the nibbles he trailed down her throat. New Year's meant the start of spring.

New beginnings.

Lenore turned her head to meet Rook's lips. She intended to make good on the endeavor.

~*~

Bonus chapter available on the Exclusive Content page of
www.wordsbydana.com

Read on for a preview of

what's next in the

Broken Gears world.

~A Sneak Preview of *Raven's Cry*~

Excitement rippled through the nobility that evening as reports of a newcomer to our small court spread. His name was Nicodemus, Duke Gregory's friend, esteemed guest, and mysterious *magus*. Dinners at the Ivory Palace were meant for the court only, but who in their right mind would refuse such a rare opportunity? Not our cunning regents, that was for certain.

Magi lived in secluded communities outside of our cities and towns. They communed with nature and went out of their way to avoid contact with the outside world, or so the most common accounts went. The tales I heard whispered that evening seemed ill-fitting and farfetched. He was wealthy, though no one knew how he had acquired his money. He was also reclusive—at least that part was in keeping with the rest of his kind—but he had built himself a dwelling more akin to what one would find in the city. Duke Gregory had only met him because his hunting party had stumbled upon the man's house when a storm forced them to seek refuge.

"It's set deep in the woods, surrounded by orchards and gardens," Countess Melody of the Bladed Mountains and Valley said. "He has a menagerie of animals and a grand estate half the size of the palace."

"I bet he's a smuggler, dark and lonely and misunderstood."

"You've been reading too many adventure stories."

"Do you think he's looking for a wife?"

I took a deep breath as I strolled through the crowd, holding back the wave of fear rising from my chest. I'd just had a revelation of my own. If I sought to slake my curiosity, I would have to... *mingle*.

I was just as curious about the newcomer, to be sure. Curiosity is in my nature, but it's so much easier to learn from books than from people. Books don't judge you or ask prying questions.

Perhaps I should leave, I thought. *I can ask around about him tomorrow. Maybe I can feign sickness.*

With such a relatively small court—Queen Gertrude and King Ansel Pendragon, three duchies, six counties, eighteen baronies, and an associated spouse for most—I knew most everyone fairly well. So I shouldn't have been nervous. You'd think so anyway. I had grown up around all of these people. I knew the names and faces, the quirks and proclivities, and the associated perks and favors owed to serve my people. The categorization of these onto lists and their subsequent utilization were my forte, but the banal face-to-face interactions in between always turned my stomach. Whoever decided small talk was a useful pastime should be shot.

At least most of the rest of the Southern Assembly was not here tonight, as the weather back home was currently turning marvelous. I envied them. I only came to Prism, the capital, because my family was visiting on business. Many northerners were here, however. They didn't love the harsh winters that blew down from the Bladed Mountains. A mixture of the Midlands Assembly—those in charge of the city of Prism and the regions around it—was here too, plus everyone's children who were of age.

Yes, I think I'll catch up tomorrow, I decided.

I had just turned towards the closest exit when an arm wrapped around my shoulders and gave them a friendly squeeze.

"Going somewhere, Cali?" From the corner of my eye, I saw a warm, teasing smile spread across a face I knew as well as my own.

"Uncle Ducky, I think I'm going to be ill," I whispered.

"Nonsense!" he guffawed. "It's just nerves. Here, some wine should sort you out."

He snapped a waiter over to us and handed me a crystal goblet of crimson courage. I sipped politely, knowing I was going nowhere.

"Have you seen him yet?" Ducky asked, his eyes scanning the room like a Gryphon on the hunt.

"No. I think I'll—"

"There he is!" Ducky thundered so suddenly I jumped, nearly spilling my wine. "Gregory, my good man!"

Ducky then whisked me towards the Duke of the North. Trailing him was obviously the man called Nicodemus.

The magus dressed in the same fashion as every other man in the room, but he glowed with power. It rested on the surface of his skin, a halo of light so faint I questioned my eyes. It remained, and so I realized somewhere in the back of my mind he truly was luminous, if only slightly. To be honest, I was so caught up in keeping my composure, I almost failed to notice this marvel.

"Richard!" replied Duke Gregory. "Didn't think I'd see you here tonight. You're missing some prime hunting days."

"Pah, business had to come first, I'm afraid. But isn't our timing fortunate?" Ducky reached a meaty, enthusiastic hand out to the newcomer. "The man of the hour. You must be Nicodemus. Duke Richard Jones, Lord and Servant-Protector of the Southern Reaches. And this beauty of heart and spirit is my niece and potential heir, Lady Calandra Allen. Currently unattached, if you can believe it. And you?"

I felt my face warm with an unwelcome blush. The villainous plot had reared its ugly head again! My older brother, Carlos, was destined to be the Count of Bone Port and the surrounding Bone Bay territory, thank the heavens. I think everyone in my family was pleased with our birth order, as I had shown little interest in marriage. Ducky, however, had his own aspirations for me and liked to dangle a much larger inheritance like a carrot.

I was nineteen then. Most ladies my age were already married. My parents, shrewd but kind people, weren't what you would call nurturing, but they also weren't monsters. They wouldn't force me into a life sure to make me miserable. Secretly, I think the way every court event exhausted me worried my family. Ducky believed having someone to help shoulder responsibility would fix everything.

To be quite honest, the idea of marriage terrified me. Or rather, I wasn't interested in anyone we knew, and the idea of getting to know new people was enough to make me run for the hills. People are so very tiresome, you know. Where my parents had begrudgingly accepted this, Ducky had redoubled his efforts and practically threw me at every new and eligible young man we came across. He never gave a copper crown about decorum.

As Ducky ushered me forward, I resisted the urge to point out that he was also unattached. It was possible the magus, like Ducky, preferred men, and I wanted to remove the attention from myself. I wanted even more to stay out of Ducky's game entirely, though it was a bit late for that.

The cloaked magus chuckled softly and smiled, reaching for my hand. I offered it to him smoothly. That, at least, was something I had done often enough to execute without thinking. When Nicodemus took my hand and bowed, I felt warmth emanate from his skin. That subtle glow limning his figure combined with the sensation of a late spring breeze washing over me, he might well have been a small star. I smiled and, for once, it was not by rote.

"Pleased to make your acquaintance," he said. His voice thrummed warmly in the low din of the grand dining room, a sound I both wanted and needed to draw closer to hear. "No titles, I'm afraid."

"Not even a surname?" I asked. In my periphery, I saw Ducky's eyes flicker towards me.

I could practically hear the wiry hairs of his beard bristle with excitement. I had broached something like actual conversation with the most intimidating stranger we had ever met! Wonders never cease.

"Not even a surname," Nicodemus replied. "My people have no need of such."

"Your people?" I asked.

Nicodemus looked around, and I followed his gaze. Nausea returned as I realized every eye in the room had swiveled onto to us, and I wished to disappear into my bejeweled shoes.

"Lady and gents, would you all mind if we moved this conversation outside? I'm feeling a bit warm," Nicodemus said.

Stars, yes! Thank goodness, I thought.

We made our way out to a veranda overlooking the royal gardens in the distance. Along the way, Ducky suspiciously managed to entangle himself and Duke Gregory in a conversation with Baroness Leliana, who had half a dozen or so eligible daughters.

I felt people watching us as we made our escape, but no one moved to join us just yet. They wouldn't risk appearing too eager. Save for Baroness Leliana, that is, but with so many daughters, who could blame her? They'd have to crowd the doorway to spy on us, and that wouldn't reflect very well on them at all. They may have been a swarm of ogling, goose-necking gossips, but heaven forbid they actually let it show!

I gulped the cool outside air, lightly scented with recently bloomed honeysuckle. My heart immediately slowed without all those faces peering over glasses and whispering behind hands.

"Your... uncle, was it? He seems quite friendly," Nicodemus began.

I could tell he was taking care not to offend me, but he clearly had questions too. Ducky was fair with neat ginger hair, and I was nearly as dark as my father with wild ebony locks that barely capitulated to the strokes of a brush.

"He's not really my uncle," I explained. "Not by blood, but in every other sense. Apologies. I'm not being clea—." I blinked at him. "Your glow is gone."

Nicodemus rubbed the back of his neck and replied, "Ah, yes. That's a little party trick Duke Gregory requested."

He gifted me another smile. It sat sheepish and crooked on his face, as if it wasn't brought out terribly often and therefore unpracticed.

What a shame, I thought, surprising myself with the sentiment.

"I understand," I said with an answering smile, soft and encouraging. There was a pause, and I sipped my wine.

"I had no idea the court was so numerous."

I was grateful for the new thread of conversation and picked it up perhaps a bit too enthusiastically.

"There are even more than this," I told him before explaining about the Southern Assembly. "We're small compared to the Arnavi, though. Those are our neighbors from across the sea. Their Nish, erm, government, is like a spider's web."

"Ah."

I seemed to have led Nicodemus into another conversational dead end. A tiny cry suddenly peeped from the edge of the veranda. Without thinking, I turned away and walked towards the sound. The sides of the veranda were latticed and overgrown with thick foliage. Carefully hunting through the leaves and vines along the stone floor, I found my prize. A baby bird, half feathered and still blind, sat caught in the exuberant plant life.

"You poor thing!" I cooed. I scooped underneath him, catching up a few leaves as I did. "Come here, darling. I'll take care of you."

"It's probably going to die anyway, you know," Ducky's voice grumbled from behind me.

He and Duke Gregory had apparently rejoined us when my back was turned. I suspected Ducky could smell the conversation dying and had come to rescue it.

"Well, perhaps not now," I replied, almost whispering. "Look at him. He *needs* me."

Ducky came into view at my side. A comforting whiff of pipe smoke and whiskey floated towards me as he drew close to my cupped hands.

"Definitely going to die," he asserted.

"Uncle Ducky, you're horrible." Nevertheless, I was smiling.

He always did this to me. I looked around for the nest and spotted a scraggly collection of twigs and straw above.

"Give me a boost," I said.

Without further protest, Ducky got on one knee and offered himself as a step stool. He held one of my hands for support as I carefully lifted the baby bird, which was cheeping plaintively in my palm, towards the nest. As gently as I could, I deposited the little dear back into it.

Brushing my hands together with satisfaction, I said, "There now. All better."

"That was very kind."

I turned, surprised at hearing Nicodemus speak. I had altogether forgotten about him and was thankful for the way the darkness hid my blush.

"I, er, I just hope he'll be alright. Or she. It couldn't have been an easy fall."

"Might I check?" Nicodemus offered, and that uncertain smile reappeared.

"Can you?" I asked. "I mean, um, by all means, please."

"I have a gift with birds," was all he offered by way of explanation.

The power rolling off of Nicodemus was palpable as he strode forward. His glow returned, brighter than before, as he reached his hands towards the nest. His dark eyes glinted through a broken wall of dark, messy tresses. This was the most alive I had ever seen anyone. You know the sparks that form in dry, cold weather? Nicodemus seemed made of those. I was honestly concerned he might set something on fire. Nothing nearly so spectacular transpired, however. He merely glowed for a few moments and then stopped. It was there and gone so quickly I wondered if I had imagined it.

"Well, that was certainly… something," Ducky said.

I burst into laughter. Never, in all the years I had known him, had I heard Ducky at a loss for words.

"If you think that's impressive, you should have seen some of the wonders he spun for us at his home," Duke Gregory said.

Nicodemus began to object when Ducky demanded, "Show us one."

"Ducky!" I scolded. "He is not a trick pony. Nicodemus, I apologize. My uncle forgets himself when he is excited." I shot Ducky a glare.

Nicodemus shook his head. "It's quite alright—"

"Then let's see something!" Ducky pressed. "Just one miracle, eh?"

Nicodemus glanced at Duke Gregory, who nodded once. The magus sighed and gave in. With a graceful twirl of his hand, he conjured the image of a perfect sunset colored rose. Dipping his head, he handed the rose to me.

"It's real!" I gasped as my fingers grasped the cool stem.

"It's not," Nicodemus assured me. "It's easier to see through once you know it's an illusion."

I concentrated, telling myself I held nothing but air. Eventually, I could no longer feel the stem between my fingers, and the rose grew translucent, but it still moved with my hand. As I mused on this phenomenon, a wretched, torn sound suddenly ripped through the uneasy peace we had found on the quiet veranda.

The scream silenced the murmuring court within first. I hurried back towards the doors and looked in, though Ducky blocked most of my view as he took a defensive stance before me. Everyone looked at one another, waiting, hoping we had perhaps imagined it. The scream came again, louder and angrier, closely followed by glass shattering above us. We shrieked as shards rained down from the crystalline dome which had, until a few moments ago, topped the royal dining room. What had caused the damage was far more terrifying, however.

A Rukk, one of the enormous, predatory birds against which we had no defense. The creature's talons were the size of a man, its beak large enough to swallow an elk whole. Looking back, I realize it was a lucky thing its wings were so large. Only that saved us from certain death. The Rukk's outstretched wings could not fit through the shattered dome. Despite the glass jabbing into its flesh, the Rukk jerked and bobbed, trying to snatch up some delicious human morsels by any means possible.

People ran in every direction, yelping in panic. Carlos and his family were, thankfully, back in Bone Port, but I needed to locate my parents. I had to ensure they were safe. Before I could spot them in the scrambling mass, a voice deeper and louder than humanly possible thundered through the room.

"STOP!"

To this day, I don't know if he was addressing us or the Rukk. The people, however, obeyed and froze in their tracks. Every head turned, and we saw Nicodemus staring up at the Rukk. His body sizzled with blue and silver light as his eyes shifted between indescribable colors. He made a sweeping gesture for us to get back. We did so without question, pressing ourselves against the walls, unable to tear our eyes from the incandescent magus. The Rukk ignored his commands, and alarmingly deep cracks began to pattern the ceiling around where the dome had been. Bits of it were already falling down around us. Thank the stars no one had been struck by falling debris.

Nicodemus raised his hands skyward and glowed brighter yet. The clouds rumbled above, and a great crack shredded the air as the sky ripped open. Sweat beaded on his brow. We all recognized what he was doing, but I don't think any of us believed it. Tales circulated about magi calling nature itself to their aid, harnessing the power of the elements, but those were the most fantastical stories of all. Before that night, I didn't know anyone who actually believed it was possible.

The heavens grew angrier, as did the Rukk. Boulder-sized chunks of stone and plaster dropped from the ceiling. The Rukk had nearly broken through, the combination of its weight and efforts severely compromising the strength of the roof above us. Nicodemus thrust his fists into the air and, with a pained heave, dragged a bolt of lightning from the tumultuous clouds, striking the Rukk with it. The Rukk shrieked so loudly it shook the windows, cracking most of them. Nicodemus grabbed more bolts, quickly pulling smaller ones, spearing them into the Rukk. It was one well-placed—or perhaps just lucky—jolt to the Rukk's skull which finally bested the horrible beast. As it slumped over dead, the bird's head slid through the shattered dome, its golden eyes staring blankly at us all.

During the next moments that passed, the stillness crackled with the question of whether or not the danger had truly passed. Nicodemus hunched with exhaustion, looked around him and took in our gaping faces. Queen Gertrude and King Ansel appeared from the crowd and tentatively crossed beneath the hanging head. Nicodemus straightened halfway up before folding over again into a weak bow.

"Your majesties…" he puffed. "I… I apologize…"

Queen Gertrude silenced him with a single raised finger.

"Speak no more except to answer this: is it truly dead?"

"Yes, my Queen. It is."

And thus was Nicodemus' introduction to the royal court of Invarnis.

~Acknowledgements~

I am hugely fortunate to be surrounded by so many wonderful, supportive people. Thank you to God for this crazy creation wonder-magic. To my family for always being willing to listen to me natter, wail, whine, obsess, and cheer over and over again. Thank you, Mike, my awesome husband, for supporting me and encouraging me to take breaks and reminding me to eat. I know I'm bad about that, but I'm better with you. And Bruin and Badger, my mini-wolves, thank you for always being ready with fuzzy snuggles and kisses when I need them.

Sarina, my patient, compassionate, relentless editor. You push me to be better at every turn. I'm both a better person and a better writer because of you. And thank you for holding my hair back while I verbally and emotionally barfed all those times.

Dad, the Hollow Tower would not exist without you. That two-hour phone discussion where you so patiently walked me through how magnets work started that chapter. And Lowell is "jolly grateful" for the enhanced arm you advised about.

To my entire reader squad—Vee, Bethany, Beverley, Jo-Ann, Meg, Dariush, Alex, Amanda, Allison, and so many more. I could not do what I do without a team like you. Your feedback, reviews, support, and encouragement is indescribably precious to me. I love you all.

To the incredible community that is Bookstagram, thank you for creating a place where authors and readers can come, be themselves, and find encouragement no matter what we're dealing with.

Congratulations to Amelia for winning the tuckerization in here—Nieva thanks you for her splendid name.

And finally, thank you, dear reader. Thank you for taking time to explore the Broken Gears world. I truly hope you enjoyed the experience. As I've said before, to share stories with you is its own kind of magic. Thank you again; you freaking rock!

~About the Author~

Dana Fraedrich is an independent author, dog lover, and self-professed geek. Even from a young age, she enjoyed writing down the stories that she imagined in her mind. Born and raised in Virginia, she earned her BFA from Roanoke College and is now carving out her own happily ever after in Nashville, TN with her husband and two dogs. Dana is always writing; more books are on the way!

If you enjoyed reading this book, please leave a review. Even it's just one line to say you liked it, that really helps.

Find Dana online at www.wordsbydana.com
Facebook: https://www.facebook.com/wordsbydana/
@danafraedrich on Twitter, Tumblr, and Instagram
Follow Dana on Goodreads or her Amazon Author page
Get extra goodies on her Patreon page:
https://www.patreon.com/wordsbydana
Sign up for exclusive access to Dana's VIP newsletter, free short stories, and giveaways on her website
Thanks!

CPSIA information can be obtained
at www.ICGtesting.com
Printed in the USA
LVHW091456031019
633100LV00001B/52/P